Barclay, William
Ethics in a permissive society

BJ
1251
.B32
1971b

Barclay, William
Ethics in a
permissive society

Ethics in a Permissive Society

ETHICS IN A PERMISSIVE SOCIETY

WILLIAM BARCLAY

Harper & Row, Publishers
New York, Evanston, San Francisco, London

 For information address Harper & Row, Publishers, Inc., 49 East 33rd Street, New York, N.Y. 10016.

FIRST UNITED STATES EDITION

LIBRARY OF CONGRESS CATALOG CARD NUMBER: 70-175157

For Jane B and Jane C
who are the modern generation

Scripture quotations are taken, unless otherwise stated, from the Revised Standard Version of the Bible, copyrighted 1946 and 1952 by the division of Christian Education of the National Council of the Churches of Christ in the United States of America.

Contents

Foreword

My first word must be a word of very sincere thanks to the Baird Trustees for entrusting me with the task of delivering these lectures. The Baird lecturers have been a distinguished succession, and it is a very great honour and privilege for me to walk in that company.

My second word must be a word of explanation. Until now the Baird Lectures have been an academic occasion, and they have been delivered to a comparatively limited audience within a college or university. But on this occasion the Baird Trustees and the BBC decided to make an experiment by putting the Baird Lectures on to the television screen. This necessarily altered their presentation. They had to be designed to reach a far larger audience and an audience of a different kind. What had formerly been an academic occasion became an experiment in communication; what had formerly been intended for a limited number had now to be aimed at the general public.

The original title of the television series was *Jesus Today: the Christian Ethic in the Twentieth Century*, and the circumstances in which they were given explain both the form and the subject of the lectures. I am quite sure that at the present time there is nothing more important than the presentation of the Christian ethic. What I have tried to do is to present the Christian ethic in its relevance for today, not in a form for the classroom or even for the pulpit, but in a form which would be relevant and intelligible for people with Christian concern, but with no specialist knowledge. It has been no small problem to do justice to the academic nature of this lectureship and at the same time to meet the need for the wider communication which its presentation on television necessitated. It has been given to me to begin this kind of experiment; I am sure that in the time to come others will do it far better than I have done.

Since the lectures were given on television they were shorter than they would otherwise have been. I have therefore added some material to this book in addition to the actual lectures, and have in some places expanded the lectures. The chapters on the ethics of the Old Testament, the ethics of Jesus, situation ethics, work, community ethics and person to person ethics are the substance of the six lectures which were actually delivered. The chapters on the ethics of Paul, on pleasure, and on money are additional material. This is not a handbook on Christian ethics. Very often subjects which need far more detailed treatment have had to be dealt with in a paragraph. But Christian ethics form a subject on which no book could ever be complete. I have tried to deal with the aspects which I believe to be most relevant for today, and often I have tried rather to open avenues for further thought than to offer any solutions. The fact that these chapters began life as television talks explains too why there is a certain amount of repetition. It could not be assumed that every listener would listen to every talk, and therefore each talk had to be complete in itself, and some things have had to be said twice.

For the Baird Lectures to be put on television was a departure. And this seemed to me to carry with it the necessity of a departure from custom in publishing them also. In former times the Baird Lectures would have been a stately and fairly expensive volume. But it seemed to me—and the Trustees agreed—that the corollary of presentation on television was publication in paperback form.

I have many people to thank for their help and sympathy. Colonel Baird and Rev R. H. G. Budge of the Baird Trust gave me constant encouragement. And I owe a greater debt than I can express to Rev Dr R. S. Falconer of the BBC and to the whole BBC team which produced these lectures on television. He and they combined kindness and efficiency to give me every support.

It is my hope and prayer that these lectures may do something to show that the Christian ethic is as relevant today as ever it was.

Glasgow University,
January 1971 William Barclay

CHAPTER ONE

The Cradle of the Christian Ethic

If you want to put it in one sentence, ethics is the science of behaviour. Ethics is the bit of religion that tells us how we ought to behave. Now it so happens that in regard to ethics we are facing today a situation which the Christian church never had to face before.

Not so very long ago, when I was young and first entered the ministry, the great battle-cry was: 'Don't bother about theology; stick to ethics.' People would say: 'Stop talking about the Trinity and about the two natures of Jesus and all that sort of thing, and stick to ethics. Never mind theology; just stick to the Sermon on the Mount, and let the abstractions and the abstrusenesses and the philosophy and the metaphysics go.' People said: 'Take theology away—I can't understand it anyway.' But thirty years ago no one ever really questioned the Christian ethic. Thirty years ago no one ever doubted that divorce was disgraceful; that illegitimate babies were a disaster; that chastity was a good thing; that an honest day's work was part of the duty of any respectable and responsible man; that honesty ought to be part of life. But today, for the first time in history, the whole Christian ethic is under attack. It is not only the theology that people want to abandon—it is the ethic as well.

That is why it is so important to look at the Christian ethic today, to see what it is all about, and to ask if it is still as binding as ever.

If you are going to understand anyone, you need to know something about his parents and about the home he came from. The Old Testament is the parent of the New Testament and the religion of the Old Testament is the cradle from which Christianity came. It is therefore necessary to look first at the ethics of the Old Testament.

i. The very first thing to say about the ethic of the Old Testament is that it is an *ethic of revelation.*

In this case, if we start out by simply looking at words, then we get off very much on the wrong foot. The word *ethics* comes from the Greek word *ethos*; and *ethos* means a *habit* or *custom.* Are we then to say that ethics simply consists of habits and customs and conventions which have become fixed and stereotyped so that things which were once the usual thing to do have become the obligatory thing to do?

Take another word; take the Greek word for law—*nomos.* If you look up *nomos* in the Greek dictionary you will find that the first meaning given for it is *an accepted custom.* Are we at the same thing again? Is law something which has become so habitual, so conventional, that it has finished up by becoming an obligation? Is it simply a case that the *done thing* has become *the thing that must be done*? Take still another word; take the Greek word for justice—*dikē*; in Greek *dikē* means *an accepted standard of conduct*—and obviously this is an entirely variable thing, quite different in one society from another, quite different in Central Africa and in the Midlands of England or the Highlands of Scotland. Are we back at the same thing again? Is justice simply stereotyped custom, habit and convention? When we talk about ethics, law, justice, are we really only talking about habits and customs—or does it go deeper than that?

In the Old Testament it goes far deeper, for, as it has been put, for the Old Testament *ethics is conformity of human activity to the will of God.* Ethics for the Old Testament is not what convention tells me to do, but what God commands me to do.

ii. Second, the ethics of the Old Testament are rooted in history. There is one thing that no Jew will ever forget—that his people were slaves in the land of Egypt and that God redeemed them. To this day that story is told and retold at every Passover time. 'You must remember that you were a slave in the land of Egypt and that the Lord your God rescued you' (Deuteronomy 7.18; 8.2; 15.5; 16.12; 24.18,22). That is the very keynote of Old Testament religion.

That saying has two implications; it means that for two reasons God has a right to speak. First, he has the right to speak because he did great things. Second, he has the right to speak because he did these great things for the Jews. The Jew would say: 'God has a right to tell me how to behave, for God has shown that he can act with power—and act with power for me.'

iii. For the Old Testament the idea of ethics is tied up with the idea of a covenant. A covenant is not in the Old Testament a bargain, an agreement, a treaty between two people, in this case between God and Israel, for any of these words means that the two parties are on the same level. The whole point of the covenant is that in it the whole initiative is with God. The idea is that God out of sheer grace—not because the nation of Israel was specially great or specially good—simply because he wanted to do it—came to Israel and said that they would be his people and he would be their God (Deuteronomy 7.6-8; 9.4,5).

But that very act of grace brings its obligation. It laid on Israel the obligation for ever to try to be worthy of this choice of God.

iv. Quite often the Old Testament puts this in another way. It talks of Israel as the bride of God (Isaiah 54.5; 61.10; 62.4,5; Jeremiah 2.2; 3.14; Hosea 2.19,20). It is as if God chose the nation of Israel to marry it to himself. That is why in the Old Testament when Israel is unfaithful the prophets talk of the nation going a-whoring after strange gods. Israel and God are married and infidelity is like adultery (Malachi 2. 11; Leviticus 17.7; 20.5,6; Deuteronomy 31.16; Judges 2.17; 8.27,33; Hosea 9.1). It is also why the Old Testament can use a word about God that we perhaps don't much like nowadays

—it talks about God being a jealous God (Exodus 20.15; 34.14; Deuteronomy 4.24; 5.9; 6.15). That is because love is always exclusive. God wants the undivided love of the nation —and if he does not get it, like any lover he is jealous.

Take it either way—take it that God entered into a special relationship with Israel in the covenant—take it that God takes the nation as his bride—either way out of sheer gratitude, out of the obligation that love always brings, the nation is—as you might say—condemned to goodness.

v. I have just been using a word which is a key word in regard to the relationship of Israel and God—the word *chose*. God *chose* Israel. The one thing about which the Jews are absolutely sure is that they are *the chosen people*; that in some way or other they specially and uniquely belong to God. This idea of being chosen has certain consequences—and they are not the consequences that you would altogether expect.

(a) First, it brings a terrifying sense of responsibility. There is a devastating passage in Amos. Amos has been reciting the sins of people after people—Damascus, Gaza, Tyre, Edom, Ammon, Moab—the long and terrible list and to each its doom. Then he comes to Israel—and the feeling is that he is going to say that Israel is the chosen people, and that therefore there is no need to worry; everything will be all right. So the voice of God through the prophet comes: *You only have I chosen of all the families of the earth*—and the hearers are prepared to sit back comfortably—and then there comes the shattering sentence: *Therefore I will punish you for all your iniquities* (Amos 3.2). The greater your privilege, the greater your responsibility. The better the chance God gives us, the more blameworthy we are if we fail him. This is one of the most dreadful *therefores*: You have I chosen—*therefore* you will I punish.

(b) Equally clearly this chosenness must issue in obedience. Moses says to the people: This day you have become the people of the Lord your God. '*Therefore* you shall obey the voice of the Lord your God, keeping his commandments and his statutes' (Deuteronomy 27.9,10). Not, chosen, therefore exempt from obedience; but, chosen, therefore for ever under obligation to obedience.

(c) If then this obedience is of the very essence of life, the law which must be obeyed becomes for the Jew the most important thing in life. As Moses said of the law when he was making his farewell speech to the people: 'It is no trifle; it is your life' (Deuteronomy 32.46,47). The law was that whereby they knew the will of God, and it was through the law that the necessary obedience could be rendered.

(d) This obedience had one obvious consequence—it meant that, if this obedience were accepted, the Jews had to be prepared to be different from all other nations. The word of God was quite clear; they were not to be like the Egyptians they were leaving; and they were not to be like the Canaanites into whose land they were going (Leviticus 18.1-5; 20.23,24). God had separated them from other peoples.

(e) And here we come to the text and the saying which more than any other are of the very essence of the Jewish religion—the voice that they heard again and again said to them over and over again: 'You shall be holy because I am holy' (Leviticus 20.26; 19.2; 11.44,45; 20.7,26). The basic meaning of the word *holy* is *different*. The Sabbath was holy because it was different from other days; the Bible is holy because it is different from other books; the temple was holy because it was different from other buildings. God is supremely holy because God is supremely different. Now the very first duty of the Jew is to be different; he is separated; he is chosen; he is God's; and therefore he is different.

This explains two of the great ethical problems of the Old Testament. There was about the Jews a complete exclusiveness. (There is a qualification of this to come, but to that we will come later.) A Jew was to make no covenant with any other nation (Exodus 23.32; 34.12-15). Intermarriage with persons of any other nation was—and is—absolutely forbidden (Exodus 34.16; Deuteronomy 7.3). Here also we have the explanation of certain things in the Old Testament which have always shocked the Christian—because the Christian so often did not try to understand them. For instance, in war the shrines of any other nation were to be utterly destroyed (Exodus 23.24; Deuteronomy 7.5; 12.3). It is here that we come on that command which is so often quoted against the Old Testament. If a city surrendered, the inhabitants of it were to be made slaves; if a city resisted and was in the end conquered—*you shall save nothing alive* (Deuteronomy 20. 10-18; 7.1-5). Men, women and children were to be obliterated. And so within the nation, if a man left Judaism and became an apostate, he was to be mercilessly destroyed (Deuteronomy 13.12-18; 17.2-7).

Things like that shock us; but just try to understand. At the back of this there was nothing personal; there was no hatred. What there was was a passion for purity. Nothing—absolutely nothing—must be allowed to taint the purity of Israel; the infection must be mercilessly rooted out. Holiness had to be protected by the extermination of the enemies—not of Israel, but of holiness and of God. There is nothing political here; there is no thought of a *Herrenvolk*, a master race who will exterminate other peoples; it is holiness that matters. The day had not yet come—it was to come—when they began to see that the best way to destroy God's enemies is not to kill them but to make them his friends; God's enemies are to be destroyed by converting them, not by annihilating them. But early on the passion for holiness produced the demand for destruction—a demand which is not to be condemned without being understood.

The second ethical problem is to be found in a feature of the Jewish law which leaves anyone who studies it initially amazed. One of the strangest things in the Jewish law is the way in which the ethical and the ritual, the moral and the ceremonial are put side by side. Things are put side by side, one thing which seems to matter intensely and another thing which does not seem to matter at all, and they seem to be treated as of equal importance. Let us take an example; here is a passage from Leviticus:

> You shall not hate your brother in your heart, but you shall reason with your neighbour, lest you bear sin against him. You shall not take vengeance or bear any grudge against the sons of your people, but you shall love your neighbour as yourself; I am the Lord.
>
> You shall keep my statutes. You shall not let your cattle breed with a different kind; you shall not sow your field with two kinds of seed; nor shall you wear a cloth made of two kinds of stuff (Leviticus 19.17-19).

This passage begins with one of the greatest ethical principles that has ever been laid down—to love your neighbour as yourself—and it ends with a prohibition of wearing clothes made of a certain kind of cloth—the reason for which is completely obscure. You have the ethical and the ritual completely mixed up.

Now a great many people criticise Judaism because it makes so much of a physical thing like circumcision, because of its food laws, and things like that. But, you see, it is crystal clear that if Judaism had not had these laws it would not have survived at all. The point is this. A good man is a good man to almost any religion or philosophy—Plato, Aristotle, Thomas Aquinas, Immanuel Kant, John Stuart Mill, a Stoic, a Christian, a Jew—all agree on what honour and honesty and courage and chastity are. C. S. Lewis spoke of 'the triumphant monotony of the same indispensable platitudes which meet us in culture after culture'. If it was just a matter of morals there was no great difference in the action of the Greek, the Roman, the Jewish and the Christian good man. What made the Jew stand out, what made him different, is his ceremonial law. You can tell him by what he eats and what he does not eat.

I have told this story before, but it so perfectly illustrates what I am getting at that I tell it again. When my daughter

Jane was young her closest friend was Diane a little Jewish girl. We used to go out on Saturday afternoons in the car, and we would stop somewhere for afternoon tea, and when the sandwiches arrived, Diane would say to me: 'Can I eat it?' At afternoon tea in an hotel Diane was a Jewess, *and she showed it*. Would to God we Christians were as willing to show our Christianity! But the point is that the Jewish ceremonial law is designed to show the essential difference of the Jew—it was his witness to his Judaism—and so far from mocking it or criticising it, it was that, we must remember, that kept Judaism alive. The Jew has always been the great non-conformist, for the Jew—all honour to him—is the man who had has the courage to be different.

We now come to what is the greatest contribution of Jewish religion to ethics. *Judaism insisted on the connection between religion and ethics*. This may seem to us the merest truism, but it was not a truism in the ancient world. We can see this connection in two things. First, one of the widespread practices in the ancient world was that of temple prostitution. The ancient peoples were fascinated by what we might call the life force. What makes the corn grow and the grapes and the olives ripen? Above all, what begets a child? This is the life force. So they worshipped the life force. But, if you worship the life force, then the act of sexual intercourse can become an act of worship; and so temples in the ancient world had hundreds and sometimes thousands of priestesses attached to them who were nothing other than temple prostitutes.

In Deuteronomy there is a passage like this:

> There shall be no cult prostitute of the daughters of Israel, neither shall there be a cult prostitute of the sons of Israel. You shall not bring the hire of a harlot or the wages of a dog (that is, a male prostitute) into the house of the Lord your God in payment for any vow; for both of these are an abomination to the Lord your God (Deuteronomy 23.17, 18).

What on earth has the price of a prostitute to do with the temple of the gods? In Greece, everything. In the temple at Corinth there were one thousand sacred prostitutes and they came down to the streets in the evening and plied their trade. In Greece Solon was the first Greek statesman to institute public brothels, and with the profits of them they built a temple to the goddess Aphrodite. The ancient world saw nothing wrong in this. Chastity and religion had no connection. Judaism for the first time made religion and purity go hand in hand.

The second thing that Judaism insisted on was that the most elaborate ritual and the most magnificent church services cannot take the place of the service of our fellow men. What does God want? the prophet asks; and the answer is not church services, but to share your bread with the poor, to take the homeless into your house, to feed the naked. To do justice and to love mercy is what God wants us to do (Isaiah 1. 12-17; 58.6-12; Jeremiah 7.8-10; Amos 5.21-24).

So Judaism insists that there can be no religion without ethics. And that to serve God we must serve our fellow men. As Micah had it, you can come to God and offer him calves a year old; you can offer him thousands of rams; you can offer him tens of thousands of rivers of oil; you can even take your own child, fruit of your own body, and offer him; not one of these things is what God wants—the only real offering is to act justly, to love mercy, and to walk humbly before God (Micah 6.6-8; Hosea 6.6). Once and for all the Old Testament unites religion and ethics, and it did it so permanently and so well that today no one would ever regard a religion as a religion at all, unless it joined the service of God and the service of men.

Before we look at some of the detail of the Old Testament ethic, there are two other general things that we ought to notice.

First, the Old Testament is not in the least afraid of the reward motive. The Old Testament is quite insistent that the prosperity of a nation is in direct ratio to its obedience to God. Given obedience to God, the rains will fall, and the harvest will be sure, and there will be victory over their enemies; and given disobedience to God the national life will fall apart (Leviticus 26; Deuteronomy 28; Leviticus 5.18,19; Deuteronomy 7.12-16; 11.13-17). There are two things to be said. First, the Old Testament had little or no belief in any life to come, and therefore it had to promise its reward in this life; that is one of the differences which Christianity made (Cp. Job 14.7-12; Psalms 6.5; 30.9; 88.5,10-12; 115.17; Ecclesiastes 9.10; Isaiah 38.18). It brought in a new world to redress the balance of the old. Second, there is a real sense in which the Old Testament prophets were right. This much is true—there is not a problem threatening this or any other country just now which is not a moral problem. Industrial unrest, for instance, is not basically an economic problem today; it is a moral problem because—dare I say it?—and to this we will return—it springs from the fact that all of us—I, like everyone else—want to do as little as possible, in as short a time as possible, with as little effort as possible, and to get as much as possible—and de'il tak' the hinmost. You cannot mend an economic problem when the attitude to life of most people makes it insoluble.

The second broad fact to note—and again to this we will return—is that the prophets were politicians. The prophets were not talkers; they were doers. They were quite clear that the only way to turn the vision into fact was through political action. The prophets were the best friends the poor man ever had, and the biggest scourges the rich man ever had. Péguy the philosopher said: 'Everything begins in mysticism and ends in politics.' Of course, a man must have the vision of a perfect society. The demand of the prophet was; 'All right! You've had the vision. What are *you* doing about it?'

So then we come to look at some detail.

i. The supreme characteristic of the Old Testament ethic is its comprehensiveness. It involved every man and covered every action. One of the most extraordinary commands of God to the Jews was: 'You must be a kingdom of priests' (Leviticus 19.6). Goodness, religion, was not the business of a few experts; it was every man's business. Some poet wrote a poem about Judaea in which he said that all Judaea was 'pregnant with the living God'. The writer called Ecclesiastes, the preacher, said: 'He has set eternity in their heart' (Ecclesiastes 3.11, RV margin). All life came within the command and the service of God.

ii. Within the family parents were to be honoured (Exodus 20.12). To strike a parent was to deserve the death penalty (Exodus 21.15; Deuteronomy 21.18-21). If we may digress for one moment—the ancient world honoured parents as a duty which was built into life. The Babylonian code, the code of Hammurabi, has as the penalty for striking a parent that a man's hand should be cut off. Plato laid it down that the punishment for such a crime was permanent banishment, and death if the transgressor returned (*Laws* 881 BD). Cicero said that Solon the greatest of the Greek lawgivers did not legislate for the eventuality of a man striking a parent, for he believed that it was inconceivable that it should ever happen (*Rosc.* 25). Chastity and purity stood very high. The ideal of marriage was high but the practice did not reach the ideal—but of that more later.

iii. There is one very notable thing in Jewish law. The law was specially designed to protect the widow and the fatherless and the poor, for they were held to be specially dear to God (Deuteronomy 10.18; 1.17; 16.19; Leviticus 19.15). But—here is the special thing—the Jews insisted that there must be one law for everyone, the same for the Jew and the resident alien within their gates (Leviticus 24.22). There are two things about a Jew which together make an amazing paradox. The Jew never forgets he is one of the chosen people; he will not intermingle with the Gentile; but at the same time no nation ever more firmly banished racialism from their society. No matter who a man was, justice was his, because God cared for him.

There is only time to dip here and there into the ethic of the Old Testament and to choose some of the outstanding things.

i. To the Jewish ethic business morality mattered intensely. One of the most extraordinary things about the ethic of the Old Testament is that the obligation to have just weights and measures is laid down no fewer than seven times (Leviticus 19.35,36; Deuteronomy 25.13-16; Proverbs 16.11; Ezekiel 45.10-12; Amos 8.4-6; Micah 6.10,11). As the writer of the Proverbs has it: 'A just balance and scales are the Lord's; all the weights in the bag are his work.' Here is the God not only of the sanctuary and the church, but of the counter and the shop floor. The weighing out of the housewife's order and the measuring of the customer's request become an act of worship for the Jew. And that is why I think that it is safe to say that you will never find a dishonest Jew who has stuck to his religion.

ii. One of the outstanding features of the Jewish law is its stress on responsibility. A man is not only responsible for what he does; he is also responsible for the wrong thing he might have prevented and the damage for which he is to blame because of his carelessness or thoughtlessness. If an ox gores someone, if the ox was not known to be dangerous, then the ox is killed and the owner goes free; but if it was known that the ox was dangerous, then not only is the ox killed, but its owner too is liable to the death penalty—for he ought to have prevented the tragedy (Exodus 21.28-32). Palestinian houses were flat-roofed and the flat roof was often used as a place of rest and meditation. So it was laid down by the law that if a man built a house he must build a parapet round the roof, 'that you may not bring the guilt of blood on your house, if anyone fall from it' (Deuteronomy 22.8).

The Old Testament is sure that I am my brother's keeper; it is quite sure that I am not only responsible for the harm I have done, but that I am equally responsible for the harm I could have prevented.

iii. Lastly, there is in the Jewish ethic a kindness that is a lovely thing. A Jew wore only two articles of clothing; an undergarment like a shirt and an outer garment like a great cloak. He wore the cloak by day and he slept in it at night. It was laid down that, if ever he pawned the outer cloak, it must be given to him back again at night to sleep in. And the law-giver hears God say: 'And if he cries to me, I will hear, for I am compassionate' (Exodus 22.26,27; Deuteronomy 24.12,13). The law cared because God cared that a man should sleep warm at nights even in his poverty.

A Jewish workman's pay was no more than four new pence a day. No man ever got fat on that and no man ever saved on that. And so the law lays it down that a man must be paid on the day he has earned his pay—'lest he cry against you to the Lord and it be sin to you' (Leviticus 19.15; Deuteronomy 24.14,15; Malachi 3.5). God cares that the working man should get his pay.

A lost ox or ass is to be returned to its owner, or kept till it is claimed. An animal which has collapsed has to be helped to its feet again (Exodus 23.4,5; Deuteronomy 22.1-4; 21.1-9). In a nest the mother bird must always be spared (Deuteronomy 22.6,7). A field must not be reaped to the edge, nor gleaned twice; the olive trees must not be gone over twice; the vineyard must not be stripped and grapes which have fallen must not be gathered, for something must always be left for the poor and the stranger (Leviticus 19.9,10; 23.22; Deuteronomy 24.20,21). A deaf man must never be cursed and a blind man must never be tripped up (Leviticus 19.14; Deuteronomy 28.18). A man who had just married must be given no business to do and must be exempt from military service for one year to be 'free at home and for one year to be happy with the wife whom he has taken' (Deuteronomy 20.5-7; Leviticus 24.5).

There are few more wonderful ethics than the ethic of the

Old Testament. It has its sternness and it has its severity; but it has its mercy and its kindness and its love. It is the very basis of the Christian ethic, and the Christian ethic could not have had a greater base or a finer cradle.

CHAPTER TWO

The Characteristics of the Christian Ethic in the Teaching of Jesus

The title of this series of lectures is *Jesus Today*, and there are a large number of people who would say quite bluntly that they do not believe that Jesus has anything to do with today at all. The alternative title is *The Christian Ethic in the Twentieth Century*, and there are an equal number of people who would roundly declare that the Christian ethic has no relevance at all for the twentieth century. Are they right, or are they wrong?

You could, if you were so disposed, put up a very strong theoretical argument that the ethics of the Bible in general and of the New Testament in particular have nothing to do with 1970.

i. The oldest parts of the Old Testament date back to about 950 BC; the latest part of the New Testament dates back to about AD 120; that is to say, bits of the Bible are just about 3,000 years old; none of it is more recent than more than 1,800 years ago. How can teaching of that age have any relevance for today?

No one would try to teach doctors today with Galen and Hippocrates as their textbooks; no one would try to teach agriculture on the basis of Varro, or architecture on the basis of Vitruvius. The ancient writers in other spheres are interesting; they are part of the history of their subject. But no one accepts them as authoritative for life and living today. Why then accept Jesus? Why accept the New Testament?

ii. Further, the Bible, the New Testament and Jesus come from a tiny country. Palestine is only about 150 miles from north to south, about as far as Perth is from Carlisle or Doncaster from London. Palestine is about forty-five miles from east to west, less than the distance from Glasgow to Edinburgh or from London to Brighton. How can an ethic coming from a tiny country like that be an ethic for the world? Further, Palestine was inhabited by the Jews, and the Jews deliberately isolated themselves from other countries and other cultures. How can an ethic that comes from a country with a deliberate policy of self-isolation be an ethic for the world? Still further, politically the Jews were failures. They were subject to Assyria, Babylon, Persia, Greece, Rome. They hardly knew what freedom and independence were. How can an ethic that comes from a tiny, isolated, subject country be an ethic for the world?

iii. Again, it is obvious that life in Palestine was nothing like what life is today. Just think. The wages of a working man in Palestine were about four new pence a day. Even allowing for the vast difference in purchasing power, four new pence a day bears no relation to the wages which a man earns in the affluent society, in which people never had it so good. In the ancient world there was no such thing as industry in the modern sense of the term, no factories, no machines, no mechanisation, no industrialisation.

Again, in that ancient world society was by our standards extraordinarily immobile. In the early chapters of Samuel we read of Samuel and his mother Hannah. She took the little boy from his home in Ramah to the tabernacle in Shiloh and left him there with Eli the priest. And then it goes on to say that once a year she made him a new little coat, and once a year she visited him with the coat (1 Samuel 2.19). You would think that it was a tremendous journey, a journey that could only be faced once a year. In point of fact Ramah was fifteen miles from Shiloh! Jesus was only once in his life more than about seventy miles from home. When you think of the difference between that and a society in which a summer holiday in Spain is a commonplace, and a flight to the moon a possibility, then you see that that society and ours are worlds apart.

How then can a teaching and an ethic given in a society like that have any connection at all with today?

Two things have to be said. Firstly, externals can change while the underlying principles remain the same. Take the case of buildings. There is a very great difference between the Pyramids in Egypt, the Parthenon in Athens, Canterbury Cathedral, Liverpool Cathedral, Coventry Cathedral, and the Post Office Tower in London. Externally they look worlds apart, and yet underlying them all there are the same laws of architecture, because, if there were not, they would simply fall down. The externals can be as different as can be; the underlying principle is the same.

Now add the second thing. The one thing that the Christian ethic is all about is personal relationships. It is about the relationship between men and men, and men and women, and men and women and God; and personal relationships don't change. Love and hate, honour and loyalty remain the same.

Someone took this illustration—when Rachel arrived to marry Jacob she arrived on a camel, in eastern robes and veiled and hidden; the modern bride arrives in a hired Rolls-Royce and a miniskirt. But the situation is exactly the same—two young people in love. You remember Thomas Hardy's lines:

Yonder a maid and her wight
Go whispering by,
War's annals will fade into night
Ere their story die.

This is why the ethics of the New Testament and of the Bible are as valid today as ever they were. It is because they are all about the unchangeable things, the relations which do not alter so long as men are men and women are women and God is God.

If this is so, one thing stands out about the Christian ethic—it is *a community ethic*. It is an ethic which would be almost impossible for a man to live in isolation from his fellow men. Love, loyalty, forgiveness, service—these are community matters; things which can only be found and exercised when people live together. When John Wesley was young and still bewildered in the faith he formed a plan to get himself a hut on the moors and to go away and live alone with God. An older and at that time a wiser Christian said to him: 'God knows nothing of solitary religion.' This business of Christian living is something which is to be found among men.

Now we must ask the all-important question. What is it that characterises the ethic of the New Testament? Or to put it in another way in view of what we have been saying—what is it that characterises the personal relationship of the Christian with his fellow men?

This has got to be pushed one step back. We have to ask first—what are the personal relationships of God with his creatures as taught by Jesus? We have to ask that for this reason: one of the main features of the Christian ethic lies in the demand for imitation. Men are to imitate Jesus. Peter says that Jesus left as an example that we should follow in his steps (1 Peter 2.21). The word he uses for example is *hupogrammos*, and *hupogrammos* was the word for the perfect line of copperplate handwriting at the top of the page of a child's exercise-book, the line which had to be copied. So then the Christian has to copy Jesus. And it is Paul's demand that the Christian should imitate God—and after all is this not a reasonable demand since man, as the Bible sees it, is made in the image and the likeness of God (Ephesians 5.1; Genesis 1.26,27)?

So then what we really have to ask is—what is the new thing that Jesus taught about God in regard to God's personal relationships with his people?

If we go to the Greek ideas about God, we find that the first and most basic idea of God is the idea of God's absolute serenity, a serenity which nothing in earth or in heaven can affect. The Greeks used two words about God. They talked about his *ataraxia*. When Jesus talked about our hearts being *troubled*, he used the verb (*tarassō*) which is the opposite of *ataraxia*. *Ataraxia* is undisturbedness; it is inviolable peace. The Stoics talked about the *apatheia* of God, by which they meant that God was by his nature incapable of feeling. It is feeling which disturbs. If you can love, you can be worried and sad and distressed about the one you love. They felt that the one essential thing about God was this serene, undisturbed, absolute, untouchable peace. To have that peace God, they said, must be without feeling.

Here is the difference which Christianity made. Jesus Christ came to tell men of a God who cares desperately, a God who is involved in the human situation, a God who in the Old Testament phrase is afflicted in all our afflictions, a God who is concerned. A detached serenity is the very opposite of the Christian idea of God. The insulated, emotionless deity is the reverse of the Christian God.

If this is so, then the basis of the Christian ethic is clear—*the basis of the Christian ethic is concern*. Here is the essence of three of the great parables of Jesus. In the parable of the sheep and the goats (Matthew 25.31-46), the standard of the final judgment of men is quite simply: Were you concerned about people in trouble? In the parable of the rich man and Lazarus (Luke 16.19-30) there is not the slightest indication that the rich man was in any way cruel to Lazarus. The trouble was that he never noticed the existence of Lazarus. Lazarus was there in poverty and pain and the rich man simply accepted him as part of the landscape; he was not in the least concerned; and in the parable he finished up in hell.

The third parable is that of the Good Samaritan (Luke 10.29-37). The whole point of the parable is the concern of the Samaritan. While the others passed by on the other side, concerned only to avoid all contact with suffering, the Samaritan was concerned and did something.

William Booth would always deny that the vast and wide-ranging work of the Salvation Army was planned. He used to say:

> We saw the need. We saw the people starving, we saw people going about half-naked, people doing sweated labour; and we set about bringing a remedy for these things. We were obliged—there was a compulsion. How could one do anything else?

But the whole trouble is that plenty of people can do something else—they can do nothing. It was this concern that haunted a man like William Booth. 1868 was the last Christmas Day he ever spent in the normal way with a meal and a party. He had come back from preaching in Whitechapel in the morning. He tried to keep Christmas, but he couldn't. 'I'll never spend a Christmas Day like this again,' he said. 'The poor have nothing but the public house, nothing but the public house.' Later in life he was to say when the agony of dyspepsia made eating almost impossible for him: 'They bring me eggs for breakfast and right now children are starving.' What haunted him above all was put in that most pathetic of phrases—he was haunted by the thought of children to whom the word *kiss* was a meaningless mystery.

First, then, the basis of the Christian ethic is the basis of the being of God and of the life of Jesus Christ—it is concern.

In this life of concern the Christian is the very reverse of the Greek. Inevitably the Greek saw life in terms of a God who was serene, isolated, untouchable, freed from all feeling and emotion. Therefore, he argued, a man must be like this. And so his great aim could be summed up in one sentence: 'Teach yourself not to care. Whatever happens, God sent it anyway. Therefore accept it.'

But the Stoics went farther; they saw life as a process of learning not to care. Epictetus gives his advice; begin, he says, with a torn robe or a broken cup or plate and say, I don't care. Go on to the death of a pet dog or horse, and say, I don't care. In the end you will come to a stage when you can stand beside the bed of your loved one and see that loved one die, and say, I don't care.

For the Stoic life was a progress in not caring; for a Christian life is a process of learning to care—like God.

Set that beside the last speech William Booth made in 1912 when he was an old man and knew that he was going to become blind:

> When women weep as they do now, I'll fight; while little children go hungry as they do now, I'll fight; while men go to prison in and out, in and out, I'll fight; while there yet remains one dark soul without the light of God, I'll fight—I'll fight to the end.

And he did. If you want to see what the Christian ethic is all about place that dying battle-cry of Booth beside the education in not caring—and you have the difference.

The Gospels have a word for this attitude of concern. They call it love. Since this is at the very heart of the Christian ethic we must look more closely at it.

We begin with a disadvantage. In English the word *love* has a highly emotional content. It is that outreach and upsurge of the heart which we feel for those who are very near and very dear to us. And so when we are told that we must *love* our neighbour, and still more, when we are told that we must *love* our enemies, we are daunted by the seeming impossibility of the task. Love, as we have learned to use the word, is not something which can be diffused over a great number of people; it is necessarily something which by its nature has to be concentrated on some very few, on some one person. The Greeks knew this. They knew all about the love which was a passion and a desire, overmastering in its intensity, and they called it *erōs*. They knew of the steadfast love of affection which comes from the experience of facing life together, the lasting love which binds two people together, even when passion is spent. They called it *philia*. They knew of the love which a child has for his parent, a son for his mother, a daughter for her father, a brother for a sister, a love into which sex does not enter at all. They called it *storgē*.

But the love which Jesus demands is none of these things; it is *agapē*. What is it, this *agapē*? We have it described to us in terms of the attitude of God to men:

> You have heard that it was said, 'You shall love your neighbour, and hate your enemy.' But I say to you, Love your enemies, and pray for those who persecute you, so that you may be the sons of your Father who is in heaven; for he makes his sun rise on the evil and on the good, and sends rain on the just and on the unjust (*Matthew 5.43-45*).

What then is the distinguishing thing about this love of God which is to be our love for our fellow men? Its characteristic is that to good and evil, to just and unjust, God gives his gifts. The sunlight and the rain are there for all men. So this means that, whether a man is good or bad, God's goodwill goes out to this man; God wants nothing but his good; God's benevolence is around him and about him.

This is what Christian love is. It is an attitude to other people. It is the set of the will towards others. It is the attitude of a goodwill that cannot be altered, a desire for men's good that nothing can kill. Quite clearly, this is not simply a response of the heart; this is not an emotional reaction; this is an act of the will. In this it is not simply our heart that goes out to others; it is our whole personality. *And this is why it can be commanded and demanded of us.* It would be impossible to demand that we love people in the sense of falling in love with them. It would be impossible to demand that we love our enemies as we love those who are dearer to us than life itself. But it is possible to say to us: 'You must try to be like God. You must try never to wish anything but good for others. You must try to look at every man with the eyes of God, with the eyes of goodwill.'

Luther noticed one thing about the love of God. In the Heidelberg Disputation of 1518 he was talking about the love of God, and he said this: 'Sinners are attractive because they are loved; they are not loved because they are attractive.' God does not love us because we are attractive and lovable people; he loves us as we are, and by his love he recreates us and remakes us. This is how we ought to love others. We do not love them because they are lovable; no one needs anyone to command him to love a winsome and attractive person. The whole point about Christian love is that it is that attitude of the mind and the will and the whole personality which can make us love the unlovely, the unlovable, the unloving, even those who hate us and hurt us and injure us, in the sense that, do what they like, we will never have anything but goodwill to them, and we will never seek anything but their good.

This is the concern of the Christian, because this is the concern of God. It is not a spasmodic emotional thing; it is not something which is dependent on the attractiveness of the other person. It has learned to look on men as God looks on them, with an eye which is not blind to their faults and their failings and their sins, but which for ever and for ever yearns to help, and the worse the man is, the greater the yearning to help. There is a sense in which the more a man hurts me the more I must love him, because the more he needs my love.

Nor is this quite the end of the matter. Luther begins the section of the Disputation from which I have already quoted like this:

> The love of God does not find, but creates, that which is pleasing to it. The love of man comes into being through that which is pleasing to it.

This is to say, human love loves that which is lovable; divine love loves that which is unlovable, and by loving it makes it lovable. This Christian love, then, to be like God's love has this attitude of unchanging goodwill, but it does not simply accept the other person as he is, as if it did not matter if he always remained the same and never became otherwise. The Christian, like God, wishes to love men into loveliness, into goodness, into love in return. It does not always work, but sometimes it can blessedly happen that we can love a person out of bitterness and out of hatred and into love. To answer hatred with hatred, bitterness with bitterness, can do nothing but beget hatred and bitterness. There are times when we will fail, but the only way to make the unloving loving is by love. And that is what Christian concern means.

But we go one step farther than this—and again it is the new thing Jesus brought—the Christian ethic is not only concern, it is *universal concern.* I suppose the greatest moral teacher the Greeks ever had was Plato; but you can only describe the ethic of Plato as an aristocratic ethic. He saw life as aimed at the production of the philosopher kings who were, as it were, right at the top of a human pyramid; and the ordinary people existed only to make life possible for the magnificent few. Greek civilisation was built on slavery, and a slave was a living tool.

It took the world about 1,800 years to begin to discover this part of the Christian ethic. As late as 1895 the Salvation Army started work in India and lived among the Indians. An English official said to the Salvationists: 'I don't know how you can bear to live among these people. To us, they're cattle, just cattle.'

That's India. All right, do you know that as late as 1865 in this country only one man in twenty-four had the vote? Just at the turn of the eighteenth century into the nineteenth century the word *democrat* was a bad word. Thomas Coke, the famous Methodist, second only to John Wesley, writes to Henry Dundas:

> When a considerable number of democrats had crept in among us, to the number of about 5,000, I was the principal means of their being entirely excluded from our Society.

Did not Queen Victoria herself write that she could never be 'the queen of a democratic monarchy'?

It took the world a very long time to see that the Christian ethic demands not only concern, but universal concern.

But in contrast with what went before there is still something else to say. The Christian ethic demands concern; it demands universal concern; and it demands *passionate* concern.

We have already looked at Plato's ethic. The other supreme Greek philosopher was Aristotle, and Aristotle produced one of the most famous of all ethical theories, the theory of the mean. We would now call it the happy medium. He taught that virtue is always the mean between two extremes. On the one side there is the extreme of excess and on the other side there is the extreme of defect, and in between there is the mean. So on the one side there is cowardice; on the other side there is recklessness; and in between there is courage. On the one side there is the miser; on the other side there is the spendthrift; and in between there is the generous man.

When you have an ethic like that the one thing you can never have is enthusiasm. You are always busy calculating between too much and too little, balancing and adjusting. It is an ethic of calculation. But the Christian ethic is the passionate ethic; it is not the ethic of the man who carefully calculates every risk; it is the ethic of the man who flings himself into life, and whose sympathy with men is a passion.

We have to add still something else to the concern of the Christian ethic; the concern of the Christian ethic is a *total concern.* As Paul saw it, man is body, soul and spirit. The body is the flesh and blood part of a man; the soul, the *psuchē*, is not what we usually mean by soul. The soul is the animal life of a man. Everything that lives has *psuchē*. An animal has *psuchē*; even a plant has *psuchē*; *psuchē* is the breath of physical life which all living things share. The spirit, the *pneuma*, is that which is unique to man; this is what man alone has; this is the part of man which is kin to God and to which God can speak.

Now here again Christianity brought something new into the world. The ancient world by and large despised and feared the body; it thought that all man's troubles and sins and sufferings came from the fact that he had a body. Plato said that the body is the prison-house of the soul. Seneca spoke of the detestable habitation of the body. Epictetus said that he was a poor soul shackled to a corpse. The ancient world hated the body. And there is still a strain in Christianity which is ashamed of the body, a strain which is still frightened of sex and of physical things, and which thinks that things like that are not quite polite and should not be spoken of.

The Christian ethic is quite sure of two things. It is quite sure that we can take our body and offer it as a sacrifice to God (Romans 12.1); that in fact is exactly what we must do. To allow the body to become weak and ill and inefficient and fat and flabby is a sin. It is just as much a sin to let our body run to seed as it is to let your soul run to seed. Physical fitness is one of the duties laid on a Christian.

Second, the Christian is as concerned with men's bodies as he is with their souls. William Booth could never forget the saying of Jesus before the feeding of the five thousand: 'Give ye them to eat' (Matthew 14.16). That is why he started his Food-for-the-Million shops and why he gave men and women free meals. That is why Bramwell Booth was in Covent Garden Market with a barrow at three o'clock in the morning begging for rejected vegetables and bones to make soup. That is why Booth said:

> No one gets a blessing, if they have cold feet, and nobody ever gets saved if they have toothache.

Booth knew that men's bodies mattered. George Whitefield was with Booth here. When Whitefield went to America he certainly took one hundred and fifty common prayer books and a lot of books of sermons; but he also took enough material things to fill two pages of print—at random—twenty-four striped flannel waistcoats, twelve dozen shirt buttons; rhubarb, senna, saffron, gentian-root, a Cheshire cheese; three barrels of raisins; pepper, oatmeal, onions, sage and two hogsheads of fine white wine! When he got on board ship he writes in his diary:

> The sick increased upon my hands, but were very thankful for my furnishing them with sage-tea, sugar, broth etc.

He reached America and we find him supplying a family with eight sows and a pig; we find him giving a cow and a calf to a poor woman; and barrels of flour to a poor baker. There are times when sermons and prayers and Bible readings are very poor substitutes for a good meal.

We will not forget that the Christian ethic ought never to forget that men have bodies and these bodies are the property of God and that they matter to God.

We have always to remember that the Christian ethic is an ethic which looks to the beyond. It remembers that there is a world to come. That does not mean that it offers pie in the sky; it does not mean that it is so concerned with heaven that earth is a desert drear. But it does mean that the Christian knows that life is going somewhere; that this life is the first chapter of a continued story; and that what happens after death is affected deeply by the kind of life that we live here.

When Dick Sheppard died after his most notable ministry in St Martin-in-the-Fields, one of the great national daily papers published a cartoon. It showed Dick's empty pulpit, and on the pulpit, an open Bible, and beneath, the caption: Here endeth the reading of the first lesson.

The Christian ethic lives in the consciousness of eternity.

You remember the byreman in Stevenson's story. Stevenson asked him if he never got tired of the muck and the mud and the dirt of the byre as his work. 'No,' he said. 'No; he that has something ayont need never weary.' The Christian ethic is lived in the light of the beyond.

It is very important to note that the Christian ethic is a positive ethic. This is to say that the Christian ethic on the whole tells us rather what to do than what not to do.

The Ten Commandments are on the whole *Thou shalt not's*. In one particular commandment—not one of the Ten Commandments—this is of the first importance. This is in what is usually known as the Golden Rule. In its negative form the Golden Rule is to be met with in many systems of ethics: Don't do to others what you would not like them to do to you. But the Christian version of it is positive: Do to others what you would like them to do to you (Matthew 7.12). The Christian version is much the more demanding. It is not so very difficult to abstain from doing things. But the Christian demand is not simply that we abstain from doing things to others, but that we actively do to them what we would wish them to do to us.

This is the Christian doctrine of love. We have to note very carefully the word the Christian ethic uses for love. It is the word *agapē*. It has no passion in it; no sex; it has no sentimental romanticism in it. It means an undefeatable attitude of goodwill; it means that no matter what the other man does to us we will never under any circumstances seek anything but his good. It is an attitude of goodwill to others no matter what they are like. It is not simply a reaction of the heart; it is a direction of the will. It can be exercised even to the person we do not like, because, even not liking him, we can still deliberately and purposefully wish him nothing but well and act for nothing but his good.

The whole point of the Christian ethic is not that it supplies us with a list of things we must not do. It says to us: Your attitude to your fellow men must be such that you wish only their good. And if you look at men like that, then the practice of the Christian ethic becomes the inevitable result.

There is another and a very important sense in which the Christian ethic is a total ethic. It is an ethic of thought as well as of action; of feelings as well as of conduct. Thus it condemns not only murder, but also the anger which brought about the murder (Matthew 5.21, 22). But we must have a care as to just how we state this inner demand, and in particular in one application of it. Jesus said:

> You have heard that it was said: You shall not commit adultery. But I say to you that everyone who looks at a woman lustfully has already committed adultery with her in his heart (*Matthew 5.28*).

If we will only think, we will not say—as some have said—

that the wrong desire is just as bad as the wrong deed. If that were so, we would be saying that it is just as wrong to have a temptation as it is to fall to that temptation. In that case we might as well fall to the temptation straight away. To have a wrong desire and to resist it cannot be as bad as to have a wrong desire and to act on it.

This saying of Jesus has worried a great many people. If we go to the Greek of it, we see what Jesus really meant. What the Greek condemns is not the person who looks at a beautiful person and has an instinctive reaction of admiration and even of desire. What it does condemn—and the Greek makes this quite clear—is the person who looks at another in such a way as deliberately to awaken and to foment desire. What is condemned is a particular kind of looking; the kind of looking which reads pornographic literature in order quite deliberately to waken desire; the kind of looking to be found at a striptease show; the kind of looking which, as the French phrase has it, undresses with its eyes the person at whom it looks; the kind of looking which smears anything with a kind of smut and filthiness. This does not condemn the kind of looking which comes to all of us simply because a man is a man and a woman is a woman and God made us so. It condemns the prying, peering looking which uses the eyes to foment desire.

What in the end Jesus is saying in these teachings of his about the inner desire is that in the last analysis the only thing which is truly sufficient, the only peak which is at the top of the Christian ethic, is the situation in which a man has come to a stage when he not only does not do the wrong thing, but does not even want to do it—for only then is he safe.

It is here that we have to look at the phrase which dominates the letters of Paul—the phrase *in Christ*. In Paul's letters everything is *in Christ*. A great New Testament scholar used an analogy to explain this phrase. He used the analogy of the air, the atmosphere. We cannot live at all physically unless the air is in us and we are in the air. Otherwise, we cannot breathe; we die. Just so, for the Christian, Jesus Christ is the atmosphere of his life. The Christian is conscious always of his presence.

We may take another analogy. There are certain abnormal psychological conditions which make a man behave in public in ways he should not behave; and one piece of psychological advice which is very often given to such people is never to go out alone, always to go out with a friend. The whole basis of the Christian ethic is that the Christian never goes out alone. He goes out always with the memory and the presence of Jesus Christ.

So then to sum up, the keynote of the Christian ethic is concern; that concern is embodied in Jesus Christ and is the expression of the very life and heart of God. It is a concern that knows neither boundaries nor limits. It is expressed in the life of the world; and in the world it is purified and inspired by the continuous memory that life is lived in the presence and in the power of Jesus Christ.

CHAPTER THREE

The Characteristics of the Christian Ethic in the Teaching of Paul

Most people think of Paul as a theologian, and a difficult theologian at that. Even within the New Testament there are people saying that Paul's letters were anything but easy to understand (2 Peter 3.16). But for Paul every theological argument ended with a series of ethical imperatives. In letter after letter the theological argument, however difficult it may be, ends with an ethical section which is crystal clear. The argument ends in the demand (Romans 12-15; Galatians 6.1-10; Ephesians 5.21-6.9; Colossians 3.18-4.6; 1 Thessalonians 5; 2 Thessalonians 3). In 1 Timothy the object of the letter is to show 'how one ought to behave in the household of God' (1 Timothy 3.15). The New English Bible margin translation of Titus 3.8 runs: 'Those who have come to believe in God should make it their business to practise virtue.' Paul is every bit as great and earnest an ethical teacher as he is a theologian. Let us then look at the ethical teaching of his letters.

i. For Paul, as for Jesus, the Christian ethic is a community ethic. The great virtues of love and service and forgiveness can only be practised in a society. Involvement, not detachment, is the keynote of the ethics of Paul.

ii. But equally definitely for Paul the Christian ethic is an ethic of difference. Paul's letters are regularly addressed to the people whom the Authorised Version calls the *saints* (Romans 1.7; 1 Corinthians 1.2; 2 Corinthians 1.1; Ephesians 1.1; Philippians 1.1; Colossians 1.2). The Greek word is *hagios*. We have already looked at this word as it is used in the Old Testament of the people Israel. It is the word which in the

Old Testament is regularly translated *holy*, and its basic idea is the idea of *difference*. That which is *hagios*, *holy*, the Sabbath, the Temple, the Bible, is that which is different. So the Christian is first and foremost to be different. That difference comes from the fact that he is dedicated and consecrated to God; and that difference is to be demonstrated within the world and not by withdrawal from the world.

When Paul does not write to the *hagioi*, the saints, the men and women pledged to be different, he writes to the *ekklēsia*, the church, in whatever place it happens to be (Galatians 1.2; 1 Thessalonians 1.1; 2 Thessalonians 1.1). This word has exactly the same implication. *Ekklēsia* is tied up with the verb *ekkalein*, which means *to call out*, and the church is composed of those who are called out from the world, not to leave the world, but to live in the world and its society, and there to be different.

The Christian, says Paul, is not to be conformed to the world, but transformed from it (Romans 12.2). The Christian lives in the world, but it is not on a worldly war that he is engaged (2 Corinthians 10.3). The Christians must be children of God without blemish, shining like lights in a twisted and perverse society (Philippians 2.15). The Christian must not live as if he still belonged to the world (Colossians 2.20).

That last demand brings us to another of Paul's consistent demands. He is always urging on his people that they should make it clear that they are changed, that they have left their old life behind them, and that they have genuinely embarked on the new way. They must no longer live as the Gentiles do (Ephesians 4.17-24). Once they were in darkness, now they are in light, and their conduct must show it (Ephesians 5.8). Once they were hostile to God and estranged from him; now they are reconciled to him (Colossians 1.21-23). Once they were dead in trespasses; now they are gloriously alive (Colossians 2.13). They must put away the conduct which was formerly characteristic of their lives (Colossians 3.7-10). They must not act with the passion of lust of heathen who do not know God (1 Thessalonians 4.5).

It would never have occurred to Paul that it would have been impossible to distinguish between the Christian and the non-Christian. He would have agreed with Richard Glover, who said that there was no such thing as secret discipleship, for either the secrecy killed the discipleship or the discipleship killed the secrecy. For the Christian every moment of life was to be a demonstration that he was a Christian.

How does that work out today? In the present situation a man does not come out of a heathen society into a Christian society, for even when the church is disregarded or ignored, the principles on which society is built are now Christian principles. What should happen now is this. Nowadays a man knows very well what the Christian ethic demands. When he becomes a pledged follower of Jesus Christ, he should move from a theoretical awareness of the Christian ethic to a committed practice of it. Knowledge should turn into action—whatever the cost.

iii. The idea of difference can be taken a step farther and confront us with something of a problem. There are times in Paul's teaching when the difference turns into severance. There are times in Paul's letters when the difference seems to become segregation. In 2 Corinthians 6.14-16 Paul writes: 'Do not be mismated with unbelievers. For what partnership have righteousness and iniquity? Or what fellowship has light with darkness? What accord has Christ with Belial? Or what has a believer in common with an unbeliever?' The Letter to the Ephesians speaks of those who are immoral and impure, and then goes on to say: 'Do not associate with them' (Ephesians 5.7). Paul warns the Thessalonians to keep away from any brother who is living in idleness. If anyone will not accept his authority, the Thessalonians are to note that man and to have nothing to do with him (2 Thessalonians 3.6,14). The Pastoral Letters speak of those whose religion is only a name, and whose profligate lives deny their profession. 'Avoid such people' (2 Timothy 3.1-5). If a man is factious, he is to be admonished once or twice. If the warning is ineffective, 'Have nothing more to do with him, knowing that such a person is perverted and sinful' (Titus 3.10,11).

This is a formidable series of warnings. What is to happen to missionary work? Are certain people to be abandoned as hopeless? Is the sinner to be left to his sin? This is clearly something which demands thinking about. Certain points can be made.

(a) We must never forget the general situation. When Paul was writing, the Christian church was no more than a little island in a surrounding sea of paganism. The tempting and the infecting influences were terrifyingly near. These Christians in the early church were only one remove from paganism, and relapse was so desperately easy.

We can see the thing coming to a head in 1 Corinthians chapters 8 to 10. There the point at issue is whether or not a Christian can eat meat that has been offered to an idol, that is, meat which has formed part of a heathen sacrifice. The problem arose in this way. In the ancient world it was only in the very rarest cases that a sacrifice was burned entire. In by far the greater number of cases only a token part of the sacrifice was burned on the altar, sometimes no more than a few hairs cut from the forehead of the beast. Part of the meat then became the perquisite of the priests, and part was returned to the worshipper. With his part the worshipper gave a feast, a party, a celebration for his friends. And—and here is the point—that feast was given in a temple. Just as we might give a party in an hotel or restaurant or club, so the Greek gave it in the temple of his god. The invitation would run: 'I invite you to dine with me on such and such a date and at such and such a time at the table of our Lord Serapis,' Serapis being the host's favourite god. Could the Christian go to such a party? Paul is clear that he cannot. Paul is clear that no man can be a guest at the table of Jesus Christ and then a guest at the table of Serapis. He cannot have it both ways. He must be off with the old love before he is on with the new (1 Corinthians 10.21,22). To try to act like this was to court infection. It could mean that a man's social life came to an abrupt end, but that was part of the price that he had to pay for being a Christian.

(b) The second thing that emerges when we consider these passages is that the person who is being condemned is the person who is deliberately and open-eyed flirting with temptation. What is being insisted on by Paul is that in that precarious situation no man should voluntarily go into company which would endanger his life as a Christian.

(c) And most of all it is the misguided Christian brother who is to be avoided. It is not a case of the Christian cutting himself off from the world and from all the missionary opportunities life in the world gave him; it is a question of cutting himself off from the Christian brother who was hell-bent on folly. Paul makes this quite clear in 1 Corinthians 5.9-13. In the church at Corinth there was a man who had been guilty of sexual misconduct with his step-mother, conduct which would have shocked a heathen, let alone a Christian. Paul insists that the congregation must take action. The man must be ejected. They are not to associate with immoral men. But, says Paul, this does not mean out in the world, or they would have to leave the world altogether. It is not outsiders they are to judge; it is their own members; and if a man claims the name of brother and behaves shamelessly, he must go.

From this certain things emerge. It is the pledged Christian who is in question. The church dare not adopt an easy-going attitude to the man who is guilty of flagrant misconduct. It is a matter of discipline, and Paul holds that if a pledged Christian refuses to accept the ethical standards of the church, then the church must in self-defence take action.

(d) But that is not the end of the story. It is discipline that is in question. Even if excommunication means apparently delivering a man to Satan, the ultimate end is to save his soul alive (1 Corinthians 5.5), and in one case at least we find Paul pleading for the receiving back of the sinner into the fellowship before his spirit is altogether broken (2 Corinthians 2.5-11). The whole process is for cure and not for destruction.

What it all means is that the church cannot continue to be the church and refuse to exercise discipline. The Christian is a man under pledge, a pledge voluntarily given, and he cannot with impunity deliberately break his pledge. And the word *deliberately* is to be stressed. All the way through it is clear that Paul is not thinking of the man who on the impulse is swept into sin and who has never ceased to repent. He is thinking of the man who, deaf to appeal and blind to duty and oblivious to love, has callously and deliberately gone his own way.

iv. A community ethic is bound to be an ethic of responsibility. The Christian is characteristically the responsible man.

(a) The Christian is responsible to the society of which he forms a part. Here Paul uses an analogy which many of the classical writers had used before him, the analogy of the body. The most famous instance of it in the classical writers is in the parable of Menenius Agrippa (Livy 2.32). There was an occasion in Rome when there was a split between the common people and the aristocrats. The split grew so wide that the common people marched out and withdrew from the city. The life of the city came to a standstill. So the rulers of the city sent an orator called Menenius Agrippa out to the people to see if he could persuade them to return. He told them a parable which ran something like this. There came a time when the members of the body grew very annoyed with the stomach. There the stomach sat, they said, doing nothing, and they had all to labour and to combine in bringing food to the stomach which itself did nothing to procure it. So the members of the body decided that they would no longer bring food to the stomach; the hands would not lift it to the mouth; the teeth would not chew it; the throat would not swallow it; and by this they hoped to have their revenge on the stomach. But the only result was that the whole body was in danger of starving to death, and thus the members of the body learned that the only way in which the body can maintain its health and well-being is for every part of it to do its share, and not to be envious and jealous of any other part.

This is exactly the picture that Paul uses in Romans 12.3-8. They are one body in Christ, and each a member of the body. Grace has given them different gifts and all these gifts must be used for the good of the whole. 'No man is an Island, entire of itself,' as John Donne said. No man lives to himself and no man dies to himself (Romans 14.7). We are, in the vivid Old Testament phrase, bound up in the bundle of life (1 Samuel 25.29). A man cannot do without society, and society cannot do without him. If a person 'drops out' from society, he does not really do so. He withdraws himself and his labour and his contribution from society, but if he is to live and eat he has to take what society still gives him. He has chosen to retain his rights and to abdicate from his responsibilities.

(b) The Christian has a responsibility to the weaker brother. He is well aware that he is his brother's keeper. This is true both mentally and physically. What may be perfectly safe for one person may be highly dangerous for another. Paul reminds us that arguments and debates which may be for one man a pleasant mental hike or an intellectual stimulus may be for another man the ruin of his faith (Romans 14.1). And the strong must always bear with the weak, for we are in this world, not to please ourselves, but to strengthen our neighbour (Romans 15.1,2). A man must always remember the effect on others of that which he allows himself. Twice Paul lays this down most practically and explicitly. 'It is right not to eat meat or drink wine or do anything that makes your brother stumble' (Romans 14.13-21). 'If food is a cause of my brother's falling, I will never eat meat, lest I cause my brother to fall' (1 Corinthians 8.13). Saul Kane in John Masefield's poem *The Everlasting Mercy* was haunted by 'the harm I've done by being me'. The New Testament is quite clear that the

Christian must always ask not only: 'What will this do to me?' but also: 'What will this do to the brother who is not as strong as I am?'

(c) The Christian has a responsibility to the state, but that we will leave for future discussion, when we come to talk about the Christian and the community.

(d) The Christian has a responsibility to the man who is going astray. He must gently restore him to the right way (Galatians 6.5). The Christian is conscious of the sin of looking on; he knows that a man can sin just as badly by doing nothing as by doing something.

(e) Three times in the New Testament there is laid down the simple, human duty of providing hospitality for the traveller and the stranger (Hebrews 13.2; 1 Peter 4.9; Romans 12.13). 'Practise hospitality,' says Paul. And little wonder. In the ancient world inns were notoriously bad. In his *Pagan Background of Early Christianity* W. R. Halliday has a vivid chapter on 'Communications' in which he describes travel. He cites a charming but very apocryphal story from the apocryphal *Acts of John* (M. R. James, *The Apocryphal New Testament*, p. 242). John and his disciples came to a deserted inn and settled down for the night. The bed proved to be infested with bugs. Whereupon John addressed them: 'I say unto you, O bugs, behave yourselves one and all, and leave your abode for the night and remain quiet in the one place, and keep your distance from the servants of God.' On the next morning when the servants opened the door 'we saw at the door of the house which we had taken a great number of bugs standing.' John then 'sat up on the bed and looked at them and said: "Since you have well behaved yourselves in hearkening to my rebuke, come into your place." And when he had said this, and risen from the bed, the bugs running from the door hastened to the bed and disappeared into the joints.' The innkeeper's terms were extortionate. Seneca writes (*On Benefits* 6.15): 'How glad we are at the sight of shelter in a desert, a roof in the storm, a bath or a fire in the cold—and how dear they cost in inns.' Many of the inns in the cities were no better than brothels, although of course in the great resorts there were palatial inns for the wealthy; but few Christians were wealthy. So the simple duty of keeping open door for the young person away from home and for the stranger in a strange place is a part of the Christian ethic.

(f) The Christian has a responsibility to Jesus Christ. The church is the body of Christ (1 Corinthians 12.27; Ephesians 1.22). That phrase may mean many things; but it means one simple and practical thing. Jesus is no longer here in the body; he is here in the Spirit. But that means that, if he wants something done, he has to get a man or a woman to do it for him. There is a helplessness of Jesus as well as a power of Jesus. Nothing can teach his children unless a man or woman will do it for him. The help which he wishes the aged, the weak, the suffering, the sorrowing to have must come through human means. He needs men to be hands to work for him, mouths to speak for him, feet to run on his errands. The Christian cannot forget his responsibility to Jesus Christ. It is no small part of the Christian ethic that the Christian is the representative of Jesus Christ.

v. The Pauline ethic is an ethic of body, soul and spirit. It is quite convinced of the importance of the body. The body can be presented as a living sacrifice to God (Romans 12.1). The body is nothing less than the temple in which the Holy Spirit can dwell (1 Corinthians 3.16; 6.19). The body can therefore neither be despised nor misused. It must be used for what it is, and the Pauline ethic has no use for the asceticism which despises marriage and refuses the good gifts of God (1 Timothy 4.1-5). This is in line with Judaism, for there is a rabbinic saying that a man will have to give account for every good thing that he might have enjoyed and did not enjoy.

This has to be seen against a background of Gnosticism. Gnosticism was a type of thought very prevalent in the time of the New Testament. It had not yet developed into the elaborate systems into which it later flowered, but it was deeply ingrained into Greek thought. It came from a desire to explain whence came the sin and the sorrow and the suffering of this world. It began with the principle that from all eternity there have been two principles—spirit and matter. God is spirit and spirit is altogether good. Matter was there from the very beginning, and matter is the stuff out of which the universe is created. But—and here is the essential point—the Gnostic believed that from the beginning matter is essentially flawed; it is evil; the universe is made out of bad stuff. But if matter is bad, then the God who is altogether pure spirit cannot touch it. The real and the true God cannot be the creator. So, according to the Gnostic belief, the true God put forth a series of emanations, each one farther from himself, each one more ignorant of himself, and in the end culminating in an emanation who was not only ignorant of, but hostile to, the real God. It was this distant, ignorant, hostile emanation who was the creator. There is only one conclusion to be drawn from all this—that the body and all that has to do with it is essentially bad. And that gives rise to two possible ways of life. The one way demands complete asceticism, where a man despises and neglects the body and stifles all its instincts and impulses. For him, sex, marriage, everything that has to do with the body is incurably evil and must be abandoned. The second way argues that, since the body is in any event evil, it does not matter what you do with it. Let it have its way; sate its impulses and glut its appetites. It does not matter what happens to it. This leads to complete immorality and to the abandonment of life to life's physical instincts. As Augustine said, he could find parallels in the Greek philosophers for everything in the Bible except the words: 'The Word became flesh' (John 1.14). Flesh, a body, was the one thing that God could never take upon himself.

This is far from the thought of Paul. But it did deeply affect Christian thinking. And the matter was complicated by a misunderstanding of the Pauline use of the word *flesh*. In Paul *flesh* does not mean the *body*. When Paul speaks of sins of the flesh he is far from meaning only physical and sexual sins. Sins of the flesh include strife, jealousy, anger, dissension, party spirit, envy (Galatians 5.20,21). What Paul means by the *flesh* is human nature apart from God. It is what man has made himself in contrast with what God meant him to be. But from the beginning this was misunderstood, and the feeling has lingered on that the body and its desires are something to be regretted, that sex is something dirty and something to be ashamed of, that the instincts of the body are something over which a veil must be drawn. It has been this which has been the cause of that sexual ignorance which has brought sorrow and disaster to so many, and which has put a muzzle on things like proper sex education.

The Christian ethic accepts the body and all that has to do with the body. The Christian ethic believes that the body is God's, and that we can dedicate it to God just as much as we can dedicate heart and mind to him.

vi. The Christian ethic is an ethic which goes beyond this world and beyond time. For the Christian life is lived out against a background of eternity.

(a) The Christian ethic is a resurrection ethic. It is quite clear that, wherever Paul started out to preach, he finished up with preaching the risen Christ (Acts 13.30-37; 17.18,31). All life is lived in the presence of the Risen Lord. All life is meant to stand the scrutiny of his eye.

(b) The Christian ethic is an ethic of judgment. As Paul saw it, all life is on the way to judgment. The destination of every man is the judgment seat of God and Jesus (Romans 14.10-12; 2 Corinthians 5.10). Anyone who continues to be guilty of the sins of the flesh will not inherit the kingdom of God (Galatians 5.21). What a man sows he will reap (Galatians 6.7,8). To be disobedient is to be doomed to the wrath of God (Ephesians 5.6). To continue to live a life of immorality and impurity is to incur the wrath of God (Colossians 3.6).

To remove the idea of judgment from Christianity is to

emasculate it. No honest presentation of Christianity can remove from it the ultimate threat.

(c) The Christian ethic as Paul presented it is never allowed to forget the coming again in judgment and in glory of Jesus Christ. The New Testament is peopled by men and women who are waiting. Nothing must be allowed to interfere with the intensity of that expectation, not even the closest relationships of life (1 Corinthians 7.25-35). The Christians wait for their blessed hope (Titus 2.13). There comes a day, and the Christian must so live that that day will not surprise and shock him (1 Thessalonians 5.2-7, 23;Philippians 2.16; 3.20; Colossians 3.4; 2 Thessalonians 1.5-10). It may be that that coming is long delayed, but however long it is delayed, it does not alter the basic fact that the Christian, as Cullmann put it, is always living in the space between the *already* and the *not yet*. The Christian is the man for whom something has happened, and for whom something has still to happen.

It is clear that all these things will have a tremendous ethical effect. To live in the presence of Christ, to see in life a journey to judgment, to rejoice in the *already* and at the same time to expect the *not yet*—these are things which are bound to give life a certain quality, and a certain ethical strenuousness, which can never be forgotten.

vii. For Paul the Christian ethic is an ethic of imitation.

(a) To begin with the highest form of it, the Christian is called upon to do no less than to imitate God. 'Be imitators of God,' says the Letter to the Ephesians, 'as beloved children' (Ephesians 5.1). Startling as this may sound, it is a summons to which man is called by the great teachers of both Greece and Israel. Plato says in the *Theaetetus* (176) that a man ought to fly away from this earth to heaven as quickly as possible, and to fly away is to become like God, so far as this is possible for a man. Before Plato, Pythagoras had taken as his maxim: 'Follow God.'

The same idea was there in Jewish thought. In the second

series of *Studies in Pharisaism and the Gospels* Israel Abrahams has an essay on 'The Imitation of God'. There he quotes from one of his best loved books, a Jewish classical devotional work by Cordovero, called *Deborah's Palm Tree*. The book begins: 'Man must liken himself to his Master.' Cordovero then quotes Micah 7.18-20:

> Who is a God like unto thee, that pardoneth iniquity, and passeth by the transgression of the remnant of his heritage? He retaineth not his anger for ever, because he delighteth in mercy. He will turn again and have compassion on us; he will tread our iniquities under foot: and thou wilt cast all their sins into the depths of the sea. Thou wilt perform the truth to Jacob, and the mercy to Abraham, which thou hast sworn to our fathers from the days of old.

Abrahams tells us that in that passage Cordovero sees the thirteen divine attributes, every one of which man must copy. 'He takes the clauses one by one, explains God's method, and then calls on his reader to go and do likewise. Thus man must bear insult; must be limitless in love, finding in all men the object of his deep and inalienable affection; he must overlook wrongs done to him, and never forget a kindness. Cordovero insists again and again on this divine patience and forbearance, on God's passing over man's many sins and on his recognition of man's occasional virtues. So must man act. He must temper his justice with mercy, must be peculiarly tender to the unworthy. His whole being must be attuned to God's being. His earthly eye must be open to the good in all men, as is the heavenly eye; his earthly ear must be deaf to the slanderers and the foul, just as the heavenly ear is receptive only of the good. For God loves all men whom he has made in his very image, and how shall man hate what God loves?' (I. Abrahams, *Studies in Pharisaism and the Gospels*, second series, pp. 145, 146). Abrahams goes on to tell how the Talmud (*Sota* 14 a) on Deuteronomy 13.4 calls on man to imitate God who clothed the naked (Adam and Eve), who visited the sick (Abraham), and who buried the dead (Moses).

'Thus the whole *torah* (the law) from Genesis to Deuteronomy bids Israel imitate God.'

To talk of man imitating God is neither blasphemous nor impossible, for God made man in his own image (Genesis 1.26,27), and the imitation of God is therefore the very function of manhood.

(b) The Christian must imitate Jesus Christ. He can be said to learn Christ (Ephesians 4.20). The Christian is the follower of Jesus.

(c) The Christian is urged to imitate the heroic figures of the faith. The writer to the Hebrews commands his readers to remember their leaders. 'Consider the outcome of their life, and imitate their faith' (Hebrews 13.7). They are to be imitators of 'those who through faith and patience received the promises' (Hebrews 6.12). Paul praises the Thessalonians because in their suffering for their faith they became imitators of the churches of Judaea who suffered before them (1 Thessalonians 2.14).

This is why a man should know something of the history of his church. This is why Oliver Cromwell, when he was arranging for the education of his son Richard, said: 'I would have him know a little history.' History, as it has been said, is 'philosophy teaching by examples'. This was indeed the very aim and object of the ancient historians. It was the aim of Thucydides not to compose a book which was a prize essay, but which would abide for all time, so that, when the same kind of events happened again, as he was certain they would, men would find guidance for the present from the examples of the past (Thucydides 1.22). Lucian in his essay on *How History ought to be Written* (44) says that the historians must above all aim at accuracy and usefulness, so that, when similar events occur and similar circumstances arise, the record of the past may teach us how to act in the present. Livy in his *Preface* writes: 'This is the most wholesome and faithful effect of the study of history; you have in front of you real examples of every kind of behaviour, real examples embodied in most conspicuous form; from these you can take, both for yourself and the state, ideals at which to aim; you can learn also what to avoid because it is impious either in its conception or in its issue.'

A. L. Rowse, a modern historian, makes exactly the same claim. For him the prime use of history is that 'it enables you to understand, better than any other discipline, the public events, affairs and trends of your time. . . . History is about human society, its story and how it has come to be what it is; knowing what societies have been like in the past and their evolution will give you the clue to the factors that operate in them, the currents and forces that move them, the motives and conflicts, both general and personal, that shape events' (A. L. Rowse, *The Use of History*, p. 16). By the study of the examples of the past we gain guidance for the present.

The Christian must know the history of his church that he may imitate its heroisms and avoid its mistakes.

(d) But by far Paul's most astonishing invitation to imitation is his repeated invitation to his converts to imitate himself. 'I urge you,' he writes to the Corinthians, 'be imitators of me' (1 Corinthians 4.16). Again he writes to the same people: 'Be imitators of me, as I am of Christ' (1 Corinthians 11.1). 'Brethren,' he writes to the Philippians, 'join in imitating me' (Philippians 3.17). Again he writes to them: 'What you have learned and received and heard in me do'(Philippians 4.9). He writes to the Thessalonians: 'You became imitators of us and the Lord' (1 Thessalonians 1.6). 'You yourselves know you ought to imitate me,' he writes again to them. His life and work in Thessalonica were designed 'to give you in your conduct an example to imitate' (2 Thessalonians 3.7,9). (This is to some extent obscured in the Authorised Version which translates *mimeisthai* by *to follow* rather than *to imitate*; it is from *mimeisthai* that the English word *to mimic* is derived.)

There are any number of preachers and teachers who can say: 'I can *tell* you what to do.' There are few who can say: 'I can *show* you what to do.' There are any number who can say:

'Listen to my words.' There are few who can say: 'Follow my example.' It was Paul's astonishing claim that he taught by being, even more than he taught by speaking or by writing.

viii. The Christian ethic demands that all Christians should not only accept an example to imitate but should also provide an example to imitate. It has been well said that 'everyone pipes for the feet of someone to follow'. In the days when I write this a little episode is being shown on television as part of the propaganda to deter people from smoking. A father and son are out fishing; they sit down to eat and to rest; the father produces a cigarette and lights it; the young boy plucks a blade of grass, puts it in his mouth, and puffs at it in imitation of smoking. The father sees what is happening, and he extinguishes his cigarette, for he suddenly realises that his son will imitate him, in the wrong things as well as in the right things.

This Paul well knows. He knows what you can only call the propaganda value of a really Christian life. And so the Christian ethic, as Paul sees it, insists that the Christian must produce an example to attract and not to repel. Paul is very conscious of the Christian duty to the 'outsider', to the man outside the church. The Thessalonians are urged to live a life of honest toil 'that you may command the respect of outsiders' (1 Thessalonians 4.12). One of the qualifications of the bishop is that he must be 'well thought of by outsiders' (1 Timothy 3.7). The Colossians are urged to conduct themselves wisely towards outsiders (Colossians 4.5). Peter is equally insistent on this. He urges Christians to 'maintain good conduct among the Gentiles' so that all malicious charges and all ill-natured slanders may be seen to be demonstrably untrue (1 Peter 2.12; 3.16). Loveliest of all is Peter's advice to a Christian wife married to a heathen husband. She is to live so beautifully that her husband will be brought to Christianity without a word being spoken (1 Peter 3.1).

Greek has two words for *good*. *Agathos* simply describes a thing as being good; *kalos* describes a thing—or person—as being, not only good, but also winsome and lovely. And it is *kalos* which in the New Testament is more frequently used (cf. Matthew 5.14-16). The Christian dare not say: 'I don't care what people say or think of me.' He must care, for his life is a sermon for or against his faith.

ix. One of the most widespread demands of Paul's ethical teaching is that Christians should live at peace together. There is hardly anything about which Paul has more to say than the danger of disharmony and the necessity of harmony.

Division has always been a disease of the church. Even at the Last Supper the disciples were disputing about which of them should be greatest (Luke 22.24). The Corinthian church had its partisan support for different leaders, a situation for which the leaders themselves were in no way to blame. Paul's rebuke is that, so long as there is jealousy and strife in their society, they have no right to call themselves Christians at all (1 Corinthians 3.1-4). The Love Feast, which should have been the sign and symbol of perfect unity, has become a thing of divisions and class distinctions. And here there is something which only the newer translations reveal. In the older translations it is said that to eat and drink at the sacrament without discerning the Lord's body is the way to judgment and not to salvation. But in the best Greek text the word *Lord's* is not included. The sin is not to discern the body; that is to say, not to discern that the church is a body, not to be aware of the oneness of the church, not to be aware of the togetherness in which all its members should be joined (1 Corinthians 11.17-32). That disunity is described in verses 17-22; to it Paul describes the illness and the weakness which have fallen upon the congregation (verse 30). The danger in question is not that of not discerning that the bread and wine stand for the body of Christ; the danger is that in a church where there is no harmony and peace between Christian and Christian the sacrament of the Lord's Supper becomes a blasphemy. In Philippi there are preachers whose aim is rather to embarrass Paul than to preach Christ (Philippians 4.2). Paul fears that, when he arrives in Corinth, he may find quarrelling and jealousy (2 Corinthians 12.20). He talks about the possibility of the Galatians biting and devouring one another (Galatians 5.15). In the Pastoral Letters there is a warning to those who 'have a morbid craving for controversy', and a warning against 'wrangling among men who are depraved in mind' (1 Timothy 6.4,5).

Again and again Paul appeals for harmony. 'Live in harmony with one another,' he writes to the Romans more than once (Romans 12.16-18; 15.5,6). The Ephesians are urged to maintain the unity of the Spirit in the bond of peace (Ephesians 4.2,3). One of the greatest hymns to Christ in the New Testament is written not as theology but as an appeal to have that mind of Christ, and so to be in unity and humility of mind (Philippians 2.1-11). The hands that are lifted in prayer should be pure, without quarrelling and without anger (1 Timothy 2.8). Titus is to tell his people always to avoid quarrels and always to show courtesy (Titus 3.2).

The ethic of Paul demands that Christians should solve the problem of living together—or stop calling themselves Christians.

x. For Paul the Christian ethic is an ethic of humility. This quality of humility is stressed all over the New Testament. In the teaching of Jesus it is the proud who will be brought low and the humble who will be exalted (Matthew 23.12; Luke 14.11; 18.14). The way into the Kingdom is the way of a child's humility (Matthew 18.4). Both James and Peter quote the Old Testament saying that God gives grace to the humble and resists the proud (James 4.6,7; 1 Peter 5.5,6; Proverbs 3.34). But the great passage on humility is the passage in which Paul draws the picture of the humility of Jesus, who gave up the glory of heaven to come and to live, not only as a man, but also as a servant, and not only to live, but in the end to die, and not only to die, but to die on a cross. The perfect pattern of humility is to be found in Jesus Christ (Philippians 2.1-11). Lowliness and meekness, says the Letter to the

Ephesians, must be the hall-marks of the Christian life (Ephesians 4.2).

This was one of the new things in Christianity. It has been pointed out that in secular Greek there is no word for humility which has not got something mean and low in it. Nowhere can the difference between the Christian and the Greek ethic be seen better than in the comparison between this Christian humility and Aristotle's picture of the great-souled man, who for Aristotle is the finest character of all (Aristotle, *Nicomachean Ethics* 4.3.1-34, 1122 a 33-1125 a 17).

Aristotle's picture is as follows. The great-souled man is the man who claims much and who deserves much. The man who claims little may be modest and temperate, but he can never be great. The man who claims much without deserving it will be merely vain, not great. To be great-souled involves greatness just as to be handsome involves size. 'Small people,' says Aristotle, 'may be neat and well-made, but they cannot be handsome.' The one thing at which the great-souled man will aim is honour. It is necessary that he should be a good man. To be great-souled is the crown of the virtues, and it cannot exist without them. When persons of worth offer the great-souled man honour, he will deign to accept it; but if honour is offered to him by common people, he will utterly despise it. He will not rejoice overmuch at prosperity, and he will not grieve overmuch at adversity. He will be largely indifferent even to honour, for nothing really matters to him. This is why great-souled people usually give the impression of being haughty. The great-souled man has a contempt for others, and he is justified in despising them.

The great-souled man is fond of conferring benefits, but he dislikes receiving them, for to confer is the mark of superiority, and to receive is the mark of inferiority. If he does receive any service, he will return it with interest, for thus he will continue to be the superior party. If he gives a benefit, he will remember it; if he receives a benefit, he will prefer to forget it. He will never, or at least only with the greatest reluctance, ask for help. To those above him he will be haughty; to those beneath him he will be condescendingly gracious. The ordinary objects of ambition will have no attraction for him. He will give the impression of being idle and slow to act, for he will be interested in nothing less than great enterprises. He can never live at the will of another, for that would be slavish. He regards nothing as great; nothing to him is to be admired. He will not bear grudges, but only for the reason that he is too superior for that. He will have no interest in receiving compliments. He will like things which are beautiful and useless rather than things which are useful; he will have a slow walk, a deep voice, and a deliberate way of speaking.

Here is the picture of the conscious aristocrat, whose characteristic attitude is contempt. The Greek picture of a great man is the picture of a man who is conscious of nothing so much as of his own superiority, a man to whom a confession of need would be a confession of failure. The blessings of the Christian view are for the man conscious of his own poverty, the man sad for his own sins, the man hungry for a goodness which he is sadly conscious that he does not possess (Matthew 5.3,4,6). The Greek great man was the man who stood above and looked down. In the Christian ethic the great man is the man who looks up to God, who knows nothing so much as his own need, and who sits where his fellow men sit.

*xi.*It is basic to the ethic of Paul, as it is to the ethic of the whole New Testament, that the Christian ethic is an ethic of love. That love is not an easy-going, emotional, sentimental thing. It is not something subject to impulse and motivated by passion. It is not something which flames and then dies, at one time a burning passion, at another time almost non-existent. It is not something which depends on our likes and our dislikes for other people. It is the steady, unvarying, undefeatable determination to love men as Jesus loved them, and never, no matter what they do in response, to seek anything but their highest good. It is the goodwill that cannot be quenched. This kind of love is going to have consequences.

(a) It will dominate the attitude of the Christian towards insult and to injury. Revenge will be something which—if it enters into the picture at all—will be in the hands of God. As for us, even for the man who counts himself our enemy, there will be nothing but concern (Romans 12.19,20). The pattern of human forgiveness is the divine forgiveness. As Christ forgave us, so must we forgive others (Ephesians 4.32; Colossians 3.13). He who has been forgiven must be forgiving. This will mean that a Christian will never try to return evil for evil. He will always try to overcome evil with good (Romans 12.21; 1 Thessalonians 5.15). The Christian will practise not so much a negative policy of non-retaliation as a positive policy which by its kindness shames men into response (Romans 12.20; Proverbs 25.21,22).

(b) This Christian love will bring into personal relationships a new tolerance. Forbearance is characteristic of the Christian attitude to others (Ephesians 4.2; Philippians 4.5). Paul was well aware that different people can quite honestly hold different points of view (Romans 14.5,6). Of this tolerance two things have to be said.

First, it is the tolerance not of indifference but of love. It is tolerant not because it does not care, and not because it thinks that it does not matter, but because in sympathy it tries to understand why the other person thinks and behaves as he does. It is the tolerance which knows that there is a great deal of truth in the saying that to know all is to forgive all.

Second, a wide tolerance in non-essentials does not at all preclude the determination to take an immovable stand, when such a stand is necessary. No one would ever dare to say that Paul was a weak character. But this inflexible Paul was able to yield on matters which he regarded as non-essential or for the greater good of the community. Everyone knows what Paul thought of circumcision, yet he circumcised Timothy simply because he knew that Timothy circumcised would find opportunities for the spread of the gospel which would be closed to Timothy uncircumcised (Acts 16.3). We know what Paul thought of the Jewish law and all its ceremonial, yet Paul was entirely willing to finance those who were taking the Nazirite vow, when James suggested that he should do so, as a demonstration that he was by no means a renegade from Judaism (Acts 21.17-26). To be inflexible and to be stubborn are by no means the same thing. To be a man of principle and to be the victim of prejudice are very different things. Christian tolerance knows the difference between principle and prejudice.

(c) Christian love is the control and the condition of Christian freedom. The Christian is free, free from the tyranny of law, free from the obligations which governed the food and the drink of the Jew, free from a legalistic slavery. But that freedom must never be used as an excuse for licence. It is the freedom of a man who loves his neighbour and who will never do anything to harm his neighbour (Galatians 5.1,13,14). It is, as Peter said, the freedom of the servant of God (1 Peter 2.16). There is in one of the Gilbert and Sullivan operas a song, 'Free, yet in fetters bound to my last hour'. The Christian is free; but the Christian is bound by the fetters of responsibility and the obligation of love.

We can see this very clearly if we set side by side two different pieces of instruction by Paul regarding food and drink. In the Letter to the Colossians he insists that the Christian must never be bound by the laws of the ascetic which tell him that he must not taste this, and he must not touch that, and he must not handle the other thing. The Christian is free to eat and drink what he likes (Colossians 2:16,21). And yet when he is writing to the Romans and to the Corinthians Paul issues the warning that a man must never claim the right to eat and to drink those things which may be the ruin of his neighbour (Romans 14.21; 1 Corinthians 8.13). The Christian is free, but that freedom is controlled by responsibility and conditioned by love. Freedom without responsibility, liberty without love are not Christian freedom and liberty, for they can do nothing but harm.

(d) There is one other sphere in which love dominates and controls. Love must dominate the presentation and the defence of the truth. It is true that the truth must be spoken, but it must be spoken in love (Ephesians 4.15). The truth can be spoken with an almost sadistic cruelty; it can be spoken to hurt and not to cure. It is true, as the Greek philosopher said, that truth can be like the light to sore eyes, but the hurt must never be deliberate. The Christian teacher, say the Pastoral Letters, must not be quarrelsome but kindly; he must be 'an apt teacher, forbearing, correcting his opponents with gentleness' (2 Timothy 2.23-25). As Peter had it, the Christian must always be ready to defend and commend his faith, but always with gentleness and reverence (1 Peter 3.15). It is perfectly possible to win an argument and lose the person. But when the teaching and the argument are carried on in Christian love, this will not happen.

xii. There remains one last area in which the ethic of Paul has something significant to say, something which is also said in the ethic of Peter. Included in the moral literature of the ancient world there were what were called House Tables, in which the duties of the members of the family to each other were explained and codified. The New Testament has its own form of these House Tables. They deal with three relationships.

1. The relationship between husband and wife (Ephesians 5.21-33; Colossians 3.18,19; 1 Peter 3.1-7).
2. The relationship between parent and child (Ephesians 6.1-4; Colossians 3.20,21; 1 Timothy 5.4,8,16).
3. The relationship between master and servant or slave (Ephesians 6.5-9; Colossians 3.22-4.1; Philemon 16; 1 Timothy 6.1,2; 1 Peter 2.18-25).

From these passages certain things emerge.

First, in life Paul sees a natural series of subordinations—wife to husband, child to parent, servant to master. These subordinations are not in the least tyrannies or dictatorships. They are simply the inbuilt mechanism without which life cannot go on and without which it would become a chaos. Christianity is not anarchy. It is based on love; it introduces a relationship of love between people; but it sees that, unless certain leaderships are accepted, life cannot proceed. This is not feudalism, or paternalism, or the maintaining of class distinctions. A man need not always be a servant, nor for that matter need he always be a leader. But the acceptance of leadership, both in the sense of exercising it and obeying it, is part of life.

Second, Paul's ethic of personal relationship is always a reciprocal ethic. This is the other side of the subordination. Paul never lays down a right without assigning a duty to it. The duty of the leader to the subordinate is every bit as clearly stated as the duty of the subordinate to the leader. The wife must be subject to her husband, but the husband must treat her with constant kindness and courtesy and consideration (Ephesians 5.22,25,28; Colossians 3.18,19; 1 Peter 3.1,5-7). The child must obey the parent, but the parent must never by unreasonable demands drive the child to resentment or to despair (Ephesians 6.1-4; Colossians 3.20,21). The servant must give obedience and service to the master, but the master must never forget the rights of the servant (Ephesians 6.5,9; Colossians 3.22-25; 4.1; 1 Peter 2.18-25). Privilege is never all on one side. Simply to possess the leadership is to be involved in responsibility for those who are led. The ethic of Paul would bind all together in a mutual responsibility in which no man would ever make a claim on any other man without at the same time recognising his duty to that man.

Third, the whole matter is dominated by the presence of Jesus Christ and by our responsibility to God. It is to please the Lord that children must obey (Colossians 3.20). The relationship between husband and wife is like that between Christ and the church (Ephesians 5.21-33). The servant works as if he was going to take his work and offer it to Christ (Ephesians 6.6-8; Colossians 3.23,24). The master must always remember that he is not his own master, but that he has a master in heaven (Ephesians 6.9; Colossians 4.1). Earth is always related to heaven; time is always related to eternity; the simplest thing becomes a religious thing. As George Herbert had it:

Teach me, my God and King,
In all things thee to see;
And what I do in anything,
To do it as for thee!

A servant with this clause
Makes drudgery divine,
Who sweeps a room as for thy laws,
Makes that and the action fine.

Work and worship have become one and the same thing.

Fourth, the new situation had its problems. It may at first sight surprise us that in the New Testament nothing is said about emancipating the slaves. Two things are to be said. First, to have suggested the emancipation of the slaves would have produced a chaos, and in the end nothing but mass executions; and even if a move for emancipation had succeeded there was no free market for labour. The time was not ripe. Second, when Paul sent Onesimus back to Philemon, he sent him back no longer as a slave only, but also as a brother beloved (Philemon 16). This is to say that Christian love and fellowship had introduced a new relationship between master and slave in which these terms ceased to have any relevance at all. So much was this the case that in the congregation the master might well find himself receiving the sacrament from the hands of his slave. If men are together in Christian love, it does not matter if you call one servant and the other master, for they are brothers. True, the time will come when that very situation will make slavery impossible, but it had to come in its own time, or there could have been nothing but trouble.

Fifth, one last thing is to be noted. The servant is now a brother beloved; master and servant may both be Christians. There is a passage in the First Letter to Timothy which indicates that there were servants who tried to take advantage of that new relationship. 'Those who have believing masters must not be disrespectful on the ground that they are brethren; rather they must serve all the better since those who benefit by their service are believers and beloved' (1 Timothy 6.1,2). There were clearly some servants who used the new relationship to attempt to slacken discipline and to get away with idleness and shoddy work. But the Christian ethic teaches that the relationship of brotherhood should make us better and not slacker workmen, for now we work not by compulsion but in partnership with each other.

The Pauline ethic may be nineteen hundred years old, but it is still as valid as ever, and not even yet have its implications been completely worked out.

CHAPTER FOUR

Situation Ethics

When we talk about ethics, we mostly mean a series of rules and laws and principles by which we act and which tell us what to do. Mostly we take it that ethics classifies words and actions into things which are good and things which are bad, and we take it that the goodness and the badness belong to the thing as such. On the whole this is meant to simplify things and to make life easy. It means that we have got, so we think, a series of prefabricated rules and laws and principles, which we accept and apply. It saves us from the difficult and the often dangerous task of making our own judgments and deciding things for ourselves.

But in 1966 an American professor called Joseph Fletcher wrote a book called *Situation Ethics*, which has proved to be one of the most influential books written this century. Fletcher's basic principle is that there is nothing which is universally right or universally wrong; there is nothing which is intrinsically good or intrinsically bad. Goodness and badness are not built in, essential, unchangeable qualities of anything; they are only things which happen to actions in different situations; they are only descriptions of things in different circumstances; they are not properties, they are predicates. According to this theory of ethics, there is no such thing as a predefinition of goodness or badness. What we have to take to any situation is not a prefabricated decision, but an act of judgment. Throughout this chapter the arguments and the illustrations are taken mainly from Fletcher's two books, *Situation Ethics* and *Moral Responsibility*.

It has to be noted that the situation ethics man does not as it were start from nothing. He knows all the rules and the principles; he knows all that the accumulated experience of human beings has found out. He knows that there are rules and principles; but he refuses to say that any principle is absolutely binding and always valid, right or wrong in itself. Bonhoeffer said: 'Principles are only tools in the hand of God, soon to be thrown away as unserviceable.' The situationist does not deny that there are principles; he does not for a moment deny the classifications of things that experience has built up; but he completely refuses to be shackled or bound by anything.

We have got to qualify all this; for to the situationist there is one thing and one thing only that is absolutely, always and universally good—*and that one thing is love*. So Fletcher's first two propositions are:

> Only one thing is intrinsically good, namely love: nothing else. The ultimate norm of Christian decisions is love: nothing else.

Quite clearly we will have to be sure of just what love is. The situationist is not talking about what we might call romantic love. In Greek there are four words for love. There is *erōs*, which means passion; there is always sex in *erōs*. There is *philia*, which is friendship-feeling; there is physical love in *philia*, but there is loyalty and companionship as well. There is *storgē*, which is love in the family circle; there is no sex in it; it is the love of a father for a daughter, a son for his mother, a brother for a sister. And there is *agapē*; this is the word. *Agapē* is unconquerable goodwill; it is the determination always to seek the other man's highest good, no matter what he does to you. Insult, injury, indifference—it does not matter; nothing but goodwill. It has been defined as purpose, not passion. It is an attitude to the other person.

This is all important, because if we talk about this kind of love, it means that we can love the person we don't like. This is not a matter of the reaction of the heart; it is an attitude of the will and the whole personality deliberately directed to the other man. You cannot order a man to fall in love in the romantic sense of the term. Falling in love is like stepping on a banana skin; it happens, and that is all there is to it. But you can say to a man: 'Your attitude to others must be such that you will never, never, never want anything but their highest good.'

Obviously, when we define love like this, love is a highly intelligent thing. We must, as the Americans say, figure the angles. We must in any situation work out what love is. What does love demand?

Suppose, for instance, a house catches fire and in it there is a baby and the original of the Mona Lisa; which do you save—the baby or the priceless and irreplaceable picture? There is really no problem here; you save the baby for a life is always of greater value than a picture.

But think of this one—suppose in the burning house there is your aged father, an old man, with the days of his usefulness at an end, and a doctor who has discovered a cure for one of the world's great killer diseases, and who still carries the formulae in his head, and you can save only one—whom do you save? Your father who is dear to you, or the doctor in whose hands there are thousands of lives? Which is love?

On the Wilderness Trail, Daniel Boone's trail westward through Cumberland Gap to Kentucky, many families in the trail caravans lost their lives to the Indians. A Scottish woman had a baby at the breast. The baby was ill and crying, and the baby's crying was betraying her other three children and the rest of the party; the party clearly could not remain hidden if the baby continued crying; their position would be given away. Well, the mother clung to the baby; the baby's cries led the Indians to the position; and the party was discovered and all were massacred. There was another such occasion. On this occasion there was a Negro woman in the party. Her baby too was crying and threatening to betray the party. She strangled the baby with her own two hands to stop its crying—and the whole party escaped. Which action was love? The action of the mother who kept her baby and brought death to it and to herself and to all, or the action of the mother who killed the baby and saved the lives of the caravan? Here is the kind of decision with which the situationist confronts us; which action was love?

The situationist is always confronting us with decisions. There is no absolute right and wrong; we have to work it out in each situation. There are principles, of course, but they can only advise; they do not have the right of veto. Any principle must be abandoned, left, disregarded, if the command to love your neighbour can be better served by so doing.

The situationist is sure that a rigid sticking to the rules is all wrong. It can produce what someone called 'the immorality of morality'. It can produce what Mark Twain called 'a good man in the worst sense of the term'. A French priest said that fanatic love of virtue has done more harm than all the vices put together. It is the situation that counts. There are times when justice can become unjust. So Fletcher tells two stories, the first from real life, the second from a play.

A friend of Fletcher's arrived in St Louis just as a presidential campaign was ending. He took a cab and the cab-driver volunteered the information: 'I and my father and my grandfathers and their fathers have always been straight ticket Republicans.' 'Ah,' said Fletcher's friend who is himself a Republican, 'I take it that means you will vote for Senator So-and-so.' 'No,' said the driver, 'there are times when a man has to push his principles aside, and do the right thing!' There are times when principles become wrong—even when they are right.

The other is a story from Nash's play *The Rainmaker*. The Rainmaker makes love to a spinster girl in a barn at midnight. He does not really love her, but he is determined to save her from becoming spinsterised; he wants to give her back her womanhood, and to rekindle her hopes of marriage and children. Her morally outraged brother threatens to shoot him. Her father, a wise old rancher, says to his son: 'Noah, you're so full of what's right that you can't see what's good.' For the situationist a thing that is labelled wrong can be in certain circumstances the only right thing.

This leads us to the second of Fletcher's basic principles. Fletcher lays it down:

> Love and justice are the same thing, for justice is love distributed, nothing else.

We can relate love and justice in different ways. Sometimes people think of love *versus* justice, as if love and justice were against each other; or love *or* justice, as if you had to choose one or the other, but could not have both; or love *and* justice as if the two things complemented each other. But for Fletcher love *is* justice; love and justice are one and the same thing. This is a new idea. Niebuhr, the great American teacher, used to say that the difference is that love is transcendent and love is impossible; while justice is something by which we can live in this present society. Brunner held that the difference is that love must be between two persons; whereas justice exists between groups. But Fletcher will have it that love is the same thing as justice. How does he make this out?

Accept the fact that the one absolute is love. Then love has to be worked out in the situations of life—and the working of it out is justice. Justice, it is said, consists of giving each man his due; but the one thing that is due to every man is love; therefore love and justice are the same. Justice, says Fletcher, is love distributed. When we are confronted with the claims of more than one person, of three or four people, we have to give them love, and it is justice which settles just how love is to be applied to each of them. Justice is love working out its problems.

So then unless love is to be a vague sentimental generalised feeling, there must be justice, because justice is love applied to particular cases. This is precisely what is so often the matter with love, the fact that it never gets worked out and never gets beyond being a feeling and an emotion. Some time ago—Fletcher cites the case—Sammy Davis Jr. the great entertainer became a Jew, and thereby repudiated Christianity. 'As I see it,' he said, 'the difference is that the Christian religion preaches, Love thy neighbour, and the Jewish religion preaches justice, and I think that justice is the big thing we need.' Sammy Davis is black, and he knew all about so-called Christian love. As Fletcher says, there are many people who would claim that they love black people, and who at the same time deny them simple justice. Fletcher goes on: 'To paraphrase the classic cry of protest, we can say: To hell with your love; we want justice.' This is exactly what happens when justice and love are not equated.

This means that love has always got to be thinking; love has always got to be calculating. Otherwise love is like the bride who wanted to ignore all recipes and simply let her love for her husband guide her when she was baking him a cake. Love has to think, wisely, deeply, intelligently. Fletcher goes on to illustrate the kind of problem love must face and solve.

Take the case of a nurse in a TV play called *The Bitter Choice*. She was in charge of a ward in a military hospital for wounded soldiers, and she acted with deliberate and calculated severity and even harshness to make the wounded soldiers hate her so much that the one thing they wanted was to get on their feet again and get out. Was this cruelty or was it a far more real love than the love which coddled and comforted until the men had no wish to leave the hospital at all?

Take the case of a doctor. A doctor is bound not to divulge any of the affairs of his patients. In his Hippocratic oath he promises:

> Whatever in my professional practice—or even not in connection with it—I see or hear in the lives of men which ought not to be spoken of abroad, I will not divulge, deeming that on such matters we should be silent.

The doctor knows that a marriage is going to take place. He knows both parties; he knows that the girl is a virgin and is pure; he happens to know that the boy has been a libertine and has syphilis. What is the duty of love? Does the doctor keep his oath? If a doctor began to talk it would create a situation that would be intolerable. Or does he tell the girl? Which is love?

Suppose in a public works a personnel manager has on his staff a clerk in bad health and rendered inefficient through illness, where does *agapē*, love, concern lie? Does he keep the clerk on? Or does he think of the workers on the production-line whose output and piece rate are being cut by the inevitable delays caused by this clerk's inefficiency due to his health condition? Which is love? Which is the Christian thing to do?

In one of Sinclair Lewis's novels there is a scientist Dr Arrowsmith. He has discovered a serum which he knows to be a certain cure for a plague that regularly attacks a Caribbean island. He cannot persuade the government and the authorities to accept his claim. Plague hits the island. Arrowsmith inoculates half the inhabitants; and deliberately refuses to inoculate the other half. He knows that those inoculated will recover and he knows that those not inoculated will die. He deliberately sacrifices them to convince the government of the effectiveness of his serum, and thus to save thousands of lives in the future. Is this love? Is this the real concern?

Fletcher quotes a war incident which happened in Italy. A priest in the underground movement bombed and destroyed a Nazi freight train. The occupying Germans then began killing twenty prisoners a day, and said that they would go on doing so until the saboteur was handed over or surrendered. The priest refused to give himself up, not because he contemplated more sabotage, but because, so he said, there was no other priest available in the district, and the people needed the absolution he could give for their souls' sake. After three days a fellow resistance fighter deliberately betrayed the priest in order to stop the massacre of prisoners. Was he right? Was what looked like an act of treachery in fact an act of love?

Love has got to calculate. And it may well be that love has

to use methods which in other circumstances would be terrible things. The argument of the situationist is that nothing is absolutely good or bad; it all depends on the situation and in certain situations even an act of treachery may be an act of love.

Let us return to the ten commandments. The situationist knows the ten commandments; he respects them; he does not merely toss them aside; but he is prepared to say that there can come times when any of the ten commandments may become a bad thing and when it may be a Christian duty to break any or all of them.

Let us look at some of the examples that Fletcher produces.

What about the commandment: You must not steal?

If a homicidal maniac had possession of a gun, surely it would be a duty and not a sin to steal it from him. Suppose a man was hellbent on murder, and he was mad. Suppose he came up to you and asked you where his intended victim was, and suppose you knew, surely it would be a duty to mislead the man rather than to give him the information you were asked for; surely a lie in this case is the right thing. Oddly enough, some ethical teachers do not think so. They think that you ought to tell the man the truth. They argue that if you do that, there will only be one sin—murder; whereas if you tell a lie and then afterwards the murderer does in spite of your lie get his victim, there will be two sins, lying and murder.

What about the commandment that you must not kill? When T. E. Lawrence was leading his Arabs two of his men had a quarrel and in the quarrel Hamed killed Salem. Lawrence knew that Salem's people would be out for vengeance, and he knew that a blood feud would arise in which both families would be involved, and that one whole family would be out to murder the other whole family. What did Lawrence do? He thought it out and then with his own hands he killed Hamed and thus stopped the blood feud. Was this right? Was this action which stopped a blood feud and probably prevented scores of people from being murdered an act of murder or an act of love?

Take the case of the commandment which forbids adultery. Here Fletcher cites two illustrations, both from films. The first is from the film *Never on Sunday*. The film was originally cited by H. A. Williams in the volume entitled *Soundings*. The point he was making was that the biggest thing in life is generous self-giving, giving as God gives. And he was saying that a good deal of what we call Christian virtue is based on fear and on the refusal totally to give oneself to another. He applies this to sexual relationships. Sexual relationships are always wrong when they merely exploit the other person. But even in relationships outside marriage there can be this total self-giving. So he tells the story of the film, a Greek film. A prostitute in the Piraeus is picked up by a young sailor. When he gets to her room he is nervous and very ill at ease. She soon sees that he is not troubled by any idea of doing wrong, but that he doubts his own virility and his capacity for physical union at all. He is a prey to destructive doubt, not to moral scruples. She gives herself to him in such a way that he acquires confidence and self-respect. I quote Williams: 'He goes away a deeper, fuller person than he came in. What is seen in this is an act of charity which proclaims the glory of God. The man is equipped for life as he never was before.' Fornication or the wonderful cure of the personality of a psychologically maladjusted man; the transgression of God's law or the fulfilment of God's will; sin or love—which?

The second illustration is from an English film called *The Mark*. In it there is a man whose abnormality is that he is a danger to small girls. The abnormality springs from the fact that he is really afraid to commit himself to an adult woman. Time goes on and he meets a woman who inspires him with enough confidence to go away with her for a weekend. They occupy separate rooms at the hotel; but it is clear that until he summons up enough confidence to sleep with her he will never be delivered from that dreadful abnormality which is on the way to destroying himself and others. In the end—I quote—they sleep together and he is made whole. Williams goes on to say: 'Where there is healing, there is Christ, whatever the church says about fornication, and the appropriate response is: Glory to God in the Highest.' Is it God or the devil? Is it love or lust? Is it sin or love? Which? (It has been pointed out to me by experts in this field that in any event such action would by no means necessarily result in a cure.)

Are we going to be driven to this conclusion that nothing is absolutely right and that apparently still less is anything absolutely wrong, and that it all depends on the situation? Is it true that goodness and badness are not qualities which are built into actions, but things which happen to an action within a situation, that they are not properties but predicates?

Let us take one last example from Fletcher. He entitles it Sacrificial Adultery. As the Russian armies drove forward to meet the Americans and the British, a Mrs Bergmeier, who was out foraging for food for her children and herself, was picked up. Without being able to get a word to the children she was taken away to a prison work camp in the Ukraine. Meanwhile her husband was captured and ended up in a prison camp in Wales. Ultimately the husband was released. He came back to Germany and after weeks of search he found the children, the two youngest in a Russian detention school and the oldest hiding in a cellar. They had no idea where their mother was. They never stopped searching for her. They knew that only her return could ever knit that family together again after all that had happened to them. Meanwhile away in the Ukraine a kindly camp commandant told Mrs Bergmeier that her family were together again and that they were trying to find her. But he could not release her, for release was only given for two reasons. First, a prisoner was released if he or she was suffering from a disease with which the camp could not cope, and was in that case moved to a Russian hospital. Second, a woman was released if she became pregnant. In that case women were returned to Germany as being a liability and no use for work. Mrs Bergmeier thought it out, and finally she decided to ask a friendly Volga German camp guard to make her pregnant. He did. Her condition was medically verified. She was sent back to Germany and received with open arms by her family. She told them what she had done and they thoroughly approved. In due time the baby was born. Dietrich they called him and they loved him most of all because they felt he had done more for them than any one of the others. And for the German guard they had nothing but a grateful and affectionate memory. So what? Right or wrong? Adultery or love? Which?

Fletcher holds that, when an act of intercourse has no love in it, inside or outside marriage, it is wrong. When it has no care, no concern, no love, no commitment, nothing but the satisfaction of desire—in or outside marriage—it is wrong. Fletcher quotes a cartoon from one of the glossy magazines of sex. A dishevelled young male is holding a dishevelled young female in his arms, emerging from the blankets and saying: 'Why talk of love at a time like this?' It is better—so Fletcher says—to live together unmarried in commitment and loyalty and responsibility than to live in marriage with no love.

What, then, are we to say to all this? The situationist claims that nothing is absolutely right and nothing is absolutely wrong; it all depends on the situation. Goodness and badness are not something intrinsic, but things that happen to actions in the doing. What are we to say?

First, we can begin with something which is a criticism not so much of situation ethics as it is of Fletcher's presentation of it. The trouble is that by far the greater number of Fletcher's illustrations are drawn from the abnormal, the unusual and the extraordinary. I am not very likely to be confronted with an Arab blood feud or a war situation in Eastern Germany. It is much easier to agree that extraordinary situations need extraordinary measures than to think that there are no laws for ordinary everyday life.

Second—and this is a much more serious matter—situation ethics presents us with a terrifying degree of freedom. There we are in front of our situation; we have no prefabricated judgment; *you*—just *you*—have to make the right decision. Brunner has said that there is nowhere you can go—not even to the Sermon on the Mount and say: 'Now I know what to do.' There is no such thing as a readymade decision. Of course, we know the things that experience has discovered and teaches, but we are left alone in complete freedom to apply them.

Fletcher is quite right when he says that basically men do not want freedom. He quotes the legend of the Grand Inquisitor in Dostoievsky's book, *The Brothers Karamazov*, which is a parable of the terrible burden of freedom. Jesus returns to this earth. The Inquisitor recognises him in the crowd, watching a religious procession, and immediately has him arrested. In the dead of night the Inquisitor secretly goes to Jesus. He tries to explain to Jesus that people do not want freedom. They want security. If you really love people, he argues, you want to make them happy, not free. Freedom is danger, openness. They want law, not responsibility; they want the neurotic comfort of rules, not the spiritual open places of decision-making. Christ, he says, must not start again all that old business about freedom and grace and commitment and responsibility. Let things be; let the church with its laws handle them. Will Jesus please go away.

There is no doubt that most people do not want to be continually confronted with the necessity of making decisions. They would rather have their decisions made for them; they would rather apply laws and principles to the situation. And it may well be that people are right.

The right use of freedom in our relationships with others depends on love. If love is perfect, then freedom is a good thing. But if there is no love, or if there is not enough love, then freedom can become licence, freedom can become selfishness and even cruelty. If you leave a man without love to do as he likes, then the damage that he can do is incalculable. It may well be that neither I nor any other person is at this stage ready for this lonely freedom which the situationist offers us. The situationists have a kind of phobia of law, but the lesson of experience is that we need a certain amount of law, being the kind of people we are.

Aristotle had his doctrine of habituation. He argued that there is a time when it is not possible to give a child freedom. It is not that the child is bad. It is that at the stage of childhood the child has not the wisdom or the experience, the ability to take the long view and to calculate consequences, which freedom demands. We have, therefore, at this stage to submit the child to discipline, to law, to control, so that the child develops the habit of doing the right thing. You only learn to play the flute by practising playing the flute according to the laws of flute-playing. You only learn to be good by practising goodness under the discipline—and sometimes even the punishment—of the laws of goodness. There is a stage at which the child has to be habituated and even compelled into goodness. Only after he has reached the stage of habituation is it possible to trust him with freedom.

Take the case of a game. A game would become a chaos if there were no rules. It may be that in some future sporting Utopia it will be possible for Celtic to play Rangers, or for Arsenal to play Manchester United, without a referee, but that stage has not yet come! The reign of law is still needed.

If all men were saints, then situation ethics would be the perfect ethics. John A. T. Robinson has called situation ethics 'the only ethic for man come of age'. This is probably true—but man has not yet come of age. Man, therefore, still needs the crutch and the protection of law. If we insist that in every situation every man must make his own decision, then first of all we must make man morally and lovingly fit to take that decision; otherwise we need the compulsion of law to make him do it. And the fact is that few of us have reached that stage; we still need law, we still need to be told what to do, and sometimes even to be compelled to do it.

Thirdly, the situationist points out again and again that in his view there is nothing which is intrinsically good or bad. Goodness and badness, as he puts it, are not properties, they are predicates. They are not inbuilt qualities; they happen to a thing in a given situation. I am very doubtful if the distinction between goodness and badness can be so disposed of.

We may grant that Fletcher has shown that there can be situations in which a thing generally regarded as wrong could be the right thing to do. But that does not prove that it is good. There is a close analogy here with dangerous drugs which a doctor may have to prescribe. When he describes these drugs, he does not pretend that they are not poisons. Poisons they are and poisons they remain. They have to be kept in a special cupboard and in a special container. They can only be used under the strictest safeguards. There are indeed occasions when the doctor will not prescribe them at all, because he is not certain that the patient has the strength of mind not to misuse them. These things have a kind of inbuilt red light, and that red light is not taken away, for the dangerous drug is never called anything else but a poison. So there are certain things, which on rare occasions may be used to serve a good end. But the red light should not be removed by calling them good things. They remain highly dangerous, and they should never be called, or regarded as, anything else.

I should personally go further. I think that there are things which can in no circumstances be right. To take but two examples, to start a young person in the name of experience on the experiments which can lead to drug addiction can never be right. To break up a family relationship in the name of so-called love can never be right. The right and the wrong are not so easily eliminated.

Fourth, the situationist is liable to forget two things.

(a) He is liable to forget what psychological aids can do for abnormal conditions. Fletcher took instances of cures being effected by what the Christian would simply regard as committing adultery. He cites the instance of the man who was a danger to small girls being cured by intercourse with a mature woman. It is to be noted that such an action would by no means guarantee a cure for a man in such a condition anyway. He quotes the play *The Rainmaker*, in which the Rainmaker deliberately seduces the farmer's daughter to save her, as he claimed, from being 'spinsterised'. This completely leaves out of account the very real possibility of sublimation. 'Sublimation', Dr Hadfield says, 'is the process by which instinctive emotions are diverted from their original ends and redirected to purposes satisfying the individual and of value to the community.' There is no need for repression with all its attendant evils. It is a perfectly normal thing for the force and the power and the surge that can flow through one instinct to be sublimated in the service of another. A man or a woman may have no outlet for the instinct of sex, and time and again that force of sex can be canalised into other channels and sublimated in the service of other things. There is many an unmarried woman who is very, very far from being a 'frustrated spinster' because she has found fullness of life in some other outlet. There is many a man who has had to do without marriage and who has sublimated his sex drive into other achievements and other service. One may speculate whether John Wesley would have been such a dynamic founder of a new church if he had been happily married. He poured into the church what he might have kept within the limits of a home. There are cures and compensations for abnormal conditions which do not involve breaking what we have learned to call the moral law—and in point of fact these cures are far more effective.

(b) And above all, the situationist is liable to forget quite simply the grace of God. Unless Christianity is a total swindle, then it must make good its claim to make bad men good. To encourage towards permissiveness is no real cure; to direct to the grace of God is. When John Wesley entered on open-air preaching, and when he saw what the grace of God could do, he wrote to his brother Samuel:

> I will show you him who was a lion till then, and is now a lamb; him that was a drunkard, and is now exemplarily sober; the whoremonger that was, who now abhors the very garment spotted with the flesh.

These, said Wesley, are the arguments for, and the proofs of, the power of the grace of God—and that power is still as strong as ever.

The situationists have taught us that we must indeed be flexible; that we must indeed look on the problems of others, not with self-righteousness, but with sympathy; that we must not be legalists; but in spite of that we do well still to remember that there are laws which we break at our peril.

In the background of our discussion of situation ethics there has always been the idea of *law*. Sometimes, in fact, it has almost seemed that the idea of law and the idea of situation ethics formed a contrast and even an antithesis. I did say at one point that the situationists seemed to have a phobia of law. Before we leave this subject, it will therefore be well to look at the conception of law in general, so that, if we do discard law, we may see what we are discarding. What then is law, and what does law do, or what is law intended to do, for society?

i. It may be said to begin with that law is the distillation of experience. Law seeks to ensure that those courses of action which experience has shown to be beneficial are followed, and to eliminate those courses of action which experience has proved to be harmful and injurious to society and its members. Law is thus a summary of society's experience of life and living. Therefore, to discard law is to discard experience. This is not by any means a full description of law, for it will clearly make a very great difference which courses of action any particular society has decided to be good or bad.

ii. This may be put in another way. It has been said that 'law is the rule of reason applied to existing circumstances'.

Fletcher has said that law is that which seeks to ensure that people will live life as a reasonable man would live it. Again, it has been said that 'law translates morals (value judgments) into social disciplines' (J. Fletcher, *Moral Responsibility*, p. 94). A society comes to a conclusion what a reasonable life is. It comes to a conclusion as to what it will take as its working values and as to what is dangerous to these values. It then frames a code of laws the intention of which is to ensure that this approved way of life and these chosen values can be followed.

iii. One of the main functions of law is definition. It defines what is to be punished and what is to be approved. It defines what is a crime and it lays down the point at which restraint will be exercised on the man who refuses to conform. There is a sense in which law not only defines but creates a crime. For instance, for long polygamy was perfectly legal as, for example, in patriarchal times in the Old Testament; then monogamy becomes the law, and that which was once legal becomes a crime. It is law's function to define that which at any time society forbids.

iv. Law has, or at least can have, two opposite effects. First, by defining the wrong things the law intends to dissuade people from doing them. It may either dissuade by making people afraid of the consequences of doing the wrong thing, or by creating in them a sense of responsibility for maintaining the society of which they are a part.

But, second, law can have an unfortunate effect. The very forbidding of a thing can create a desire for that thing, as Paul so vividly shows in Romans 7: 'If it had not been for the law, I should not have known sin. I should not have known what it is to covet, if the law had not said, "You shall not covet".' The thing is no sooner forbidden than it becomes attractive. This was what the boy Augustine discovered about the stolen pears:

> There was a pear tree near our vineyard, laden with fruit. One stormy night we rascally youths set out to rob it and

> carry our spoils away. We took off a huge load of pears—not to feast upon ourselves, but to throw them to the pigs, though we ate just enough to have the pleasure of forbidden fruit. They were nice pears, but it was not the pears that my wretched soul coveted, for I had plenty better at home. I picked them simply in order to become a thief. The only feast I got was a feast of iniquity, and that I enjoyed to the full. What was it that I loved in that theft? Was it the pleasure of acting against the law, in order that I, a prisoner under rules, might have a maimed counterfeit of freedom by doing what was forbidden? . . . The desire to steal was awakened simply by the prohibition of stealing.

The sweetness of the pears lay in the fact that they were stolen pears. In the days before consenting homosexuality was legalised, Westermarck quoted a homosexual as saying that 'he would be very sorry to see the English law changed, as the practice would then lose its charm' (E. Westermarck, *Christianity and Morals*, p. 374; qtd. J. Fletcher, *Moral Responsibility*, p. 103).

Law is a double-edged force. Its prohibitions may dissuade, but they may encourage.

v. Law is for the protection of society. Law is meant for the control of the man who would injure society. Law is ordinary people uniting and banding themselves together to control the strong, bad man. A number of small boys may make common cause against the bully, against whom singly they would be helpless; so they combine to control him. So law is a defensive and protective alliance by the mass of ordinary people to control and restrain the man who for his own ends would injure or exploit or dominate society. Law exists for the protection of the ordinary citizen.

vi. I have left to the end one very important view of law. It is a view which is largely, but not quite universally, accepted. It is the view that it is always public morals with which the law is concerned, and never private morals, unless these private morals are an offence to public decency or a threat to public welfare. In other words, there are many things which are immoral, but which are not illegal. Or, to put it in another way, there is a wide difference between *sin*, with which the law is not concerned, and *crime*, with which the law is deeply concerned. To take the case of sexual morality, so long as a sexual act is by common consent between two adults, so long as it cannot be held to have hurt or injured either, and so long as it is carried on in a way that does not offend public decency or interfere with public order, then it is not the concern of the law. This has always been the law in regard to prostitution in this country. It has never been illegal to have sexual intercourse with a prostitute. What is illegal is solicitation, which is an offence against public order. Very recently, the situation has become the same in regard to homosexual practices, which until then were illegal as such.

This point of view is stated in the words of the Church of England Moral Welfare Council:

> It is not the function of the State and the law to constitute themselves guardians of private morality, and thus to deal with sin as such belongs to the province of the church. On the other hand, it is the duty of the State to punish crimes, and it may properly take cognizance of, and define as criminal, those sins which also constitute offences against public morality.

Similarly, the Wolfenden Report says:

> It should not be the duty of the law to concern itself with immorality as such . . . It should confine itself to these activities which offend against public order and decency, or expose the ordinary citizens to what is offensive and injurious.

On this view the law has nothing to do with a man's private morals, but everything to do with his public conduct. It is not only what we might call public pronouncements which take this point of view. There is a letter from C. S. Lewis to Mrs Edward A. Allen, written in 1958, which takes exactly the same view:

> I quite agree with the Archbishop that no *sin*, simply as such, should be made a *crime*. Who the deuce are our rulers to enforce their opinions about sin on us?—a lot of professional politicians, often venal time-servers, whose opinion on a moral problem in one's own life we should attach very little value to. Of course, many acts which are sins against God are also injuries to our fellow-citizens, and must on that account, but only on that account, be made crimes. But of all the sins in the world I should have thought that homosexuality was the one that least concerns the State. We hear too much of the State. Government is at its best a necessary evil. Let's keep it in its place (*Letters of C. S. Lewis*, ed. W. H. Lewis, p. 281).

So the official and the personal point of view combine to hold that private morality is no affair of the State or of the law, unless it has public effects. For the moment we shall leave this, and we shall very soon return to it.

The trouble about this whole question is that it presents us with a series of tensions, which are built into the problem of the connection between morality and law.

i. There is the tension between freedom and law. Here the situationists are very definite. Fletcher writes: 'Nothing we do is truly moral unless we are free to do otherwise. We must be free to decide what to do before any of our actions even begin to be moral. No discipline but self-discipline has any moral significance. This applies to sex, politics or anything else. A moral act is a free act, done because we want to . . . Morality is meaningless apart from freedom' (J. Fletcher, *Moral Responsibility*, p. 136).

On the face of it, this is true. But—and it is a very big but—who of us is, in fact, free? Our heredity, our environment, our upbringing, the traditions we have inherited, our temperament, the cumulative effect of our previous decisions all have an effect upon us. Again it is of the first importance that freedom does not only mean that a man is free to do a thing; it must also mean that he is free *not* to do it—and that is exactly where our past comes in. Most of us have made ourselves such that we are not free. The whole trouble about freedom is that for many of us it is an illusion.

If a man was really free, then we might agree that he must be given an unrestricted choice; but in the human situation, as it is, man, as he is, cannot do without law to persuade and even to compel him to do what is right. This is not to plead for a régime of law and it is not to reject a régime of freedom, for here we are certainly confronted not with an either/or but with a both/and. Freedom and law go hand in hand, and it may be the truest proposition of all that it is by the influence of law that people come in the end to be really free. And, to be fair, this is precisely where Fletcher comes down, for in the end he writes: 'In the language of classical biblical theology in the West, grace reinforces law and sometimes even bypasses it, but it does not abolish it, nor can it replace it, until sin itself is no more' (J. Fletcher, *Moral Responsibility*, p. 94).

ii. There is the tension between immorality and illegality. We have already made the point that there are many things which are immoral but which are not illegal. For instance, to take a crude example, prostitution is immoral, but it is not illegal. We have seen that the common, one might say the orthodox, view is that the law has nothing to do with private morals, but only with public morality. Not everyone agrees with that. So prominent a jurist as Lord Devlin did not agree with the Wolfenden Report. He said that it was wrong to talk of 'private morality' at all. He holds that 'the suppression of vice is as much the law's business as the suppression of subversive activities'. There is no doubt that this is a very difficult doctrine, if for no other reason than that it would be hard to get people to agree as to what vice in fact is. Fletcher quotes a section from the Sycamore Report from America: 'Let Christians face squarely the fact that what the body of authoritative Christian thought passed off as God's revealed truth was in fact human error with a Pauline flavour. Let us remember this fact every time we hear a solemn assertion about this or that being God's will or the Christian ethic.' The difficulty would be to define vice.

But suppose we do accept the Christian ethic as it is in the teaching of Jesus; suppose we accept it ourselves and suppose that we are convinced that it is the best prescription for the life of society. Are we then quite happy if the law progressively makes what we think wrong easier? Are we quite happy about the legalising of consenting homosexuality? Are we quite happy about the easing of divorce regulations? Would we be quite happy to find it enacted that unmarried students living together and begetting a child should then become eligible for the same grants as married people? The trouble is that once a thing is not forbidden, it may be felt not only to be permitted but to be encouraged. It could be argued that what the law permits, it approves. Take the case of the university-student relationship. No longer is the university *in loco parentis*, in the place of the parent; paternalism is out. But take especially the case of the residential universities. It is argued that in his rooms the student has the right to do as he likes, to live his own life, and that the university has no right to interfere with his 'private' life. But what if he makes his rooms a centre of what some people would still call seduction? What if he does have a girl in bed with him all night? What if he does make his rooms a centre for experiment in the taking of drugs? Is the university in such a case to be strictly neutral? Must the university stand by and see at least some students emerge from its life intellectually wiser and morally worse? Of course, if we say we no longer accept any Christian standards, then the question does not arise. But this we have not yet said, and so long as these standards are accepted, then sheer and absolute permissiveness is not possible. It is here, in fact, that the public aspect of private morality comes in. A man can live his own life, but when he begins deliberately to alter the lives of others, then a real problem arises, on which we cannot simply turn our backs, and in which there is a place for law as the encourager of morality.

iii. There is the tension between the individual and the community. This is the tension between individualism and solidarity. In the early days of Judaism there was such solidarity that the individual as an individual had hardly any independent existence. When Achan's sin was discovered his whole family was stoned along with him (Joshua 7). They say that to this day if you ask a man in a primitive society what his name is, he will begin by telling you, not his name, but his tribe. But in our time it is the individual who is stressed. Self-development, self-expression, self-realisation have become the watchwords of modern society. Too much law means the obliteration of the individual; too much individualism means the weakening of law. It so happens that today we are living in a time of individualism, but a man will do well to remember that it can never be right to develop himself at the expense of others.

We may well come to the conclusion that one of the great problems of the present situation is to adjust the delicate balance between freedom and law, and between the individual and society. And the only solution is that a man should discover what it means to love his neighbour as himself.

CHAPTER FIVE

The Teaching of the New Testament about Work

Work—a curse or a blessing—which is it? Here are two poems with precisely opposite ideas of work. The first is four lines of doggerel which were written by a charwoman who was very tired and who was dying:

Don't pity me now;
Don't pity me never;
I'm going to do nothing
For ever and ever.

The one thing in the world she wanted was to be done for ever with work. Dr Johnson, who was nothing if not honest, once said: 'We would all be idle if we could.'

But here is Rudyard Kipling's dream of what he wanted when life had ended:

When earth's last picture is painted,
  and the tubes are twisted and dried,
When the oldest colours are faded,
  and the youngest critic has died,
We shall rest and faith we shall need it—
  lie down for an aeon or two
Till the Master of all Good Workmen
  shall put us to work anew.

And those that were good shall be happy:
  they shall sit in a golden chair;
They shall splash at a ten-league canvas
  with brushes of comets' hair.

They shall find real saints to draw from,
Magdalene, Peter and Paul,
They shall work for an age at a sitting,
and never grow tired at all.

And only The Master shall praise us,
and only The Master shall blame;
And no one shall work for money,
and no one shall work for fame,
But each for the joy of the working,
and each in his separate star,
Shall draw the Thing as he sees It
for the God of Things as They are.

Here are two opposite points of view. In the one case the end of life is the end of work—and thank God! In the other case the end of life is the opportunity to work as never before—and praise God! It so happens that these two points of view can both be found in the Bible, though not with equal emphasis. The conclusion of the old Genesis story is that Adam and Eve are for ever shut out of the garden, and the condemnation is: 'In the sweat of your face you shall eat bread' (Genesis 3.17-19). The idea is that, if man had not sinned, he would have lived for ever in the sun-kissed paradise with nothing to do but to enjoy the garden.

On the other hand, almost the whole Bible, apart from this story, bases its entire thought on the teaching and the assumption that man is meant to work and to work honourably and well. 'There is nothing better,' said the preacher, 'than that a man should enjoy his work' (Ecclesiastes 3.22). In the teaching of Jesus parable after parable is based on the fact that a good servant must be a good workman.

Paul was quite clear that if a man refused to work, he had no right to eat (2 Thessalonians 3.10), and it is his own claim and his boast that he supported himself with his own two hands, and took nothing for nothing from anyone (1 Thessalonians 2.9; 2 Thessalonians 3.8). And there is the astonishing case of Jesus. Jesus was no less than thirty years of age when he emerged into public life (Luke 3.23). It was as the carpenter of Nazareth that people knew him (Mark 6.2). For thirty of his thirty-three years on earth he was a village workman. There is a legend that he made the best ox-yokes in Galilee and that men beat a track to his shop to buy them. In those days they had signs over their shops as they have now, and it has been suggested that the sign on Jesus' shop door was an ox-yoke and the writing: 'My yokes fit well.' 'My yoke is easy' (Matthew 11.30)—not in the sense that it is no bother, but in the sense that shoes are easy, that they fit well. It is quite certain that, if Jesus had not done the work of the shop in Nazareth well, he would never have been given by God the work of saving the world. Jesus began by being a working man.

This was one of the basic differences between the Jewish and the Greek and Roman world. To a Jew work was essential; work was of the essence of life. The Jews had a saying that he who does not teach his son a trade teaches him to steal. A Jewish rabbi was the equivalent of a college lecturer or professor, but according to the Jewish law he must take not a penny for teaching; he must have a trade at which he worked with his hands and by which he supported himself. So there were rabbis who were tailors and shoemakers and barbers and bakers and even perfumers. Work to a Jew was life.

But the Greek and Roman civilisations were based on slavery. According to Plato, no artisan could be a citizen of the ideal state. Aristotle tells us that in Thebes no man could become a citizen until ten years after he had stopped working at a trade. Cicero lays it down that no gentleman will work for a wage; no gentleman will buy or sell either wholesale or retail. 'No workshop can have any culture about it.'

Unquestionably the Christian tradition came from the Jewish tradition. Work for the Jew and for the Christian is the making of life. Work and life are the same thing. We can begin by saying certain quite general things about work.

i. First, our work is what we are and where we are. There is nothing commoner than for a person to wish that his work was other than that it is. The worker in industry or in a factory might wish to be a minister or a doctor, and there are times when the minister and the doctor covet enviously a job that begins at 9 a.m. and finishes at 5.30 p.m. instead of a job that goes on for twenty-four hours a day. Carlyle was one of Scotland's great thinkers and writers; his father was a stone-mason and a famous builder of bridges; and Thomas Carlyle used to say that he would rather have built one of his father's bridges than written all his own books.

There was a famous Jewish rabbi called Zusya. Sometimes he used to wish that he was other than he was. And then he said very wisely: 'In the world to come they will not ask me, Why were you not Moses? They will ask, Why were you not Zusya?' A man's duty is literally to be himself.

Rita Snowden quotes a poem in one of her books; she says that it was written by a girl of nineteen years of age, but she does not name the author:

Lord of all pots and pans and things
Since I've no time to be
A saint by doing lovely things
Or watching late with thee,
Or dreaming in the dawnlight,
Or storming heaven's gates,
Make me a saint by getting meals
And washing up the plates.

Thou who didst love to give men food
In room or by the sea,
Accept this service that I do—
I do it unto thee.

So then our work is first and foremost what we are and where we are. This is not to say that no man ought to change his job, or want another job; but it is to say that the best way to a greater job is to do the one we have supremely well. It is the strange paradox that the man who gets the greater job is the man who is so intensely interested in what he is doing that he does not think of any other job.

ii. The New Testament is quite sure that there is no better test of a man than the way in which he works. Again and again this is the keypoint of the parables of Jesus. All that a man has to show God is his work—and that does not mean *what* he has done so much as *how* he did it.

L. P. Jacks used to tell of an old Irish navvy who worked on the construction of railways long before the days of mechanical shovels and bulldozers and excavators, in the days when all they had was a shovel and a barrow. The old navvy's spade was so well used that it shone like stainless steel when he cleaned the mud off it at night. Some one once asked him jestingly: 'Well, Paddy, what will you do when you die and when God asks you what you have to say for yourself?' 'I think', said Paddy, 'that I'll just show him my spade.' L. P. Jacks was the author of many books, and he wrote his manuscripts by hand. When he wrote he always wore an old tweed jacket, and the right cuff of the jacket was worn away with rubbing against the desk as he wrote. 'If it comes to that,' Jacks used to say, 'I think I'll show God the cuff of my jacket.'

Work is the test—not the importance of the work from the prestige point of view, but the fidelity with which it is done. It has been truly said that God does not so much need people to do extraordinary things as he needs people who do ordinary things extraordinarily well.

iii. The test of a man is work; and we can put that in another way—the test of a workman is, Does he earn his pay? Or, to put it better, does he try to earn his pay? We have in these days come perilously near to a situation in which a man is thinking, not of earning his pay, but of getting more and more pay for less and less work. If this was an ideal world, we would all be more interested in the quality of the work we produced than in the pay we got for it. It is hardly possible to rise to that height, except for the creative artist whose work is a thing of the spirit. But we are at a stage just now when the right to be paid is demanded, when the right to bargain for more is demanded, when the right to take action for the highest possible pay is demanded, and when the obligation to earn that pay is seldom admitted. Rudyard Kipling, a long time ago now, wrote a poem with this verse in it:

From forge and farm and mine and bench,
Deck, altar, outpost lone,
Mill, school, battalion, counter, trench,
Rail, senate, sheepfold, throne,
Creation's cry goes up on high
From age to cheated age:
'Send us the men who do the work
For which they draw the wage.'

iv. There is one thing which would go far to make work what it ought to be, and to cause it to be done in the spirit in which it ought to be done; and that is, if we could look at our work as a contribution owed to the community.

One of the most famous of all economic principles is the principle associated with the name of Adam Smith—the principle of the division of labour. By that principle no one tries to do everything, but each person does his own job. The baker does not try to make clothes and the tailor does not try to bake bread. The shoemaker does not try to fillet fish and the fishmonger does not try to sole shoes. Each man does his part and the whole makes up an efficient society. It is a case of each for all and all for each. This is not only good economics; it is also good Christianity. For this is the principle of the community as a body in which each part has its own part to play.

But the trouble today is that there is little or no community in life. Each section of the community is out to further its own interests, often regardless of the interest of the other parts of the community, and, it would seem, always regardless of the interest of the community as a whole. If men and women worked to contribute to the community instead of to extract from the community, the community would be in a much more healthy state than it is today.

It is easy—and it is unfair—to point out all the faults and to give the impression that the duty is all on one side. Just as a man has obligations which he must satisfy and responsibilities which he must fulfil, he has certain things which are due to him; and, if these things are not given to him, there is bound to be trouble—and that trouble extends far beyond its own generation, for there is such a thing as racial memory. We see racial memory at work in animals. For instance, a dog will turn round and round before he lies down to sleep, because at one time his ancestors lay down in the long grass and they had to make a comfortable hollow before they slept. So in society today we get discontents and fears and resentments which are not the result of present conditions at all, but which are the result of injustices and inhumanities which happened two or three generations ago. The trouble in society is that if we sow the wind we reap the whirlwind. It often happens that men are fighting again—quite unconsciously—the battles their fathers and their grandfathers fought—and in the present conditions quite unnecessarily. So, then, just as there are certain things due *from* a man there are also certain things due *to* a man.

The teaching of Jesus has certain implications; they are specially prominent in the Parable of the Labourers in the Vineyard (Matthew 20.1-16).

i. There is first of all *the right of a man to work*. It is astonishing how recently the working man acquired any rights at all. As late as the 1890s there was no unemployment benefit and no old age pensions. Hundreds of thousands of artisans were out of work. They were sleeping six on a bench on the Embankment between Temple and Blackfriars; they huddled together for warmth in the arches of Blackfriars Bridge; they were sleeping by the score in Spitalfields graveyard and in the shop doors of Liverpool Street. Frank Collier tells how the Salvation Army began to investigate this problem. And on a single evening in June 1890 there were in the middle of the night 368 men sleeping out in the single mile between Westminster and Blackfriars, living through the hell of empty days on a pennyworth of bread and a pennyworth of soup per day.

When I went to my first and only parish in Renfrew in the early thirties, we were almost at once plunged into that terrible depression which hit the world in the middle thirties, and of my twenty-seven elders nineteen were unemployed. It was then that I saw men's skill rotting in idleness. It was then that I knew what Sir Henry Arthur Jones the philosopher meant when he said that the saddest words in all Shakespeare are: 'Othello's occupation's gone.' This is something which in a Christian country must never happen again. It is the racial memory of these days which produced and produces things like restrictive practices and the failure to work all out. There is the unconscious memory and the unconscious fear that these workless days might come back.

ii. There is next *the right of a man to a living wage.* Again in 1890—which, mark you, is still within the lifetime of people still alive—Richard Collier quotes an instance of a mother and two children under nine working sixteen hours a day to produce 1,000 matchboxes for a wage of 1s. 5¾d. All right—that cannot happen now—but it happened—and it takes more than one generation to eradicate the memory of that.

iii. There is *the right of a man to reasonable working conditions.* This was something which eighty years ago did not enter into an employer's calculations. Richard Collier tells of how matches were made at that time to sell at a penny per dozen boxes. At that price they had to be made of yellow phosphorus, of which three grains are lethal. The workers dipped the matches in the phosphorus and the operation put them in peril of their lives. They would touch their faces. They would think that they had toothache. It was phosphorus attacking the jaw. 'Soon the whole side of the face turned green, then black, discharging foul-smelling pus. This was "phossy jaw"—necrosis of the bone—and the one outcome was death.' In a workshop in which phosphorus was used, if the light was put out—I quote—'in the eerie darkness, the victim's jaw, even her hands, glowed greenish-white like a spectre's, as the phosphorus rotted her while she lived'—and people were brought to see this as a sight. You cannot do that to people without leaving this racial memory which it will take generations to remove. When we remember the nineteenth century, the wonder is, not that industrial relations can be difficult, but that they are as good as they are. When people who were treated like that find themselves in a position to defend themselves and to have their demands met, no one can blame them for taking the chance. The simple fact is that it is impossible to build an industrial community on an industrial ethic which is unchristian. Our forefathers did just that, and it is our task to mend the situation—but first we must understand it.

But now we must bring the matter home. What is work to me? What place has it in my life? What ought work to be to me? What place ought it to have in my life?

It can be that my work is everything, and that for it I live. Carlyle said: 'Blessed is he who has found his work; let him ask no further blessedness.' Sir Henry Coward the musician said at the end of his career that there was no reason to thank or congratulate him on his work, because all his life he had been paid for doing the work that he would gladly have paid to be allowed to do. Paul Tournier the great doctor said that every doctor must feel that he is a collaborator with God. A man can find God and life in his work. You remember Kipling's M'Andrew, the Scots engineer down in the bowels of the ship who tended his engines and thought of God:

From coupler-flange to spindle-guide I see thy hand, O God,
Predestination in the stride o' yon connectin' rod.

These and such as these find real life in their work. But that is far from being true of everyone. You remember how Robert Louis Stevenson tells in his *Inland Voyage* about the man who drove the hotel bus at Maubeuge: the man said: 'Here I am. I drive to the station—well—and then I drive back to the hotel; and so on every day all the week round. My God, is that life?' Or you remember Charles Lamb, for thirty-three long years a clerk in the East India Company offices, as he talks of

the dry drudgery of the desk's dead wood.

For long enough now Christian ethics has been piously teaching that in our everyday work we must find our joy, our pride, our self-satisfaction, our self-fulfilment. We have been comfortably quoting John Keble:

The trivial round, the common task,
Would furnish all we ought to ask;
Room to deny ourselves; a road
To bring us, daily, nearer God.

It is time that we stopped talking pious platitudes and took a fresh look at our philosophy of work. Of course, it is still possible for a man to find his life in his work. A minister of the gospel can do so. As Peter Green used to say: 'Had I nine lives like a cat, I should have been a parish priest every time.' A doctor, a teacher, an artist, a craftsman, a motor mechanic who has the thrill of seeing a recalcitrant engine bursting into life—this is all right. But this is not by any means all. In the first place, I doubt if more than 10 per cent of people really choose what they are going to do. They leave the school, and they take the first thing that comes to hand—not because they want to, but because they have to. In the second place, the more developed industry becomes, the more automation takes over, the cleverer we become, the more jobs there are in which a man is a machine-minder, a presser of buttons, a manipulator of switches, a doer of one repetitive action as the article which is taking shape glides past him on the conveyor belt. The plain fact is—we cannot find life in that kind of existence. And it is going to become commoner and commoner. The machine replaces the craftsman; an automatic process replaces individual skill; and a man is left doing things in which it is not possible to take a pride.

We have then frankly to admit that under modern conditions a man's work may well be the process by which he earns a living for himself and for his family—and nothing more. And the consequence is that nowadays there are many, an increasing number, who will have to find their real life outside their work.

There are plenty of people who have already solved this problem. There are men who earn a living through the day and who come alive when they sing in a choir or act in a dramatic society in the evening. There are people who through the day earn so much money, and then come home to find life in a Boy's Brigade or a Scout Company, in work for epileptics or spastics, or for the old or the homeless. There are people who have a hobby which is their life.

There are any number of people who have, so to speak, lived double lives. Charles Lamb was the slave of his desk in the office, but he escaped to write the essays the world still reads. C. L. Dodgson was teaching mathematics and writing textbooks, *An Elementary Treatise on Determinants* or *Curiosa Mathematica*, but he was writing *Alice in Wonderland* at the same time. There are people who have a sphere of service or of interest or of art into which they can escape and live.

But there are others who have not, who cannot see beyond the picture house, the television set, the bingo hall, the football match—all good enough things but not things in which a man can invest his life. So certain things are needed.

i. What we are really saying is that a situation is arising when a man needs education for leisure as much as he needs education for work. This must mean the rebirth of education, so that education does not only teach the things necessary to make a living, but also the things which make men able to live.

There is a sense in which education has broken down. There are areas with schools out of which a child will come never having written one single line in answer to any question, unable to put a paragraph together on paper. There are levels of education out of which the child will come with no reading desire other than the strip cartoon or the comic.

When G. K. Chesterton was a child he had a cardboard toy theatre with cut-out characters. One of the characters was a man with a golden key; he never could remember what character that man with the golden key represented; but that character was always identified in his mind with his father, whom he saw as a man with a golden key who unlocked all sorts of doors leading to all sorts of wonderful things. The dream of education is that education should be a golden key to unlock the doors, not simply to the skills which are necessary to make a living, but to the things of the human spirit, of art, of music, of drama, by which men and women will find life.

ii. Man has a body as well as a mind; and a good deal of the juvenile delinquency which exists is due to men forgetting this fact. It is incredible that many new towns were planned in which there was literally nothing to do; and in which if there was any grass the only thing allowed on it was a notice telling you to keep off it. Eric Fromm the psychologist has said quite truly that everyone—especially a young person—has in him a certain dynamism, a certain almost crude life force, and if that force, that energy, is not directed towards life, it will certainly be directed into destruction. *Destruction is the outcome of unlived life*. We cannot put a young person in a concrete desert with nothing to do, or in the end he will heave a brick through a window or start a fight through sheer boredom. In the new society there must be plenty to do when the hours of work are done.

iii. In the new world, in which the time after work matters so much, the church must become the centre of the community. Of course, a church is a place where men praise and pray, but a church should be far more than that; the church should be the place to which men turn to find the satisfaction of every honest need in life. It is one of the great truths that the better we know a person the more deeply and truly we can worship with him. We can pray best with the man with whom we have played best. The man beside us in church should not be a holy stranger but a living friend.

Long ago, George Bernard Shaw of all people wrote a piece about the church. It is obviously dated now, but in principle it remains the same:

> If some enterprising clergyman with a cure of souls in the slums were to hoist a board over his church door with the following inscription: Here men and women after working hours may dance without getting drunk on Fridays; hear good music on Saturdays; pray on Sundays; discuss public affairs without molestation from the police on Mondays; have the building for any honest purpose they choose on Tuesdays; bring the children for games, amusing drill and romps on Wednesdays; and volunteer for a thorough scrubbing down of the place on Thursdays, he could reform the whole neighbourhood.

The church with the seven-day open door must be part of the new era.

iv. One last thing—we have seen that work can be the biggest thing in life, but that for many life will need to begin after the day's work is done. We have been suggesting ways in which this new leisure can be and must be used; but we cannot leave it there. So far our suggestions have been basically selfish. The one thing that could give meaning to life is service—the service of the community. If the mature would remember what they could do for the young, from teaching them judo to teaching them the Bible; if the young would remember what young hands can do for the lonely, the aged and the helpless; if the strong would remember the weak, and if those who have too much would remember those who have too little; if there was an inbuilt obligation to service there would be no problem at all, for it is in living for others that a man finds life for himself.

Originally it was at this point that this lecture ended. But not long after it had been televised it was pointed out to me by a university colleague whose views I respect, and who had been leading a discussion group, that it had one basic omission. All through it I have assumed as a first principle that work is an essential part of life, that the Christian ethic presupposes the fact that a man will work. But—I was challenged—what about those who have dropped out from work, or who wish to do so? And I do not mean those who have dropped out through laziness, or through unwillingness to work, or through inability to work. I am not thinking of the person who, without disrespect, can be called the professional lay-about. I am thinking about the person who feels that on nothing less than conscientious grounds he is under obligation to drop out, the person whose decision to drop out is in its own way a religious decision.

There are beyond any doubt young people who feel what is far more than a resentment against society. They feel that society is such that they cannot take part in it. Society, they say, is literally and spiritually polluted. Society is utterly materialised. Society, to use the common phrase, is a rat race. Society grows rich on the manufacture of armaments and the like. Society is the battle of the *have's* to avoid sharing with the *have not's*, to cling on to their possessions and to retain their vested interests at all costs. There are people who honestly and sincerely feel that they are compelled to drop out of such a society. It is not because they are lazy spongers that they opt out; it is because they feel intensely that they do not want to be involved in that which society has become and will become. What have we to say to people like that?

i. It has to be said that anything like a complete drop-out is, in fact, an impossibility. Whether society is good or bad, a man cannot do without it. He has to use the services with which society supplies him. Somehow he has to eat and to live and he depends on society to enable him to do so. In the nature of things we have to use the services which society implies, even to accepting support from the society for which we refuse to work. Completely to opt out of society is not possible. We may disapprove of society, but we cannot sever ourselves completely from it.

ii. One of the great questions in regard to this is—drop out into what? Is the drop-out to be a drop-out into a completely non-productive, negative form of life, where endless talk takes the place of action? Very few would drop out, say, into a monastic order, where with discipline and devotion a man might withdraw from society to pray for the society from which he had withdrawn. Is the drop-out to be from all that the world calls a career into some form of service, the rewards of which are in material terms negligible, but the effect of which is to relieve, as far as we can relieve them, the hunger and the pain and the sorrow of the world? Would a man drop out of life in order in some way to dedicate his life to the end of racialism, the end of war, the end of poverty? This is the acid test. To drop out into utter inactivity is to fail in one's obligation as a human being to other human beings. Protest can often be right; this kind of abdication can hardly ever be right. A man does not shed his responsibilities by ignoring them. A man may deny that he has any obligation to an effete and polluted society; he cannot deny his obligation to humanity.

iii. What I have just said involves and implies something else. A man of really conscientious mind has to decide what he can do and what he can not do. He may come to the conclusion that the society in which he lives is a rotten society from top to bottom. But this does not mean that there are not many things in this society which a man can do without involving himself in the pollution of society, and in doing which he may be the means of purifying—or it might be destroying—this society. The doctor, the social worker, the youth leader, often the teacher, the parson are often just as incensed at society as the man who has decided to drop out. The man who drops out has to ask himself if the best way to register his protest is to do nothing. Can you really build life on a negative? Is withdrawal the only way? Is there literally nowhere in society where a man can keep his heart pure and his hands clean? Is there nowhere he can strike a blow for the ideals in which he so intensely believes?

Suppose a person does feel that society is corrupt and materialised and inhuman, suppose that he does feel that he must withdraw from an industrialised society, must he include in his sweeping condemnation the shepherd with his sheep, the ploughman with his plough, the nurse with her patients, the surgeon bringing men back from death to life, the priest slaving his life out in some slum parish? I am not able to believe that there is absolutely nothing that the idealist can find to do. I am quite certain that he can find something to do which will not wound his conscience or outrage his principles.

iv. It would be quite wrong to level the charge against all who drop out, but it is true that many who drop out involve themselves in practices which are more than doubtful. A man may feel so distressed about the evils of society that he drops out from it, and may at the same time involve himself in the ruinous experiments of drug-taking. He may wish to end war and at the same time he may eagerly take part in demonstrations which are in themselves small wars. He may talk about love, and he may be a source of very grave anxiety to those who have loved him most and to those to whom he owes the greatest debt of love. It is very hard to see how ideals which are so high that they compel a man to abandon society can lead him to the kind of life which some of such people have chosen to live.

Further, it is a disturbing fact that there is an element of waste in all this. It often happens that those who drop out from society are people of considerable intellectual ability. They are often young people of very great gifts and of very high potential. Unquestionably, such people have a genuine distress in face of the kind of society by which they are surrounded. If that is so, it would be to be expected that their first desire would be to change it. And the only way to change society is from the inside. It is easy to understand the reformer, the rebel, the revolutionary, even the wrecker. It is much more difficult to understand the person whose protest consists in doing nothing. A man on strike certainly withdraws his labour, but he only does so that the conditions of his labour may be reformed and improved, if not for himself, then certainly for those who are to come after him.

v. One other simple thing remains to be said. If a person drops out from the life of society, all the chances are that in the end he will find himself fighting one of the greatest enemies of human life—boredom. There comes a time in life when work of some kind becomes a human necessity. There are many definitions of man, and in the end it may well be true to say that man is naturally a working animal. In every life there are times for doing nothing. It might well be an excellent thing if at some time in every man's life there was such a period; but over the years man was meant to do something, and in the end he will not be happy unless he does.

It would be impossible to question the ideals and the sincerity of many of those who drop out from society. But I do not think that they have chosen the right way, because I do not think that life can be built on a negative, and I do not think that a permanent protest can be based on doing nothing, and I believe that man is better to be even the active enemy of society than the passive abandoner of society.

CHAPTER SIX

The Christian View of Pleasure

There are few things harder to define than pleasure. The same thing can be a delight to one person and a penance to another. There is in pleasure a completely subjective element. To one person one kind of food is appetising and desirable, to another person the very same thing is nauseating. One kind of music will thrill one person and will appear to another person only an unpleasant noise. One person will enjoy games and sport; another person will think them a childish waste of time. One person will read avidly a certain kind of book; another person will find the same kind of book almost unreadable. One person will love travel; another person will find it an exhausting weariness. Pleasure varies from person to person—but there must be some kind of principle behind all the variation.

The simplest thing to say is that pleasure is the opposite of work, but that will hardly do. In the first place, there are people who are never happier than when they are at their work. Their work is a joy to them. Take it away and you would take from them that which in life they enjoy most of all. And secondly, there are many pleasures which involve a great deal of hard work. Many a man works harder at some game at which he wants to excel than at his day's work. Many a man puts a great deal of thought and time and effort into his hobby. There are people whose pleasures look very like hard labour.

We may go a step further. We may say that the effort which pleasure involves is effort which is voluntarily made, and which is made for the sake of no material reward. For instance, a man might spend a great deal of time and thought and effort and money building up a stamp collection in which he found delight; that would be pleasure. But, if he stopped stamp-collecting and started stamp-dealing, he would be doing much the same kind of things, but it would be work. A man may spend a great deal of time and money on a game, and so long as it is a game it will be pleasure. But he may decide to become a professional; he may decide to make his living by that game. In that case he will be doing much the same kind of things, but it will be work. It is then true that the absolutely voluntary nature of the activity is an essential part of pleasure.

But still another step must be taken. A man may spend a great deal of time and thought and money on some activity; it may be quite voluntary; it may have no material reward. But it may not be in the normal sense of the word pleasure. For instance, a man may give a great deal of time to church work, to youth work, to social service. He does it voluntarily; he does it for no material reward; but that is not what we normally mean by pleasure.

So we have to come back to the essential meaning of the word. Pleasure is that which is *pleasant*; and that which is pleasant is that which is *pleasing*. Pleasure is that which a man does simply and solely to please himself. Pleasure is what a man does when he does what he likes. He is not doing it because he has to; he is not doing it to earn money and to support his family; he is not doing it to be of help and service to others; he is doing it for no other reason than that he likes doing it.

We no sooner begin to think of pleasure than we remember that there have often been Christians to whom pleasure is a bad word. There were those who thought the same long before Christianity came into the world. Antisthenes the Cynic philosopher once said that he would rather be mad than pleased, that he would prefer madness to pleasure. There have been those who would have said that there was no such thing as a good pleasure, if pleasure is taken as referring to anything in this world.

The monks and the hermits of the fourth and fifth centuries were like that. H. B. Workman describes them in his book, *The Evolution of the Monastic Ideal.* They made a cult of discomfort. They trained themselves to do without food. A Cilician monk called Conon existed for thirty years on one meal a week. They trained themselves to do without sleep. Adolus never slept except the three hours before dawn. Sisoes spent the night on a jutting crag so that if he fell asleep, he would pitch to his death. Pachomius never lay down, but slept, when he did sleep, standing in his cell. Some lived on grass; some lived in cells so small that they could neither stand up nor lie down. Some were famous for their 'fleshlessness'. It was said of Macarius that 'for seven years he ate nothing cooked by fire', so that 'the bones of his face stood out naked beyond the wont of men'.

They made a cult of filth. The dirtier they were, the holier they were. It was said of Simeon Stylites, as a mark of great holiness, that his body 'dropped vermin as he walked'. Jerome wrote to Paula: 'Why should Paula add fuel to a sleeping fire by taking a bath?' And Paula replied: 'A clean body and a clean dress mean an unclean soul.' Anthony never changed his vest or washed his feet. The great Roman lady Melania boasted that after her conversion she never allowed water to touch her, except the tips of her fingers, in spite of her doctor's advice.

They made a cult of killing all human emotion and all human relationships. There is nothing uglier than their view of the relationship between men and women. Augustine would never see any woman except in the presence of a third party. An Egyptian monk Pior was ordered by his superior to see his sister. He obeyed, but he kept his eyes shut tight all the time he was in his sister's presence. A dying nun refused to see her brother. Melania, to whom we have already referred, lost her husband and two of her three sons in one week. Her reaction was to thank God: 'More easily can I serve thee, O Lord, in that thou hast relieved me of so great a burden.' When Paula was about to enter the convent, her children wept and besought her not to leave them. 'She raised her eyes to heaven, and overcame her love for her children by her love for God. She knew herself no longer a mother.' A certain Mucius entered a convent with his eight-year-old son. They were separated. To test Mucius the boy was systematically beaten. 'The love of Christ conquered, nor did he grieve over the lad's injuries.' One day when the lad was in tears, Mucius was ordered to throw him into the river. And 'this new Abraham' would have done so, had the monks not stopped him.

It is easy to see what people like that would have thought of the word pleasure. And that tradition has never wholly died.

It took England a very long time to escape from the Puritan tradition. The best account of Puritan England is still to be found in Chapter 8 of John Richard Green's *A Short History of the English People* and in the second chapter of Thomas Babington Macaulay's *The History of England from the Accession of James the Second*.

The publication of the Authorised Version of the Bible did something to England. 'Theology', said Grotius, 'rules there.' 'There is great abundance of theologians in England,' Casaubon said to a friend. 'All point their studies in that direction.' As J. R. Green put it: 'The whole nation became, in fact, a church.' But at first there might be gravity and solemnity and seriousness, but there was no gloom. Colonel Hutchinson was one of the people who signed the death warrant of Charles the First; he was a Cromwellian and a Puritan. His wife left a most beautiful biography of him, which was published early in the nineteenth century. Hutchinson was serious enough, but he was expert in hawking, in fencing and in dancing. He loved 'gravings, sculptures and all the liberal arts'. 'He had a great love for music, and often diverted himself on a viol, on which he played masterly.' John Milton and John Milton's father were Puritans. But John Milton's father composed madrigals to Oriana. He saw to it that his son knew French and Italian as well as Latin, Greek and Hebrew. John Milton played the lute and the organ, and he could admit to loving the theatre of Shakespeare and Ben Jonson.

Early Puritanism was not what Puritanism was to become. More and more the seriousness and the gravity turned to gloom. More and more the elect stressed and felt their difference from the world. As J. R. Green puts it: 'Humour, the faculty which above all corrects exaggeration and extravagance, died away before the new stress and strain of existence.' A grim legalism descended on life. 'The godly man learned to shrink from a surplice, or a mince-pie at Christmas, as he shrank from impurity or a lie.'

Macaulay tells how the Book of Common Prayer was banned from public and even from private use. 'It was a crime in a child to read by the bedside of a sick parent one of those beautiful collects which had soothed the griefs of forty generations of Christians.' Any picture which showed Jesus or Mary was burned. Works of art and beautiful churches were brutally defaced. All public amusements were prohibited and an ordinance was passed that every Maypole in England should be hewn down. All theatrical shows were banned. Playhouses were dismantled, spectators fined, and actors whipped at the cart's tail. Rope-dancing, puppet-shows, bowls, horse-racing, wrestling-matches, games on the village green were all banished from life. The Long Parliament of 1644 put an end to Christmas Day and enacted that 25th December should be observed as a national fast, on which men bemoaned the sins their fathers had previously committed on that day 'by romping under the mistletoe, eating boar's head, and drinking ale flavoured with roasted apples'. Fiddlers were put in the stocks; dancing and hockey on the village green were ended. It was when he was engaged on what he called 'the ungodly practice' of playing tipcat that the voice came to Bunyan: 'Wilt thou leave thy sins and go to Heaven, or have thy sins and go to Hell?' Bell-ringing and tipcat had become crimes of the first magnitude.

Henry Graham's *Social Life of Scotland in the Eighteenth Century* provides a picture at least as gloomy, especially in the chapter on religious and ecclesiastical life. In 1715 a Dumfriesshire Presbytery spent months investigating the charge against a minister that on a printing machine which he had in his manse he had printed copies of a 'profane' song called 'Maggie Lauder'. The Presbytery of Edinburgh denounced those who 'immediately before public worship, and then after it was over, take recreation in walking in the fields, links, meadows and other places, and by entering taverns, ale-houses and milk-houses, drink tipple, or otherwise spend any part thereof, or despise and profane the Sabbath by giving or receiving social visits, or by idly gazing out of windows beholding vanities abroad'. Simply to talk in the street, to go for a walk, to pay a visit, even to look out of the window had become a sin.

In Scotland in the eighteenth century one of the popular institutions was the 'penny wedding'. The people were very poor, and on the occasion of a wedding all contributed a very small sum that there might be an entertainment, especially an entertainment with dancing. In 1715 the Kirk Session of Morton in Dumfriesshire condemned the penny weddings. It talks about 'the great abuse that is committing at wedding dinners, and in particular by promiscuous dancing betwixt young men and women, which is most abominable, not to be practised in a land of light, and condemned of former time of Presbytery as not only unnecessary but sensual, being only an inlet of lust and provocation to uncleanness through the corruptions of men and women in this loose and degenerate age, wherein the devil seems to be raging by a spirit of uncleanness and profanity, making such practices an occasion to the flesh, and thereby drawing men and women to dishonour God, ruin their own souls, and cast reproach upon the holy ways of religion'. Anyone taking part in a penny wedding was to be fined by the church and publicly rebuked at the church service. To people with minds like that any entertainment in which men and women shared was an evil thing.

A certain Mr John Willison was a popular preacher and writer in those days. He gave advice to his people about how they must live so as not to forget God. When they put on their clothes, they must think of the nakedness of their souls and for the need of the robes of imputed righteousness. When they comb their head they must think of their sins, which are more than the hairs thereof. When they sit at supper, they must think of the joy of some day supping with Abraham, Isaac and Jacob. As they see themselves stripped of clothing, as they prepare for bed, they must think that they came naked into the world and that they will leave it naked. And, as they cover themselves with the blankets, they must think of lying in the cold grave and being covered with the earth.

There was little room for pleasure in a day spent in thoughts like that.

It must have been desperately hard to be a child in those days. John Wesley drew up the rules for his famous school at Kingswood near Bristol. No games whatever were to be allowed in the school. 'He who plays when he is a child will play when he is a man'—and that is not to be thought of. There were no holidays at all. From the day he entered the school until the day he left it, the child had no holiday. All in the school, adults and children alike, rose at four in the morning. The first hour was spent in reading and meditation, in singing and in prayer. On Fridays they fasted until three o'clock in the afternoon. After thirty-five years of it Wesley wrote in his diary: 'The children ought never to play, but they do every day, and even in the school. They run about in the wood, and mix and even fight with the colliers' children ... They are not religious: they have not the power and hardly the form of it.' W. M. Macgregor, telling of this in his book, *The Making of a Preacher*, wonders at any man trying to lead his fellow men to God and understanding them so little!

George Whitefield recounts in his *Journals* an incident which happened on board the ship on which he was sailing to America:

> Had a good instance of the benefit of breaking children's wills betimes. Last night, going between decks (as I do every night) to visit the sick and to examine my people, I asked one of the women to bid her little boy say his prayers. She answered his elder sister would, but she could not make him. Upon this I bid the child kneel down before me, but he would not, till I took hold of his two feet and forced him down. I then bid him say the Lord's Prayer (being informed by his mother he could say it if he would), but he obstinately refused, till at last, after I had given him several blows, he said his prayer as well as could be expected and I gave him some figs for a reward.

Susannah Wesley said about bringing up children: 'The first thing to be done is to conquer their will . . . I insist on conquering the will of children betimes.'

When we remember this kind of attitude, we can very easily see how the church at least in some of its parts inherited a suspicion of pleasure, and how pleasure came to be looked on as something which is wrong as such. And to this day there are still lingering remnants of this attitude.

It would be true to say that a man is known by his pleasures, and so is a society. The things which a man enjoys will provide a clear indication of his character, and the things which it calls sport will reveal the character of a nation. It will then be important to look at the pleasures of that Roman society to which the Christian ethic was first preached.

The basic fact in the whole situation was that by the time Christianity entered the world Rome was mistress of the world, and the Roman citizen was convinced that work was beneath him. The work of the world, as far as he was concerned, was done by slaves. This meant that in Rome there were about

150,000 people who had literally nothing to do; and there were another 100,000 whose work was finished by noon. Some safety-valve had to be found for this mass of people; somehow they had to be kept fed and amused. Hence there came the famous phrase that all that the populace now wanted was 'bread and circuses' (Juvenal, *Satires* 10.77-81). Fronto said that the Roman populace was absorbed in two things—food and the shows.

It has been pointed out that Rome had more public holidays than any society in history has ever had. On these public holidays everything stopped, and the populace thronged to state-provided amusements. In the time of Augustus, 66 days were public holidays each year; in the time of Tiberius, 87; in the time of Marcus Aurelius, 135; in the fourth century, 175. When the Colosseum was dedicated under Titus, there were 100 consecutive days of shows and holidays. When Trajan celebrated his Dacian triumph there were 123 consecutive days of public holiday and entertainment. The hardest work that the Roman did was his pursuit of pleasure. Let us then see what these pleasures were.

There have been few times in history with such a passion for gambling. Juvenal said that it was not a purse that men brought to the gambling tables; it was a treasure chest. Nero, Suetonius tells us, gambled at the rate of the equivalent of £4,000 on each pip of the dice, for dicing was the favourite game. At a dinner-party Augustus usually presented each guest with £10 so that, if he so wished, the guest could gamble to pass the time.

Equally, there can have been few ages in history so dedicated to gluttony. By this time the Romans had formed the habit of taking emetics before a meal, and even between courses, to enjoy the food better. Vitellius held power for only a few months during the chaos which followed the death of Nero. He served a dish in a platter called The Shield of Minerva. Suetonius says: 'In this he mingled the livers of pike, the brains of pheasants and peacocks, the tongues of flamingoes, the milt of lampreys.' When Vitellius entered Rome and assumed for his brief space the imperial power, his brother gave a banquet, at which there were served two thousand fish and seven thousand birds. Seneca (*Moral Letters* 95.15-29) compares the modern luxury with the old Spartan fare. Nowadays, he says, it is not a question of finding dishes to satisfy the appetite but rather to arouse it. Countless sauces are devised to whet men's gluttony. Food was once nourishment for a man; now it is a further burden to an already overburdened stomach. Hence the characteristic paleness, the trembling of wine-sodden muscles, the repulsive thinness due to indigestion rather than to hunger; hence the dropsy; hence the belly grown to a paunch by repeatedly taking more than it can hold; hence the yellow jaundice; the body rotting inwardly; the thickened and stiffened joints . . . The halls of the professor and scholar are empty, but the restaurants are besieged with crowds. There is a medley of bakers and a scurry of waiters. 'How many are kept busy to humour a single belly!' And note it is not a Christian preacher but a Stoic philosopher who is responsible for this indictment. There is a curious resemblance between that world and the world of the latter half of the twentieth century, a world of betting-shops and plush restaurants, a world in which abject poverty and the lushest kind of wealth existed side by side.

It was the age of the degeneration of the theatre. The theatre had become sexual, bawdy and depraved. But it had become something worse. It had become cruel. Many of the plays were about some criminal character and his exploits. In many cases the criminal in the play was played by an actual criminal. And the play ended with the criminal on the stage being crucified or torn limb from limb in the full sight of the audience.

It was the great age of chariot-racing. The greatest of the arenas was the Circus Maximus which was about two hundred yards long and about sixty yards wide; it had room for

385,000 spectators. The race was usually seven laps. The chariots might have up to eight or ten horses. This meant that the chariots went fourteen times round the turning-posts, and it was there that what one writer called 'the bloody shipwreck' could happen, for the drivers drove standing in the chariot with the reins wrapped round their bodies, and the flying wheels and the trampling hooves at the turning-points caused many a disaster. The public and even the Emperors were fanatical supporters of the whites or the blues or the greens or the reds. A charioteer could finish up a millionaire. Diocles rode 4,257 races and won 1,462 victories and retired with £375,000. It was not only the prospect of disaster that lured in the crowds; it was the betting in which the millionaire betted in his thousands and the man on the dole staked his last penny. There was even a transfer system whereby the most famous riders were lured away from one faction to another. Chariot-racing in Rome and big-time sport today bear a close resemblance, not least in the way that the financial rewards of sport make nonsense of all real values.

It was, as all the world knows, the age of the gladiatorial games. It was at these that the people received their greatest thrill. The rag man in Petronius' story looks forward to the games which Titus is going to give. 'He'll give us cold steel and no shrinking, and a good bit of butchery in full view of the arena.' That 'carnival of blood' had a strange fascination. Alypius, the friend of Augustine, gave up the games when he became a Christian, but on one occasion his friends dragged him to the arena with them. At first he held his hands over his eyes and refused to look; but the atmosphere got him, and soon he was shouting and swaying and roaring with the rest. There were the Samnites who fought with a great shield and a short sword; there were the Thracians who fought with a little shield and a long curved scimitar; there were the heavy-armed myrmilliones, so called from the fish-badge on their helmets; there were the *retiarii*, the net men, who fought with net and trident; there were the horsemen with their long lances, and the charioteers with the wheels of the chariots with projecting scythe-like blades.

The numbers of the gladiators constantly grew. Julius Caesar had 320 pairs of gladiators; Augustus claimed to have put 10,000 men into the arena. At Trajan's Dacian games 4,941 pairs of gladiators fought in under 120 days. Sometimes they fought each other. Sometimes they fought with beasts. When Titus dedicated his great amphitheatre in AD 80, 5,000 animals were exhibited as shows and more than 9,000 were killed. And in Trajan's Dacian triumph in AD 107, 11,000 animals were killed.

Sometimes the gladiators were slaves; sometimes they were criminals; sometimes they were prisoners captured in war; sometimes they were men who fought because they wanted to. Sometimes a great gladiator fought for years and retired wealthy and honoured. The great ambition of a gladiator was some day to be presented with the wooden sword which signified honourable retirement. Then he would hang up his armour in the temple of Hercules and maybe retire to a little country estate and live to see his son become a citizen—and sometimes he came back to the arena, for there were gladiators who had fighting in their blood.

There were even artificial sea-battles. Artificial lakes, sometimes 1,800 feet long and 2,000 feet wide, were dug out and flooded; and there were sea-fights in which as many as 19,000 marines took part.

The Christian ethic first came to a society which was thrilled by murder in the name of sport. And it is the mark of the power of the Christian ethic that, while the gambling and the gluttony and the pornography continue, the bloodthirsty cruelty is gone.

It is now time to see if we can lay down certain principles by which pleasures may be judged. We can approach this from two different angles. We can approach it from the *negative* angle, and we can lay down certain principles on which certain things have to be rejected; and we can approach it from the *positive* angle, and we can lay down certain tests which a true pleasure must satisfy.

i. No pleasure can be right if its effects on the person who indulges in it are harmful. There are pleasures which can injure a man's body and which in the end can have a permanent ill-effect on his health. There are pleasures which can coarsen a man's moral fibre. There are pleasures which can weaken a man's character and lower his resistance power against that which is wrong. Any pleasure which leaves a man less physically fit, less mentally alert, less morally sensitive is wrong.

There are obvious instances of this. The excessive use of alcohol lowers a man's power of self-control and renders him liable to do things which he would not have done if he had been soberly master of himself. The taking of drugs and stimulants can end in leaving a man a physical and mental wreck. Over-indulgence in eating and drinking can leave a man a burden to himself, with his physical fitness seriously impaired. Promiscuous sexual relationships can leave a man with the most tragic of diseases, diseases which will not only ruin his own life, but will descend to any children he may beget.

One of the simplest tests of pleasure is: What does it do to the man who indulges in it? If it is actively harmful, or even if it has a built-in risk in it, it cannot be right.

ii. No pleasure can be right if its effect on others is harmful. There are pleasures which can result in the corruption of other people, either physically or morally. To teach others to do wrong, to invite them to do so, or to make it easier for them to do so, cannot be right. It is no small sin to teach another to sin. When Burns went to Irvine to learn flax-dressing he met a man whose influence was altogether bad. Afterwards he said of him: 'His friendship did me a mischief.' It is precisely this that Jesus unsparingly condemned. 'Whoever causes one of these little ones who believe in me to sin, it would be better for him to have a great millstone fastened round his neck and to be drowned in the depth of the sea. Woe to the world for temptations to sin! For it is necessary that temptations come, but woe to the man by whom the temptation comes!' (Matthew 18.6,7). If Jesus is right it is easier for a man to be forgiven for his own sins than it is for him to be forgiven for the sins which he taught to others. A man may have a certain right to ruin his own life; he has no right at all to ruin the life of someone else.

A person always needs the first impulse to sin. True, that impulse will often come from within his own heart. But almost always it needs someone's push to turn the inner desire into outer action. And tragically often the wrong thing can be given a spurious attraction. To take drugs can be painted as adventurous and free. An illicit relationship can be presented as a beautiful friendship. Experiment with things which experience has proved to be disastrous can be looked on as the assertion of freedom. To lead or persuade or seduce someone else into any kind of conduct which is hurtful and harmful is a grave and terrible responsibility.

iii. A pleasure which becomes an addiction can never be right. The formation of a habit is one of the most terrifying things in life. The first time a person does a wrong thing he does it with hesitation and with difficulty. There are many forms of self-indulgence which are actually unpleasant when they are first tried, but which in the end can become a tyranny. The second time the thing is done it will be easier, and so on. The initial unpleasantness will give place to pleasure, and the day will come when a man discovers that he cannot do without the thing. It has become an addiction. One of the old Greeks said that there were only two questions about any pleasure: 'Do I possess it?' or, 'Am I possessed by it?' 'Do I control it?' or, 'Does it control me?' The minute a man feels that some pleasure is gripping him in such a way that he cannot do without it, he will be well advised to break it before it breaks him. Addiction can happen with quite ordinary things like tobacco; it can happen with more serious things like alcohol; it can happen with drugs, so that a man becomes 'hooked' on some drug, the slave of the evil thing. It is better to have nothing to do with a pleasure which is liable to become an addiction. It is essential, the moment we become aware of the growing addiction, to stop.

iv. A pleasure is wrong, if to enjoy it the essentials of life have to take less than their proper place. A pleasure can cost too much, even if it is a good thing in itself. A man may spend on a game time and money which should have gone to his home and family. A man may practise a public generosity which leaves too little for his own home. A man may be so active in the service of the community, of youth, even of the church, that he has too little time left for his own wife and his own children. Anything in life that gets out of proportion is wrong. Whenever any pleasure annexes time and money which should have gone to things and to people in life of even greater importance, then, however fine it is in itself, it is wrong.

v. Any pleasure which can be a source of danger to others must be very carefully thought about. Here we are back at Paul's insistence that he will eat and drink nothing which might cause his brother man to fall into error (Romans 14. 21; 1 Corinthians 8.13). He will put an obstacle in no man's way (2 Corinthians 6,3). This is not something on which we can lay down definite rules and regulations. It is something for a man's own conscience to decide within the context of the life that he has to live. But a man is a selfish man if he insists for his own pleasure on that which may ruin his brother.

vi. We may end this series of principles with what is the most far-reaching test of all. *The ultimate test of any pleasure is, does it, or does it not, bring regret to follow, and that pleasure which brings regret is wrong.* Epicurus was one of the very few philosophers who declared that pleasure is the supreme good in life. And we use the word *epicurean* to describe a person who is a devotee of pleasure. But when we do so, we do grave injustice to Epicurus. For Epicurus always insisted that it is essential to take the long view of pleasure, that it is essential to ask, not, what does this feel like just now? but, what will this feel like in the time to come? Epicurus was therefore himself the least epicurean of persons. He believed in a diet of bread and water, for such a diet has no ill consequences to follow. He believed in justice, in honour, in honesty, in chastity and in fidelity, for only when life is lived in these things are there no regrets. Epicurus believed that, if you do make pleasure the supreme good in life, you must take the long view of pleasure.

This is the final guide. We must always ask, not simply, will I enjoy this at this moment? but also, how will I feel about this in time to come? This even the prudent man of the world will ask, but the Christian will ask not only what the thing will feel like in time to come, but also what it will feel like in eternity to come. And if that be so, the supreme test of pleasure is, can it bear the scrutiny of God?

We now turn to the positive side of the matter, and we try to lay down certain principles regarding the Christian view of pleasure.

i. Pleasure is a necessary element in life, because, if there is no pleasure, one essential part of the total personality of a man is not being satisfied. Certainly, in life there is the basic need to work; but equally certainly, there is the basic need to play. The desire to play is instinctive. No one needs to teach animals to play. No one needs to teach children to play. Long before they come to the games which have their special rules and which a child has to be taught, children have invented their own games and their own play. 'All work and no play makes Jack a dull boy,' the proverb says. It does not only make him a dull boy; it makes him an unnatural boy as well.

Life must have its work, and equally life must have its leisure. Leisure can on occasion mean doing nothing, but more often leisure means doing things. Man has two instincts. He has the gregarious instinct; he wants to do things with other people; he wants activity in friendship; and thus the conception of the game, and especially the team game, is born. But man has also the instinct of competition, and in the game the instinct of competition is harmlessly and healthily satisfied. Thus pleasure fills an essential gap in the life of man. Without it a man's personality cannot be fully developed.

ii. Within this general background pleasure has at least two definite aims and uses. *Pleasure relaxes the mind.* The mind can become tired just as the body can become tired. It comes to a stage when it works slowly and laboriously like a machine running down. It comes to a time when it works inefficiently, and when it makes mistakes. Anyone who uses a typewriter knows that the tireder he gets the more typing errors he makes and that there comes a time when the only sensible thing is to stop. In industry there tends to be, when work is really hard, a decreasing efficiency from Monday to Friday. The relaxation of the mind is essential.

John Cassian tells a famous story about the apostle John. John was one day stroking a tame partridge. Just then a famous philosopher came to visit him, and the philosopher was dressed as a hunter, for he was going on to hunt after he had visited John. He was astonished to find so famous a man as John playing with a tame bird, and he said so. He said he would never have expected to find John doing a thing like that. 'What is that you are carrying in your hand?' John said. 'A bow,' said the philosopher. 'Do you,' asked John, 'carry it always and everywhere bent, taut and at full stretch?' 'No, indeed,' said the philosopher. 'If I kept it at full stretch all the time, it would soon lose its elasticity; and the arrows would fly neither true nor straight nor fast.' John answered that it is exactly the same with the human mind. Unless there are times when it is relaxed, the mind cannot follow its search for truth as it ought. 'The bow that is always bent will soon cease to shoot straight.' And the mind which is always at full stretch will soon cease to be efficient.

Everyone needs some relaxation. He may find it doing nothing; he may find it in a hobby; he may find it in a game; he may find it in music; he may find it in reading a detective novel; he may find it by going fishing or by spending an hour with his stamp collection or with his model railway. When a man is engaged on these things at the right time, he is far from wasting his time. He is recharging the energies of his mind.

iii. Pleasure refreshes the body. Two of the great masters of the spiritual life have pointed out that sometimes, when a man feels that there is something spiritually wrong with him, the trouble is physical and not spiritual at all. Philip Doddridge has a sermon on 'Spiritual Dryness' in which he writes:

> Give me leave to offer you some plain advice in regard to it . . . And here I would first advise you most carefully to enquire whether your present distress does really arise from causes which are truly spiritual? Or whether it does not rather have its foundations in some disorder of body or in the circumstances of life in which you are providentially placed, which may break your spirits and deject your mind? . . . The state of the blood is often such as necessarily to suggest gloomy ideas even in dreams, and to indispose the soul for taking pleasure in anything; and, when it is so, why should it be imagined to proceed from any peculiar divine displeasure, if it does not find its usual delight in religion? . . . When this is the case, the help of the physician is to be sought rather than that of the divine, or, at least, by all means together with it; and medicine, diet, exercise and air may in a few weeks effect that which the strongest reasonings, the most pathetic exhortation or consolations, might for many months have attempted in vain.

The advice of Doddridge is plain—if you think that there is something wrong with your mind and your soul, check on your body first. Richard Baxter has a sermon 'Praise and Meditation' in which he writes:

> I advise thee, as a further help to this heavenly life, not to neglect the care of thy bodily health. Thy body is an useful servant, if thou give it its due, and no more than its due; but it is a most devouring tyrant, if thou suffer it to have what it unreasonably desires; and it is as a blunted knife, if thou unjustly deny it what is necessary to its support . . . There are a few who much hinder their heavenly joy by denying the body its necessaries, and so making it unable to serve them; if such wronged their flesh only, it would be no great matter; but they wrong their souls also; as he that spoils the house injures the inhabitants. When the body is sick and the spirits languish, how heavily do we move in the thoughts and joys of heaven!

So two of the great masters of the spiritual life lay it down that the surest way to injure the spiritual life is to neglect the body. The truth is that many a man might work better if he played more. Pleasure is that which relaxes the mind and refreshes the body, and it is no credit to a man, only a sign of grave unwisdom, if he says that he has no time for it.

In his 1520 manifesto, *Concerning Christian Liberty*, Luther writes:

> It is the part of a Christian to take care of his own body for the very purpose that, by its soundness and well-being, he may be enabled to labour, and to acquire and preserve property, for the aid of those who are in want, that thus the stronger member may serve the weaker member, and we may be the children of God, thoughtful and busy one for another, bearing one another's burdens, and so fulfilling the law of Christ.

It is as if Luther said that, if not for his own sake, then for the sake of others and of the service that he must render them as a Christian man, a Christian ought to care for his body.

But general principles have always to be tested by particular applications. There are then certain pleasures which we must look at in the light of the Christian ethic. We choose three, because they are built into modern society.

1. There is, first, gambling. There has never been an age which did not gamble, for gambling seems little short of a human instinct. But the figures for the present time are staggering. Something like £1,000,000,000 a year changes hands in betting transactions. In 1965 the various figures were as follows: On greyhound racing bets amounted to £110,000,000; on football pools, £73,000,000; on horse-racing, £615,000,000; on fixed odds football betting, £65,000,000; on bingo, £35,000,000. There were then 15,500 betting shops. 12,000,000 people engage in the football pools every week. (It is interesting to note that, when the government has taken its tax, and when expenses have been met, about 8s. in the £1 remains for distribution in winning dividends.) There were 12,363 bingo halls, and the membership of the bingo clubs totalled more than 14,250,000. The charge for taking part in bingo, apart altogether from stake money and club membership money, amounted to £11,700,000. These are staggering figures (cf. R. H. Fuller and B. K. Rice, *Christianity and the Affluent Society*, pp. 80, 81). When we consider this whole matter, there are two facts in the general background at which we must look.

(a) The most universal form of gambling is football pools. These pools began thirty or forty years ago. That is to say, they began at the time when unemployment was always a threat and when life for the working man was permanently insecure. In those days in the early and middle thirties such gambling did not arise from anything like a gambling fever. It arose from a very simple and a very pathetic dream of some kind of security on the part of the working man. If only he had enough to meet that threat of the loss of his work without sheer terror. He was living always on the edge of the precipice of unemployment, and it was here he saw his way of escape. That is not so now. In the age of the affluent society, the desire is not for subsistence; it is for luxury—which is a very different thing. The element of pathos is no longer there.

(b) In the present social structure there is another factor. It is the simple fact that there is hardly any way of becoming really rich other than by one of these immense wins which are publicised. Under the present tax structure, if a man had an income of £24,000 a year, he would pay £18,000 in income tax; if he had an income of £100,000 a year, £83,000 of it would be consumed in tax. The only way to get wealth and to get it quickly, and to get it and keep it, is by a big pools or betting win.

These factors help to build gambling into the social background of the time. There is in the Bible no definite instruction about gambling; we cannot quote this or that text; we have to approach the matter from first principles.

i. The gambler had better begin by facing the fact that all the chances are against him. His chances of losing are far greater than his chances of winning, and his chances of a really big win are very slim indeed.

ii. There are few activities which gain such a grip of a man. It is a common saying of wives that they would rather that their husbands drank than that they gambled. Gambling can become a fever which can leave a man penniless. To go into a casino and to watch professional gamblers at work is a grim experience. There is a bleak and deadly silence and a look on faces which have nothing remotely to do with what we would ordinarily call pleasure.

iii. It is not irrelevant to remember the effect of gambling on sport. Horses and dogs can be doped; more rarely, players can be bribed. Gambling is often allied to crime.

iv. From the point of view of the Christian ethic, the case against gambling can be based on two things.

(a) Basically, gambling is an effort to gain money without working. It is an attempt to become wealthy with no contribution whatever to the common good. The gambler produces nothing and hopes to gain much. Gambling is a deliberate attempt to bypass the essential social principle that reward should go to productive labour. Gambling literally attempts to get money for nothing.

(b) In gambling all winning is based on someone else's losing. In order that one should win another must lose. One person's good fortune is based on another person's ill fortune. One man's winnings are paid out of another man's losses, losses that all too often the loser can ill afford.

It may be argued that the harmless 'flutter' which a man can well afford, that the raffle, the sweepstake and so on can do no harm. They are the very things which can start a man on a way of excitement which can end in very serious harm. It would be well that the Christian and the church should have nothing whatever to do with gambling, which has reached the proportion of a social menace.

2. There is drug-taking. Drug-taking may well be the supreme problem of the present generation.

i. We live in a drug-conscious society. We live a pill-dominated life. People expect to be supplied with a tranquilliser which will pacify them, or a stimulant which will rouse them; and we can even have the bizarre situation of one man at the same time being supplied with a tranquilliser to soothe him, and a stimulant to remove the depression which the tranquilliser caused. No one doubts there is a legitimate and beneficial use of these things. But the root trouble about them is that they are fundamentally a deliberate evasion. They seldom cure; all they do is to hide or mask the symptoms under a cloak of synthetic calm. They are basically and fundamentally an attempt to escape from reality—and the trouble is that reality has a way of catching up with us. No drug on earth can permanently tranquillise a man into peace or stimulate him into action. Their action is temporary; they leave the man unchanged—and there lies the problem. They are an attempt to solve a problem by running away from it.

ii. Serious as that problem is, it is much less serious than the problem of the dangerous drugs. The trouble about these drugs is that they do provide an experience which can be in itself a thrill in the initial stages. Young people think it clever to experiment. There are dope peddlers who cash in on the situation, and surely no hell can be too grim for people who grow wealthy by ruining others body and soul. Let us make no mistake about it. The way to the hard and deadly drugs is through the drugs which are allegedly less harmful. As I write this, there is an article in today's *Scotsman* in which a man's story is told. He began with cannabis offered to him in the bar of a public house; he went on to the amphetamines and to methadrine; he proceeded to heroin and to intravenously injected barbiturates; he ended up a morphine addict. His best friend is a victim, assured of death, of drugs because of 'the slow suicide of the hard drugs', and he would never have got to that stage of the ruin of body and soul if he had not started by experimenting with cannabis. No man in his senses can experiment for a thrill with that which can end by being lethal in the most terrible way.

The Christian ethic must be set against this. Certainly freedom is important, but freedom does not include giving people freedom to destroy themselves and giving people freedom to peddle death.

3. We come now to the third of the pleasures characteristic of our present society, the pleasure of drink, of alcohol. This is by far the commonest pleasure, and by far the most controversial. To take only one form of drinking, in one year the production of beer was 29,500,000 barrels, and the amount drunk was 1,032,000,000 gallons. In the ten years between 1955 and 1965 the convictions in the police courts for drunkenness increased by 60 per cent. There are at least 400,000 alcoholics in Britain, of whom one in every five is a woman. In the case of gambling and drug-taking, the actual evidence from scripture is scanty and meagre; in the case of drink it is plentiful and abundant, but by no means consistent. Let us

begin by setting out the scriptural evidence, and let us begin with the Old Testament.

i. For the Old Testament people the staple articles of diet were corn and wine and oil. To talk of corn and wine and oil was for them what talking of bread and butter is to us. The question of abstinence from wine did not arise. In the time of famine even the children call to their mothers: 'Where is the bread and wine?' (Lamentations 2.12). Whenever the people of Palestine wished to talk of their basic food, it was bread and wine of which they spoke (Genesis 27.37; 1 Samuel 16.20; 25.18; 2 Samuel 16.1; 1 Chronicles 12.40; 2 Chronicles 2.10,15; Nehemiah 5.11,18; 10.37,39; 13.5,12; Job 1.13; Jeremiah 40.10,12). It is well to remember that they drank wine in the proportion of two parts of wine to three of water.

ii. It was a sign of the punishment of God when the bread and wine failed. This is what happens when the nation disobeys God and goes its own way (Deuteronomy 28.39; Isaiah 16.10; 24.9). In the day of punishment, when joy is in its twilight and gladness is banished, 'there is an outcry in the streets for lack of wine' (Isaiah 24.7,11). In the blessed days the invitation is to come and buy milk and wine (Isaiah 55.1). It is God who gives the corn, the wine and the oil, and it is God who can withhold them (Deuteronomy 28.51; Hosea 2.9; Haggai 1.11).

iii. The tragedy is when a man labours and then is never allowed to enjoy his wine and oil (Hosea 9.2; Joel 1.10). The definition of peace and prosperity is when a man works in his own vineyard and enjoys the fruits of it (Amos 5.11; Micah 6.15; Zephaniah 1.13).

iv. The corn, the wine and the oil are the gift of God. 'May God give you plenty of corn and wine and oil,' is Isaac's blessing (Genesis 27.28). The promised land is a land of grain and wine (Deuteronomy 33.28; Isaiah 36.17). 'Honour the Lord and your vats will be bursting with wine' (Proverbs 5.10; Deuteronomy 7.13). It is the fault of Israel that she does not see that it is God who gives the corn, the wine and the oil (Isaiah 65.8).

There is no doubt that in the Old Testament the corn, the wine and the oil are the gifts of God. Certainly, they may be sinfully misused; certainly, they have their dangers; but they are freely to be enjoyed.

There is another side of the picture. Drunkenness was to blame for the shame of Noah (Genesis 9.21-24); the incest of Lot (Genesis 19.20-38); it played its part in the murder of Uriah (2 Samuel 11.13) and of Ammon (2 Samuel 13.23-29). It was a law for the priests: 'Do not drink wine or strong drink when you go into the tent of the meeting' (Leviticus 10.9; Ezekiel 44.21). The rebellious son who is a glutton and a drunkard is guilty of a sin punishable by death (Deuteronomy 21.20). Part of the Nazirite vow was temporary abstinence from wine (Numbers 6.3; Amos 2.12) Jeremiah tells of the Rechabites who were under a permanent vow of abstinence (Jeremiah 35). It is exactly this double view which presents us with our problem.

i. There are many passages in the Old Testament where the excellence of wine is praised and its use commended. It was a regular part of the equipment of the temple, although not for the priests on duty (1 Chronicles 9.29). It was part of the first-fruits to which the Levites were entitled (Deuteronomy 18.4). It was part of the tithes which were to be 'eaten before the Lord' (Deuteronomy 14.22-27). 'Wine or strong drink or whatever your appetite craves . . . you shall eat before the Lord and rejoice.' Wine was a regular part of the daily sacrifice (Exodus 29.40). Wine was a standard part of the sacrificial system (Numbers 15.5-10; 28.7-14).

Wine is the symbol of that which is best and most joyous. Only love is better than wine (Song of Solomon 1.2,4; 4.10; 7.9). Wine is part of Wisdom's feast (Proverbs 9.2,5). Wine cheers gods and men (Judges 9.13). God gave it to gladden the heart of man (Psalm 104.15). It is to be given to those who faint in the wilderness (2 Samuel 16.2). Wine in plenty was to be a picture of the golden age to come. 'They shall plant vineyards and drink their wine' (Amos 9.14; Joel 2.24; 3.18;

Isaiah 25.6; 62.8). 'They shall be radiant over the goodness of the Lord, over the grain, the wine and the oil' (Jeremiah 31.12). 'Go your way,' says the Preacher. 'Eat your bread with enjoyment, and drink your wine with a merry heart, for God has already approved what you do.' 'Bread is made for laughter and wine gladdens life, and [an odd sentiment to find in Scripture!] money answers everything' (Ecclesiastes 9.7; 10.19).

The Old Testament has much to say about the joy and the delight of the God-given wine.

ii. But there is another side in the Old Testament. The Old Testament was acutely aware of the danger of wine. Very naturally the prudent Wisdom literature emphasises this. 'Wine is a mocker, strong drink a brawler; and whoever is led astray by it is not wise' (Proverbs 20.1). 'He who loves wine and oil will not be rich' (Proverbs 21.17). 'The drunkard and the glutton will come to poverty' (Proverbs 21.17; 23.20). There are two long passages in Proverbs which must be quoted in full:

Who has woe? Who has sorrow?
Who has strife? Who has complaining?
Who has wounds without cause?
Who has redness of eyes?
Those who tarry long over wine,
those who go to try mixed wine.
Do not look at wine when it is red,
when it sparkles in the cup,
and goes down smoothly.
At last it bites like a serpent,
and stings like an adder.
Your eyes will see strange things,
and your mind utter perverse things.
You will be like one who lies down in the midst of the sea,
like one who lies on the top of a mast.

'They struck me,' you will say, 'but I was not hurt;
they beat me but I did not feel it.
When shall I awake?
I will seek another drink' (Proverbs 23.29-35).

It is not for kings, O Lemuel,
it is not for kings to drink wine,
or for rulers to desire strong drink;
lest they drink and forget what has been decreed,
and pervert the rights of all the afflicted.
Give strong drink to him who is perishing,
and wine to those in bitter distress;
let them drink and forget their poverty,
and remember their misery no more (Proverbs 31.4-7).

It is only to be expected that the prophets with their strong ethical bent would be very much aware of the dangers of wine. 'Wine and new wine,' says Hosea, 'will take away the understanding' (Hosea 4.11). 'Princes become sick with the heat of wine' (Hosea 7.5). 'Wine is treacherous' (Habakkuk 2.5).

To the sin of drunkenness the prophets are merciless. 'Woe to the proud crown of the drunkards of Ephraim,' says Isaiah (Isaiah 28.1). 'They also reel with wine, and stagger with strong drink; the priest and the prophet reel with strong drink; they are confused with wine; they stagger with strong drink; they err in vision; they stumble in giving judgment. For all tables are full of vomit; no place is without filthiness' (Isaiah 28.7,8). 'Woe to them who rise early in the morning that they may run after strong drink, who tarry late in the evening till wine inflames them' (Isaiah 5.11). 'Woe to those who are heroes at drinking wine, and valiant men in mixing strong drink, who acquit the guilty for a bribe, and deprive the innocent of his right' (Isaiah 5.22). Isaiah rebukes those who say: 'Let us eat and drink for tomorrow we die.' 'Come, let us get wine. Let us fill ourselves with strong drink, for tomorrow will be like today, great beyond measure' (Isaiah 22.13; 56.12).

There then is the Old Testament evidence. To put it briefly—the Old Testament looks on wine as one of the good gifts of God; it nowhere demands total abstinence from it; but there is no book which is more intensely aware of its dangers, and which more unsparingly condemns its misuse.

Finally, we turn to the evidence of the New Testament. In the New Testament the material is not so extensive, but we meet with the same general attitude. Jesus himself was not a total abstainer; they could slanderously call him a glutton and a drunkard (Matthew 11.19; Luke 7.34). The miracle of Cana of Galilee shows Jesus willing to share in the simple joys of a wedding-feast (John 2.1-11). Paul can send advice to Timothy: 'No longer drink only water, but use a little wine for the sake of your stomach and your frequent ailments' (1 Timothy 5.23).

But the voice of warning is there. The bad servant in the parable eats and drinks with the drunken (Matthew 24.49). 'Do not get drunk with wine,' says Paul, 'for that is debauchery' (Ephesians 5.18). When the New Testament lists sins, sins in which the Christian must have no part, revelry, drunkenness, carousing regularly appear among the forbidden things (Romans 13.13; 1 Corinthians 6.10; Galatians 5.21). There are even times when drunken conduct invades the church and its Love Feasts (1 Corinthians 11.21; 2 Peter 2.13), and there are those who have to be warned against drunkenness at night (1 Thessalonians 5.7). In particular those who hold office in the church are warned against any excess. There must be no association with a drunkard (1 Corinthians 5.11). The older women are not to be addicted to drink (Titus 2.3). The deacons are not to be slaves to wine, and the bishop is not to be a drunkard (1 Timothy 3.8; 3.3; Titus 1.7).

One passage must have special treatment. The saying in Colossians 2.21 is often used as evidence for total abstinence—'Do not handle; do not taste; do not touch.' It is precisely the reverse. In the passage Paul is dealing with those who are preaching a false asceticism, and who are trying to introduce new food laws which will prohibit people from eating this, that, and the next thing. And this saying is the saying of the *heretics*, who are trying to mislead the people. It is the heretics and the misguided and misleading teachers who say, 'Do not handle; do not taste; do not touch,' and this the Revised Standard Version makes quite clear by putting the sentence into quotation marks, in order to show that it is a quotation from the false teaching of the heretical teachers. This sentence tells us, not what to do, but what not to do.

This, then, is the New Testament evidence. Once again there is nowhere any demand for total abstinence, neither in the words nor in the example of Jesus or of his followers. but there is a strong warning against the misuse and the danger of drink. In this case we have no rule and regulation on which to fall back. We must work out our own conclusion.

Before we begin to work out a view of this question of total abstinence or of the Christian attitude to the use of alcohol, we may note that this is a comparatively new question. We have already seen that neither in the Old Testament nor in the New Testament did the demand arise. Nor were the reformers against the use of alcohol. Luther enjoyed his wine and his beer. When he was hidden away in the castle of the Wartburg, he wrote to Spalatin: 'As for me, I sit here all day long, at ease with my wine. I am reading the Bible in Greek and Hebrew.' John Kessler tells how he and another Swiss student met Luther in an inn, not at first aware that it was Luther. Luther paid for their dinner. Kessler tells the charming story: 'Then he (Luther) took a tall glass of beer and said in the manner of the country, "Now you two Swiss, let us drink together a friendly drink, for our evening Grace." But as I went to take the glass from him, he changed his mind and said, "You aren't used to our outlandish beer; come, drink wine instead".' Luther says in a 1522 Wittenberg sermon that the work that was in progress was none of his doing; it was the work of the Word of God. 'I simply taught, preached and wrote God's word; otherwise I did nothing. And while I slept (cf. Mark 4.26-29), or drank Wittenberg beer with my friends Philip (Melanchthon) and (Nicholas von) Amsdorf, the Word so greatly weakened the Papacy that no prince or emperor ever inflicted such losses upon it. I did nothing; the Word did everything.' It did not occur to Luther to abstain from alcohol. Nor did it strike the early Methodists. Charles Wesley writes to his wife Sally that 'a glass of wine helps him in his indispositions. And he always carries his own Madeira with him on his journeys' (Frederick C. Gill, *Charles Wesley, the first Methodist*, p. 174). When George Whitefield set off for America, amidst a host of other stores he took with him 'a firkin of butter, a Cheshire cheese, a Gloucestershire cheese, one hundred lemons, two hogsheads of fine white wine, three barrels of raisins' (Arnold Dallimore, *George Whitefield*, p. 144). The practice of Thomas Chalmers of Disruption fame is interesting. His resolution was 'not to take more than three glasses of wine at a sitting'. Dr McDonald of Ferintish was so famous a preacher that he was known as the Apostle of the North. Cunningham the historian tells us of him: 'Twelve or fifteen glasses of whisky daily rejoiced his heart and simply produced a pleasant glow upon his countenance' (Ian Henderson, *Scotland: Kirk and People*, pp. 100, 101). From another source we learn that in September 1824 in Glasgow, Thomas Chalmers' cellar was composed of: 71 bottles of Madeira; 41 of port; 14 of sherry; 22 of Teneriffe; 10 of claret; and 44 of whisky.

On the other hand, William Booth was inflexibly opposed to the use of alcohol. In the conditions of his day he could not use it. Richard Collier describes the London scene: 'London's 100,000 pubs, laid end to end, would have stretched a full thirty miles. In East London alone, the heart of Booth's territory, every fifth shop was a gin-shop; most kept special steps to help even tiny mites reach the counter. The pubs featured penny glasses of gin for children; too often child alcoholics needed the stomach-pump. Children less than five years old knew the raging agonies of delirium tremens or died from cirrhosis of the liver. Others trudged through the Sunday streets bringing yet more gin to parents who lay drunk and fully clothed in bed, vomiting on the floor. These were the by-products of a £100 million a year trade, whose worst victims slept on heaps of soot beneath the arches of Blackfriars Bridge, living only for the next glass' (Richard Collier, *The General next to God*, p. 53). On practical grounds, Booth was unalterably opposed to the use of alcohol, and his Salvationists were and are pledged to total abstinence.

i. The prevalence of the use of alcohol in all grades of society is ample proof of its attraction. It makes entertaining easy; it relaxes tensions and eases the atmosphere of a social occasion. There is the occasional medical use of it, of which even Paul's advice to Timothy is an example. We need not argue about the attraction; it is there.

ii. But in addition to the attraction there are obvious dangers.

(a) There is the fact that the effect of alcohol on a man is quite unpredictable. One man may be able to take it in even large quantities with no visible ill effect; another man may be liable to become drunk on the smallest quantity; another man may have that built into his composition which makes him an alcoholic, and he may be such that any use of alcohol will have the most disastrous effects. None of these effects can be predicted in advance. Only experiment shows how a man will react, and it can be argued that the experiment carries with it such a risk that it is unwise to make it.

(b) There is the danger of excess. It is quite true that the danger of excess arises with any pleasure, and that scripture warns against gluttony just as strongly as it warns against drunkenness. But drunkenness is a specially ugly thing in a drunken person, and a specially unhappy thing for those with whom he lives and who share his life and home.

(c) With alcohol there arises the question of addiction. One of the characteristics of alcohol is that, as time goes on, it requires an ever-increasing amount of it to produce the same effect. What in the beginning was a pleasure becomes in the end an overmastering desire. The habit is formed, and the habit is desperately hard to break. A man will do well to think whether it is wise to begin something to which he may well end by becoming a slave.

(d) There is the matter of expense. Drinking is nowadays one of the most expensive pleasures; and a man may well find himself spending money on a luxury which should have been kept for the necessities.

(e) There are the general effects of alcohol. It can impair a man's efficiency and dull his brain. It can slow down his reflexes and his reactions, which is why the law is so stern to those who drive a motor car under its influence. It can slur a man's speech. But it has one effect which is more serious in its own way than any of the others. Alcohol does not only relax tensions; it also relaxes a man's self-control and renders him liable to do and to say things which in his sober senses he would not do or say. In particular, it loosens a person's moral control, and sexual immorality and alcohol very often have a very close connection. Alcohol, especially if it is used to excess, can make a man behave in ways in which he would not ordinarily behave. There is therefore in alcohol an inbuilt danger.

All this is true, but all this does not settle the matter. All that has been said could be said of almost any pleasure that has got out of control. There are many drugs which are at one and the same time dangerous drugs and useful drugs. There are many habits which are useful in moderation but harmful in excess. If the man who takes alcohol risks danger to his stomach and to his liver, the man who smokes risks danger to his lungs, and the man who consistently eats too much and moves too little risks the stomach ulcer and the thrombosis. The physical danger argument is not a good argument, for a man might answer quite simply that he is aware of the danger and that he chooses to face it.

In the last analysis the only argument against the misuse of alcohol is the argument from responsibility for our brother-man. We have here the old tension between freedom and responsibility. Paul is quite clear that no man has any right to lay down what any other man may eat or drink (Colossians 2.21). The classic passage is in Romans 14.1-8. There Paul refuses to arbitrate between those who hold different ideas of what it is right to do. If a man holds that what he does is as far as he is concerned right in the sight of God, then no one can criticise. On the other hand, there is the responsibility never to cause a brother to stumble or fall by what we eat or drink (1 Corinthians 8.13; Romans 14.20,21). The liberty of the strong must never become a stumbling block to the weak (1 Corinthians 8.9). Certainly, all things are lawful, but all things are not helpful, and nothing must be allowed to master us (1 Corinthians 6.12).

But even this does not free us from making our own personal choice. The biblical writers, Paul, Jesus himself knew the dangers of drink as well as we do, for every age has known what drunkenness means, and yet, while they unhesitatingly condemned excess, they never demanded total abstention. The decision is left to us, and on soul and conscience we must make it, and some will decide one way and some another—and they have liberty to do so.

The one thing to avoid is a censorious self-righteousness. W. M. Macgregor, in *The Making of a Preacher*, says: 'Nearly sixty years ago I knew a crusty, ill-tempered woman, who lived alone in one very dismal room, with no apparent means of support but her parish allowance and occasional charity. Her neighbours resented her caustic tongue, so her solitude was seldom invaded, but at vague intervals she started on a pilgrimage among old acquaintances, from each of whom she exacted a contribution of at least one penny, and on the proceeds of the tour she got satisfactorily drunk. The deliberation of what she did gave it an ugly look, and she was appealed to and denounced as peculiarly a sinner, but only once, as I was told, did she retort: "Wad ye grudge me my one chance o' getting clean out o' the Pans wi' a sup of whisky?"' Her one chance of escape from the Pans, the grim slum in which she lived, was occasionally to drink.

Whatever else we say, and whatever stand we adopt, those of us who have comfortable and happy homes should not be too hard on the person whose only club is the pub; those of us who have many friends should not be too hard on the lonely one who turns to the public house for company; those of us who have no fears and tensions should not be too hard on the person who seeks to relax with drink.

We can do no more than leave the verdict in suspense for each man to make his own decision. We are not the keeper of any man's conscience. But let the man who emerges with one verdict not condemn the man who emerges with another.

In life there must be pleasure, and the ideal pleasure is that which is harmless to the person who indulges in it and to all other people, which brings help to him who practises it and happiness to others.

CHAPTER SEVEN

The Christian and his Money

It will be well to look at the situation against which we are discussing the Christian and his money. I am indebted for many of the facts I shall quote in the earlier part of this discussion to *Christianity and the Affluent Society*, by Reginald H. Fuller and Brian K. Rice (pp. 63-149). That book was published in 1966; its statistics therefore come from 1965, but they are the statistics of a situation which has not altered, except to become intensified. So then let us look at the present situation.

i. We are living in what has been called the affluent society. F. R. Barry in his book *Christian Ethics and Secular Society* (p. 267) does not deny that poverty still exists, but he says that for the great majority of Christians 'the call is now to the sanctification of wealth'. Brian K. Rice (*op. cit.*, p. 170) writes: 'Affluence in the hands of fallen man is a double-edged blessing and the source of much evil.' Affluence, wealth, are the key-words.

The Board of Trade prepares the cost of living index, and that index is based on the price of things which may be deemed as part of the equipment of an ordinary household. In 1900 neither butter nor electricity was included in that list. In 1962 washing-machines and television sets appeared. In 1938 it took sixty-five weeks' wages to buy a motor car; it now takes thirty-six and a half weeks' wages. Two homes out of every five have a car, and one in ten have more than one car. The national hire purchase debt in 1965 was £1,378,000,000, £21 16s. for every man, woman and child in the country.

There are about fourteen million combined television and sound licences, and another three million licences for sound only. In the ten years before 1965 the number of homes with refrigerators rose from 8.1 per cent to 41 per cent. In 1965 five million people holidayed abroad at a cost of £200,000,000 and about a quarter of them had a second holiday at home. Even their holiday photographs cost £70,000,000! The country spends about £1,330,000,000 a year on tobacco, of which £1,000,000,000 goes in tax. Eighty-six per cent of the homes in the country have television. (And perhaps two million sets have never had a licence paid for their use.) £100,000,000 a year is spent on toiletries and cosmetics, £40,000,000 on hair preparations, and £70,000,000 on hair-dressing. Every day £2,000,000 is spent on advertising.

That is the kind of society in which we live; that is the meaning of the affluent society.

ii. But there is another side to this society. As Brian K. Rice says that it might be put: 'The things which are flourishing amidst our prosperity are venereal disease, mental disorder, bad debts, juvenile delinquency, drug addiction, strikes, bankruptcy, crime.' Let us look at only a few of the facts.

At any one time there are 200,000 mentally disturbed patients in hospital. In fact, half the people in hospitals are in some form or other mental patients. There are 7,000 suicides a year, and ten times as many people attempt suicide each year. There are probably 500,000 in Britain who have tried to take their own lives. And Britain's suicide rate is comparatively low. In Austria the suicide rate is 24·9 per thousand people; in Denmark, 23·5; in Finland, 22·9; in Switzerland, 22·6; in Sweden, 21·1; in Britain 12·3. Suicides from overdoses of drugs increased from 787 to 1,038 in one year. In the last fifteen years suicides by use of the barbiturate drugs have increased ten times over, and attempted suicides by use of the barbiturates amount to 8,000-10,000 a year.

At any moment there are 30,000 people in gaol. Before the

war there were 3,000 crimes of personal violence per year; now there are more than 20,000.

In spite of the affluent society there are 1,500,000 households with no indoor lavatory; 3,640,000 without a fixed inside bath; three million with no hot water tap; and 246,000 without even a cold water tap. Two thousand people sleep rough in London every night.

Side by side with the affluence there are terrible things, and there is poverty and bad housing, which look all the worse for their comparison with the general affluence.

iii. There is another paradox. In one sense this situation is one with the greatest possible opportunities. There is a health service with the best attention available to all. There is now no reason why any young person with the necessary ability should not receive a university education. There are almost limitless possibilities of increased production, with higher wages, more things to possess, increased leisure. In one sense to look ahead is a dazzling prospect.

iv. But there is another side to this, and for this other side Brian K. Rice supplies certain facts from America which provide very serious food for thought.

The outstanding development in America is the arrival of the computer and of electronic systems. The speed with which this has happened is shown by the fact that in 1958 there were only 450 computers in America. Here is a selection of the things which have happened and are happening.

In America the computer and the electronic systems are putting anything from 40,000 to 70,000 people out of work every week. There are in that very advanced and very wealthy country between thirty million and forty million people living in poverty and squalor 'in slums, migratory labour camps, depressed areas, Indian reservations'. At least thirty million go hungry in America. Why?

A company in Michigan which supplies electricity to 50,000 homes dismissed 300 meter-readers and half its office staff, because customers are now linked to a computer which registers the current used, makes out the account, and addresses the envelope. In a motor-car factory there is a computing machine which can make up the wages of 26,000 employees, differing rates, overtime and everything else, in half an hour. There is a machine which can print a 300-page book in three hours. A government department handling pensions has been able to reduce its staff from 17,000 to 3,000. There is a radio factory in Chicago where by electronic processes 1,000 radio transistor sets can be produced each day, and the whole process is tended by two men—instead of 200 as formerly. There is a bottling plant which can clean, refill, cap and crate 200,000 bottles per day, with a total staff of three men. The New York telephone exchange is twenty storeys high and handles millions of calls a day. The total staff is five, two on duty and three on stand-by. Macey's store experimented with a robot machine which can sell thirty-six different garments, in ten styles and sizes, which accepts coins or notes, and gives change, and which screams if any one tries to feed it with counterfeit money.

What is happening is obvious. Since the war 400,000 coal-miners have lost their jobs; 250,000 steel-workers; 300,000 textile-workers; and the whole process is just beginning.

Brian K. Price quotes a labour leading figure: 'There is no element of blessing in automation. It is rapidly becoming a real curse to society, and it could bring us to a national catastrophe.' What happens—it is Mr Price's question—when man is unnecessary? It has already been suggested that the day will come when a married man with one child will be paid one hundred dollars a week to *stay at home*. 'Society must accept,' so it has been said, 'that work as we know it must eventually disappear. Man as a working instrument is heading towards obsolescence.' And the result already is that there is poverty and unemployment in America on a scale almost unknown in Britain.

This is the background of our present situation. We have not yet in this country encountered the full problem. If we are wise enough to do so, we can learn from the experience of others how to face it. But here are the paradoxes of the affluent society in which men make and spend and give and save their money.

Let us then go to the Bible and see what it teaches about wealth and possessions. We begin with the Old Testament, and we find in it an abundance of material.

i. It has been said—and it is as true or as false as most epigrams—that prosperity is the blessing of the Old Testament and adversity of the New Testament. The Old Testament expects to find the good man flourishing and prosperous; the New Testament expects to find him afflicted and in trouble.

It is true that in the Old Testament there is a strong line o thought which does connect prosperity with goodness and adversity with wickedness, just as Job's comforters did. It is indeed very significant that after all his afflictions Job does finish up with renewed and increased prosperity (Job 42.10-17). 'I have been young and now am old,' said the Psalmist, 'yet I have not seen the righteous forsaken, or his children begging bread' (Psalm 37.25). The reward for humility and fear of the Lord is riches and honour and life (Proverbs 30.8,9). The blessing of the Lord makes rich (Proverbs 10.22). Wealth and riches are in the house of the man who fears the Lord (Psalm 112.3). Wisdom has long life in her right hand, and honour and riches in her left. Riches and honour are with her, lasting wealth and prosperity (Proverbs 3.16; 8.18). The Old Testament does connect goodness and prosperity.

ii. In the Old Testament there is a line of thought which sees the way to happiness as having neither too much nor too little. The wise man prays to God: 'Give me neither poverty nor riches, lest I be full and deny thee, and say, "Who is the Lord?", or lest I be poor, and steal and profane the name of my God' (Proverbs 30.8,9). This would be very much in line with the Greek doctrine of the happy medium.

iii. The Old Testament is sure that prosperity is a gift from

God, and that no man should forget that it is so. The preacher talks of the man to whom God has given wealth and possessions and the power to enjoy them. 'This,' he says 'is the gift of God' (Ecclesiastes 5.19). And if wealth is the gift of God, a man must use it in stewardship for God.

iv. Wealth does not fall into a man's lap with no effort from him. 'A slack hand causes poverty,' says the wise man, 'but the hand of the diligent makes rich' (Proverbs 10.4). As the Greek Hesiod had it: 'The gods have placed sweat as the price of all good things.'

v. There is a kind of security that wealth can bring. 'A rich man's wealth is his strong city, and like a high wall protecting him' (Proverbs 18.11; 10.15). There are things from which wealth can protect a man. There is an old Scots saying: 'Sorrow is not so sore, when there is a loaf of bread.' To be left alone is always a sore thing, but to be left alone and in destitution is still worse.

vi. But even if there is a kind of security in wealth, there is also an essential inadequacy in it too. 'The righteous man will flourish, but the man who trusts in riches will wither' (Proverbs 11.38). Wealth is no substitute for character and goodness. It is durable riches that wisdom gives (Proverbs 8.18). When it comes to a matter of meeting the judgment of God, riches do not profit; it is righteousness which delivers a man from death (Proverbs 11.4). Even if riches do increase, a man is not to set his heart upon them (Psalm 62.10). There is no permanence about them; riches do not last for ever (Proverbs 27.24). Wealth may be a gift from God, but wealth is not everything.

vii. At best wealth is a secondary good. A good name is to be chosen rather than great riches, and favour is better than silver or gold (Proverbs 22.1). Better a little that the righteous has than the abundance of many wicked (Psalm 37.16). The sleep of the labouring man is sounder than the sleep of the rich (Ecclesiastes 5.12). It is only a short-sighted man who concentrates everything on the search for wealth

(Proverbs 28.22). When a man dies he will carry nothing away (Psalm 49.16). He came naked into the world, and naked he will leave it (Job 1.21). As a man came from his mother's womb, so he will go back again. He takes nothing of his toil that he can carry away in his hand. He has toiled for the wind (Ecclesiastes 5.15,16). A man should be wise enough to cease the struggle for wealth. 'When your eyes light upon it, it is gone; for suddenly it takes to itself wings, flying like an eagle towards heaven' (Proverbs 23.4,5).

He will be a foolish man to give his life to that which he cannot take with him, and to that which he can lose at any moment.

viii. There are occasions when wealth can hinder rather than help. A man can keep riches to his hurt (Ecclesiastes 5.13). There is no profit for the man who gets riches in the wrong way. 'In the midst of his days they will leave him, and at his end he will be a fool' (Jeremiah 17.11). Wealth can make a man careless of God and of his fellow men. How can God know? he will ask. The wicked take their careless ease, but the day of reckoning comes (Psalm 73.12). Some day the righteous will laugh at the man 'who would not make God his refuge and sought refuge in his wealth' (Psalm 52.7).

ix. Undoubtedly wealth gives a man power over his fellow men. 'The rich rules over the poor, and the borrower is the slave of the lender' (Proverbs 22.7). Wealth gives a man a certain popularity. 'The poor is disliked even by his neighbours, but the rich has many friends' (Proverbs 14.20). Wealth can bring with it pride and arrogance, and these are the sins which go before a fall. 'The poor may have to use entreaties, but the rich answers roughly' (Proverbs 28.11). The wise man never glories in his riches, any more than the wise man in his wisdom, or the mighty man in his might (Jeremiah 9.23). The rich man tends to be a man who is full of violence (Micah 6.12). Wealth can do things to a man which make him a far worse man, and to possess it is not a sin, but a danger to character.

x. On at least one occasion in the Old Testament the rich man is synonymous with the wicked man. It is said of the suffering servant that they made his grave with the wicked, and with a rich man in his death (Isaiah 53.9).

The writers of the Old Testament know that wealth is a gift from God, but they also know that it can separate a man from God and from his fellow men. They know that wealth is a good thing for a man to enjoy, but a bad thing for a man to put his trust in, or to give his life to.

We shall gain further light on this, if we look at what the Old Testament has to say about the poor.

The Old Testament uses three words for *poor*. It uses the word *dal* which means poor and weak and even emaciated. It is, for instance, the word that is used of the lean cattle in Pharaoh's dream (Genesis 41.19). The Revised Standard Version usually translates it *poor* (Proverbs 22.9,16,22; Amos 4.1; 5.11; 8.6); but sometimes it translates it *weak* (Psalm 41.1, margin; Psalm 82.3,4). It uses the word *ebion*, which the Revised Standard Version regularly translates *needy* (Job 5.15; Psalm 69.33; 140.12; Proverbs 14.31; Jeremiah 20.13). This word expresses the state of the man who is not only poor, but whose poverty has brought to him oppression and abuse. It uses the word *ani*. This is what we might call the most developed word. It describes the man who is poor, without influence, oppressed. This man has no human help and no human resources; and in such a state his only help is in God, in whom he has put his trust. So it comes to mean the poor and humble man, whose whole and only trust is in God (Psalm 34.6; 40.17; 68.10; 86.1; Proverbs 14.21; Isaiah 66.2). Here there emerges something which is very much a dominant part of the pattern—the fact that the poor man is specially the concern of God.

i. There is laid upon men the special duty of remembering and helping the poor. Both the wise man and the psalmist speak of the happiness of the man who remembers the poor (Psalm 41.1; Proverbs 14.21). It is part of a good man's duty to maintain the rights of the poor and the needy (Proverbs 31.9). The good man does not regard the rich more than the poor (Job 34.19). The command of God is: 'Give justice to the weak and the fatherless; maintain the right of the afflicted and the destitute. Rescue the weak and the needy; deliver them from the hand of the wicked' (Psalm 82.3,4). Only if a king judges the poor with equity will his throne be established for ever (Proverbs 29.14). As the Old Testament sees it, it is an essential part of a good man's duty to remember, to help and to defend the poor.

ii. In the Old Testament there is also consistent condemnation for those who neglect or ill-treat the poor. It is the wicked who persecute the poor (Psalm 10.2). Part of Isaiah's condemnation of the wicked is that the spoil of the poor is in their houses (Isaiah 3.14,15). 'Woe to those who make iniquitous decrees . . . to turn aside the needy from justice, and to rob the poor of my people of their rights' (Isaiah 10.1-2). It is the activity of the wicked 'to ruin the poor with lying words, even when the plea of the needy is right' (Isaiah 32.7). He who oppresses the poor to increase his own wealth will come to nothing else than want (Proverbs 27.6). 'A righteous man knows the rights of the poor, but a wicked man does not understand such knowledge' (Proverbs 29.7).

It has been said that the voice of the prophets is often nothing other than 'a cry for social justice'. The care of the poor is an essential duty laid on the man who wishes to see the world as God meant it to be.

iii. In the Old Testament the care of the poor is laid down, not only as a duty to man, but also as a duty to God. It is something which has to be done, not only for the sake of the poor, but also for the sake of God. Jeremiah says of a good king: 'He judged the cause of the poor and the needy: then it was well. Is not this to know me? says the Lord' (Jeremiah 22.16). The wise man says: 'He who oppresses the poor insults his Maker, but he who is kind to the needy honours him' (Proverbs 14.31). 'He who is kind to the poor lends to the

Lord' (Proverbs 19.17). If a man closes his ear to the cry of the poor, God will close his ear to his cry (Proverbs 21.13). 'Do not rob the poor because he is poor, or crush the afflicted at the gate; for the Lord will plead their cause, and despoil the life of those who despoil them' (Proverbs 22.22,23).

To help the poor is to help God; to be heartless to them is to incur his anger. How could it be otherwise, for to injure the child is always to anger the child's father, and to help the child is always to delight the child's father's heart?

iv. As we would expect from all this, the Old Testament is sure that God cares for the poor in a very special way, and rescues and delivers them. This is a favourite thought in the Psalms. 'The Lord hears the needy' (Psalm 69.33). 'God stands at the right hand of the needy' (Psalm 109.31). 'The needy shall not always be forgotten, and the hope of the poor shall not perish for ever' (Psalm 9.18). 'This poor man cried and the Lord heard him' (Psalm 44.6). God in his kindness provides for the needy (Psalm 68.10). 'God delivers the needy when he calls, the poor and him who has no helper' (Psalm 72.12). 'The Lord executes justice for the needy' (Psalm 140.12). 'He raises up the poor from the dust' (1 Samuel 2.8). 'With righteousness God will give justice to the poor' (Isaiah 11.4).

The poor man is under the care of God. The Old Testament does not despise wealth; it does not deny that there are things that wealth can do. But it will never make wealth the principal good, and it will always insist that to gain wealth wrongly and to use wealth selfishly are both to sin against God.

We now turn to the New Testament, and in particular to the teaching of Jesus.

i. When we study Jesus' teaching about money, the first thing that emerges is that the assumption of New Testament teaching is that the Christian will live an ordinary life, so far as the work and the obligations of life are concerned. It is assumed that he will be doing a job, earning a pay, paying his way and supporting those who are dependent on him. There are those who have withdrawn from the world, and who have taken the vow of poverty, chastity and obedience. At first sight this seems the very essence of Christianity. But here a paradox emerges. If there are people who vow themselves to poverty, who divorce themselves from the ordinary work of this world, and who live on the charity they receive, if they forswear all possessions, it simply means that the rest of the world must keep on working to enable these people to withdraw from the world and to supply the charity on which they live. If everyone withdrew, and if everyone forswore all earthly possessions, then the whole structure of society would collapse, and, if no one had anything, there would be no one to give anyone anything, and all charity would necessarily come to an end. So we have the odd situation that it is necessary for the 'ordinary' Christians to keep on working in order to make it possible for the 'super' Christians to withdraw from the world. This is not the Christian way. New Testament teaching involves the assumption that the Christian is living a normal life, doing the world's work, and accepting the world's obligations.

This is what Jesus did. The first thirty years of his life were spent in Nazareth (Luke 3.23), where he was well known as the village carpenter (Mark 6.3). He accepted the normal duty of paying taxes, both to the government (Matthew 22.15-22) and to the Temple (Matthew 17.24-27). He and his friends had their own store of money, and it was the task of Judas Iscariot to look after it. When it was a question of feeding the crowds, Philip's first reaction was that the food would have to be paid for (John 6.7). The whole implication is that Jesus and his friends accepted their normal obligations and paid their way.

ii. Exactly the same was true of Paul. He was a qualified tradesman (Acts 18.3) and it was always his claim that, wherever he stayed, he was a burden on no one, because he was self-supporting (1 Corinthians 4.12; 1 Thessalonians 2.9; 2 Thessalonians 3.7,8; Acts 20.34). He earned his money, supported himself, and paid his debts with his own work—and he wanted it that way.

iii. Nevertheless the New Testament is clear about the danger of riches. The New Testament never says that it is a sin to possess money, but it does say that it is a grave danger. 'Woe to you that are rich,' Jesus said, as Luke has it. 'Woe to you that are full now' (Luke 6.24,25). In the story of the rich young ruler (Matthew 19.16-30; Mark 10.17-31; Luke 18.18-30), a story to which we shall return, Jesus warns men that it is desperately difficult for a rich man to get into the kingdom of God. It is not money itself, but the love of money that is the root of all evils (1 Timothy 6.10). The danger is always there.

iv. The danger that a man can become too fond of money can even enter the church. The bishops and the deacons are both warned that they must not be greedy for gain (1 Timothy 3.3,8; Titus 1.7). Those who tend the flock are warned that they must not do so for shameful gain (1 Peter 5.2). There are those in the Christian fellowship who are there to exploit their fellow Christians (2 Peter 2.3). The writer to the Hebrews writes: 'Keep life free from the love of money' (Hebrews 13.5). The attraction of money is something from which the Christian was not, and is not, immune. The sin of covetousness was something of which the New Testament was very much aware (Mark 7.12; Luke 12.15; Romans 1.29; 2 Corinthians 9.5; Ephesians 5.3; Colossians 3.5; 1 Timothy 2.5; 2 Peter 2.3). *Pleonexia*, the Greek word for covetousness, means *the desire to have more*, and that is a desire which is deeply rooted in human nature.

v. There was nothing of inverted snobbery in the attitude of Jesus to wealth. He did not glorify poverty as such. He had friends in every walk of life. James and John came from a family who were well enough off to own their own fishing-boat and to employ hired servants (Mark 1.19,20). Nicodemus brought spices which must have cost a very large sum of money for the anointing of Jesus' body (John 19.39).

Zacchaeus was a wealthy man, and he was not called upon entirely to divest himself of his belongings (Luke 19.1-10). There were certain women who followed Jesus, and who cared for his needs, and of them Joanna, the wife of Chuza, Herod's steward, certainly must have belonged to the upper and the wealthy classes (Luke 8.3). Even if we insist on the dangers of riches, we cannot fly to the other extreme, and make poverty itself a virtue.

vi. One of the dangers of riches, as the New Testament sees it, is that they may beget arrogance in their possessor, and subservient snobbery in those who come into contact with him. In the Pastoral Letters Timothy is instructed to charge the rich in this world's goods not to be haughty (1 Timothy 6.17). James draws the picture of the rich man arriving in the Christian congregation and being treated with a servile snobbery at the expense of the poor (James 2.1-7). And he condemns the rich man who lives in luxury while his employees remain unpaid (James 5.1-6). The New Testament is well aware of the attitude of mind which riches can produce, both in the mind of the man who has them and in the minds of the people who encounter them.

vii. The New Testament is sure that riches are a bad thing in which to put our trust; they are a very insecure foundation for life.

(a) A man has to learn that the value of his life cannot be assessed by the size of his bank balance. The rich man in the parable (Luke 12.13-21) thought that he had enough laid by to enable him to enjoy life for many years to come, but that very night, when he was making his future plans, God required his soul from him, and all the material things of which he had been so proud became a sheer irrelevance. A man cannot take his material possessions to heaven along with him.

(b) Riches are a diminishing asset. The moth and rust can damage them, and the thief can steal them (Matthew 6.19-21). They are no more permanent than the flower which blossoms and fades (James 1.10,11). It has been said that there are people who know 'the price of everything and the value of nothing'. It is when he is confronted with eternity that a man sees the true value of things, and he is a foolish man who puts his confidence in things so easily lost and so quick to deteriorate.

(c) The desire for riches can blind a man to the higher things. 'The cares of this world and delight in riches' are like the fast-growing weeds that choke the life out of the seed (Matthew 13.22; Mark 4.9; Luke 8.14). As William Lillie says in his *Studies in Christian Ethics*: 'The pursuit of money takes the place of the worship of God.' 'No man', said Jesus, 'can serve two masters . . . You cannot serve God and mammon' (Matthew 6.24). A man's god is that to which he gives himself, his time, his energy, his thought, his life, that which dominates and pervades his life. And if a man's one concern is with wealth, then wealth is his god.

(d) Whatever else is true, a man cannot take his wealth with him when he dies. He came naked into the world, and naked he will leave it (Job 1.21; Ecclesiastes 5.15,16; 1 Timothy 6.7). He will therefore be well advised to seek for the true riches, and to lay up the real treasure, which will last beyond time and into eternity. He should do good, and be rich in good deeds, and thus lay a foundation for the future life which is life indeed (1 Timothy 6.17,18).

As the New Testament sees it, and as experience confirms it, trust placed in any material thing is misplaced trust, and even in this life the mistake will be discovered. To see nothing beyond the material world is the way to disappointment in time and in eternity.

There is still certain material in the New Testament at which we must look before we begin to make our own general pattern.

i. There is a New Testament parable which has at least something to tell about Jesus' attitude to wealth—the parable of the rich man and Lazarus (Luke 16.19-31). This is the story of two men. One was rich. He was dressed in the finest clothes and ate the finest food; there was nothing in the world that he did not possess. The other was Lazarus, a beggar with ulcerated sores on his body, so helpless that he could not even keep off the dogs. Daily he was placed at the gate of the rich man's house and he did at least get the crumbs that fell from the rich man's table. Then the scene changes; it is no longer this world but the world to come. And in that other world the rich man is in agony and in torture, and the poor man is in bliss and blessedness—and there is no altering of their positions.

What is this parable saying? There has just been a reference in the preceding passage to the Pharisees 'who are lovers of money' (Luke 16.14). So this parable has something to say about money. What it is condemning so unsparingly is *irresponsibility*, lack of awareness, lack of concern. There is no indication that the rich man was in any way cruel to Lazarus in an active way. He let him lie there; he let him have the crumbs that fell from his table. The trouble was that he never noticed him. To the rich man Lazarus was part of the landscape. If ever he did notice him, it never struck him that Lazarus had anything to do with him. He was simply unaware of his presence, or, if he was aware of it, he had no sense of responsibility for it.

This parable is a vivid illustration of the fact that a man may well be condemned, not for doing something, but for doing nothing. As someone has put it: 'It was not what the rich man did that got him into gaol; it was what he did not do that got him into hell.' Hugh Martin writing on this parable in *The Parables of the Gospels* says that Dale called this parable 'the indignation of infinite love at white heat', and that Alexander McLaren called it 'the sternest of Christ's parables'. The condemnation is for the man who has money and who is quite unaware of those who have not, for the man who has no sense of responsibility for those who are less fortunate than he is. There is many a man who will spend on a dinner in a plush restaurant, even on the drinks at such a dinner, a sum exceeding the weekly old age pension for a man and wife. In one year Great Britain spent forty-five times as much on defence as it did on free aid to dependent territories. In one year something like £40,000,000 was given in such aid and something like £930,000,000 was spent in betting and gambling.

The New Testament unsparingly condemns irresponsibility, whether that irresponsibility be personal or national. It insists that no person or nation has a right to live in luxury while others live in poverty. It could be argued that we are forced to help others through the very heavy taxation system which now exists. This is perfectly true. But a fiscal obligation cannot take the place of a personal awareness. The simple fact, platitudinous as it may sound, is that no man has the right to live like the rich man while Lazarus is at his gates.

ii. The second passage which is very relevant for our discussion is the record of the cleansing of the temple by Jesus (Matthew 21.12,13; Mark 11.15,16; Luke 19.45,46; John 2.13-17). Here is the only incident in the New Testament when we find Jesus moved to violence; it must therefore have been an incident of special significance.

Jesus drove out of the temple courts the changers of money and the sellers of sacrificial victims. At the Passover time the temple tax was paid. The temple tax was about half a shekel. It does not sound much, but it has to be remembered that the average day's pay in Palestine in the time of Jesus amounted to about four new pence; and this means that the temple tax represented about two days' pay—a quite considerable sum. Since it was the ambition of every Jew to keep one Passover in Jerusalem the city was crowded with Jews who had come from all over the world. Since they came from all over the world, they brought all kinds of currency—Roman, Greek, Egyptian, Tyrian, Phoenician. For all normal purposes all the coinages were equally acceptable. But the temple tax had to be paid either in shekels of the sanctuary or Galilaean half-shekels. This was because these were the only two coins which did not have a king's head on them. To the Jew a coin with a king's head on it was a graven image, especially if the king was deified. So the temple authorities had set up stalls in the temple where the other currencies could be changed into the right currency in which to pay the tax. It was on the face of it a convenient arrangement, but, for every coin changed the changers made a charge equivalent to about one new penny, and if the transaction involved the giving of change, another new penny was charged. So a pilgrim might well be charged an extra two new pence to enable him to pay his tax in the right currency—and remember that two new pence was about half a day's wage for a working man. It was blatant exploitation of simple people.

As for the sellers of pigeons, they had, if anything, an even better ramp. A man might bring his own pigeons to the temple to sacrifice, birds which he had bought outside. But every animal for sacrifice had to be without blemish and so there were temple inspectors, and if the animal had been bought outside the temple, they would certainly find a flaw in it and direct the worshipper to the temple stalls where victims which had already been examined were for sale. Again it seems a convenient arrangement, but outside the temple a pair of pigeons could cost as little as one new penny, and inside the temple they could cost as much as seventy-five new pence. Again it was sheer conscienceless exploitation, and exploitation practised in the name of religion.

Jesus was moved to the use of force. He whipped the sellers, put their animals out of the temple and overturned the tables of the money-changers. And what moved him to this violence was the sight of deliberate and highly profitable exploitation. The making of money by the exploitation of people's credulity or trustfulness, or, worse, by the exploitation of their need, incurs the wrath of Jesus—and it still happens.

iii. There is another parable of Jesus which has much to say about wealth, the strangest of all Jesus' parables, the parable in which every character is a rogue, the parable usually called the parable of the unjust steward (Luke 16.1-13). This parable tells how a steward was discovered to be dishonest and therefore faced the prospect of dismissal. In the east a steward had unlimited control over his master's property. So with the prospect of dismissal facing him, and with the end of his comfortable life in sight, this steward went one by one to the people who owed his master debts. He was not yet dismissed, and he had authority to deal with these debts and debtors. In each case he came to an agreement with the debtor to falsify the account. In each case the debt was recorded as considerably less than it was. In this way the steward hoped to be able to gain entry into the household of all the debtors in time to come, partly because they would be grateful to him, and no doubt partly—for he was a clever scoundrel—because, since he had made them sharers in his defalcations, he had them in his power. And when the master found out about it, instead of being angry, he looked on it as a clever bit of roguery, and congratulated the steward on his shrewdness in providing thus for his future.

That is an extraordinary parable. It is so extraordinary that it is clear that by the time Luke recorded it, its original lesson was lost, because Luke attaches no fewer than four different lessons to it—and all of them are relevant to the question of the Christian and his money. Let us look at the lessons which Luke has attached to it.

(a) He begins with the comment of the master: 'The sons of this world are wiser in their own generation than the sons of light' (Luke 16.8). What Luke means by this is that Christians would be very much better Christians if they were as keen to be Christians as the rascal of a steward was to cling on to his comfort and his money. It is perfectly true that this would be a very different world, and the church would be a very different church, if so-called Christians put as much time and thought and energy into being Christian as they do into making money, or even into practising a hobby or playing a game. If the

Christian put as much effort into maintaining his standards as a Christian as the worldly man puts into maintaining his standards of worldly comfort, he would be a very much better Christian than he is. There are things in which the children of this world can be an example to the children of light.

(b) His second comment is: 'And I tell you, make friends for yourselves by means of unrighteous mammon, so that when it fails, they may receive you into the eternal habitations' (Luke 16.9). This is a very difficult saying, but William Lillie seizes on one unmistakable thing about it. He says: 'Whatever else this means, it teaches that money is to be used as a means, and not as an end in itself' (William Lillie, *Studies in New Testament Ethics*, p. 97). It was not the money itself that the steward was interested in; he was interested in the friends which money could win him, and the comfort it could ensure for him. It is a cynical enough view of life—you can buy friendship, is the principle behind it—but the whole parable is designed to show how a cynical worldling can in some ways be an example to a Christian. So this tells us that money is meant to be used and not to be kept, and that it must never be regarded as an end in itself, but always as a means to an end—and the end towards which it is a means will be all important.

(c) The third lesson is: 'He who is faithful in a very little is faithful also in much; and he who is dishonest in a very little is dishonest also in much. If then you have not been faithful in the unrighteous mammon, who will entrust to you the true riches? And if you have not been faithful in that which is another's, who will give you that which is your own?' (Luke 16.10-12). This is a much simpler lesson. It is the principle that a man's conduct in money matters is no bad test of the man. If, we might almost say, a man can be trusted with money, he can be trusted with anything. A man's character, his honesty or his dishonesty, his straightness or his crookedness, can be seen, and nowhere better, in his daily business and financial dealings. The life a man lives in business is in its own way a preparation for eternal life

(d) The fourth lesson is: 'No servant can serve two masters; for either he will hate the one and love the other, or he will be devoted to one and despise the other. You cannot serve God and mammon' (Luke 16.13). In Matthew this is part of the Sermon on the Mount, and appears in a quite different context (Matthew 6.24). We may well conclude that Jesus said this more than once. It says quite definitely that there is only room in life for one supreme loyalty, and that supreme loyalty must be to God. And, if a man's supreme loyalty is to God, there will never be anything wrong with either the way he makes his money or the way in which he spends it.

iv. The fourth place in which we will find guidance about the Christian and his money is the story of the collection which Paul made from the Gentile churches for the church at Jerusalem. This whole subject is dealt with most illuminatingly in *Christianity and the Affluent Society* by R. H. Fuller (pp. 46-59). With Paul, Christianity went out to the Gentiles. The day came when it became a kind of agreed division of labour that Paul should go to the Gentiles and that Peter and James and John should have the Jews as their special sphere. The one thing that the older apostles did enjoin upon Paul was to remember the poor, and that was something to which he required no urging (Galatians, 2.9,10). Some four or five years passed and Paul formed a scheme. Jerusalem was always a poor church, and Paul initiated a movement whereby all the Gentile churches he could contact would join in making a special gift collection for the church at Jerusalem. After all, Jerusalem was the mother church. It was from Jerusalem that the whole Christian religion flowed, and it was very right and proper that the younger churches, who had received such spiritual blessings from Jerusalem, should give Jerusalem all the material help they could. (The story can be pieced together from 1 Corinthians 16.1-4; 2 Corinthians 8 and 9; Romans 15.25,26.)

The first passage, short as it is, is very instructive for Christian giving through the church:

> On the first day of every week, each of you is to put something aside and store it up, as he may prosper, so that the contributions need not be made when I come (*1 Corinthians 16.2*).

Giving is to be *systematic* giving, so that there will not have to be a sudden emergency sermon and appeal. Far better a regular putting aside than a desperate effort when the deadline is fast approaching. The giving is to be *proportionate*. A man is to give as he prospers. The 'flat-rate' kind of giving is quite inappropriate, for what may be much for one man is likely to be negligible for another. The giving is to be *universal*. Each of them is to do it. So often the financial welfare of the congregation depends on the generosity of something under half of its members. It should be something in which all are involved, as they are able.

This collection for Jerusalem lay very near to Paul's heart. It was not only of great practical help to Jerusalem; it had a very great symbolic value for the whole church. It stood for at least three things.

(a) It symbolised the oneness of the church. It avoided any atmosphere of congregationalism. Just as there must be a relationship between individual and individual, so there must be a relationship between community and community, between congregation and congregation, between church and church. No congregation must think only of itself; it must be one for all and all for one. It is, for instance, very doubtful if wealthy congregations have any right to embark on schemes for things which are non-essentials, however much artistic value they may have, when there are congregations whose essential work is hindered through lack of funds. Any community whose outlook is limited to its own congregation is not a church.

(b) It symbolised the fact that no spectacular manifestation of spiritual gifts can take the place of concern for others. To put it technically, no number of *charismata*, spiritual gifts, can ever be a substitute for *agapē*, Christian love. The Corinthian church was taken up with spectacular things like speaking with tongues; and such things may well lead to spiritual pride, instead of love's concern.

(c) The third point is well made by R. H. Fuller. This collection symbolised the fact that spiritual fellowship, if it is really genuine, 'will always be given material expression, in terms of dollars and cents, of pounds, shillings and pence'. If we talk of the necessity of fellowship with others, that fellowship is quite unreal unless it issues in practical giving. James thought it the very negation of Christianity, if kind words and kind thoughts did not become concrete in kind deeds (James 2.14-17).

We have now looked at the biblical material about money and wealth and possessions. Let us go on to see if we can deduce from it certain general principles by which we may guide our own use of them.

i. We must right at the beginning dispose of the saying so common with preachers and evangelists that money does not matter, and that it is of no importance. It is very unlikely that anyone who has ever had the experience of having no money would ever say such a thing. Here is a letter which appeared some time ago in the correspondence columns of a newspaper:

> Ask the man in the street, who has only a few shillings in his pocket, and who has to count every penny before spending it, if he is happy, and the answer will be, No. He'd be much happier being able to order a slap-up lunch and to buy a good suit, and only the possession of money can enable him to do so.
>
> In all my life I have never met a needy person who was happy.

Lack of money is at the root of most marital problems too. It may be that that letter is too sweeping; but it has never been a pleasant thing to have too little, not to be able to get for one's family what other families get, not to be able to afford the occasional celebration or holiday, always to be haunted by a feeling of insecurity for the future. Even in the affluent society there are still people for whom life is like that. No honest person is going to say that money does not matter.

ii. If we assume that money and possessions must have a certain importance in life, we may go on to say that there is one basic principle which must govern our relationship to them. It is a test which goes as far back as the Greek philosophers. It is the question: *Do I possess my possessions, or am I possessed by them?* 'You cannot serve God and mammon,' the saying of Jesus has it (Matthew 6.24). The Greek word for *serve* is a strong word; it is *douleuein*, which comes from the word *doulos*, which means a *slave*. A man ought to be a slave to God, in the sense that in regard to God he should have no will of his own; he should regard himself as the possession of God; but a man should never be the slave of his possessions. And that is what some people are. Take away their luxuries and their comforts, and you take away their life. Their life is spent planning how they can maintain and increase their standards of comfort.

This is where the story of the rich young ruler comes in (Matthew 19.16-31; Mark 10.17-31; Luke 18.18-30). That story culminates in Jesus telling the young man that, if he wants the satisfaction he wistfully longs for, he must sell all that he has and give the proceeds to the poor, whereat he goes sorrowfully away for he was very wealthy. The question immediately arises: Is Jesus' command meant for everyone who wishes to be a Christian? Must every Christian give away all his possessions to the poor?

There is a very old Gospel called the Gospel according to the Hebrews. That Gospel may well be as old as some of our own Gospels. It never got into the New Testament; it is largely lost and only fragments remain. One of these fragments is in Origen's commentary on Matthew, and it is another version of this story. In it two rich men come to Jesus. The story runs:

> The second of the rich men said to Jesus: 'Master, what good thing must I do to have life?' 'Fulfil the commandments of the Law and the Prophets,' Jesus said to him. 'I have done so,' the rich man answered. Jesus said to him: 'Go and sell everything you have, and distribute the proceeds to the poor, and come, follow me.' The rich man began to scratch his head, for he did not like this advice at all. The Lord said to him: 'How can you say, "I have kept the Law and the Prophets"? It is written in the Law that you must love your neighbour as yourself. And in point of fact many of your brothers, sons of Abraham, are clothed in filth and are dying of hunger, and your house is packed with good things, and not a single thing goes out of it to them.'

What was wrong with the rich young man was not his possessions, but his possessiveness. He was in fact possessed by his possessions. And the only cure for him was a radical change in his approach to the whole matter of possessions, a surgical eradication of the passion of possessiveness from his life. He claimed to have kept the commandments, and his claim was a lie, and his wealth was the very thing which prevented him from keeping them. If he had used his possessions to help and comfort others, this commandment would never have been given to him, but such was his possessiveness that he had either to abandon his possessions or abandon any attempt to follow the way of Jesus.

It is not wealth that is condemned; it is a certain attitude to wealth. It is the attitude in which a man has become so possessed by his possessions, so dominated by the desire to make and to have, to hold more and more, that a Christian use of possessions has become impossible for him.

iii. In the passage which follows the story of the rich young ruler it is not said that it is impossible for a rich man to get into the kingdom of God, but it is said that it is very difficult (Matthew 19.23-26; Mark 10.23-27; Luke 18.24-27). It is quite clear that money, wealth can be a real danger to a man's life.

It is a plain fact that the more money a man has, the more temptations he has. There are a great many things which are no temptation to a poor man because they are impossible for him. He has no temptation to luxurious living. Caviare and champagne are no temptation to a man who has all he can do to get bread and butter. It is no temptation to a man to keep two homes when it takes him all his time to keep one. There is no temptation to idleness to a man who simply cannot afford to take a day off work. It is the simple fact that there are many more sins available to the man who has money in his pocket. The possession of money can be a real test of a man's moral fibre. To say that we 'never had it so good' is also to say that we never had it so dangerous. The affluent society is also the society in peril. A new range of temptations opens to the man who can pay for them. The temptation to get drunk is only open to the man who can pay for enough liquor to get drunk. The more complex and sophisticated life becomes, the stronger its foundations must be. The wealthier a man is, the more he needs God. It is not the struggle with hard times that has brought disintegration to nations; it is the inability to cope with prosperity and luxury. Roman history tells the story of Hannibal, the great Carthaginian general, and his armies. He and his armies were well-nigh invincible. Then they spent one winter in Capua, that city where luxury and pride were notorious; and the army of Carthage was never the same again. The supreme danger comes when a man or a nation possesses things which it is not morally fit to possess. 'You've never had it so good' could end by being, not the proud claim of a politician, but the death sentence of a nation.

iv. Let us look more in detail at the dangers of wealth.

(a) It can beget a false sense of independence. A man can come to feel that he can buy his way into, or out of, anything. Sir Robert Walpole said that every man has his price, and there are those who consciously or unconsciously think that every situation has its price. It is quite true that there are doors which money can open and escape routes which money can supply; but a man will not come to the end of life without grimly discovering that there are some things which have no price-tag—and these things are the most important of all.

(b) There are times when money can cost too much. No traitor was ever happy. Judas Iscariot discovered this, when he discovered that the price of thirty pieces of silver was suicide (Matthew 27.3-5). There is a drug-market, a vice-market, a pornography-market, and money made on these markets costs too much. There is the wave of petty pilfering, which in industry alone is reckoned to cost £70,000,000 a year. There are expensive schools in which girls do not qualify for the school aristocracy until they have stolen something from a department store. George Macdonald told of a draper who made a fortune by keeping his thumbs inside the measure and so giving an inch or two short with every yard of cloth. 'He took from his soul,' said George Macdonald, 'and put it in his siller bag.' A fortune in money is a poor substitute for a man's soul.

(c) The more a man possesses in this world, the more difficult it will be for him to leave it. Jesus said: 'Where your treasure is, there will your heart be also' (Matthew 6.21). Once, after they had been to the house and policies of a wealthy man, Dr Johnson turned to his friend and said: 'These are the things which make it difficult to die.' A man can be so entangled with this world that he forgets that there is any other world.

(d) One of the curious results of wealth is that it is very liable to produce in a man, not the comfortable feeling that he has enough, but the constant desire for more. 'Enough', as someone said, 'is always a little more than a man has.' 'Riches', as the Roman proverb had it, 'are like salt water. The more you drink, the more you want to drink.' It is a curious thing that it may well happen that the more a man has, the more he will want to get, and the less he will want to give.

v. There remain five great principles to be stated, which, if they are kept in mind, will save any man from the dangers of wealth.

(a) *How did we get our money?* Did we get it in a way which harmed or injured no one, but helped and enriched the community? Did we get it in utter honesty, with every item open to the light of day? Did we get it without exploitation, and by giving value for it in honest work and service? Did we earn it always to the welfare and never to the hurt of the community, or of any individual in the community? To apply these tests would be never to go wrong in the getting of money.

(b) *How do we regard money?* Do we regard it as the *master* whom we serve? Do we regard it as an ascetic might do as an *enemy* with which we will have nothing to do? Or do we regard it as a *friend*, by the use of which we can enrich life for ourselves and for others?

Once Mr Okamura, the secretary of the Kobe YMCA, was telling that great Christian Kagawa about the difficulties of his association, about the debts which had accumulated, about the schemes which were frustrated for lack of money. Kagawa put his hand in his pocket, and took out a letter. The letter contained a cheque for £1,000 which Kagawa that morning had received from his publisher in payment for a book of his that was just about to be published. He handed the cheque to Okamura. Okamura said: 'I can't possibly take it.' Kagawa said: 'You must.' Kagawa literally forced it on him. Okamura went home and wrote a letter trying to get Kagawa to take the cheque back. 'You mustn't give money away like that,' he wrote. Kagawa wrote back: 'Why shouldn't I? When your friend is dying, there is only one thing to do—give him your life-blood.' If we regard money as something to be shared, it becomes our servant for good. If we regard it as something to be hoarded, it becomes our master. If we regard it as something to be used in love, it becomes one of the world's great powers.

(c) *How do we use money?* This has brought us inevitably to the question of how we use money. Do we use it selfishly? Do we make it to spend it on ourselves and on our family? Do we desire it to make life ever more lush for ourselves? When John Wesley was at Oxford his income was £30 a year. He lived on £28 and gave £2 away. His income later increased to £60, £90, £120 a year. He continued to live on £28 and to give the rest away. His rule was 'to *save* all I can that I may *give* all I can'. If a man's main question was, How much can I give? he would never go wrong.

(d) There is one principle which must never be lost sight of. People are always more important than things; men are always more important than money; workers are always more important than machines. This is exactly the principle that was lost sight of in the days of the industrial revolution. At that time working conditions, living conditions, wages conditions all took second place to production and profits. There were people who saw what was happening. It was argued that the cotton mills could not go on without child labour. Thomas Carlyle thundered: 'If the devil gets into your cotton mills, then close them.' It is for this disregard for people, for men and women, for basic human rights that we are suffering today in industrial suspicion and unrest. We can never even begin to have a proper view of money and possessions until we accept as a first principle the priority of persons. And this is not only good Christianity, it is also good economics, for in the end it is only the happy worker who is the good worker.

(e) There remains one last principle. There are times when to give money is not enough. To give money may be at times an evasion of a still greater responsibility. I am not one of these people who play down the generosity in giving of people with money by saying: 'It's easy to write a cheque.' It may be —but there are many who can write cheques, and who do not.

Nevertheless it must be said that there is need for something beyond impersonal giving. It was said of a man who was generous with money but who stopped there: 'With all his giving, he never gave himself.' And there are times when the giving of oneself is the greatest gift of all—for that is the gift that Jesus gave to men.

CHAPTER EIGHT

The Christian and the Community

Every man necessarily lives in two worlds. He lives within the four walls of the place that he calls home, and where his companions are the members of his own family. This is his private world. But equally a man has to go out of his house and home and has to live in a public world. He is not only a member of a family; he is also a member of a community, a state, a world. He is not only a private person; he is a public citizen.

A man's attitude to the world can take more than one form.

i. He can be totally immersed in the world. He can plunge into it and live as if there was no other world. His attitude may be: 'Eat, drink and enjoy yourself, for tomorrow we die.' 'Gather ye rosebuds while ye may,' as Herrick had it. Pile up kisses, as Catullus said, for when this world is done there remains nothing but a night which knows no ending and a sleep which knows no awakening.

But there is another way of being immersed in the world, and a commoner way than that. To be immersed in the world need not mean to be devoted to the pleasures of this world; it need not mean to eat and drink and be merry. There are many people who are immersed in this world in the sense that they are unaware that there is any other. They are not in the least immoral; they are not in the least dedicated to pleasure. They simply go in and out, and live decent respectable lives, and never think of any other world or any other life. They are hardly aware that there is any such thing as religion, or any such place as the church. They are not in the least hostile to religion. They regard it—if they think of it at all—as something which is quite irrelevant, something of which they have no need at all. A. J. Gossip used to say: You've seen a little evangelical meeting going on down some cul-de-sac of a street, while the crowds stream past on the pavements of the main road with never a look and never a second glance and never a thought. That is what the church is to many people—perhaps now to the majority of people. To be immersed in the world is not by any means necessarily to be a pleasure-lover; it is simply to be unaware of any horizons beyond this life.

ii. A man can take the opposite course and completely renounce this world. There has always been a strain of so-called Christian thought which had no use for this world at all; and there always have been people who quite deliberately and as completely as possible divorced themselves from the world. Thomas à Kempis said that the greatest saints deliberately avoided the society of men and tried to live to God and with God alone. The third and the fourth centuries were the great days of the monks and the hermits, when they deliberately turned their backs on life and on men and went to live in the desert, if possible not even within sight of another hermit.

There was one hermit who for fifty years lived on the top of Mount Sinai. He would not even see travellers and pilgrims who had come specially to visit him. 'The man who is often visited by mortals', he said, 'cannot be visited by angels.' There was the famous St Simeon Stylites, known as the pillarman. He tried living in a cavern; he tried digging a grave and living in it with nothing but his head exposed. Finally, in AD 423, he built himself a pillar six feet high and began to live on the top of it. He never came down. For no less than thirty-seven years he lived on the top of his pillar, which was gradually heightened until it was sixty feet high. He was the first of many pillar-saints who chose this way of isolating themselves from the world. There were the people called the shut-ins, the *inclusi*. They chose a niche in some monastery and literally got themselves bricked in, leaving only a narrow slit for the bare minimum of food and drink to be passed in to them. It is on record that one of them lived thus for twenty-five years. 'Are you alive?' someone asked through the narrow opening. 'I believe', he answered, 'that I am dead to the world.'

Men like these attempted to live as if the world did not exist. It was in many ways the most selfish of lives, for they were so concerned to save their own souls that they simply isolated themselves from all other men. They were, as it has been put, so heavenly-minded that they were no earthly use. Their renunciation was complete—and it was a caricature and parody of Christianity.

iii. So then there are people who are immersed in the world, and there are people who in the name of Christianity have renounced the world and who have as far as possible severed all connection with the world. From the point of view of the Christian ethic neither immersion in the world nor isolation from the world can be right. Jesus was quite clear that his men were not of this world (John 17.14,16). So much so were they not of this world that he warned them that the world would hate them as it had hated him (John 15.18,19; 17.14). It is therefore clear that no follower of Jesus can be immersed in the world. On the other hand, Jesus was equally clear that God loved the world (John 3.16). He did not pray that his men should be taken out of the world but that they should be kept from the evil of the world (John 17.15). And in the end he deliberately and of set purpose sent them out into the world (John 17.18).

The Christian must have an attitude to the world which combines involvement and detachment. This is not so unusual as it sounds. I think it would be true to say that this combination of involvement and detachment is characteristic of the work of many people, for instance, of the minister and of the doctor. Of course minister and doctor must be deeply involved, deeply identified with the people whom they wish to help. But they must at the same time be able to stand back and to view the facts in such a way that their judgment is not clouded by too much sentiment and too much softness. Sometimes it is necessary to be stern in order to be merciful and to be hard in order to be kind.

This involvement and detachment are characteristic of the Christian's attitude to the world. He is involved in the world and its life as Jesus was; but at the same time to him the world is not everything. It is the threshold to a larger and a wider life which begins when this life ends. In the world he lives, and lives to the full, but always with the conviction that it is something beyond this world which in the end gives this world its value and its significance.

Now we turn directly to the New Testament, and we are at once faced with the fact that the New Testament expects, and indeed demands, that a man should be a good citizen. Jesus was ready and willing to pay the temple tax that any Jew had to pay (Matthew 17.24-27). He does not question the fact that a man has a duty to the Emperor as well as having a duty to God, and that both must be fulfilled (Matthew 22.15-22).

Paul was proud to be a Roman citizen, and had no hesitation in claiming his rights as a citizen (Acts 21.39; 22.25). He writes to the Romans about the relationship of the Christian to the state, and he is quite clear that the state is a divine institution and that it is a Christian duty to give obedience to it. The magistrate is God's servant, and if a man does the right thing he has nothing to fear; it is only the criminal and the wrongdoer who have anything of which to be afraid. The taxes of the state ought to be paid and the authority of the state ought to be respected as Paul sees it (Romans 13.1-7). It is the duty of the Christian to remember in his prayers those who are in charge of public affairs from the Emperor downwards (1 Timothy 2.2). Peter is equally sure of the duty of citizenship. 'Fear God,' he says, 'and honour the Emperor' (1 Peter 2.17).

Then all of a sudden in the Book of the Revelation we get a thunderous volte-face, for in that book Rome is the great harlot, drunk with the blood of the saints and the martyrs (Revelation 17.1-7). The Roman Empire for the John of the Revelation has become the very essence and incarnation of devilish and Satanic power. What has happened? Why the difference?

In her great days, Roman justice and Roman impartiality were famous. The people whom Rome conquered were not resentful; they were grateful. The seas were cleared of pirates and the roads of brigands. A man might make his journeys in safety and live his life in peace, thanks to the *pax Romana*, the Roman peace. Quite spontaneously, men began to talk of Roma, the spirit of Rome, as something divine, and even as far back as the second century BC men were building temples for the worship of divine Rome. If things had stopped there, there might have been no great trouble. But it was the next step that made the difference. It is all very well to worship the spirit of Rome, but after all the spirit of Rome is an abstraction; and that abstraction is incarnated in the Emperor, and bit by bit the worship came to be transferred to the Emperor as the embodiment of Rome, and by the early days of the Christian era temples for the worship of Caesar the Emperor were quite common.

At first the Emperors really and truly did not want this. They were embarrassed with the whole business. But bit by bit the Roman state began to see a far-reaching use for this Caesar worship. The Roman Empire was a huge area stretching from the Danube to North Africa and from Britain to the Euphrates. It was very difficult to get some focus, some one thing, which would unify all the many tribes and nations in it. And suddenly the Roman government realised that they had just that in Caesar worship. We talk about the Crown being the one thing that holds the Commonwealth together; and it is just the same as if to unify the Commonwealth we set up a universal worship of the Queen. So the Roman government laid it down in the end that every citizen should once a year burn a pinch of incense to Caesar and say: Caesar is Lord; and then he would get a certificate to say that he had done so. Be fair to Rome. After a man had done this he could go off and worship any god or goddess he liked, so long as the worship did not affect public order or public decency. The worship of Caesar was a test of a man's political loyalty far more than of his religion. But the one thing that the Christians would not say was: Caesar is Lord. For them, Jesus Christ is Lord—and no one else. So persecution broke out and as William Watson the poet put it:

So to the wild wolf hate were hurl'd
The panting, huddled flock whose crime was Christ.

And this is where the Revelation comes in. In Paul's time there was nothing like this. By the time of the Revelation compulsory Caesar worship was on the way.

All this has to be said, for the point is that the Christian is the good citizen, and the Christian is the obedient citizen—but there are limits and beyond these limits he will not go. In the Christian life there is only one supreme loyalty; that loyalty is to Jesus Christ, and that loyalty takes precedence over loyalty to family, loyalty to state, and loyalty to everything else, and so there can come a time when the Christian duty is disobedience to the state, and the Christian must hold that when that time comes he must act on it. It may not come once in a lifetime; it may not come once in a century—but it can come—and that is something which we cannot forget.

Let us then look at the relationship between the church and the Christian, and the state. That relationship has in its time taken many forms.

i. Sometimes the church has dominated the state. One of the great figures of the early church was Ambrose the Bishop of Milan. He was a close friend of Theodosius the Roman Emperor who was a Christian. Theodosius was a good and a generous man but he was cursed with a temper which at times made him act like a madman. There had been trouble in the city of Thessalonica, which resulted in the assassination of the governor. Theodosius reacted with violence. He waited until the people were gathered in the amphitheatre at the games; then he sent in his troops and 7,000 men, women and children were murdered where they stood. It was not long before the fiery tempered emperor repented of what he had done. He had in fact tried to cancel his order, but it was too late to do so. He came to Milan; he came to worship at the cathedral, for worship meant much to Theodosius; but Ambrose was standing at the cathedral door to bar his way. The bishop would not allow the emperor into the cathedral. For a year Theodosius had to do penance; for a year he was refused entry to the sacrament; and at the end of it he had to sit among the common penitents, and had even to lie prostrate in the dust before the cathedral door, before the bishop would accept him at all. There was a time when the Christian church could order the emperor of the world to lie prostrate in the dust.

The same happened to Henry the Second after the murder of Thomas Becket, the Archbishop of Canterbury. Becket had stood for the rights of the church. 'Who,' said Henry, 'will rid me of this turbulent priest?' Some of his courtiers took him at his word and murdered Becket in his own cathedral. The day came when Henry, clad in a hair-shirt, and living on bread and water, had to walk barefoot in the rain to the place where Becket had been murdered, and had to lie on the ground and be scourged by the bishop, the abbot and the priests, before he was received back into the church.

There have been times in history when the church dominated the state, and when kings and emperors bowed before an authority higher than their own. But these times are surely gone for ever, although we might argue that it was the church which even in our own day compelled the abdication of Edward the Eighth, because he wished to make queen a woman whom the church did not regard as a fit person to be queen of Britain. The church still has power, but not the utterly dominating power that once it had.

ii. There have been times when the church was utterly independent of the state, and when the church claimed that it was acting under an authority to which the state also was subject. This has been particularly the Scottish point of view. We see it fully displayed in John Knox's conflicts with Queen Mary. Mary resented his interference, but Knox's answer is: 'Outside the preaching place, Madam, I think few have occasion to be offended at me; and there, Madam, I am not master of myself, but must obey him who commands me to speak plain, and to flatter no flesh upon the face of the earth.' He is the bearer of a message from God and nothing and no one will stop him from delivering it. 'Yea, madam,' he says, 'it appertains to me to forewarn of such things as may hurt that commonwealth.' King and queen and commoner must listen to the conscience of the nation. The queen wept, but Knox makes answer: 'I must sustain your Majesty's tears, albeit unwillingly, rather than dare hurt my conscience, or betray my commonwealth through my silence.' The truth must be spoken. The Master of Maxwell warns him that, if he continues to oppose the queen, he will suffer for it. 'I understand not, Master, what you mean,' said Knox. 'I never made myself an adversary to the Queen's Majesty, except in the head of religion, and therein I think you will not desire me to bow.' When it comes to a message from God, come what may, that message must be given. One of the queen's councillors reminds him that he is not in the pulpit now but in the queen's presence. Knox thunders back: 'I am in the place where I am demanded of to speak the truth; and therefore I speak. The truth I speak, impugn it whoso list.' When the queen complains of the tone of his preaching, Knox tells her that as a man he may be no more than a worm, but he is a subject of this commonwealth, and God has given him an office which makes him 'a watchman over the realm and over the Kirk of God gathered in the same.' Here is the attitude that queen and commoner must listen to the word of God which must be spoken, and spoken without fear.

The classic expression of this is in the words of Andrew Melville to James the Sixth. The Commission of Assembly had appointed a deputation to visit the king at Falkland. There were James Melville, Patrick Galloway, James Nicolson and Andrew Melville. At first it was decided that James Melville should do the speaking, since he was likely to speak with a moderation to which the king might listen. But the king was 'crabbed and choleric' and Andrew Melville broke in. He caught the king by the sleeve, calling him 'God's silly vassal'. Then he said:

> Sir, we will humbly reverence your Majesty always, namely in public, but since we have this occasion to be with your Majesty in private, and the truth is that you are brought into extreme danger of your life and crown, and with you the country and the Kirk of Christ is like to be wrecked, for not telling you the truth, and giving you a faithful counsel, we must discharge our duty therein, or else be traitors both to Christ and you! And, therefore, sir, as divers time before, so now again, I must tell you, there is two kings and two kingdoms in Scotland. There is Christ Jesus the King, and his kingdom the kirk, whose subject King James the Sixth is, and of whose kingdom not a king nor a lord nor a head, but a member.

It was in the same tone that Melville had already spoken to the Regent, the Earl of Morton. Morton had complained that Scotland would have no peace while Melville was there and had threatened him with exile. Melville replied:

> Tush, sir! Threaten your courtiers in that fashion. It is the same to me whether I rot in the air or in the ground. The earth is the Lord's; my fatherland is wherever well-doing is

> . . . Yet God be glorified, it will not lie in your power to hang nor exile his truth.

Here in the Scottish tradition is the complete independence of the church. It is not rebellion or revolution; it comes from the highest kind of loyalty, but it comes from the conviction that the differences are gone when men stand in the presence of God, and that God's man must speak no matter who is listening. King, queen and commoner are all subjects of God.

iii. There have been times when the church surrendered to the state and became subservient to the state. There is extant one extraordinary letter from Thomas Coke, John Wesley's right-hand man, written to the then Home Secretary Henry Dundas. The date is 8th November 1798. There was trouble in the Channel Islands. France was threatening invasion, and the able-bodied male population had been ordered to engage on military exercises on Sundays. Certain of the Methodists refused to exercise on Sundays; they were quite willing to do double time throughout the week but not—in their opinion—to desecrate the Sunday. Thomas Coke had many friends in high places, and he is writing to try to avert a bill which would institute real persecution against those who refused to exercise. He has no use at all for Democrats. 'When a considerable number of Democrats had crept in among us, to the number of about 5,000, I was a principal means of their being entirely excluded from our Society.' He has still less use for pacifists. 'The preamble of the Law, I think, says that some have refused to bear arms at all. I have heard of only one in Jersey who answered this description; and he has been already banished from the Island. We plead not for such. We look upon them at best to be poor Fanatics or arrant Cowards, and have no objection to their Banishment. They have no right to the protection of the Laws, who will not themselves be ready to protect those laws when in danger.' And then Coke astonishingly finishes: 'I can truly say, Sir, that though I very much love our Society, I love my King and Country better' (John Vickers, *Thomas Coke, Apostle of Methodism*, p. 224).

A subservient church is a national disaster. It was said of Ambrose that he was 'the personified conscience of all that was best in the Roman Empire'. 'Who', he said to Theodosius, 'will dare to tell you the truth, if a priest does not dare?' The nation which has no independent church has lost its conscience.

iv. There have been times when the state refused the church any say at all in the affairs of the state, because the state held that such things were none of the church's business. When Hitler came to power, at first he did not threaten the church as such, but he took good care that no real Christian ever held any power. He deliberately got rid of them, for he openly admitted that he wanted no one in his government who knew any other loyalty than loyalty to the state.

When Niemöller, the great independent Christian, went to Hitler and told Hitler that he was troubled about the future of Germany, Hitler replied bleakly: 'Let that be my concern.' Goebbels, the notorious minister of propaganda, said to the church at large: 'Churchmen dabbling in politics should take note that their only task is to prepare for the world hereafter.' He had no objections to preachers being concerned with heaven so long as they left Germany alone.

Article 88 of the Constitution of the People's Republic of China states: 'Citizens . . . of China enjoy freedom of religious belief.' That means exactly what it says. There is no freedom to meet, to worship, to preach, to attempt to initiate any activity or to criticise any policy. So long as belief remains a purely internal thing which has no effect on conduct or relationships with other people or relationships with the state, there is freedom of *belief*. But if belief threatens to become action, then it is quickly strangled (Richard C. Bush Jr, *Religion in Communist China*, pp. 15-22).

In Victorian days Lord Melbourne made his famous statement that religion is an excellent thing, so long as it does not interfere with a man's private life. And the totalitarian states have no objection to religion so long as religion keeps its mouth shut about earth and confines itself to dreams of heaven—and that, of course, reduces the church to a status of sheer irrelevancy.

v. Lastly, we must look at the relationship of church and state in the thought of Martin Luther, for it could well be said that no view has had more influence on history, even in our time, and no view has been more mistaken. We may find Luther's view in two places. In the one place he divides people into two groups; in the other he divides life into two areas.

We may begin with his treatise on *Secular Authority; to what extent it should be obeyed,* which was addressed to John, Duke of Saxony, in 1523 (Volume 3 in the Philadelphia Edition of the Works of Luther, pp. 228 *et seq.*; given most conveniently in E. G. Rupp and Benjamin Drewery, *Martin Luther*, pp. 107-112). This divides people into two groups. There are those who are true believers, and who belong to the Kingdom of God, and those who are not believers and who belong to the kingdom of the world. If all men were true Christians, no king, lord, sword or law would be necessary. They would do everything the law demands and more. On the other hand there are those who do not accept Jesus Christ and his way. 'The unrighteous do nothing that the law demands, therefore they need the law to instruct, constrain and compel them to do good.' So for those who are not Christ's, 'God has provided . . . a different government outside the Christian estate and God's kingdom, and has subjected them to the sword, so that, even though they would do so, they cannot follow their wickedness, and that, if they do, they may not do it without fear nor in peace and prosperity.'

It is impossible to try to rule the world by the gospel and its love. If anyone tried to do so, 'he would loose the bands and chains of the wild and savage beasts, and let them tear and mangle everyone.' Before you can apply the Christian way to everyone, everyone must be a Christian—and to make everyone Christian is something that you will never accomplish. To attempt to govern the world by the gospel would be to act like a shepherd who put into the one fold wolves, lions, eagles and sheep all together, and told them to help themselves. The result would be chaos. Christians as Christians need no law, but the non-Christian does. Therefore the sword is necessary. 'Because the sword is a very great benefit and necessary to the whole world, to preserve peace, to punish sin and to prevent evil, he (the Christian) submits most willingly to the rule of the sword, pays tax, honours those in authority, serves, helps, and does all he can to further the government, that it may be sustained and held in honour and fear.' The Christian is therefore under obligation to serve and to cherish the sword of government, just as he serves and cherishes any other of the divinely given institutions of life, such as matrimony or husbandry. 'There must be those who arrest, accuse, slay and destroy the wicked, and protect, acquit, defend and save the good.'

So then it is Luther's argument that so long as there are two kinds of people—those in and those not in the kingdom of God—it is impossible to arrange society on the principles of Christian love. There must be law and force; there must be the sword of the magistrate. And in order to see that there is safety and good order the Christian is bound to respect and honour and, if he is qualified, to serve the state. 'Therefore, should you see that there is a lack of hangmen, beadles, judges, lords or princes, and find that you are qualified, you should offer your services and seek the place, in order that necessary government may by no means be despised and become inefficient or perish.' Quite simply, Luther is saying that you cannot govern an unchristian world by Christian love, and in such a world you have to use the sword and all that the sword stands for against the wicked man.

The second passage is much more far-reaching. It is contained in Luther's sermons on the Sermon on the Mount (*Luther's Works*, the American Edition, vol. 21, pp. 106-115). This is from a sermon on Matthew 5.38-42, where Jesus teaches us to abandon the principle of an eye for an eye and a tooth for a tooth, and tells us not to resist evil, but to turn the other cheek, to give the cloak as well as the coat, and to go not one mile but two.

In this sermon Luther's point is that the Christian lives in two spheres. In this passage, Luther says, Jesus is teaching how the individual Christian must live *personally*. As a Christian individual, apart from his official position, Christians 'should not desire revenge at all. They should have the attitude that, if someone hits them on one cheek, they are ready, if need be, to turn the other cheek to him as well, restraining the vindictiveness not only of their fist but also of their heart, their thoughts, and all their powers as well.' The Sermon on the Mount is for the Christian as a person and as an individual.

But the Christian is not only an individual person; he is a *person in relationship*; and here the situation is very different. Luther's point of view is so important that we must allow him to speak for himself, and we must quote him at length:

> There is no getting around it, a Christian has to be a secular person of some sort. As regards his own person, according to his life as a Christian, he is in subjection to no one but Christ, without any obligation to the emperor or to any other man. But at least outwardly, according to his body and property, he is related by subjection and obligation to the emperor, inasmuch as he occupies some office or station in life or has a house and a home, a wife and children; for all these are things which pertain to the emperor. Here he must necessarily do what he is told and what this outward life requires. If he has a house or a wife or children or servants, and refuses to support them, or, if need be, to

protect them, he does wrong. It will not do for him to declare that he is a Christian and therefore has to forsake or relinquish everything. But he must be told: 'Now you are under the emperor's control. Here your name is not "Christian", but "father" or "lord" or "prince". According to your own person, you are a Christian; but in relation to your servant you are a different person and you are obliged to protect him.'

You see, now we are talking about a Christian-in-relation; not about his being a Christian, but about this life and his obligation in it to some other person, whether under him or over him or even alongside him, like a lord or a lady, a wife or children or neighbours, whom he is obliged, if possible, to defend, guard and protect. Here it would be a mistake to teach: 'Turn the other cheek, and throw your cloak away with your coat.' That would be ridiculous, like the case of the crazy saint who let the lice nibble at him and refused to kill any of them on account of this text, maintaining that he had to suffer and could not resist evil.

And then there comes the passage which is the crux of the whole matter:

Do you want to know what your duty is as a prince or a judge or a lord or a lady, with people under you? You do not have to ask Christ about your duty. Ask the imperial or the territorial law. It will soon tell you your duty toward your inferiors as their protector. It gives you both the power and the might to punish within the limits of your authority and commission not as a Christian but as an imperial subject.

Luther then quotes the case of those who were called to arms by infidel emperors.

In all good conscience they slashed and killed, and in this respect there was no difference between Christians and heathen. Yet they did not sin against this text. For they

> were not doing this as Christians, for their own persons, but as obedient members and subjects, under obligation to a secular person and authority.

So,

> When a Christian goes to war or when he sits as a judge's bench, punishing his neighbour, or when he registers an official complaint, he is not doing this as a Christian, but as a soldier or a judge or a lawyer . . . A Christian should not resist any evil; but within the limits of his office, a secular person should oppose every evil. The head of a household should not put up with insubordination or bickering among his servants. A Christian should not sue anyone, but should surrender both his coat and his cloak when they are taken away from him; but a secular person should go to court if he can to protect and defend himself against some violence or outrage. In short the rule in the Kingdom of Christ is the toleration of everything, forgiveness, and the recompense of evil with good. On the other hand, in the realm of the emperor, there should be no tolerance shown to any injustice, but rather a defence against wrong and a punishment of it, and an effort to defend and maintain the right, according to what each one's office and station may require.

It is quite true that Luther does in the treatise—but not in the sermon—indicate that there are limits, and that the prince has no right to demand that which is wrong. But this is not the main impression which his teaching leaves. His teaching leaves the impression that in the secular realm the government is supreme, and that from it, and not from Christ, the Christian must take his duty. And it is this very fact which allowed Hitler to come to power and begat Belsen and Dachau.

The Lutheran church did not stand out, for it was conditioned to accept the civil power.

The whole thing is to be seen at its most terrible in Luther's attitude to the Peasants' Revolt in 1524-5. The peasants revolted. They had therefore in Luther's eyes broken the command of Jesus to render to Caesar the things that are Caesar's (Matthew 22.21). They had broken the scriptural law regarding obedience to the state as Paul stated it in Romans 13. They have therefore, in Luther's words, 'forfeited body and soul, as faithless, perjured, lying, disobedient knaves and scoundrels are wont to do.' They are makers of sedition and therefore outside the law of God and the empire. In regard to any peasant, 'The first who can slay him is doing right and well . . . Therefore let everyone who can, smite, slay, and stab, secretly or openly, remembering that nothing can be more poisonous, hurtful, or devilish than a rebel. It is just as when one must kill a mad dog.' They can be slaughtered without even a trial. 'Here there is no time for sleeping; no place for patience or mercy. It is the time of the sword, not the day of grace . . . Strange times, those, when a prince can win heaven with bloodshed, better than other men with prayer!'

It might not be too much to say that Luther's ethic of church and state was the greatest disaster in all the history of ethics, for it opened the way for a kind of Christianity which allowed the state to do terrible things, and in too many cases made no protest. It is impossible to divide life into spheres like that. A Christian is a Christian in any sphere of life, and in things sacred and things secular alike Jesus Christ is Lord for him.

It would not be right to leave the matter thus vague and abstract and generalised. We have to ask ourselves just where the Christian ethic may in fact have to show itself. I think that there are three areas in modern life where there is special need for Christian ethical witness.

i. The first is the area of *racialism*. There are certain simple facts which will show how real this problem is. There are one million coloured immigrants in Britain already. By 1980 the number will naturally increase to three million. There are something like 15,000 university students and 48,300 students from overseas in the technical colleges. Two per cent of the post-graduate students in the country are from overseas. At the present time 3 per cent of the school-leavers are coloured; by the mid-seventies that number will rise to 15 per cent. And now here is the really serious fact. Youth employment officers state that they have to spend as much time placing immigrant school-leavers in jobs as they have to spend searching for suitable jobs for handicapped children. It is almost as difficult for a coloured person to find work as it is for a handicapped person (R. H. Fuller and B. K. Rice, *Christianity and the Affluent Society*, p. 137). Fuller and Rice record a curious kind of parallel problem. In India today there are two million unemployed high-school graduates and 200,000 unemployed BA's. The racial problem is not something that can wait.

There is a very real sense in which the ancient world was a divided world. It was particularly so in two areas. The Jew was divided from the Gentile. To a Jew a Gentile child was unclean from birth. 'The daughter of an Israelite may not assist a Gentile woman in childbirth since she would be assisting to bring to birth a child for idolatry.' Even in the commonest things of life this appeared. A Gentile might not cut the hair of a Jew. A Jew could not eat bread baked by a Gentile or drink milk from a cow milked by a Gentile, unless a Jew was present at the milking. Suspicion of the Gentiles was acute. 'Cattle may not be left in the inns of the Gentiles since they are suspected of bestiality; nor may a woman remain alone with them since they are suspected of lewdness; nor may a man remain alone with them since they are suspected of shedding blood.' (The quotations are from the Mishnah tractate *Abodah Zarah* 2.1,2,6.)

There was the division between the Greek and the barbarian. Originally to the Greek the barbarian was a man who spoke another language, a man who unintelligibly said *bar bar*, barking like a dog, instead of speaking the beautiful and flexible Greek language. We twice get that meaning in the

New Testament as the translation of the Authorised Version makes clear. In the First Letter to the Corinthians Paul is speaking about the gift of speaking with tongues and about its unintelligibility, and he says: 'Therefore if I know not the meaning of the voice, I shall be unto him that speaketh a barbarian, and he that speaketh shall be a barbarian unto me' (1 Corinthians 14.11 AV). In the narrative of the shipwreck in Acts Luke tells how Paul and his party were shipwrecked on Malta and then goes on to say: 'And the barbarous people showed us no little kindness' (Acts 28.2). A barbarian in Greek was often simply a man who spoke an unintelligible language. But the word came to indicate not simply a person who spoke a different language, but a person from an inferior culture. So Heraclitus can speak of people with 'barbarian souls'. The barbarian was different from the Greek. And so the great Greek writers like Plato, Demosthenes, Isocrates can use a series of phrases. They can say that the barbarians are 'foes by nature'; that they are 'natural and hereditary foes'; that they are foes 'by nature and tradition'; that between them and the Greek there is a 'perpetual and truceless warfare' (cf. T. J. Haarhoff, *The Stranger at the Gate*, pp. 8,13, 60,61,65,66). But there was another side to the Greek, and to the Roman. Terence, the Roman dramatist could say: 'I regard no human being as a stranger.' Diogenes could claim to be a citizen of the world. He may have invented the word *cosmopolitan*. Alexander the Great could talk of his desire to marry the East to the West, and to mingle as in one great loving-cup all the races of mankind.

In the ancient world there was division all right; there were cleavages; but there was no colour-bar as such. There were divisions of religion, of culture, of tradition; but the sheer contempt for a man as a human being, which is the basis of the colour-bar, was not there—and it is here today, and not only in South Africa.

The area of racial relationships is another area in which men have sown the wind and are reaping the whirlwind. Many years ago now an authoress called Janet Mitchell wrote a book which included an account of a visit to America. One of the high-lights of her tour was to be a visit to Paul Robeson, the great singer and actor, to whom she had an introduction. She was staying with friends in Chicago, and she was talking enthusiastically of her coming visit to Paul Robeson. She noticed that the atmosphere had become a little chilly. 'What's the matter?' she asked. Her friends answered: 'We wouldn't talk too much about visiting Paul Robeson, if we were you.' 'Why on earth shouldn't I talk about it?' Janet Mitchell said. 'He's one of the greatest singers and actors in the world.' 'That may be,' her host answered. 'But Paul Robeson's a nigger.' If you treat any man or any body of men like that, you are building up a store of trouble that is some day going to erupt—and it has erupted.

Somewhere I read the story of an artist who was commissioned to design a stained-glass window illustrating the children's hymn:

> *Around the throne of God in heaven*
> *Thousands of children stand,*
> *Singing, Glory, glory, glory.*

The design was finished; the painting which had to serve as a pattern for the window was completed, and the committee in charge were to see it next day. That night the artist had a dream. He saw in the dream a stranger in his studio, and the stranger was working with brushes and palette at his picture. 'Stop!' he shouted. 'Stop! You'll spoil my picture!' The stranger turned. 'It is you,' he said, 'who have spoiled it.' 'I?' said the artist. 'I spoil my own picture?' 'Indeed you have,' said the stranger. 'How do you make that out?' said the artist. And the stranger answered: 'Who told you that the faces of all the children in heaven were white? Look! I am putting in the little black faces, and the brown ones and the yellow ones.' Morning came. The artist woke and rushed into his studio. The picture was as he had left it. He seized his brushes and paints and sketched in the faces of the children of every colour and of every nation. And when the committee saw it later in the morning, they said: 'Perfect! It's just what we wanted! It's God's family at home!' Who indeed said that the faces of all the children in God's family are white?

All this is true, but I do not think that it would be fair to leave things there like that. You cannot settle this matter on a wave of emotion; there is more to it than that. I can say in principle that racialism is entirely wrong, and that integration is entirely necessary, but I do not know how I might feel if I lived in a country in which the white population was in a tiny minority. But this we can say with certainty. There should and there must be equality of opportunity and equality of treatment for all. This might well mean that immigration into any country might need to be controlled, until the country can absorb the newcomers; until they can be properly housed; until there are decent jobs for them to do; and until they can be truly integrated into its education and its work and its life. But, if the principle is accepted that man as such is dear to God, the right way to treat him will soon be worked out.

ii. The second area in which the Christian must demonstrate the Christian ethic is in the area of *social conditions*, in the social environment in which he lives.

It is here that the church has much to live down. There is no doubt that for long the church was connected with the establishment and with the *status quo*. The church was held to be, and appeared to be, the supporter of things as they are. It had in the nineteenth century much to do with the upper and the middle classes, and little to do with the working man.

One of the most terrible things I ever read is in William Purcell's life of Studdert Kennedy. In the days of Kennedy's father, in the time of the industrial revolution, in the square of St Peter's church in Leeds, a poor wretched man publicly burned the Bible and the Prayer Book, because he felt that the church was more than anything else responsible for the conditions in which he had to live. It was at that time that a country farm-labourer was asked if he attended the Communion, and answered: 'No. That kind of thing is for the gentry'—and the tragedy is that it was very largely true, before John Wesley came.

The social gospel is not an addendum to the gospel; it is the gospel. If we read the Gospels, it becomes clear that it was not what Jesus said about God that got him into trouble. What got him into trouble was his treatment of men and women, his way of being friendly with outcasts with whom no respectable Jew would have had anything to do. It has always been fairly safe to talk about God; it is when we start to talk about men that the trouble starts. And yet the fact remains that there is no conceivable way of proving that we love God other than by loving men. And there is no conceivable way of proving that we love men other than by doing something for those who most need help.

What then is the Christian duty now? The Christian duty depends on one principle which cannot be evaded. If we think that conditions should be changed, if we think that in any area of life conditions are not what they should be in a so-called Christian country, then there is only one way to alter them—through political action. There is no other possible way through which the change can be effected. And this leaves us facing the inevitable and inescapable conclusion—the Christian ought to be deeply involved in politics. He ought to be active in local government; he ought to be an active member of his trade union; he ought to be active and responsible in national politics. This is not to say that he is to be a member of any particular political party, for no party has a monopoly of what is right. The Christian should be in all parties, acting everywhere as the conscience of the community and the stimulus to action.

We often complain of the action of local government and of trade unions; it is a first principle that no man has a right to complain of the work of others, unless he is prepared to do it better himself. It is the simple fact that time and time again decisions are taken and issues are settled by a small and militant minority who are there, while the rest absent themselves and refuse to accept their responsibilities. We cannot complain, if we leave it to others to take the decision in which we should ourselves have shared. No leaven ever leavened any loaf unless it got inside it; and the Christian will never be the leaven of society until he is completely involved in it. Luther once said an extraordinary thing in his treatise *Concerning Christian Liberty*. He thinks of all that God has given him in Christ; and then he thinks of the obligation that this love and this generosity have laid upon the man who has accepted them, especially the obligation to be among men as one who serves, as Jesus was. Then he says: 'I will therefore give myself as a sort of Christ to my neighbour, as Christ has given himself to me; and will do nothing in this life except what I see will be needful, advantageous and wholesome for my neighbour, since by faith I should abound in all good things in Christ.' Here is the voice of the man who *must* give himself to the community. Every Christian ought to feel like that, and therefore every Christian ought to give himself to the service of the community in which he lives.

iii. The third area in which the Christian ethic is involved is the area of *war*.

In the ancient world war was a very gentlemanly engagement; it was fought by mercenaries, who had their rules and kept them. It is on record that during one campaign it was discovered that in a house between the armies there was a picture by Polygnotus, the greatest of the Greek artists. The war was suspended until the picture had been removed to a place of safety. But the very nature of war has changed. During the Spanish Civil War a journalist described a city street, bombed, littered with broken glass and all kinds of debris. Along the street came a little boy dragging a wheelless wooden engine at the end of a piece of string. There is a burst of fire and a scurry; and when the dust settles the boy is dead. That is war.

But not even that is war today. That bears no relationship to the potential of modern warfare. Something happened at Hiroshima and Nagasaki, something after which the world can never be the same again. A method of fighting was discovered and used which could kill thousands, which could lay waste a city, and which could cause genetic damage to generations yet unborn. It is said—and it is unquestionably true—that this country and America and the Western democracies at least would never use the atomic bomb as an offensive weapon, and have it only as a defensive deterrent. But one thing is clear—it is not a deterrent, *unless in certain circumstances the nation possessing it is prepared to use it.* And this is exactly what I believe a Christian can never consent to do. I can in no circumstances conceive it to be in accord with Christian principles to use such methods.

If I am asked if I would defend my wife or my daughter or anyone else if I saw them attacked, the answer of course is, Yes. And the difference is this. In such a case I would be dealing with the person who was committing the assault. And there is no possible relationship between dealing with a criminal in the act of his crime and raining death and destruction over thousands of people completely indiscriminately, and so killing men, women and children, without distinction.

We are told that we must not kill. That commandment is not abrogated when the killing is not individual but mass murder. We are told that we must defend Christianity—or Western civilisation—as if they were the same thing—from forces which might destroy it. In the first place, I do not believe that Christianity can be destroyed. In its early days it survived the whole might of the Roman Empire and emerged. In the second place, if Christianity has to be defended by such means, then I for one would want nothing to do with it. It is impossible to defend the faith whose watchword is love and whose emblem is a man upon a cross, by a policy of destruction. I do not love my enemies when I drop a bomb on them. And—in the end—it may seem a naïve statement, and it may seem an oversimplification, but I cannot imagine Jesus in any circumstances pressing the switch which would release a bomb. I think that the time has come for the Christian and the church to say that they are finished with war.

The Christian both as a man and as a Christian must be involved in the community. It was never more difficult to be a Christian within the community than today—and it was never more necessary.

CHAPTER NINE

Person to Person Ethics

There never was an age in history when it was so difficult for a person to remain pure and chaste and good as it is today.

That is the first sentence that I wrote to begin this talk tonight; but no sooner had I written it than I began to doubt very much if it is true. The proverb has it that the more things change, the more they remain the same; and the plain fact of history is that it has never been easy to be good and to be pure and to be chaste. So, then, I want to begin by looking at the world into which Christianity came, and to see what the person to person ethic was like in it. I want to take only certain typical incidents and sayings from that ancient world, and it is because they are typical—not because they are unusual—that I take them.

First of all, let us look at Greece. In one of his speeches (*Against Naeaera* 122) Demosthenes sets out what he takes to be the rule of life. Demosthenes did not say this because he was condemning it, or because it was unusual, but because he was stressing that it was normal day-to-day practice:

> We keep prostitutes for pleasure; we keep mistresses for the day-to-day needs of the body; we keep wives to be the mothers of our children and the guardians of our home.

In Greece relationships before marriage and outside marriage were the normal practice, an accepted part of life. It is the supreme ordinariness of the thing which makes it so shocking.

Second, let us turn to Rome. Let us take the case of Messalina in Rome as Juvenal the Roman satirist tells it to us—and remember it is not a Christian moralist but a Roman poet who is telling the story. Messalina was no less a person than the Empress of Rome, the wife of Claudius the Emperor. She would, says Juvenal, wait until Claudius was asleep. Then with one maid and a night-cowl over her head she would slip out to her own special cell in the public brothels and serve there as a common prostitute. I quote: 'There she stood with nipples bare and gilded . . . Here she graciously received all-comers, asking from each his fee; and when at last the keeper dismissed his girls, she remained to the very last before closing her cell, and, with passion still raging hot within her, went sorrowfully away. Then, exhausted by men but unsatisfied, with soiled cheeks and begrimed with the smoke of the lamps, she took back to the imperial pillow all the odours of the stews' (Juvenal, *Satires* 6.114-132). A Roman Empress delighting to act as a common prostitute—and, just about AD 50—that is the world into which Christianity came.

Third, let us look at divorce in that ancient world. Broadly speaking, there was no process of divorce; all that a husband had to do was to tell his wife to go, for in that ancient world a woman was a thing, not a person, and had no legal rights at all. In the Roman world divorce was staggeringly common. Seneca said that women were married to be divorced and were divorced to be married (*De Beneficiis* 3.16). He said that women counted the years by the names of their husbands rather than by the names of the consuls. Hiberina, says Juvenal, naming a reigning beauty, would as soon be satisfied with one husband as with one eye (*Satires* 6.53,54). Martial tells of a woman who was living with her tenth husband (Martial, *Epigrams* 6.7). Juvenal tells of a woman who had eight husbands in five years (Juvenal, *Satires* 6.230). And Jerome tells us of what must have been the unsurpassable record, the case of a woman who was married to her twenty-third husband, she being his twenty-first wife (Jerome, *Letters* 2).

Fourth, we turn to the Jewish world. There is not in the

Jewish world the same all-embracing immorality; but the state of divorce was serious. Jesus forbade divorce, except for the case of adultery (Matthew 5.32; 19.9; Mark 10.11,12; Luke 16.18; I Corinthians 7.10,11). The Jewish law was clear. It is stated in Deuteronomy 24.1-4 that a man can give his wife a bill of divorce, if he has found some matter of uncleanness or some indecency in her. The bill of divorce was no more than a single sentence dismissing her and giving her freedom to marry anyone who would have her. Now, of course, everything depends on the interpretation of the phrase *some matter of uncleanness*. And on this in Judaism in the time of Jesus there were two schools of thought. There was the school of Shammai, which said exactly the same as Jesus, that adultery was the only possible ground of divorce. But there was the school of Hillel, and it said that *a matter of indecency* could mean going out with her hair unbound, spinning in the street, talking to another man, spoiling his dinner, speaking disrespectfully of her husband's parents in her husband's presence, being a scolding woman (and a scolding woman was defined as a woman whose voice could be heard in the next house!) (Ketuboth 7.6; Gittin 9.10). It is easy to see which school would be most popular, and in Palestine in the time of Jesus girls were afraid to marry because the tenure of marriage was so insecure.

It is, of course true that in every age and generation and in every society there have always been people living in honour and in fidelity and in purity and in chastity; but in the days of the first Christians the atmosphere was such that it can have been no easy task to escape the moral infection which pervaded society.

It is further to be added that the ancient world was riddled with homosexuality. It would be difficult to name one of the great Greeks who did not practise this kind of love—Plato, Aristotle, Sophocles and even the great Socrates. The thing had reached such a stage in Greece that when Plato talks of love it is homosexual love he means. The ordinary love of women was regarded as low and dishonourable and for a man of culture only the love of a boy was considered worthy. It is a simple fact that of the first fifteen Roman Emperors fourteen were practising homosexuals. It is not for nothing that Paul warned his people against it (Romans 1.26,27; I Corinthians 6.9; I Timothy 1.10). It would be hard for a man in New Testament times to regard as wrong that which the greatest and the wisest practised.

When we look back on those early days, we can see that we are not really called upon to face anything that previous generations have not faced. So then let us look at some of the areas of this person to person ethic.

i. Let us begin by looking at the sphere of the family. Someone has said that what life does to us, everyone of us, is equivalent to dropping us down the chimney of some house at random, landing us in the middle of a group of people, and then saying: 'Get on with these people as well as you can.' The problem of the family is quite simply the problem of living together.

When we study the New Testament family ethic, the first thing that strikes us about it is that in every case it is what can only be called a reciprocal ethic. This is to say that no privilege is ever given without a corresponding responsibility. In the New Testament family ethic the duty is never, literally never, all on one side. So wives have to obey their husbands, but the husband is always to treat the wife with love and with consideration. Children are to obey their parents, but parents are never to behave unreasonably to their children in such a way as to anger or discourage them. Always there is a double duty; never is the duty all on one side (Ephesians 5.21-6.9; Colossians 3.18-4.1).

In the family there are two main relationships. First, there is the relationship of parent and child. On the side of the parent, there are two main things to be said. The first is quite simply that those of us who are parents must always remember that times do change. A certain famous authoress tells how once she said to her small daughter: 'When I was your age, I was never allowed to do a thing like that.' And the child answered: 'But you must remember mother that you were *then* and I'm *now*.' There is a *then* and there is a *now*, and they are not the same, nor can they be made the same. The parent has to remember all the time that he cannot keep things as they are.

The second is even more important. When Paul was writing to the Colossians his plea to parents is to avoid treating their children in such a way that the children become discouraged (Colossians 3.21). It may well be that this is the most important rule of family life. The child may come to feel that the parent is always 'going on' at him—and often he is not far wrong. What most human beings, young or old, need in this world more than anything else is encouragement. Benjamin West became one of the great British painters, and he tells us how. When he was young his mother went out, leaving him in charge of his little sister Sally. In the absence of his mother the boy came across some bottles of coloured ink and some brushes and he was determined to try to paint a picture of his little sister Sally. The result may well be imagined; there was ink here, there, and everywhere. His mother came back to the house; she took one look at the mess and she took one look at the boy's attempted picture. 'Why,' she said, 'it's Sally!' And she took Benjamin in her arms and kissed him. And as Benjamin West said all his life afterwards: 'My mother's kiss made me a painter.' If she had done what so many of us would have been tempted to do, there might have been no Benjamin West. Our first instinct to those who are young should be encouragement. We do not realise how much the young person worries with the modern tensions in education and in life. In the 15-19 age-group suicide is the third most common cause of death. And one of the greatest encouragements is simply to treat the child as a reasonable human being. The days of doing a thing 'because I say so' are long past. Anyone will obey more quickly and act better, if he does so intelligently, and if he knows and understands why the order is given.

In the sphere of parent and child, the young person should remember the duty of gratitude. It is the plain fact of nature that of all creatures man takes the longest before he can sustain his own life, and there are long years when, not positive injury, but simple neglect would have killed us. Only love can repay love, and yet it happens again and again within the family that we hurt most of all those whom most of all we ought to cherish. When James Barrie looked back across the years to his relationship with his mother Margaret Ogilvie, he said: 'When I look back, I cannot see the smallest thing undone.' I do not think that I ever met anyone who could say that—but that is the aim. For one of the saddest things in life is to look back and to say: 'If only I had done this or that . . .'

One last thing, in regard to the parent-child, child-parent relationship. A home should be a place from which the child is equipped to go out, and to which he will always return. Some parents find it very hard to grasp the fact that their basic duty is to enable the child to leave them and to live his own life. Smother-love and mother-love can be very easily confused. If we bring up our children in such a way that they are eager to go out and glad to return, then our task will be well done.

ii. The second area of the home and family life is marriage. There is no doubt that for the Christian ethic in its ideal form, marriage is given for life. In the Mark account of the words of Jesus (Mark 10.1-12) no exception at all is made to that rule. In the parallel Matthew account (Matthew 5.32) the one exception is divorce for infidelity.

We have to have a care what we do here. First, we have to face the fact that sexual infidelity is far from being the only thing that can wreck a marriage. It is one of the curious facts of language that the word *immorality* has come almost exclusively to mean sexual immorality. There is many a person in marriage who is blameless from the legal sex point of view, but who has nonetheless succeeded in making marriage a hell for the other partner. Fletcher quotes a passage from Dorothy Sayers:

> A man may be greedy and selfish; spiteful, cruel, jealous and unjust; violent and brutal; grasping, unscrupulous, and a liar; stubborn and arrogant; stupid, morose, and dead to every noble instinct; and yet, if he practises his sinfulness within the marriage bond, he is not thought by some Christians to be immoral (J. Fletcher, *Moral Responsibility* pp. 133, 134).

There are other things than adultery which can kill a marriage and the love which should be in it.

The second thing we have to be careful about is that we do not try to make the words of Jesus into a law, and thus forget that the greatest thing of all is love. We have always to remember that we have to take to any situation the whole of the message of Jesus, not just one sentence from it. I am not thinking of the kind of situation in which two people have entered into marriage without thought and without facing the realities; nor am I thinking of the kind of situation in which the partners in a marriage wish to break the marriage up simply because the initial romance and glamour are gone, and they have not the moral fibre and the staying power to face the routine of the every day. I am not thinking of the kind of situation in which people think of life together in terms of soft lights and sweet music and never realise until too late that there are such things as kitchen sinks, and pots and pans, and crying babies and washing of nappies. Still less am I thinking of the kind of situation in which one of the partners of the marriage allows a relationship to develop which is in itself the way to disloyalty.

But if it should so happen that two people find living together an impossibility; if they have consulted the doctor and the minister or the priest and the psychologist and the psychiatrist; if they have taken all the guidance that there is to take, and if the situation is still beyond mending, then I do not think that it is an act of Christian love to keep two such people tied together in a life that is a torture; nor do I think that it is right for them only to be allowed to separate and never to be allowed to try to start again. In such circumstances I believe that divorce is the action of Christian love, for I do not think that Jesus would have insisted that two utterly incompatible people should be condemned to drag out a loveless existence, heartbreaking for themselves and disastrous for their children. Nor do I believe that they should be forbidden to remarry and to remarry with the blessing of the church. Nor do I think that I would wish to talk much about innocent and not innocent parties, for when a marriage breaks up I should doubt if there is any such thing as an altogether innocent and an altogether guilty party.

iii. But now we must come to what is the most difficult side of this whole matter. What has the Christian ethic to say about sexual intercourse before and outside marriage? I think that the situation in regard to sexual intercourse before marriage is more difficult today than it has ever been in history. For that difficulty there are certain reasons.

(a) There is first of all the quite simple fact that the voices which once spoke for chastity no longer do so. Joseph Fletcher, the Christian occupant of a Chair of Christian Ethics in America writes: 'The cult of virginity seems to me to be making its last stand against the sexual freedom which medicine has now made possible' (*Dialogues in Medicine and Theology*, ed. Dale White, p. 141). 'A growing number of church people', he says, 'are challenging fixed moral principles or rules about sex or anything else.' So virginity was only a cult, and is now a doomed cult, and men like Fletcher accept this as inevitable. In 1959 the British Medical Association published a handbook, entitled *Getting Married*, written by Eustace Chesser and Winifred de Kok, and in it there was the following sentence: 'Chastity is outmoded and should no longer be taught to young people.' It is true that in 1959 there were so many protests that the book had to be withdrawn, but the significant thing is that it got to the length of being published at all. One of the very significant things today is that, if we may put it so, the defences are being breached from the inside.

(b) There are certain physical facts in the situation. Two facts have come together to form an explosive combination. People mature much more quickly today. Fifty years ago the average age of the beginning of menstruation was seventeen; today it is thirteen. Further, marriage has to be delayed in many cases today, and, when a man is at his most sexually dynamic, he may be a student on a long course which to say the least of it makes marriage imprudent. This is to say that there is the dangerous situation that sexual maturity is earlier and marriage is later.

(c) Third, there are the enormous changes in the methods of contraception and the efficacy of these methods. In this country it was not until 1877 that the thing became an issue at all. In that year Charles Bradlaugh and Mrs Annie Besant published an elementary manual of birth-control and were promptly prosecuted and found guilty, although the verdict was reversed on a legal technicality. It was not until 1921 that the first birth-control clinic was opened at Walworth; it was not until 1930 that the first Ministry of Health clinic was opened, and it was not until 1934 that information was offered, and it was offered only to women suffering from abnormal conditions. This is to say it was not until 1934—and that is a year after I began in the ministry—that birth-control methods were made at all public and then only in the most limited way.

Contraception found its peak in the pill, which is easy to take, normally safe in action and almost infallible in effect. The methods of contraception have been so refined and rendered so effective that it is now not necessary for anyone to have a baby unless they want to.

(d) There is the astonishing prevalence of abortion. Throughout the world there is the incredible number of 30,000,000 abortions per year. Even in this country there are perhaps about 160,000. It is a staggering fact that in countries like Belgium and West Germany, which have so-called liberal abortion laws, twice as many babies are aborted as are born. Fletcher has gone to the length of saying that he would wish to see the day when no unwanted and no unintended baby was born (J. Fletcher, *Situation Ethics* p. 39).

(e) There is the enacting of increasingly permissive legislation. There is, for instance, the legislation which permits homosexual practices between consenting adults. There is the easing of divorce; and there was the suggestion that married grants should be extended to students who live together without being married. There is the enacting of legislation which makes it easier to do the wrong thing—and that is always dangerous.

As Fletcher has pointed out, in the old days there were three fears which went far to keeping a grip of sexual intercourse before and outside marriage—the fear of detection, the fear of infection, and the fear of conception (J. Fletcher, *Moral Responsibility*, pp. 88, 89). The fear of conception is taken away by the new methods; the fear of infection—so it is believed—is taken away by the new antibiotics; and the fear of detection will become less and less when the consequences seem less and less serious.

It is then clear that for the modern young person Christian chastity is much more difficult than once it was. What makes the situation much harder is that the church is not speaking with one voice on this. Fletcher quotes the case of Professor Leo Koch of Illinois University. Koch was a biologist and in 1960 Koch was dismissed for saying that premarital intercourse was ethically justifiable. What Koch said was this:

> With modern contraceptives and medical advice readily available at the nearest drugstore, or at least a family physician, there is no valid reason why sexual intercourse

> should not be condoned among those sufficiently mature to engage in it without social consequences and without violating their own codes of morality and ethics (J. Fletcher, *Moral Responsibility* pp. 128, 129).

And that is Fletcher's own point of view—the point of view of a Professor of Christian Ethics. It would be easy to ask Fletcher to be a little more definite and accurate. What does he mean by *mature*? It is obviously impossible to measure maturity by age. There are many people, who by their birth certificate ought to be mature, and who in fact are unstable, impulsive, insecure and neurotic. One would like Fletcher to define a little more clearly what he means by *by consent*, for it is the most obvious thing in the world that it is not difficult to buy consent. What sounds so straightforward and obvious is in fact full of difficulties.

What then are we to say to all this?

i. In the first place, such sexual permissiveness is in fact fraught with very gráve danger. The facts are alarming. There are more than 150,000 new cases of venereal disease every year. In one year 37 young people under fourteen contracted venereal disease, as did 235 who were fifteen, and 1,357 who were sixteen. It is further to be noted that the fear of infection has returned, for some of the antibiotics formerly used are no longer effective, because strains of disease resistant to them have emerged.

It is further estimated that of boys of seventeen 1 in 4 has had sexual experience, and of girls of the same age 1 in 8; of boys of nineteen 1 in 3 has had sexual experience and of girls of the same age 1 in 4. Two out of three babies born to girls under twenty are conceived out of wedlock. Every thirteenth child to be born is illegitimate. In certain areas it is calculated that two out of three girls who have reached the age of twenty-five are no longer virgins. It is estimated that from 4 per cent to 6 per cent of men are practising homosexuals and the same percentage of women are lesbians. The divorce rate is running at over 40,000 divorces per year, and in the United States 1 in 4 marriages ends in divorce.

These are alarming figures. Permissiveness may be right, or permissiveness may be wrong, but quite certainly it is dangerous—and that is a basic fact not to be forgotten.

ii. No one can study the teaching of Jesus and of the New Testament without seeing that that teaching stands for purity and chastity. Fornication, which is sexual intercourse between unmarried people, is condemned at least eighteen times. It is one of the basic demands on the Gentiles that they do not practise it (Acts 15.20). It is not even to be thought of or spoken of by the Christian (I Corinthians 6.18; Ephesians 6.3). Adultery, which is sexual intercourse with a married person other than one's own marriage partner, is condemned at least fifteen times. In Jesus' words it is one of the sins which comes from the evil of the heart (Matthew 15.14).

Often the story of the woman taken in adultery (John 8.1-11) is cited as an example of the gentleness of Jesus, and from one point of view so it is. But how does it end? It ends by Jesus saying: 'Go, and *sin no more.*' There is no question of Jesus saying: 'It's quite all right. Don't worry.' There is no question of the woman getting the impression that the whole thing did not matter very much, and that forgiveness was easy to come by, and that she could easily do it again. The demand is: '*Sin no more.*' He leaves us in no doubt that he believed that she had sinned. She was forgiven—but she was firmly told that it must never happen again.

There is no way of making Jesus a supporter of a permissive society. If we support sexual intercourse before marriage or outside marriage, then I do not see how we can continue to call ourselves Christian, for a man cannot be a Christian and flatly contradict the teaching of Jesus Christ. It is one thing honestly to say that we will abandon the demands of Christian morality; it is quite another thing to abandon them and to deceive ourselves into thinking that we are still keeping them.

iii. It is for this reason that while it is right to stress the dangers of the permissive society, the argument from danger is not in itself a good argument, because it seems to imply that, if the danger could be removed, if there was no risk of a child, and no peril of infection, then the objection would be removed too. It tends to imply that the objection is to the attendant dangers and not to the thing itself. But, if sexual intercourse before and outside marriage is against the teaching of Jesus, then the thing is not only dangerous, it is wrong in itself—and that is what we are arguing.

iv. Let us go on with the argument. The supporters of the new morality place great stress on the fact that, as they put it, sexual intercourse has two functions—baby-making and love-making. They then argue that, since modern methods of contraception, especially the pill, have next to completely eliminated the production of a child, then there is no reason why the sexual act should not be used as love-making between people who are in love, but who are not married.

v. We may take in here something else with which few will disagree. Beyond all argument the Christian ethic teaches that it is always wrong to use a person as a thing; it is always wrong to use a person simply as the means of gratification or as a way of getting pleasure. Therefore, any act of sexual intercourse which is nothing other than the satisfaction of sexual desire is essentially wrong. That is why a marriage which is based on no more than desire is bound to fail, for the partners in it are basically using each other as things, and not as persons.

vi. Now we come to what is almost the final step in the argument. The sexual act is in the literal sense of the word *unique*. It is unique for two reasons. First, it has a unique potentiality, because through it a child, a new life, can be brought into the world. Second, it is unique, because it does something physically to a woman which cannot be undone, and which means that she literally will never be the same again. The breaking of the hymen is an irreversible fact. This means that there is no comparison whatever between an act of sexual intercourse and, say, a kiss. This is love-making of a different kind, love-making with a unique potential and love-making with a unique effect.

It can be said to be love-making at its peak. And such love-making ought only to be engaged in when people are totally, completely and utterly committed to each other. It can only rightly happen when people are so totally committed to each other that they have become one new person (Genesis 2.24; Matthew 19.5). The Old Testament uses the verb *to know* for the act of sexual intercourse. Adam knew Eve (Genesis 4.1). It is an act of complete and total mutual knowledge which can come only with complete and total self-giving. If it is less than that, it is not so much wrong as tragically less than what it ought to be. It is not the expression of a moment of passion, however intense; it is the expression of a permanent commitment, and only the willingness to enter into commitment gives the right to enter upon that unique act.

It could be put in this way. Whatever we say about the two functions of sexual intercourse, the love-making and the baby-making, it remains true that the biological reason for the sex instinct is the begetting of a child. That is why it was ever given to us. This is the very economy and arrangement of nature. Therefore, even when it is an act of love-making, it may properly only be engaged in by those who would gladly and willingly use it to beget a child, even although at that particular moment it is not their intention to do so. It is the expression of a commitment of which a child is the symbol and the proof.

It thus becomes clear that the great fault of premarital sexual intercourse is quite simply that it demands privilege without responsibility; it demands rights without commitment. This is why sexual intercourse is wrong even between people who say that they are so much in love that marriage is certain and that they are only anticipating what will in any event happen. We know too well how in the uncertainty of life even such a love can somehow find an interruption and even such an anticipated marriage may not take place. The utter commitment is still not entered on and therefore the unique act is wrong. The ultimate commitment must be fully there before the ultimate privilege is given and taken. Even if such a view involves self-discipline, it leads to the deepest satisfaction in the end. There is something tragic in making that which is sacred commonplace, and that which is unique ordinary. There are things—and these the greatest things—whose value only fully comes when we do not take them until the time to take them has fully come.

There are still certain other things to say. There are few nowadays, except in the Roman Catholic church, who would question the use of methods of birth-control within marriage. No one would wish to go back to the nineteenth century, when Charles Dickens' wife, before he left her, had ten children and five miscarriages in rather less than twenty years. But today the problem faces us as to whether methods of birth-control, and in particular the pill, are to be made available to those who are not married. We have already made it clear that we believe that for the Christian who will accept the Christian ethic sexual intercourse before and outside marriage is wrong. For the Christian, therefore, the question does not arise. The Christian girl will neither want nor use the pill before marriage. But, if a girl were to come to me, and if she quite deliberately refused to accept the Christian ethic of sex, if she said that she intended to have sexual intercourse before marriage, I would argue with her, I would plead with her, I would pray with her, I would do all that I possibly could to persuade her to accept the Christian way. But if at the end of the day she would not listen, if no matter what I or anyone else said, she insisted on going her own way, then I would make the pill available to her, for I think that anything is better than to bring into the world an unwanted child. I think that those who oppose this are often illogical, for such people do not often insist that the older-fashioned instruments of birth-control should be withheld from the unmarried. In principle, there is no difference at all. If one is withheld, all should be withheld. But, if I cared deeply for someone, and if in spite of all I could say that someone refused to accept the Christian view of sex, and proposed to engage on it before marriage, I would wish to do all I could to save her and to save the child who might be born from the tragic consequences which could arise, and for that reason I should make the best methods of birth-control available to her.

It is hardly possible to leave this subject without a word about sex education. It is here that Christianity got off to a bad start. We have already had occasion to mention Gnosticism, which was a way of thought deeply ingrained into the Greek mind. It came from a deep suspicion of the body, and from the idea that, if a man could only be freed from the body, life's problems would be solved. It painted a picture of a world which from the beginning had been made out of bad stuff. It did not think of a world made from nothing, but a world made from material which in its very essence was faulty. Of such a world the true God could not be the creator, and so the Gnostics believed the world to have been made by an inferior god, ignorant of, and hostile to, the true God. If that is believed, then the world and all that is in it become evil. If matter is evil as such, then the body is evil as such. And if the body is evil as such, then all the body's instincts, and especially the sex instinct, are evil. This was originally a heresy, but it left its mark on the Christian church. Always the church has been suspicious of the body, and therefore sex has always been looked on as a kind of wicked thing. This meant that it was never spoken of; it was a kind of unfortunate necessity. There never was any sex teaching, for sex was something at best to be whispered about in corners, or to be made the subject of a smutty joke. This attitude still lingers.

It always was a wrong attitude, and today it is not only wrong, it is also highly dangerous. The sex instinct is a God-given instinct, implanted in us by the Creator. It is something entirely natural, and an integral part of human life.

Knowledge of sex must be taught. It must be taught quite objectively. Its mechanism must be taught, for only then will its dangers and its glories be realised. It is high time that the day when young people got their knowledge of sex through furtive whispered conversations and through dirty stories came to an end.

It will, I believe, better be taught on two levels. On the physical level it will be better taught at school, for often the teacher can speak freely of that which is embarrassing to the parent, and there are some things which are more easily taught in a group. Factually the school is the place for the teaching of sex. But the home is the place where the greatness of purity and chastity and fidelity can alone be taught. Let the school teach the facts, and let the home teach the ideals. It need not be an exclusive division. Often the good teacher will transmit the ideal, and often the good parent will already have talked with the child. But here is somewhere where school and parent can really co-operate.

It is often objected that the child will try to experiment with the new knowledge that he has gained. For a few years it could be so, for at the moment we have not yet escaped from the situation in which that which has been so long secret is being unveiled. But, given time, and no very long time will be necessary, such teaching will become a normal part of the child's life in which healthy knowledge will take the place of unhealthy curiosity, and there will be a far better base to build on, a base in which the dangers are known, the facts realised, and, if we teach rightly, the ideals glimpsed.

If ever there was a time to uphold the standards of the Christian person to person ethic this is it. It is now that the Christian light should be shining like a light in a dark place. The plain fact is that the church has lost the very reason for its existence, if it pursues a policy of conformity to the world.

The world wants the church to be the church. Some years ago *Punch* had a cartoon. It showed the padre walking out of an RAF mess, leaving two officers behind. The one officer turns to the other and says: 'I can't stand this unholier than thou attitude.' The world may not agree with a church that insists on being different—but it will respect it. But it will have neither respect nor use for a church which is always trying to conform to the world. B. K. Price writes: 'The Swedish Lutheran church is to set up a special commission to reconsider a pronouncement made in 1959 which branded premarital sexual relationships as sin. A spokesman said that the commission would study whether this pronouncement should be modified in view of a widely-discussed demand that the church align itself more closely to "reality" ' (R. H. Fuller and B. K. Price, *Christianity and the Affluent Society*, p. 116). Fuller and Price were writing in 1966, and I do not know the result and verdict of the commission; but to align the church to the world, in the name of aligning it to reality, is the quickest way to suicide for the church.

There is a letter from C. S. Lewis to his brother (*Letters of C. S. Lewis*, ed. W. H. Lewis, p. 177) in which Lewis tells of a visit to Oxford of Charles Williams. Williams was a close friend of Lewis, and Williams fanatically loved and worshipped purity: Lewis writes:

> On Monday Charles Williams lectured, nominally on *Comus*, but really on chastity. Simply as criticism it was superb—because here was a man who really cared with every fibre of his being about 'the sage and serious doctrine of virginity', which it would never occur to the ordinary modern critic to take seriously. But it was more important still as a sermon. It was a beautiful sight to see a whole roomful of modern young men and women sitting in the absolute silence that can *not* be faked, very puzzled but spellbound . . . What a wonderful power is the direct appeal which disregards the temporary climate. I wonder if it is

> the case that the man who has the audacity to get up in any corrupt society and squarely preach justice or valour or the like always wins?'

It may be that what the church needs to get the people back is not compromise, but a message of uncompromising purity.

Bibliography

This is not intended to be a complete bibliography. I have only listed the books which have been specially helpful to me in the preparation of these lectures.

ALEXANDER, A. B. D.: *Christianity and Ethics:* Duckworth, London, 1914

The Ethics of St. Paul: James Maclehose and Son, Glasgow, 1910

ALLAN, D. J.: *The Philosophy of Aristotle:* Home University Library, Oxford, 1952; Oxford Paperback University Series, 1970; Oxford University Press, New York (paper)

ARMSTRONG, A. H.: *An Introduction to Ancient Philosophy:* Methuen and Co. Ltd., London, 1947; University Paperbacks, 1965; Beacon Press, Boston (paper)

ATKINSON, R. F.: *Conduct, an Introduction to Moral Philosophy:* Basic Books in Education, Macmillan, London, 1969

BARKER, C. J.: *The Way of Life:* Lutterworth Press, London, 1946

BARNES, KENNETH C.: *He and She:* Darwen Finlayson, Beaconsfield, Bucks, 1958; Penguin Books, Harmondsworth, 1962

BARRY, F. R.: *Christian Ethics and Secular Society*: Hodder and Stoughton, London, 1966

BONHOEFFER, D.: *The Cost of Discipleship,* tr. R. H. Fuller: SCM Press Ltd., London, 1948; Macmillan Company, New York

Ethics, ed. E. Bethge: SCM Press Ltd., London, 1955; Macmillan Company, New York

VAN BUREN, PAUL: *The Secular Meaning of the Gospel;* SCM Press Ltd., London, 1963; Macmillan Company, New York

CARY, M. AND HAARHOFF, T. J.: *Life and Thought in the Greek and Roman World:* Methuen and Co. Ltd., London, 1940; University Paperbacks, 1961; Barnes & Noble, Inc., New York

CATHERWOOD, H. F. A.: *The Christian Citizen:* Hodder and Stoughton, London, 1969

CAVE, S.: *The Christian Way:* James Nisbet and Co., London, 1949

DEMANT, V. A.: *An Exposition of Christian Sex Ethics:* Hodder and Stoughton, London, 1963

DEWAR, L. AND HUDSON, C. H.: *Christian Morals, a Study in first Principles:* University of London Press Ltd., Hodder and Stoughton, London 1945

DOWNIE, R. S. AND TELFER, ELIZABETH: *Respect for Persons:* George Allen and Unwin Ltd., London, 1969; Schocken Books, Inc., New York

EARP, F. R.: *The Way of the Greeks:* Oxford University Press, London, 1929; AMS Press, New York

EWING, A. C.: *Ethics:* The Teach Yourself Books, English Universities Press Ltd., London, 1953; Free Press, New York

FERGUSON, J.: *Moral Values in the Ancient World:* Methuen and Co. Ltd., London, 1958; Fernhill House, Ltd., New York

FIELD, G. C.: *Plato and his Contemporaries:* Methuen and Co. Ltd., London, 1930; University Paperbacks, 1967; Barnes and Noble, Inc.

FLETCHER, J.: *Situation Ethics:* SCM Press, Ltd., London, 1966; Westminster Press, Philadelphia
Moral Responsibility: SCM Press Ltd., London, 1967; Westminster Press, Philadelphia

FLEW, R. NEWTON: *Jesus and his Way:* Epworth Press, London, 1963; Alec R. Allenson, Inc., Naperville, Ill.

FOOT, PHILIPPA, ed: *Theories of Ethics:* Oxford Readings in Philosophy, Oxford University Press, London and New York, 1967

FRANKENA, WILLIAM K.: *Ethics:* Foundations of Philosophy series, Prentice-Hall Inc., Englewood Cliffs, New Jersey, USA, 1963

FULLER, R. H. AND RICE, B. K.: *Christianity and the Affluent Society:* Hodder and Stoughton, London, 1966; Wm. B. Eerdmans, Grand Rapids, Mich.

GALBRAITH, J. K.: *The Affluent Society:* Hamish Hamilton, London, 1958; Penguin Books, Harmondsworth, 1962; Houghton Mifflin Co., New York

HUBY, P.: *Greek Ethics:* New Studies in Ethics, Macmillan, London, 1967; St. Martin's Press, Inc., New York

HUDSON, W. H.: *Ethical Intuitionism:* New Studies in Ethics, Macmillan, London, 1967; St. Martin's Press, Inc., New York

HUTTON, M.: *The Greek Point of View:* Hodder and Stoughton, London, n.d.; Kennikat Press, Inc., Port Washington, N.Y.

INGE, W. R.: *Christian Ethics and Modern Problems:* Hodder and Stoughton, London, 1930; Greenwood Press, Inc., Westport, Conn.

JONES, W. H. S.: *Greek Morality in Relation to Institutions:* Blackie and Son Ltd., London, 1906

KAMENKA, E.: *Marxism and Ethics:* New Studies in Ethics, Macmillan, London, 1969; St. Martin's Press, Inc., New York (paper)

KEELING, M.: *Morals in a Free Society:* SCM Press Ltd., London, 1967

KNOX, J.: *The Ethic of Jesus in the Teaching of the Church:* Epworth Press, London, 1962; Abingdon Press, Nashville

LEHMANN, P. L.: *Ethics in a Christian Context:* SCM Press Ltd., London, 1963; Harper & Row, Inc., New York

LILLIE, W.: *An Introduction to Ethics:* Methuen and Co. Ltd., London, 1948; University Paperbacks, 1961; Barnes & Noble, Inc., New York

Studies in New Testament Ethics: Oliver and Boyd, Edinburgh and London, 1966

LODGE, R. C.: *The Philosophy of Plato:* Routledge and Kegan Paul, London, 1956; Humanities Press, Inc., New York

LONG, E. L.: *A Survey of Christian Ethics:* Oxford University Press, London and New York, 1967

MABBOTT, J. D.: *An Introduction to Ethics:* Hutchinson University Library, London, 1966; Doubleday & Co., Inc., New York

MACINTYRE, A.: *A Short History of Ethics:* Routledge and Kegan Paul Ltd., London, 1967; Macmillan Company, New York

MACKINNON, D. M., ROOT, H. E., MONTEFIORE, H. W., BURNABY, J.: *God, Sex and War:* Fontana Books, Collins, London, 1963

MACQUARRIE, JOHN: *Three Issues in Ethics:* SCM Press Ltd., London, 1970; Harper & Row, Inc., New York

MOORE, G. E.: *Ethics:* Home University Library, Oxford, 1911; Oxford Paperback University Series, Oxford, 1966; Oxford University Press, New York (cloth and paper)

NIEBUHR, REINHOLD: *Moral Man and Immoral Society:* Charles Scribner's Sons, New York, 1932; SCM Press Ltd., London, 1963

OUTKA, G. H. AND P. RAMSEY: *Norm and Context in Christian Ethics:* Charles Scribner's Sons, New York; SCM Press Ltd., London, 1968

PATON, H. J.: *The Moral Law, Kant's Groundwork of the Metaphysic of Morals,* translated and analyzed; Hutchinson University Library, London, 1948; Barnes & Noble, New York

PAUL, L.: *Coming to Terms with Sex:* Collins, London, 1969

RAMSEY, I. T., ed.: *Christian Ethics and Contemporary Philosophy:* SCM Press Ltd., London, 1966; Macmillan Company, New York

RAMSEY, P.: *Basic Christian Ethics:* Charles Scribner's Sons, New York, 1950

Deeds and Rules in Christian Ethics: Scottish Journal of Theology, Occasional Papers No. 11, 1965

RAMSEY, P., *ed.*: *Faith and Ethics:* Harper & Row, New York, 1957; Torchbook Series, 1965

RANKIN, H. D.: *Plato and the Individual:* Methuen and Co. Ltd., London, 1964; University Paperbacks, 1969; Barnes & Noble, Inc., New York

RHYMES, D.: *No New Morality:* Constable, London, 1964

RITCHIE, D. G.: *Plato:* T. and T. Clark, Edinburgh, 1902

ROBINSON, J. A. T.: *Christian Freedom in a Permissive Society:* SCM Press Ltd., London, 1970; Westminster Press, Philadelphia

Christian Morals Today: SCM Press Ltd., London, 1964; Westminster Press, Philadelphia

ROSS, W. D.: *Aristotle:* Methuen and Co. Ltd., London, 1923, 5th ed., 1949; Barnes & Noble, Inc., New York

The Right and the Good: Clarendon Press, Oxford, 1930; Oxford University Press, New York

Foundations of Ethics: Gifford Lectures, Aberdeen, 1935, 1936; Clarendon Press, Oxford, 1939

ROUBICZEK, P.: *Ethical Values in an Age of Science:* Cambridge University Press, London and New York, 1969

RUSSELL, B.: *Marriage and Morals:* George Allen and Unwin, London, 1929; Paperback University Books, 1961; Liveright Publishing Corporation, New York

SAUNDERS, J. L.: *Greek and Roman Philosophy after Aristotle:* Readings in the History of Philosophy Series, The Free Press, New York; Collier-Macmillan, London, 1966

SCHNACKENBURG, R.: *The Moral Teaching of the New Testament:* Herder and Herder, New York, 1965

SCOTT, E. F.: *The Ethical Teaching of Jesus:* The Macmillan Company, New York, 1924

SELBY-BIGGE, L. A.: *British Moralists:* Clarendon Press, Oxford, 1897; Dover Books, New York, 2 vols., paperback, 1965

Sex and Morality: A Report presented to the British Council of Churches, 1966; SCM Press Ltd., London, 1966

SINCLAIR, T. A.: *A History of Greek Political Thought:* Routledge and Kegan Paul, London, 1951, 2nd ed., 1967

TAYLOR, A. E.: *Plato, the Man and his Work:* Methuen and Co. Ltd., London, 1926; University Paperbacks, 1960; Barnes & Noble, Inc., New York

Aristotle: Thomas Nelson and Son Ltd., London, 1943; Dover Publications, Inc., New York (paper)

THIELICKE, H.: *The Ethics of Sex,* tr. J. W. Doberstein: James Clarke and Co. Ltd., London, 1964; Harper & Row, Inc., New York

Theological Ethics, vol. 1, *Foundations,* ed. W. H. Lazareth: A. and C. Black, London, 1968; Fortress Press, Philadelphia

VIDLER, A. R., ed.: *Soundings, Essays, concerning Christian Understanding:* Cambridge University Press, London and New York 1963

WADDAMS, H.: *A New Introduction to Moral Theology:* SCM Press Ltd., London, 1964, rev. ed., 1965; Seabury Press, Inc., New York

WALKER, K. and FLETCHER, P.: *Sex and Society:* Penguin Books, Harmondsworth, 1955

WALSH, J. J. and SHAPIRO, H. L.: *Aristotle's Ethics:* Wadsworth Studies in Philosophical Criticism, Wadsworth Publishing Co. Inc. Belmont, California, USA, 1967

WARNOCK, MARY: *Ethics since 1900:* Oxford University Press, London and New York; Home University Library, 1960; Oxford Paperbacks University Series, 1966

WHITE, D., ed.: *Dialogue in Medicine and Theology:* Abingdon Press, Nashville and New York, 1967

WILLEY, B.: *The English Moralists:* Chatto and Windus Ltd., London, 1964; University Paperbacks, Methuen and Co. Ltd., London, 1965; W. W. Norton and Company, Inc. New York

WINTER, G., ed.: *Social Ethics:* SCM Press Ltd., London, 1968; Harper & Row, Inc.

71 72 73 74 75 10 9 8 7 6 5 4 3 2 1

BOOKS BY ROBERT BYRNE

The Dam 1981

Byrne's Standard Book of Pool and Billiards 1978

The Tunnel 1977

Mrs. Byrne's Dictionary of Unusual, Obscure, and Preposterous Words [Editor] 1974

McGoorty 1972

Memories of a Non-Jewish Childhood 1970

Writing Rackets 1969

THE DAM

THE DAM

Robert Byrne

ATHENEUM NEW YORK 1981

LIBRARY OF CONGRESS CATALOGING IN PUBLICATION DATA

BYRNE, ROBERT 1930–
THE DAM.

I. TITLE.
PS3552.Y73D3 1981 813'.54 80-22109
ISBN 0-689-11123-1

PUBLISHED SIMULTANEOUSLY IN CANADA BY MCCLELLAND AND STEWART LTD.
MANUFACTURED BY AMERICAN BOOK–STRATFORD PRESS, SADDLE BROOK, NEW JERSEY
DESIGNED BY MARY CREGAN
FIRST EDITION

For Russell Byrne

Contents

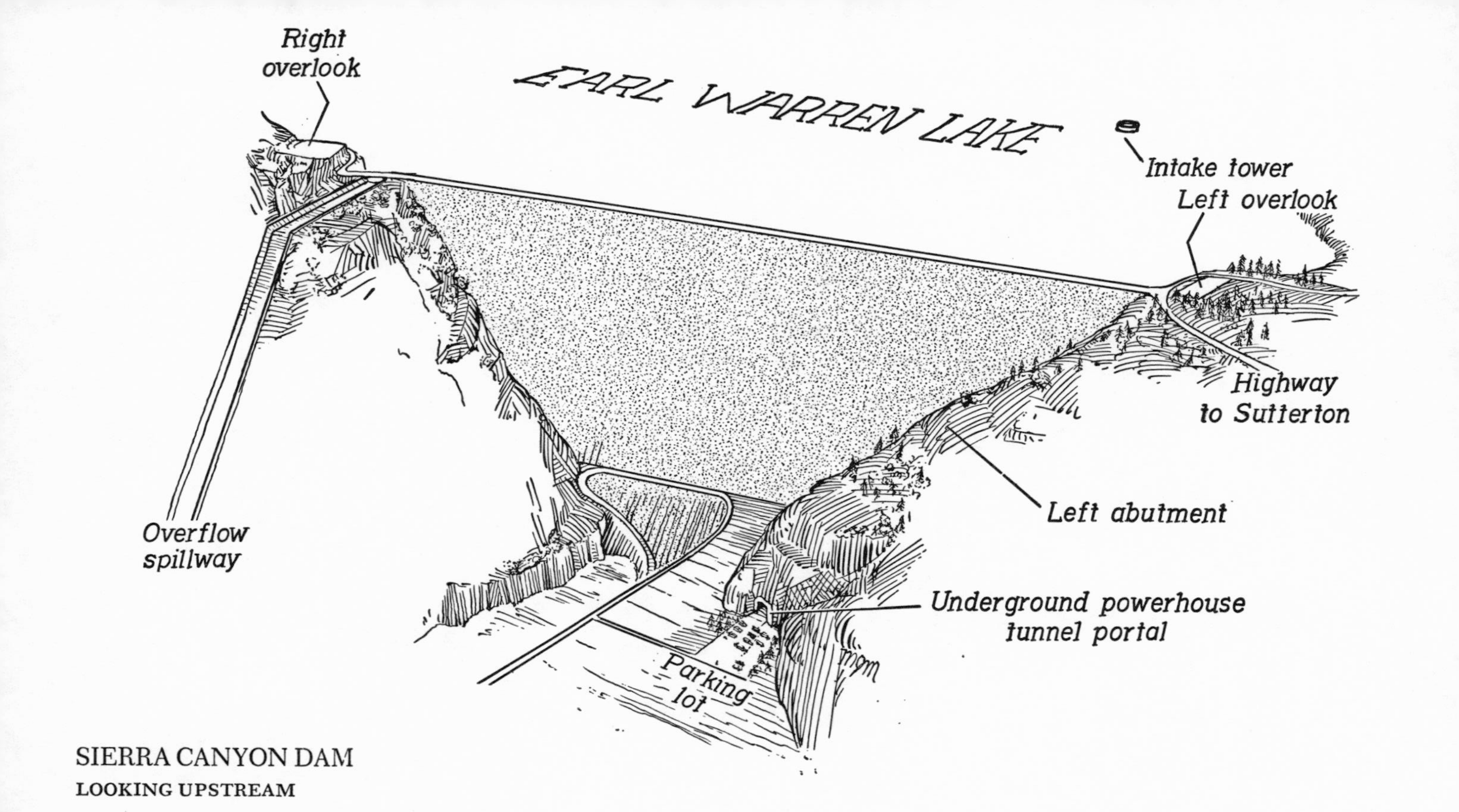

SIERRA CANYON DAM
LOOKING UPSTREAM

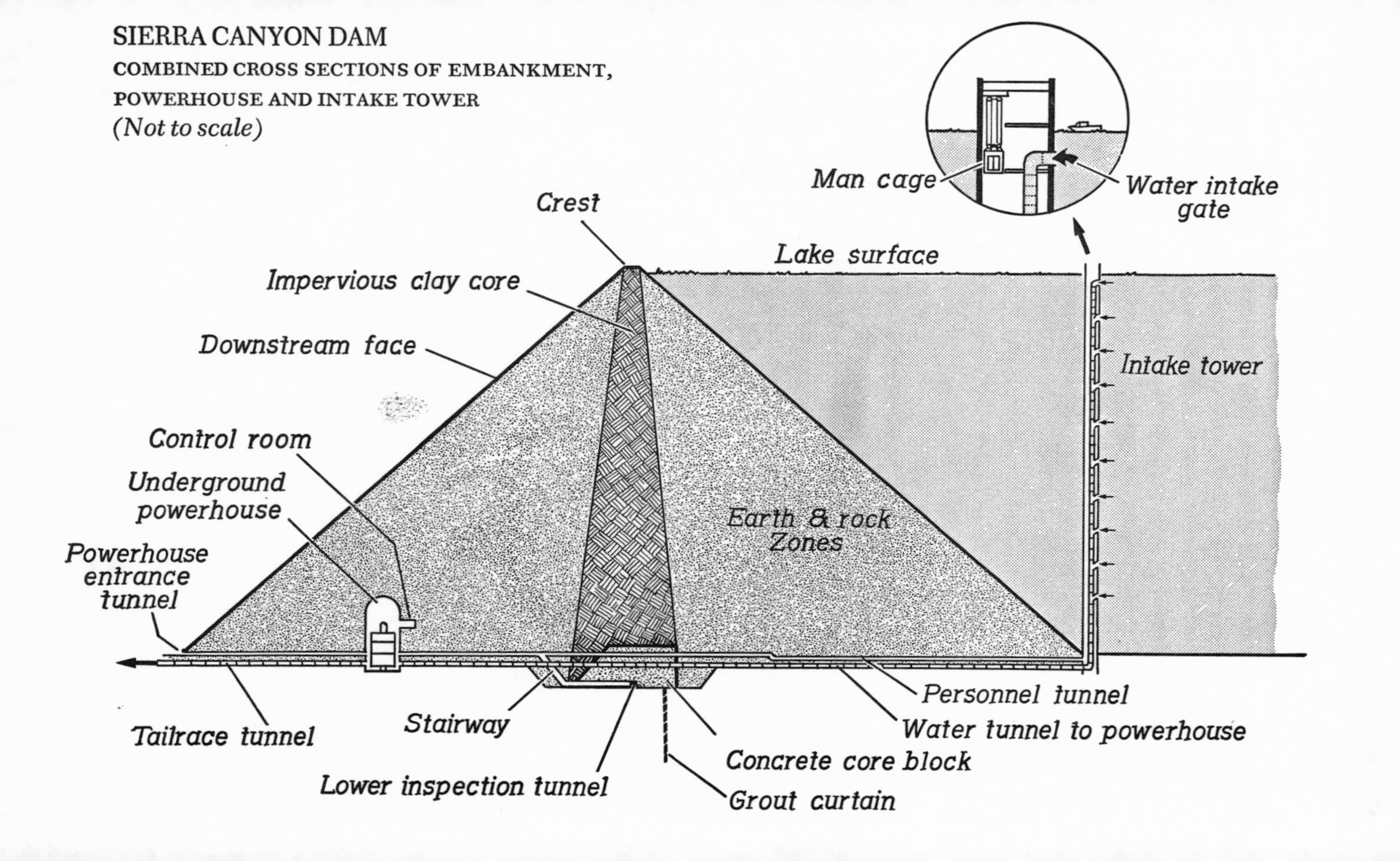
SIERRA CANYON DAM
COMBINED CROSS SECTIONS OF EMBANKMENT, POWERHOUSE AND INTAKE TOWER
(Not to scale)
Man cage
Water intake gate
Crest
Lake surface
Impervious clay core
Downstream face
Intake tower
Control room
Underground powerhouse
Earth & rock Zones
Powerhouse entrance tunnel
Personnel tunnel
Water tunnel to powerhouse
Stairway
Tailrace tunnel
Concrete core block
Lower inspection tunnel
Grout curtain

I

The Fear

1

FIVE YEARS AFTER ITS COMPLETION, Sierra Canyon Dam, at eight hundred and twenty-five feet, the highest dam in the United States and the highest earth and rock dam in the world, was subjected to a series of minor earthquakes. Seismograph needles in northern California trembled at 8:20 A.M., when the first of twenty-nine foreshocks was recorded. The main tremor, which struck five hours later, had a magnitude of 5.5 on the Richter scale and rattled dishes over an area of two hundred square miles. The rolling motion lasted for seven seconds and was disconcerting mainly to people who were indoors at the time. Most of those outdoors ascribed the quiver to the passing of trains or trucks. Fishermen and water skiers on Earl Warren Lake behind the dam noticed nothing.

The only terror was experienced by a hiker crossing a hillside meadow five miles southwest of the dam, the epicenter of the quake. He was thrown off his feet by the heaving ground and grabbed handfuls of grass to keep from rolling down the slope. "It was like trying to hang on to a raft in rough water," he told a reporter from the Sacramento *Bee*, "and wondering if there was a waterfall ahead. A crack opened up in the ground and I could see the sides rubbing together. I heard limbs falling off trees and rocks rolling downhill."

The crack in the meadow delineated a previously unknown rift in the surface rock, now called Parker's Fault after the hiker who first saw it. The fault ran in a northeasterly direction and could be traced on the surface for nearly half a mile. Geologists found that the ground had shifted six inches horizontally and three inches vertically. According to a study made by the United States Geological Survey, there was a possibility that Parker's Fault ran under Sierra Canyon Dam.

Large reservoirs that fluctuate in size have been known to cause seismic disturbances. The USGS study included a graph on which was plotted every earthquake detected in the vicinity of the dam since its construction, along with the surface elevation of the lake, which was at its lowest in the fall and highest in the spring. No correlation was found; that is, the earthquake that endangered the dam was not caused by the dam.

Despite the scarcity of measurable property damage, the earthquake made headlines in Caspar, Butte, Sutter, and Yuba counties. Hard-digging reporters described the orchards outside Wheatland, where fruit was shaken from trees. A thousand turkeys panicked in a pen at Rio Oso, and three hundred were so seriously wounded in the back-and-forth stampedes that they had to be slaughtered.

Only two people suffered injuries requiring medical care. An electrician kneeling on a kitchen floor in Grass Valley took six stitches in the cheek after being hit by a falling wall clock. A woman in a Roseville supermarket had a toe broken when her feet were engulfed by a collapsing display of canned peaches. With so little hard news to go on, newspapers had to run editorials on what might have happened had the quake been bigger or in a different place. The Yuba City–Marysville *Valley Herald* observed that modern civilization exists at the whim of the forces of nature, compared to which the works of man are puny.

One thing that might have happened was a failure of the dam, a thought that crossed the mind of Wilson Hartley, Chief of Police of Sutterton, a town of 6,500 on the Sierra Canyon River downstream from the dam. Hartley was the local officer in charge of public safety, which meant that it was up to him rather than the county Sheriff to supervise the evacuation of Suttertonians in case of a disaster or a threatened disaster. In his files was an Inundation Map furnished to him under state law by the Office of Emergency Planning in Sacramento. It was required of the owner of every large dam to confront the possibility of instantaneous failure and to make estimates of the resulting flood. The map showed how high the flood crest would be and how long it would take to reach key points downstream. Such information was valuable to communities with time to react, but in the case of Sutterton it was good only for morbid jokes around the office. The flood Hartley and his staff would be faced with would be five hundred feet deep and would be upon them in minutes. They would hardly have time to reach for their rosaries.

When the quake hit, Hartley was sitting at his desk. He put his pen down and stared at the office window, which had begun shaking noisily. A small vase of cut flowers his secretary had put on his desk that morning wobbled from side to side and fell over. He picked it up with his left hand and with his right rescued a sheaf of papers before they were soaked by the spreading puddle of water. The first thought that entered his head was that Mitchell Brothers had set off a particularly illegal blast at their quarry, but when the window and floor continued to tremble he knew it was more than that. He rose to his feet trying not to imagine the worst.

A policeman appeared in his doorway. "Did you feel that? We just had an earthquake."

"I think you're right," Hartley answered. "Now we might get a bath."

They moved to the window. Even though the dam was almost half a mile away, they had to look upward to see it looming above the trees of an intervening hill. The dam was almost unimaginably massive, higher than an eighty-story building, more voluminous than Grand Coulee and Boulder dams combined. Only the knifelike straightness of its mile-and-a-half-long crest, outlined sharply against the sky, identified it as man made. Its vast downstream face was like a prairie tilted at thirty degrees.

The two men studied the dam. "It's still there," Hartley said. "Looks tight as a drum."

"The mountains will cave in before the dam goes. When they built that sucker, they built it to last."

"That's what the engineers say, anyway. All the same, if I could do it without making the town nervous I'd drag my office to higher ground."

As they turned away from the window, the overhead light flickered and went out.

Four days after the earthquake, a Pan American flight from London landed at Los Angeles. Among those waiting for the passengers was a newspaper reporter with a notebook in his hand and a tape recorder suspended from his shoulder. "He's a crusty bastard," the city editor had told him when making the assignment, "but's he's sharp and he speaks his mind. Ignore his insults and you'll get some quotes we can use." The reporter watched with interest as the man he was after appeared in the doorway of the plane. Shrugging off the assistance of a stewardess and wielding his aluminum crutches expertly, he swung his legs across the step between the fuselage and the movable corridor and maneuvered himself into a wheelchair. Theodore Roshek, president of the international engineering firm of Roshek, Bolen & Benedetz, Inc., was easy to recognize, and not just because of his handicap. His thin, angular face was always topped by a gray felt hat with an unfashionably wide brim. Full black eyebrows, which contrasted with his white hair, gave his deep-set blue eyes an unnerving intensity. He sat erect in the chair, leaning slightly forward, as if he were a commander at the bridge of a warship. It occurred to the reporter that if Roshek could walk it would be with the stride of a man crossing a room to poke someone in the nose.

The interview was conducted as the wheelchair was pushed by an aide from the concourse gate to the street, where a limousine was waiting.

"Excuse me, Mr. Roshek, I'm Jim Oliver of the Los Angeles *Times*."

"My deepest sympathy," Roshek said, not turning his head. "I read the *Herald-Examiner* myself. Now there is a hell of a paper."

"I hope you don't mind a few questions. May I use my tape recorder?"

"Please do. It might cut down on errors."

"Your firm designed Sierra Canyon Dam. . . ."

"Right. We also supervised construction. We have a twenty year contract to provide inspection and monitor performance. Not that it needs inspection. It's probably the safest dam ever built."

Oliver, a short man, had to walk as fast as he could to keep up with the wheelchair. He explained that the *Times* was doing a background piece on the earthquake and was soliciting comments from a number of authorities.

For the first time, Roshek looked at him. "The earthquake? Are you just getting around to that? Newspapers dealt with news when I was your age. I'd rather talk about something more current, wouldn't you? Do you think the Dodgers will ever score again?"

"We tried to reach you in London."

Roshek turned away. "I was busy. I thought you were calling about a subscription."

"Did the earthquake cause you any concern?"

"Yes. I have a summer place below the dam. The fireplace may be cracked."

"The designer of the dam has a place downstream," the reporter said, scrawling a few words in a notebook. "That's an interesting point."

"I always sleep like a baby when I'm there. Must be the mountain air."

"Then you don't think the public was in danger."

"No. Well, yes. The public is always in danger. Did you get here by car? Have you no regard at all for your safety? Fifty thousand people were killed last year in the United States by cars. I just took a ride in a plane . . . that probably wasn't too smart, either."

"The fact remains that an earthquake took place next to the world's highest dam."

"The fact remains, and so does the dam. It's not the world's highest. It's the world's highest earth and rock embankment. Several concrete arches are higher. Grand Dixence in Switzerland is nine hundred and thirty-two feet. Nurek, if the Russians ever get around to finishing it, will be over a thousand. A scrupulous regard for accuracy, that's what I like about the daily press."

"Is Sierra Canyon Dam earthquake-proof?"

"Earthquake-resistant. Nothing is earthquake-proof. You get as much safety as you're willing to pay for, but never perfect safety. The little shake we had last week was five point five on the Richter, hardly enough to set a coop full of chickens clucking, and was centered five miles from the dam. The dam is designed to take six point five at five miles. There hasn't been a quake that big in that neck of the woods for a hundred thousand years."

"The little shake, as you call it, shut the power plant down for forty-five minutes."

"That was the result of too much of a good thing. There are hundreds of sensors of one kind and another in the dam and power plant. The rotating shafts of the turbine generators are three feet in diameter, and if they quiver more than a couple of millimeters in any direction, everything shuts down automatically until the situation can be assessed. You don't take chances with million-dollar generators, nor with dams."

"You say you designed the dam to stand up against an earthquake of a certain size at a certain distance. It may be that way on paper, but isn't it true that the contractors who built it may not have followed the plans and specifications in every detail?"

"Who gave you that question, the Sierra Club? A great bunch. I'm a member myself. Don't look so surprised . . . they're not all bad. My wife is a big fan of their weekend hikes. The dam was built as designed. I made sure of it by spending three years of my life on the site watching every move the contractor made. I needed only canes then and got around fairly well. I wasn't quite the physical wreck you see before you now. That was six, seven, eight years ago. I took a personal interest in the design because I wanted to prove that embankment dams of that height are perfectly safe as well as practical, and I took a personal interest in the construction because I wanted to make sure the thing would never help you sell papers by falling apart. If anything, the design is conservative. This is my car, so I'm going to say goodbye. It's been a pleasure! Sorry I didn't give you a better story. If you are bound and determined to write about the threat to the public from dams, you'll have to go outside California. California has a whole department that does nothing but worry about dams and another one that figures out what to do in case one fails. Most states have no inspection system at all. Once dams are built, they forget about them. I'm telling you God's truth! It is a scandal, my boy, that deserves the attention of your fine paper. March right into Otis Chandler's office and dump it in his lap. And tell him he'll be getting an announcement next week of my thirty-fifth wedding anniversary. We expect a gift that reflects his net worth. Goodbye! Drive carefully!"

The six water districts that jointly owned Sierra Canyon Dam, responding to a directive from the California State Division of the Safety of Dams, convened a panel of engineering consultants to determine if the earthquake "had in any way compromised the structural integrity of the dam or its appurtenances." While no structural damage was found, almost a third of the measuring and recording devices that had been implanted during construction were put out of service by the tremor. This was not considered serious by the panel because the remainder still left the dam the most extensively instrumented in the world. It was found not to be practical to try to replace the severed wires and plastic tubing that led from sensors in the embankment to the banks of dials in the drainage and inspection galleries beneath the dam. However, so that the behavior of the dam in future earthquakes could be studied more profitably, the board recommended the installation of five additional strong-motion accelerographs, two force-balance accelerometers, three pore-pressure sensors, and ten soil-stress cells.

Inspection and drainage tunnels were contained within a concrete core block that ran like a spine through the heart of the embankment at foundation level. The shocks sustained by the dam opened construction joints in the core block, allowing brown water to flow into the tunnels in the weeks following the earthquake. This caused considerable concern, but a program of grouting—involving the injection through drilled holes of a mixture of sand, water, and quick-setting cement—reduced the flow and eventually eliminated it entirely. The temporary crisis was not made public.

As a safety precaution during the following spring, the reservoir was filled at a slow, controlled rate and its highest elevation held to twenty feet below maximum. It was not until the fifth year after the quake that the lake reached capacity. On May 19, for only the second time in the ten-year life of the dam, water poured over the concrete spillway on the right abutment, providing a sensational display for tourists. A three-inch deep sheet of water flowed in shimmering waves down the thousand-foot-long concrete chute, ending in an explosion of spray. No one who heard the roar, who felt the cold wind and mist, or who photographed the rainbows will ever forget it.

On May 22, the water gliding ponderously into the spillway to begin the long plunge reached a depth of eleven inches, a historic high. Water also reached a historic high in the drainage and inspection tunnels that were buried like intestines deep within the embankment. It was particularly wet in the lowermost tunnels, which rested on bedrock eight hundred and twenty-five feet below the crest of the dam. Water stood an inch deep on the walkways, the most inspector Chuck Duncan ever had to wade through in making his weekly rounds. Water was trickling, dripping, and flowing from every drainage hole, crack, and crevice and running down the endlessly descending flights of concrete stairs in a series of miniature waterfalls. There was more water than usual, but not so much more that Duncan was moved to make a note of it. The tunnels were always sloppy when the lake was high, and the form he had to fill out with meter readings provided no space for editorial comments from a beginning-level technician.

Duncan hated the eerie lower tunnels, which were so small he could almost touch both walls at once. He hated the long climb and the stale air, the dampness, and the tomblike silence. The light bulbs on the crown were too widely spaced to alleviate the gloom and had shorted out more than once, forcing him to depend on a flashlight. How in the hell was a person with just two hands supposed to write on a clipboard while holding a flashlight? Worst of all was knowing that the full weight of the dam and the lake was directly overhead—thinking about that sometimes made sweat form on his back and stomach despite the coldness of the air. There was no point in looking for another job, not if he wanted to go on living at home. Sutterton offered nothing that paid as well year round for somebody only two years out of high school. If he could stick it out long enough to build up some seniority, the dirty job of taking readings in the lower tunnels could be dumped onto somebody else.

A heavy steel door marked the entrance to Gallery D, a hundred-foot-long side tunnel that housed almost half of the dam's monitoring instruments. It was hard to open because differential settlement had twisted the jamb out of alignment. With his clipboard tucked under his arm, Duncan used both hands to wrench the door free. He swung it against the wall and fastened it with a length of wire so it couldn't close behind him with a clang of doom the way it had once before.

Standing before the bank of dials at the end of Gallery D was like standing in a rainstorm. Grinding his teeth and shivering as water dripped on his head and shoulders, Duncan quickly jotted down figures for the dials he could see and made educated guesses for a few that were obscured by falling water. What the heavy seepage and the meter readings revealed about the condition of the dam was for other people to decide. His only concern was filling in all the blanks on the form and getting the hell out. Once back on the surface, he would take a break, light a cigarette, and think about his upcoming Friday-night date with Carla, now just a week away. Carla of the gyrating hips and flickering tongue, who had put him off on his first try on the grounds of indigestion. Next time, with the help of a joint or two, he would score with her for sure.

2

AFTER ONLY THREE WEEKS IN SOUTHern California, the newest employee of Roshek, Bolen & Benedetz, Inc., found himself in a position that struck him as wholly extraordinary—naked on a shag rug in Santa Monica. A month earlier, Phil Kramer was mowing a lawn in Wichita, Kansas. "Just because you finally got your degree," his mother had said, "doesn't mean you don't have to take out the garbage and cut the grass." Each time he pushed the clattering machine past the front porch, he stopped to read the framed document propped against the steps:

The Regents of
THE UNIVERSITY OF KANSAS
have conferred upon
PHILIP JAMES KRAMER
the degree of
DOCTOR OF PHILOSOPHY
CIVIL ENGINEERING

How he loved that piece of paper! Invested in it were seven years of canned food, examinations, and lecturers with speech impediments. He had thought those years would never end, and now, miraculously, he was lying on the floor of a young woman's apartment two blocks from the Pacific Ocean. Better yet, he was without the protection of his clothes. He wasn't exactly sure what was going to happen when Janet came out of the bathroom, but whatever it was, it was bound to be good. He had a sneaking suspicion that he was going to get laid. What she *said* was going to happen was a massage.

"You've taken me to two expensive restaurants," she said, "you fixed my car, and you moved my sofa. Now I'm going to do something for you. I'm going to give you my Class A deluxe total body massage."

"Here? At the dining-room table?"

"No. There, on the living-room floor. On the shag rug in front of the fire. Take off your clothes and lie down while I heat some oil and change into my masseuse outfit."

He walked to the rug and hesitated. What if she was kidding?

"Don't be bashful," she said. "You will love it."

To get him started, she reached up to his neck and slipped the knot of his tie. Deftly she unbuttoned his shirt from top to bottom. He frowned, slowly pulling his shirttails out of his slacks. "Isn't this a little strange?" he asked. "I mean, we haven't—"

"Just do as I say." Before disappearing into the bathroom she tossed him a towel. "Here. This is for your modesty."

He waited face down on the rug, resting his chin on the backs of his hands, feeling the glow of the fire on his skin, the towel draped over his posterior. What struck him as so extraordinary was that they had not yet made love. This was only their third evening together, and while the urgent nature of recent kisses and caresses suggested that they would soon be lovers, he didn't think that when the moment came he would be relegated to such passivity. Not that he was naturally aggressive. He was in fact shy, especially in crowds and with women. As a youth, his premature height and unmanageable hair had made him feel ungainly and even absurd. That self-image plus a religious mother and a touch of acne had conspired to safeguard his virginity until he was a sophomore in college. Said the freshman girl who helped him seduce her: "He's only shy at first. In bed he talks your leg off." Five years and eight girls later, he was still unsure of himself. He knew he wasn't a sex object, even naked on a rug. Too tall and nervous. His hair looked too much like a shock of hay that had been hit by a tractor and not quite knocked all the way over. A sprinkling of freckles across his nose undermined his credibility. He had learned to live with the harsh truth that he was cerebral rather than physical and that any girl who went for him would probably be known for her brains.

He had met Janet Sandifer at a weekend seminar sponsored by IBM on new computer languages. He glanced at her several times during coffee breaks, but he didn't have the courage to start a conversation until she smiled at him. She had a trim, compact figure and a face that held his eyes like a magnet. She was three years out of UCLA, she told him when they were trading facts about each other, where she had earned a dual degree in computer science and mathematics, and now worked as a computer systems analyst for a firm in Torrance that designed and manufactured scientific instruments. Three raises and two promotions made her feel that it was no longer important or inevitable that she become somebody's mother.

Phil closed his eyes and smiled. Things certainly were going well for him. It was a wonderful feeling to be finished with school at last, and lingering in his ears were the words of praise he had received from the faculty for his dissertation on computer prediction of dam failures. He had landed exactly the job he wanted with one of the world's most highly regarded engineering firms, and he was fast learning how much he didn't know about hydroelectric design.

The only thing that had gone wrong in Phil's life recently was the crazy response that the Roshek, Bolen & Benedetz computer had made when he tried his failure prediction program on Theodore Roshek's most famous structure, Sierra Canyon Dam. The readouts on the cathode ray tube plainly indicated that the dam was about to burst like a water-filled balloon, which meant that there was something wrong with the computers, the dam, or the program. The computers were in robust health; the dam was a universally revered example of exquisite design. So the disease had to be in the program. He would describe it to Janet when they had finished ravishing each other. She might be able to spot some flaws in the premises or the logic.

She was kneeling beside him, dressed in a kind of short Japanese robe, spreading warm oil on his back. Phil put an arm around her waist, but she pushed it away. "There is something you have to understand," she said. "I'm not trying to seduce you. I'm just trying to give you a massage. It's one of the nicest things one person can do for another, but it doesn't necessarily involve sex. Your only role is to enjoy it. Close your eyes."

She pressed her fingers into the muscles of his neck and

shoulders, using a combination of kneading and stroking motions. She urged him several times to relax. "My God, you're as tight as a coiled spring. Haven't you ever been massaged before?"

"Massage isn't too large in Kansas. Neither is public nudity."

"This is private. The door is locked and the drapes are drawn."

"Alone is private. Two is public."

He lifted his head to look at her. She pushed it down. "You're a square, did you know that? Are all engineers like you?"

"I don't know. I never massaged an engineer. The only girl in engineering school weighed two hundred pounds and wore steel-toed work shoes. We called her Puss in Boots."

She scratched his scalp with ten fingertips at once, molded his shoulders with pressure from the palms and heels of her hands, tightened her fingers around his biceps and forearms, drew her fingernails down the length of his arms, made circles on his palms. She inserted her fingers between his, caressed them, rolled them, and wiggled them. When she finished with his arms, she returned to his back, straddling his legs for better leverage. Pressing hard, she slowly pushed her fingertips from the small of his back to his neck.

"It feels unbelievably good," Phil said. "Where did you learn how to do it?"

"When I was very young, I went with a creep who thought massage was the end of the world . . . instead of merely unbelievably good. I was still in undergraduate school. Once he took me to a place in Malibu where everybody took off their clothes and practiced on each other. The instructor was a guru type who said that through massage you could get in tune with the Universal Oneness, or some such shit. That's when I bailed out."

Phil wondered what she would do when she worked her

way down to the towel. Would she skip over it discreetly and proceed directly to his legs out of respect for his puritanical upbringing, or would she cast it rudely aside as the creep and the guru would have done? She cast it aside and attacked his buttocks as if they were two mounds of bread dough. But she was so expert at what she was doing, so matter-of-fact, that he never felt the feared flush of embarrassment.

Her fingers stroked his upper legs and the sensitive areas behind the knees. Tenderly she pinched his flesh, squeezed it in her fists, pummeled it with the edges of her hands, and drew long lines on it with a touch so light that her fingertips contacted only the hair and not the skin.

"I don't know how much more of this pleasure I can take," Phil said. "I want to reciprocate. I feel selfish just lying here. I want to caress *you*."

"That's not the idea. The idea is that I am giving you a gift. You are supposed to accept it and enjoy it. Concentrate on the feeling and keep your mouth shut."

He found out how pleasurable a foot massage can be. She pressed her thumbs against his instep and arch, manipulated each toe lovingly in turn, rubbed her palms and fingers across his heels and soles, first lightly, then firmly. Finally another question that was growing in his mind was answered.

"Roll over," she said.

He did. She didn't cover him with the towel. She massaged his scalp again, this time from the front. With the touch of a butterfly she traced lines across his eyelids, his lips, his cheeks, and his neck. His chest was next, then his stomach, then his abdomen. Her hands brushed his genitals on their way to his upper legs, and after they had worked their way down to his ankles they returned up the inside of his legs to the top, where they closed gently around him. Her hands left him for a moment, and he could hear the rustle of cloth. He felt her hair against his forehead and her lips on his.

He slipped an arm around her and drew her body close.

"I've changed my mind," she whispered. "Now I'm trying to seduce you."

It was easy.

3

THE LOS ANGELES HEADQUARTERS OF Roshek, Bolen & Benedetz occupied three floors of the 500 Tishman Tower on Wilshire Boulevard. Most of the senior company officers were on the top floor, where also were located the advance planning and project development departments. On the middle floor were sections specializing in highways, structures, and tunnels. The lower floor was devoted to computer services, hydroelectric, nuclear, and mining. There were over a hundred employees on each floor, more than half of them engineers, who worked at desks or drafting tables in a central area surrounded by a ring of offices. Departments working on petrochemical developments, pipelines, ocean facilities, and foundations were in other buildings in the Los Angeles area, and one of the proposals being evaluated on the upper floor was the construction of an office tower that would consolidate all operations under one roof.

On Tuesday morning, May 26, Phil Kramer was at work an hour early, sitting at a terminal feeding his remodeled dam failure program into a computer. The revision was the result of five evenings of collaboration with Janet. She knew nothing about dams, but she knew how to forge a chain of logic and she knew how to ask questions that made him alter some of his numerical assumptions. It was she who suggested that the original mathematical model was too small and too simple to be applicable to Sierra Canyon. The model had to be expanded to accommodate the sheer size of the structure and the greater-than-average volume of data the instrumentation provided. The work they had done together had resulted in a program that was no longer appropriate for an "average" dam. It was tailor-made for Sierra Canyon.

When he had completed the required preliminary operations, Phil typed "List Gallery D meter points." A touch of the Execute key brought a column of two dozen code letters onto the screen. By touching the four Cursor control keys in a certain sequence, he brought the green indicator line to the top of the column. Phil opened a copy of the latest inspector's report from Sierra Canyon. The readings had been taken three weeks earlier, when the surface of the reservoir was still five feet below the lip of the spillway at the crest of the dam. With his left hand holding the report open and his right working the keyboard, he entered a number after each of the letters on the screen. When the column was completed, another appeared.

Thirty minutes later, all of the available data had been fed into the system. Phil instructed the computer to make estimates of the dam's condition under his "best case" assumptions. Four minutes later, columns of figures appeared relating to ten-thousand-cubic-yard blocks of the dam. Since there were ninety million cubic yards of material in the dam, there were nine thousand coded blocks, but the instructions were such that only those with an above-normal seepage, pressure, settlement, or shift were identified. Twenty blocks came on the screen under the heading "Exceed Values Predicted in Design." Five were labeled "Critical." "Conduct Visual Inspection," the computer suggested. Touching another sequence of keys brought to the screen code letters for the dam cross-sections containing the critical blocks.

Phil pursed his lips and shook his head, wondering if he should junk the program and start from scratch. Apparently it was even more skewed than before. First he wanted to see just how far off it was. He asked the computer to calculate the "worst case." This time forty-seven blocks appeared under the "Exceed Values" heading, and twelve were called "Critical." The characters faded and were replaced with the command "Take Immediate Action." Phil asked for successive displays of the critical cross-sections. As the triangular images came on the screen, dotted lines moved from right to left indicating the plane of maximum weakness—in each case it was at the lowest elevation, apparently the interface between the embankment and the foundation rock.

A new message appeared on the screen: "Garbage coming out? Don't cry. Recheck garbage going in."

It was one of the phrases Phil had included in the program to relieve the tedium.

Janet greeted him cheerfully when he phoned her at work. "How is everything over at Colossal Engineering?"

"Wonderful. According to the giant brain, our finest dam is dissolving in forty-seven places at once. I'm calling to advise you to dump any shares of Colossal that might be in your portfolio."

"You know I can't afford a portfolio. I keep my shares in a drawer."

"Janet, the results are worse than before. I don't think

anything's wrong with the logic. My initial assumptions, the arbitrary coefficients, must be too pessimistic."

"I can't help you there. Until you dropped this dam on me, the biggest thing I ever analyzed was a silicon chip. Why don't you explain it to old what's-his-name—Roshek? He could probably spot the flaw in a second."

Phil laughed. "You must want to get me killed. That guy scares me to death. You should see the way he swings through here in the morning on his crutches. You can hear him coming down the hall from the elevators like something out of a monster movie. It's funny, the way everybody stops talking and starts working. That old man, I swear, can look around the room and just with a glance knock a man right off his stool."

"You've got to talk to somebody. You can't just sit there worrying about it."

"Should I call the senior partners together and tell them that according to my calculations Sierra Canyon Dam is on its way to Sacramento? They would fall on the floor laughing. They would say, 'Gee, those must be swell calculations.' I'm fresh out of college. I'm not supposed to act as if I know anything. My eyes and ears are supposed to be open and my trap shut."

"You're too bashful. You've got an ingenious program and you should feel more confident about it. Don't you have a boss you could talk to?"

"Two. One doesn't know enough about computers and the other doesn't know enough about dams. I suppose I could go to Herman Bolen, who interviewed me before I was hired. A pretty nice guy, I think, but a little on the pompous side."

"Talk to Bolen. If the dam collapses tomorrow, you don't want to have to say that you knew it was going to but were too embarrassed to mention it. Oh-oh, I've got to hang up —here comes my supervisor looking at her watch. You think you've got a movie monster at *your* place. . . ."

Phil spent the rest of the morning as well as his lunch

break trying to summon up enough courage to ask Bolen's secretary to make an appointment. Twice he put his hand on his desk phone and withdrew it in the face of dreadful visions. "Are you crazy?" Bolen might rage at him. "I have better things to do than talk to children about their hallucinations. Do you seriously think I give a good goddamn about your old school project?" No, Phil corrected himself, Bolen wasn't the type to rage. He was more likely to belittle him with paternalism. "Your little computer program is very nice. You should look at it again in a few years when you've had some experience. Now if you'll excuse me, I'm expecting the Chancellor of West Germany." Another possibility was that Bolen would fire him on the spot for wasting valuable computer time and for not devoting a hundred percent of his attention to his assigned work. He certainly didn't want to risk losing his job.

Phil was part of a four-man team designing a rock-fill dam for an agricultural development in Brazil. Most of his time was spent double-checking the drawings and computations of others, which was educational and to which he didn't object. He was sure that if he applied himself and avoided serious mistakes he would be given more responsibility and original work to do. Already there was a possibility that he would be asked to accompany the team leader on a trip to the jobsite later in the year. A junket to Brazil! There would have been no chance of that had he taken his father's advice and joined one of Wichita's small consulting firms. He would be stuck laying out sewer connections for tract homes and hoping for a driveway design job as a change of pace. He was glad he had decided to take a crack at a big firm in California. As the days went by, the danger receded that he would make a fool of himself and have to slink back home in disgrace. Quit worrying, he scolded himself. You've got a good brain, a decent education, and a willingness to work. Bolen is the type who puts a high value on things like that. You're not nearly as tongue-tied as you used to be. So *what* if you look too young to be taken seriously? Time would correct that condition.

He put his hand on the phone again. Bolen was nothing to fear. He might be impressed with a new employee who looked beyond his immediate assignment, and would think of him when a promotion was to be made. Phil thought of the various pieces of advice his father had given him on how to succeed in the business world. Present yourself as a person who solves problems rather than causes them, but if you have a problem you can't solve, take it to someone who can, and make sure your facts are right. Phil frowned. His facts were three weeks old. He'd better call the dam and get the latest meter readings. Another thing his father believed was that the higher a person is on the ladder the easier he is to deal with. Bolen was certainly high enough: the second rung from the top.

Phil picked up the phone and put in a call to Sierra Canyon.

Herman Bolen had the second largest and second best equipped office in the company. There was all-wool carpeting, a private bathroom, and floor-to-ceiling walnut paneling—the real McCoy, not plastic or veneer. The left side of his desk resembled the instrument panel of his private plane. At the touch of a button he could summon his secretary, ring fifty phones around the world, get a weather forecast or a stock quote, rotate the louvers outside the windows, light a cigar, heat a cup of coffee, or manipulate numbers in every manner known to mathematics.

He didn't mind being number two when number one was Theodore Roshek. Roshek was a brilliant engineer with an inhuman capacity for work; he deserved his prestige and his larger share of the profits. Herman Bolen wasn't envious at all. He was, in fact, grateful to the older man. If Roshek hadn't taken a chance on him years ago, he would probably still be lost in the Bureau of Reclamation labyrinth, a federal drudge nobody ever heard of. As it was, thanks to Roshek, his own hard work, and a run of luck in the form of illnesses that had struck down rivals inside the firm, he was now enjoying considerable power and prestige. He was making more than he ever dreamed he would—more than a hundred thousand dollars after taxes in the previous year. He had played a role in some of the twentieth century's most notable engineering achievements, as could be gathered from the framed photographs and artist's renderings on the walls: Mangla Dam, the Manapouri Power Scheme, the Iraqi Integrated Refineries, the Alaska Pipeline, the Sinai Canal, Sierra Canyon Dam.

He worked well with Roshek. Roshek could turn on the charm when he had to, but his normal manner was harsh and cutting. Bolen's was soft and fatherly. He smoothed the feathers that Roshek ruffled. Not that life was perfect. Bolen mourned the retreat of his hair and the advance of his waistline. His body, pear-shaped and high in fat content, was gaining weight relentlessly—the current rate, according to his desk-top calculator, was approximately 0.897 pounds per month. *Reading* about exercising and dieting was, obviously, not enough. He touched a button. Instantly appearing on a small glass screen was the time to a hundredth of a second in twelve time zones. In Los Angeles it was 5:06.34 P.M. Time to call it a day.

There was a light knock on his door, followed by the gray head of his secretary. "Mr. Kramer is here to see you," she said.

"Who?"

"Mr. Kramer, the young man from downstairs. He asked early this afternoon for an appointment. Tall, with the reddish hair? The hydro design section? Computers?"

"Oh, oh, oh, yes. Send him in."

For some preposterous reason he thought she meant that Jack Kramer, the old-time tennis pro, was in the outer office. He had once seen Kramer play a very fine match against Pancho Segura . . . good grief, over thirty years ago! *Phil* Kramer was the lad who had just come aboard. Bolen had interviewed him himself, recruited him, recommended that he be hired. Likable young fellow, and well mannered. Presentable. Bright future if he applied himself. Just the kind of raw material that Bolen, Roshek & Benedetz was looking for. *Bolen,* Roshek & Benedetz? *Roshek,* Bolen & Benedetz . . .

Kramer was thanking him for his time with a trace of awkwardness as he sat down on the edge of a chair. "You said that if I ever had any trouble I should feel free to come to you."

Bolen smiled in a friendly fashion. The boy was nervous and had to be put at ease. "I said that and I meant it. I know how hard it is to come right out of college into a huge organization. It's a kind of cultural shock. The shock of the real world, eh? When I graduated from St. Norbert's, I enlisted in the Seabees! There was a shock for you!" He chuckled at the memory, mirth that wasn't shared by his young visitor, who sat staring at him, frowning. Bolen joined his hands and leaned forward, lowering his voice. "Now, then, what seems to be the problem? We are both engineers. If you can state the problem in specific terms, we'll solve it."

"Well, Mr. Bolen, yes, there is a problem. I think that one of the firm's structures . . . that is, according to some computer modeling I've been doing . . . Sir, I think that Sierra Canyon Dam is, or *could* be, and I might be completely wrong, probably *am* completely wrong, and I'm hoping you can show that I'm off base in thinking that the dam is . . . well, is . . . I hate to go over people's heads, but I thought before mentioning this to anybody I would talk it over with somebody who . . ."

"Mr. Kramer, just lay out the problem in an orderly manner. Sierra Canyon Dam is what?"

Phil composed his thoughts before beginning again. "In graduate school I worked out a computer program to analyze the performance of embankment dams with the goal of being able to detect conditions that might precede . . . um, failures. It's a mathematical model built up of data from ten dams on pore pressure, settlement rates, seismic response, seepage under various hydrostatic loads, and so on. There's a built-in comparison with conditions that prevail when dams fail, which I got from studying Baldwin Hills and Teton."

"I remember reading about it on your résumé. We chatted briefly about it during our interview. Nice piece of work for a student. Imaginative. But as for its *practical* value . . ." What was he working up to?

"I use a three-dimensional matrix that has been very productive in the chemical process field. Not just the *amount* of pressure, seepage, settlement, and movement in different parts of the embankment, but their *relationship* to each other, how each one affects the others, and, most important, the *rate of change* of the values as the reservoir rises."

Bolen nodded and tried to adopt an expression that would convey both sympathy and a slight impatience. "I like the general concept, but there are too many unknowns to get the solution you want. Baldwin Hills and Teton dams weren't well monitored before they failed. The trouble with your approach would lie, it seems to me, in assigning meaningful numerical values to such things as relationships and rates of change."

"I made a lot of assumptions."

"Ah . . ."

"Mr. Bolen, on my own time I've been trying my program on Sierra Canyon. What happens is that . . ." He paused. "The dam, according to the model, is not . . . is not doing too well."

Bolen shook his head and smiled faintly. "Now, really, Mr. Kramer . . ."

"It sounds ridiculous, I know, and that's how it struck me at first. When I made this appointment to see you, I was intending to ask your advice on revising the program.

But this afternoon I began to wonder if maybe I'm not onto something."

"Oh?" Bolen was beginning to regard the young engineer in a new and less flattering light. He was clever, but there was something immature about him. He seemed to lack a sense of propriety and proportion. Bolen couldn't help thinking back to the beginnings of his own career and how impossible it would have been for him to approach a senior officer with such a wild tale. Times change and not always for the better.

"I had been using readings from three weeks ago, when the lake was five feet from the top. This afternoon I used values from last Friday, May 22, when the water was eleven inches deep going over the spillway. The computer showed that . . . that . . ."

"That the dam is failing."

Phil exhaled. "All the way from the maximum transverse section to the right abutment."

While Bolen searched for a remark that was suitably sarcastic without being contemptuous, he asked how Phil got Friday's figures.

"I called the dam," Phil said.

"You *what?*"

"I called the dam and talked to the man in charge of maintenance and inspection. A Mr. Jeffers. I wanted to have all the facts I could when I saw you. The lake is higher right now than it's ever been—eleven inches deep going over the spillway."

"You called Jeffers? And told him you were with R. B. & B.?"

"Yes, sir. I asked him if there was excess seepage in Gallery D. He said the inspector hadn't mentioned anything. I asked him about the meters that weren't registering and—"

"I hope to God you didn't tell him that the dam was failing."

"No, sir. I was surprised to learn from him that in the earthquake five years ago—"

"I've heard enough." Bolen raised his voice slightly and lifted his hand for silence. He could be firm and decisive when he had to be. "This is a serious matter. Something must be done and I'm not sure what."

"Well, the spillway gates could be opened to start lowering the reservoir and a special inspection could be made of—"

"I don't mean the dam," Bolen said, practically shouting. "I mean *you!* I don't know what should be done about *you.*" Surprised at his own vehemence, he lowered his voice to a whisper. He didn't want Charlene sticking her head in again. "I hired you and so I feel a special responsibility. The failure lies with you, not with the dam."

"I was only trying to—"

"You are behaving like a partner in the firm without putting in the required twenty years of hard work. The only failure we need concern ourselves with is a loss of perspective. Have you ever even *seen* Sierra Canyon Dam? Have you ever worked on the design or construction of a dam of any kind, even in the summer months? I thought not." Bolen studied the young man, seated across from him, whose eyes were round in shock and whose cheeks were turning red. He couldn't help feeling sympathy for him. There was something affecting about his naïveté. He was sincere. He was open. He probably expected to be complimented for his efforts instead of bawled out. Kramer had talent and could become an asset if brought along properly. Bolen adopted his well-practiced soothing manner and said, "I want you to attend to the duties for which you were hired. Don't use the computers for anything not authorized by Mr. Filippi or myself. Don't mention what you've done to anybody or, I can assure you, you'll be the butt of jokes for years to come. Years from now, you and I can have a private laugh about it. Above all, don't call the site again. Leave the dam in the hands of those of us who have lived with it since the day it was conceived. You have a lot to learn, Mr. Kramer, before you can think about telling us how to run the company. All right? Agreed?"

Kramer gestured with his hands, then let them fall helplessly to his lap. "The readouts scared me," he said in a soft voice. Now he was having trouble meeting Bolen's eyes. "I still think an inspector should be sent down to Gallery D. The readings there are high by anybody's standards."

"You have the courage of your convictions, I'll give you that, even if they are wrong." Bolen waved vaguely toward the door to indicate that the meeting was over. He watched Kramer struggle to his feet like a man who had been flogged. The poor kid was obviously one of those people who couldn't hide their emotions, a trick he'd have to learn if he wanted to go very far in the engineering profession. Bolen stopped him at the door with a final comment designed to cheer him up. "I won't mention this to Mr. Roshek. He would take a dim view of one of his own employees, especially one without experience, raising doubts about a dam that happens to be one of his special favorites. This will just be between the two of us."

Kramer nodded and closed the door behind him.

Thirty minutes later, after checking the Sierra Canyon report himself, Bolen touched a button on his console. A phone rang five hundred miles away in an underground powerhouse.

"Jeffers."

"Herman Bolen. I was afraid you'd be gone for the day."

"Hello, Herman! Hey, we work day and night up here in the mountains. Not like you city slickers."

"I'll trade places with you anytime. You breathe this air for a while."

"It's a deal. You ought to pay us a visit, at least, to see the water spilling over the top. It's quite a show. Makes

Niagara look like a leaky faucet. I shot a roll of film today; I'll send you some prints if they turn out."

"Do that. Larry, did you get a call from our Mr. Kramer this afternoon?"

"Yeah, what was that about? He seemed all excited, especially when he found out that a lot of the instruments haven't worked since the quake."

"You volunteered that?"

"I sort of mentioned it in passing. I figured a man in the company would already know. I called Roshek to find out what was up, and damned if the girl didn't put my call through to him in Washington! I didn't mean to bother him there. He didn't know Kramer or what he was up to, and seemed a little pissed about the whole thing."

Bolen had been doodling on a scratch pad. The lead broke when he heard about the call to Roshek. Now he would have to try to reach the old man himself so he wouldn't think something was being hidden from him. "Thanks for getting him riled up," Bolen said. "He's difficult enough when he's happy."

Jeffers laughed. "Sorry about that. Did he call you?"

"No, but I'm sure he will. Kramer is a young engineer we just hired . . . green, right out of college. I prefer a man with a little experience, myself. We gave him a research job to do, checking some hydro stuff in our files. We didn't intend for him to start phoning around the country. God knows what kind of bill he ran up!" He chuckled to give the impression that the affair was trivial. "But in looking at some of the figures he rounded up, I see that drainage in Gallery D is a little on the high side. Wouldn't you say?"

"Up from last year, maybe, but not much. We're going to have plenty of water all year to run through the turbines, if that's what you're worried about. The reservoir isn't leaking away."

"My thought is that the dam is under maximum stress for the first time in years. A lot can be learned that would help in some other designs we're working on. I want you to do me a favor, Larry. Make a visual check of Gallery D. Personally."

Jeffers moaned. "Jesus, Herman, do you know what a drag it is to go down there? Two hundred steps! Like climbing down the stairwell of a fifteen-story building. Duncan was down there last Friday, anyway. . . ."

"I'm sure Duncan is a very fine inspector, but he can't bring your wealth of experience to the task. Go yourself, Larry, and report back to me. I don't mean a written report, just phone and describe what you see. You might as well record the instrument readings while you're at it to make sure Duncan is doing his job."

"You mean tonight? I had three Chinese engineers in here today with some guy from the State Department and they wanted to climb around on every fucking thing. I'm bushed."

"Yes, I'm afraid I mean tonight. If there is anything down below that needs attention it should be tended to right away, the reservoir elevation being what it is. If by some miracle our young Mr. Kramer has hit on something, we don't want him coming around later saying 'I told you so.' "

Jeffers sighed. "I'll check it out later. First I'm going to have some dinner and read the paper. I'll phone you tomorrow if I see anything unusual."

"Phone me in any case. I want direct confirmation."

"Okay, boss, whatever you say. Hello to the wife."

4

BARRY CLAMPETT INTRODUCED HIMSELF to Roshek and apologized for the short notice and the inconvenient hour. "When the President heard you were in town for the engineering convention" Clampett said, "he thought it would be a good idea to call you and arrange a meeting. First let me relay his regrets at his inability to be here. I'll have to speak for him."

"When the President of the United States issues an invitation," Roshek said, settling into a chair and leaning his crutches against the desk, "a man doesn't think about whether it comes at a convenient hour."

"You'd be surprised," Clampett said, "how many men there are who think about exactly that." He lit a cigarette.

It was nine o'clock and the sky was dark. Through the windows Roshek could see lights burning in other government buildings. Either the federal bureaucracy worked long hours or it forgot to turn the lights out when it went home. The Washington Monument, gleaming under floodlights, could be made out through the leaves of trees. Roshek eyed the man opposite him. Bland. Slick. An unblinking gaze that was probably taught to him by a consulting psychologist. Inoffensive and menacing at the same time. But wishy-washy at bottom, the kind of man who can't tell the difference between how he feels on an issue and how he is expected to feel.

"What's up?" Roshek asked. "I know you've been running a security check on me. Friends and neighbors have told me they've been questioned by FBI agents, those guys you apparently stamp out with cookie cutters." Clampett fit the pattern himself.

"I hope they haven't been too obtrusive."

"I just wonder if it's necessary. My firm has done a lot of design work for the military over the years. I must have every kind of clearance in the book."

"Except one. The kind required for a man who may enter the public eye."

The public eye? Roshek had heard rumors that he was being considered for an appointment, but had dismissed them as poppycock.

Clampett opened a folder on his desk. "What we need to know has little to do with national defense or patriotism. It has to do with things of a . . . of a personal nature. Things that could embarrass the Administration if unearthed by the opposition." He removed a sheet from the folder and studied it. "Theodore Richard Roshek. Born May 22, 1919. Graduated maxima cum laude MIT 1939. Worked for Bureau of Reclamation on design and construction of Shasta Dam and Fort Peck Dam. Served with distinction in World War II with the Army Engineers. Married Stella Robinson 1946. No children. Formed own consulting firm 1947, now ranked by *Engineering News-Record* as the twelfth largest in the country. Partial use of legs due to misdiagnosed polio in 1953."

"I hope you didn't pay too much for that information. Most of it is in *Who's Who in Engineering*."

Clampett smiled briefly, then asked, "Do you have a personal bank account of more than a thousand dollars in any foreign country?"

"I wish I did."

"Have you ever taken a loan from or made a loan to a person or company with connections to organized crime?"

"Of course not! What are you driving at?"

Clampett snubbed out his cigarette and fixed his gaze on the man seated across from him. "The President is exploring the advisability of forming a Department of Technology. This would require a major reorganization. The Bureau of Reclamation, the civilian functions of the Corps of Engineers, Transportation, Environment, Energy, and so on, a dozen different scientific and industrial research-funding programs, all would be put under one umbrella. The way federal funds are allocated now among competing needs is chaotic, I don't need to tell you. Setting priorities based on reason rather than politics is the underlying philosophy of the new approach. It's a philosophy the President believes voters will like. Now the key to the viability of the concept may be to present it along with the man we want to put in charge. You, Mr. Roshek, are one of a small handful of engineers and scientists being considered for the job. The title would be Secretary of Technology."

Roshek listened to the statement with growing astonishment. A Cabinet post! He had never seriously considered such a possibility. Chief Engineer of the Bureau of Reclamation, that's what he thought he was going to be offered. His voice broke slightly when he tried to reply: "I—I'm flattered, of course . . . this is quite a surprise. I'm honored that the President—"

"The proposal is still in the trial-balloon stage. Other candidates will be interviewed."

Roshek's mind was racing. Being in charge of federal grants and funding for science and technology, supervising the setting of policy and priorities would give him tremendous power. The nation would bear the stamp of his ideas and beliefs for years to come. . . .

"Your corporation," Clampett went on, "would have to be turned over to your partners for a period of time, with your shares held in trust to avoid overt conflict of interest."

"I beg your pardon? Oh, yes, of course." Bolen struck Roshek at times as a man who always finished second. Benedetz was a money man, a paper-shuffler with the outlook of a bookkeeper. But the two of them could probably be left in charge for a while without doing irreparable damage.

"Your technical qualifications are superb," Clampett said in a flat tone of voice. "You have a reputation as a man of imagination at the conceptual stage, conservatism at the execution stage. Your designs, our sources tell us, are noted for strength as well as aesthetics. These things can be sold."

"Sold?"

"To voters. To Congress. Your public image as it would be presented through the media would be of an experienced, decisive man of backbone and integrity. Now that I've met you, I would say that you could be presented as a kind of pillar of rectitude that perhaps"—here he permitted himself another small smile—"even the Washington *Post* would shrink from challenging. You see, Mr. Roshek, in matters like these image is as important as substance if you are to survive the Senate confirmation hearings. A number of people are as qualified as you. We will select the one we can most easily merchandise as ideal for the job."

As Clampett talked, Roshek considered the financial

implications. Putting his shares in the corporation in a temporary trust was a cosmetic measure that would cost him nothing. Foreign governments would love to do business with a firm whose de facto head was a key member of the United States Cabinet. When his term was over, the lines of influence he would have established would give him the inside track on military contracts beyond counting. Within five years Roshek, Bolen & Benedetz would be ranked with the biggest consulting firms in the world, right up there with Bechtel, Fluor, Parsons. . . .

"To avoid misunderstandings," Clampett said, "we see you as a gray eminence with the vision and strength of will to forge a great new division of government; then in two or three years you step down for personal reasons. We bring on a much younger man who can be presented as forward-looking, dynamic, full of fresh ideas. In the 1984 elections the new man will be immune to criticism because he will not yet have had a fair chance. You see? To reduce points of attack, a certain amount of stagecraft is required. Do you gamble, Mr. Roshek? In Las Vegas?"

"An occasional game of poker with friends. Small stakes."

"Have you ever been drunk?"

"Not since V-J Day."

"Do you visit prostitutes?"

"For God's sake . . ."

"These are the areas our great free press will dig into once your name is brought forward. We have no moral interest in your secret vices, may I make clear, unless they can't be *kept* secret."

Roshek tightened his lips, surprised that he was submitting himself to such a line of questioning. He had a sudden notion to tell Clampett to shove the whole thing up his ass and the President along with it.

"I tried a whore once in my life," he said after some consideration, "between my sophomore and junior years in college. It was the worst two bucks I ever spent."

"Is your marriage solid?"

"Is my marriage solid! Now that makes me laugh! How long have I been married to Stella? A hundred and fifty years?"

"Thirty-five."

"Stella is the perfect corporate wife. She would love a few years as a Washington hostess." They hadn't slept together in four years, but Roshek couldn't see that that was any concern of Clampett's.

"Have you ever struck anyone in anger?"

"No, but a lot of people have deserved it."

Clampett closed the folder and pushed it to one side. "Is there anything else we should know about? Anything at all that might be used against us . . . and you? Think hard. There are a lot of muckrakers in the country and they never sleep."

"Is that so? I always have the feeling that they sleep too much. Let's see . . . no, I believe we've covered everything." Eleanor hadn't been mentioned. Surely the snoops had found out about her, but in case they hadn't he wasn't going to volunteer her name.

Clampett drummed his fingers several times as if waiting for a confession. He fastened his unwavering gaze on Roshek. Roshek stared back.

"In the past year," Clampett said, "you have been seeing quite a bit of a Miss Eleanor James in San Francisco."

"That's none of your business."

"It is if you want your name to remain in nomination for one of the most important positions ever created in the federal government."

"Jesus. What about you, Clampett? Do you fool around at all?"

Another small smile. "I like your spirit. Your combativeness. One of your business associates"—he gestured toward the folder—"described you as 'a tough old buzzard.' The President feels that's the kind of man we need."

"That was probably Steve Bechtel. He calls me that to

my face. All right, I'll tell you about Eleanor James. I've developed quite an interest in ballet in the last five or ten years, maybe because I can't stand up myself without falling on my face. I contribute money to the San Francisco Ballet and I know the dancers and the staff. In my opinion it's one of the best companies of its kind in the world. Eleanor James is a dancer. She wants to start her own studio in Marin County but needs financing. I've met her several times to discuss the possibility of making her a loan. End of story."

"I see. The meetings take place at such San Francisco restaurants as The Blue Fox, the St. Tropez, and La Bourgogne, followed by further discussions, no doubt of a technical nature, at her apartment that sometimes last till dawn."

"Your French needs help. Listen, this girl is the most wonderful thing that ever happened to me. I'm not giving her up."

"We are not suggesting abstinence, merely discretion. You are sixty-two, she is thirty-two. Public restaurants are hardly the place for a married man under consideration for high government office to conduct business meetings with an attractive, unmarried woman thirty years his junior. Don't you agree? All right, enough." Clampett rose and extended his hand. "I can tell the President that you will accept the nomination if it's offered? Good. You'll be hearing from us soon."

5

THE TWISTING, TWENTY-MILE-LONG groove that the Sierra Canyon River has worn through the foothills northeast of Sacramento is too narrow for most of its length for more than a county road and a loose string of cabins and cottages. Twelve miles upstream from the mouth of the canyon, the valley widens enough to accommodate the tree-lined streets of Sutterton. Before the dam, Sutterton was a quietly aging village with a population of less than a thousand. Named after John Sutter, whose sawmill a few dozen miles away was the scene of the gold strike in 1848, the town flourished and floundered under successive waves of prospectors, miners, loggers, railroad builders, and pensioners. By the 1930s it had subsided into little more than a point of departure for fishermen and hunters.

Architecturally the town offers little. There is a gargoyle on the Catholic church. The wooden tower atop City Hall is a curious example of carpenter Gothic, and the cracked bell that hangs therein was shipped around the Horn from a Belgian foundry, now defunct. Three buildings with foundations dating from the 1870s are California State Historical Landmarks, which means that their owners can be strangled in red tape should they try to upgrade them. What is now the Wagon Wheel Saloon began as a brothel where, according to a widely believed local legend that is almost certainly false, Mark Twain and Bret Harte once knocked each other's teeth out.

In the 1960s the town was assaulted by a new wave of invaders: geologists, surveyors, soil analysts, hydrographers, and civil engineers looking for the best possible site for a dam of record-breaking size. Close on their heels, as enabling legislation was enacted, permits obtained, and court challenges beaten back, came representatives of the Corps of Engineers, the Bureau of Reclamation, the Bureau of Land Management, the Department of Agriculture, the Forestry Service, the California Division of Water Resources, the State Department of Fish and Game, the California Division of Highways, and thirty-seven other local, county, regional, state, and federal agencies that claimed an interest in or jurisdiction over one part of the project or another.

Preparation of plans and specifications and supervision of construction were assigned by the owners of the project, the Combined Water Districts, to its engineering consultant, Roshek, Bolen & Benedetz, Inc. A year before the design of the dam was completed and final authorizations received from the regulatory agencies, R. B. & B. awarded two preliminary contracts that had to be started early if they were to be completed on time: the driving of a diversion tunnel to carry the river around the site and the excavation of a cavern in which the powerhouse would be built.

The fifteen-foot-diameter diversion tunnel entered the mountainside at river level and emerged four thousand feet downstream. Workmen experienced in underground drilling, blasting, and rock removal started from both ends and worked toward each other. Temporary barriers —cofferdams—of earth were built to keep the river away from the tunnel portals while work was under way. Diverting the river into the finished tunnel was a well-publicized event that was witnessed by hundreds of people from the overlooks and by thousands on Sacramento television. The feat was accomplished in September, when the river flow was seven thousand cubic feet per second, a tenth of what it reached during the annual spring flood. At a signal from a flagman, a fleet of thirty trucks and bulldozers dumped load after load of rock into the river, building the banks on each side toward each other until the channel was pinched off. The water rose quickly, but before it could overtop the barrier and wash it away, it found the opening of the diversion tunnel. Cheers were heard in the canyon when the water first entered the tunnel and again when it emerged from the downstream portal.

In the year following the award of the two-hundred-million-dollar contract for construction of the dam, the population of Sutterton doubled, and it doubled again in the second year. The newcomers were specialists in such things as heavy-equipment operation and maintenance, concrete production and placing, steel erection, and earthmoving. They were part of a nationwide fraternity of men whose skills and temperaments led them from one big construction job to another and whose children were used to being strangers in suddenly overcrowded small-town schools.

After the river was diverted, scrapers, power shovels,

loaders, and bulldozers stripped away the topsoil along the axis of the dam from one side of the canyon to the other. Exposing bedrock required excavating a trench two thousand feet long, five hundred feet wide, and a hundred and fifty feet deep. Cracks in the foundation rock were sealed by pumping grout under pressure into hundred-foot-deep drilled holes. A solid concrete core block eighty feet high and a hundred and fifty feet wide was built along the bottom of the trench. Inside the core block were drainage and inspection tunnels, access to which was by stairs leading downward from the underground powerhouse.

When foundation work was finished, the dam took shape rapidly. Fifty scrapers and trucks shuttled twenty hours a day between the site and nearby quarries and borrow pits. Impervious clay was placed in the center while earth and rock, in precisely specified zones, were placed on either side. The material was spread into foot-deep layers by bulldozers and graders and packed down by rollers.

For nearly four years the residents of Sutterton were jolted by explosions, vibrated by passing trucks, and coated with dust. Few complained. The dam was putting the town on the map, and people were crowding in with money practically falling out of their pockets. New gas stations, car lots, realty offices, souvenir shops, and trailer parks sprang up like weeds. The highway south of town eventually was lined with every fast-food franchise known to man, plus one that was invented on the spot: Dorothy's Damburgers.

A popular form of entertainment was watching construction operations from the overlooks on the hillsides, one of which was equipped with bleachers, loudspeakers, and chemical toilets. According to a statement broadcast every hour whether anyone was listening or not, the dam required placement of ninety million cubic yards of material, enough to duplicate the Pyramid of Cheops thirty times over or to fill two cereal bowls for every human being in the world.

"Although Sierra Canyon is not a concrete dam," the voice intoned, "enough concrete is required for the core block, the powerhouse foundations, the spillway, the intake and outlet works, and a highway across the top—a million cubic yards in all—to build a sidewalk from San Francisco to New York and back with enough left over to continue it to the vicinity of Milpitas. The lake that will form behind the dam will at its maximum elevation have an area equal to eighteen thousand seven hundred and seventy-five football fields.

"The chimney-like structure you see under construction directly beneath you is located just upstream from the upstream toe of the dam and will be eight hundred and forty-five feet high, with its top twenty feet above the surface of the lake. It is the ventilation-intake tower, which among other things will provide a means of emergency ingress and egress for powerhouse personnel. Inside will be a massive vertical pipe leading to the powerhouse turbines. Water will be admitted through remotely controlled gates at ten elevations.

"The Combined Water Districts hope you enjoy your visit and ask you not to throw garbage over the guardrails. Keep children and pets under control at all times. This message will repeat in fifty-five minutes or upon the insertion of a quarter."

Sidewalk superintendents in the bleachers who took their duties seriously became familiar with a certain blue pickup truck. The driver was the chief designer of the dam and the project's resident engineer, Theodore Roshek, who had taken it upon himself to make sure the contractor followed every line of fine print in the specifications. Construction crews learned that it was useless to try to cut even the smallest corner, because Roshek would wave his canes, turn red, and threaten to shut the job down. Was a small mistake already buried under the fast-growing embankment? Dig it up. Was faulty concrete poured and set? Break it out and pour it again. He was constantly on the move, either in his pickup or on foot, despite the discomfort he felt when walking over rough ground. Each week he spent three days in Los Angeles tending to the affairs of his consulting firm and four days at the dam. During those four days, it was agreed by the project's seventeen hundred and sixty workmen, he succeeded in making life miserable for everybody.

When the dam was completed, a platform draped with bunting was set up in front of City Hall and a dedication ceremony was held featuring oratory, six massed high-school bands, barbecued chicken, German potato salad, and Popsicles. Several of the speakers mentioned Roshek. The contractor's project manager said that the engineer's nit-picking and hairsplitting, his policy of never giving the contractor the benefit of the doubt, and his refusal to negotiate even trivial points had resulted in an overall loss of four million dollars for his company over the life of the job. The audience laughed. Contractors were always claiming to lose money, even when they were driving to their private planes in their Cadillacs. The laughter changed to applause when he added that the result of "that s.o.b.'s meanness" was the best-built dam in the history of the world.

The Mayor of Sutterton, an overweight, perspiring man with a penetrating voice and the largest hardware store within fifty miles, read from a script written by his wife, who had once studied journalism at Chico State. Before describing how Sutterton intended to march bravely forward into a future garnished by economic benefits, he thanked "a great engineer for his unstinting efforts. Theodore Roshek leaves behind more than a dam that is justly famous. He leaves behind more than a legacy of dedication and personal integrity. No, my friends, he leaves behind a good deal more. Those of you who have come to know him as I do realize that he navigates on what my grandfather used to call 'gimpy' legs. His labors over the past four years haven't done those gimpy legs any good. In fact, he told me this morning at breakfast that they are a hell of a lot worse than when he arrived amongst us, you should pardon my French. Now maybe you can see what he is leaving behind. Invested in the great dam that rises behind me like the very aspirations of civilization itself are not just the best years of Theodore Roshek's life, not just the essence of his audacious and unquenchable genius, but a big chunk of his health as well."

6

LAWRENCE JEFFERS WAS A HAPPY SOUL, given to whistling while he worked and talking to himself. Chief of Maintenance at Sierra Canyon Dam was a job that suited him perfectly. He wasn't stuck in an office where his personal habits would drive other people crazy. He was alone most of the time, talking and whistling to electrical equipment and uncomplaining trees. He loved the friendly foothills of the Mother Lode country, he loved fishing in the lake behind the dam from the houseboat he had built himself, and, yes, he loved the dam. His boat was *The Blonde Beauty,* which is what he called his only daughter, Julie. In two weeks he would join the girl's mother, whom he hadn't seen in the two years since their separation, to watch their beautiful daughter graduate from college. It would be a ceremony he was sure would make him cry. He hated to see a grown man cry, especially when it was himself, but tears, of late, had a way of leaking out whether he wanted them to or not.

It was after 10 P.M. when Jeffers carefully nosed his car into the powerhouse access tunnel at the foot of the dam. Lights strung on the utility lines on each side outlined the constant left curvature of the roadway as it descended into the mountainside. Jeffers honked his horn every few seconds in case a vehicle was coming up the slope, but at this hour a control-room engineer and possibly one technician were likely the only ones on duty. He would say hello to them on the way out, but first he wanted to get the damned trip to Gallery D over and done with.

Three hundred feet from the portal, the tunnel opened into the Sierra Canyon powerhouse, a cavern carved out of solid rock that was big enough—in the words of the leaflet that was handed out to tourists—to house the State Capitol Building. Jeffers didn't drive onto the generator deck, but rather turned his car down a steep ramp that led to the floor below. He had a lot of walking to do, and wanted to get as close as he could to the drainage galleries. At the bottom his headlights fell on the six massive turbines, each one taking the thrust of three thousand cubic feet of water per second. At the center of each was a constantly rotating three-foot-diameter steel shaft that led to a generator one floor above. The generators turned out a hundred and forty thousand kilowatts each, and together could meet the peak demands of a city of more than a million people. The specific facts came readily to Jeffers's mind—he had been reciting them for years to visitors ranging from Senators to busloads of school kids.

Above the sound of his engine as he drove slowly across the steel decking alongside the turbines, he could hear the muffled thunder of the torrents hurtling through the penstocks, spinning the blades of the turbines, and surging through the tailrace tunnel to the river below the dam. There was an electrical hum as well, but so perfectly were the massive rotors balanced there was no detectable vibration.

He parked behind the sixth turbine at the end of the chamber, put on his mud-splattered hard hat, went up a flight of steel steps and pulled open a steel door marked "DANGER, NO ADMITTANCE." Inside was a rack of flashlights. He picked one, checked to make sure it worked, and set out through an eight-foot-diameter tunnel that seemed to recede into infinity. The sixty-watt bulbs at twenty-foot intervals on the crown might have been enough for a young man who didn't need glasses, but not for Jeffers. He kept his flashlight on, and the beam danced ahead of him as he walked. Thank God he had worn his boots, he thought, for there was water everywhere, seeping through hairline cracks in the concrete tunnel lining, falling in misty veils from construction joints, running freely out of drainage holes drilled through the concrete to keep pressure from building up. The trough alongside the walkway was full of water running swiftly toward the next catch basin, where pumps would lift it into the dam's network of drainage pipes for discharge downstream. Jeffers pulled his jacket tightly around him and fastened the top two buttons; the stale air was cold as well as damp.

Soon he was so far from the powerhouse he could no longer hear the electrical hum of the generators. The only sounds were the soft dripping and trickling of seepage water and his own footsteps. Now and then he stopped and cast his beam on a dial or down a side passage. The side passages turned the drainage galleries into a maze, where in case of a power failure a man without a flashlight would have a terrible time finding his way out. It had happened once to Chuck Duncan, who spent two nightmarish hours groping his way through blackness.

Jeffers didn't give a thought to the lake over his head, a lake that constantly probed for points of weakness in the dam that blocked the canyon, that tried to find ways through it, around it, and under it, that pushed against it relentlessly and with crushing force in an effort to push it downstream, to roll it over, and to split it apart. Neither did he worry about the water that was percolating into the tunnel on every side. All dams leaked, and Sierra Canyon was only slightly wetter than others of comparable size. Seepage water was no threat to safety . . . unless it suddenly increased, or was muddy, or was coming in under pressure. It was simply a nuisance that had to be pumped or drained away. It represented an economic loss as well—water that leaked out of a reservoir was water that couldn't be sent through a turbine to generate electricity.

What Jeffers was thinking about was an article he had read in the Sacramento *Bee* during dinner about electric cars. Oh, how the public loved the idea of electric cars—or was it only the newspapers? Drive an electric car a hundred miles at forty miles an hour, then plug it in for twelve hours. While you sit on a curb and read a book! Yes, but it doesn't pollute the air, the posy-pluckers say. Like hell it doesn't! To recharge it, there has to be a generating plant somewhere burning all that nice Arab oil. What you're doing with electric cars is moving the pollution from tailpipes to a smokestack. In the meantime you waste a whole shitpot full of energy lugging those heavy fucking batteries around. God, people can be stupid.

The tunnel took a sharp bend downward. Jeffers stood at the top of the long flight of stairs and probed ahead with his flashlight. Two hundred steps without a single landing to break the monotony, steps that merged at a distant point far below with the overhead lights and the gray tunnel walls. "Let's go," he muttered, beginning the descent, "you need the exercise."

California was headed for a terrible energy crunch, Jeffers said to himself, imagining a microphone in front of him, and not ten years down the pike, either. Right now!

The state needs more nukes, no two ways about it. And here was our loony Governor making love to solar. Solar! Jesus Christ! Solar might be all right to heat a few swimming pools, but what California needs is *power!* Lots of power! Nukes are the only way to go and to hell with Jane Fonda. Here was the President of the United States—*the President of the United States!*—wanting more nukes and a snot-nose of a rich-bitch actress not wanting any, and what happens? No nukes! The world is standing on its head and the public is paying the price.

He stopped and examined the tunnel walls, streaked where seepage flows had left mineral deposits. The top of a fuse box was carrying a four-inch-deep buildup of rust-colored sludge. He turned and resumed the downward trek. A soreness was beginning to grow in his upper legs. The climb back out was going to be murder.

"Hydro power is best, you don't have to be a genius to see that." He talked out loud to dispel a feeling of isolation. Around him was a sea of faces from the Chamber of Commerce and the Rotary Club, nodding in agreement. "It's cheap, it's clean, it doesn't use anything up, and it gives you flood control as well as water for irrigation and recreation. So why aren't we building a hundred dams at this point in time? I'll tell you why, my friends, my fellow Americans. Because the fucking Sierra Club and the fucking Friends of the Earth and the fucking Environmental Defense Fund don't want us to, that's why. Don't flood the valley, they say, crying tears as big as horse turds as they build summer homes along the river. Why not? If we don't flood the valley, nature will do it herself every year. Don't spoil the wild river, which the elitist snobs might someday want to look at and write a poem about. Now, my friends, I like wild rivers. I do! But I like electricity, too. And I hate Arabs. Look out for the snail darter, an endangered species, and the three-toed wart frog, and some other fucking thing nobody but a Harvard bone dome ever heard of. What is more important, snails and frogs . . . or people? That, ladies and gentlemen, is the choice that must be made."

He had reached the bottom. He looked at his boots and saw that he was standing in six inches of water. Jesus, why hadn't Duncan reported this? There must be a pump out of commission. In a side chamber were three electric pumps, and two of them weren't working. Jeffers opened the metal door of an electrical wall box. Two circuit breakers had tripped and cut the current. Probably overheated, he reasoned as he clicked them back into position and heard the motors hum to life. They have to work around the clock when the lake is high; maybe a couple of more should be put in. Anyway, the gallery should be dry again in a day or two . . . unless water was coming in faster than he realized. He pushed deeper into the tunnel toward a bank of instruments fifty feet farther along.

He imagined himself surrounded by reporters who bent their heads and scribbled on pads as he spoke. He used a loud voice and gestured broadly to emphasize his points. "Take Earl Warren Lake. Every weekend people come in droves in their campers, gas guzzlers, RVs, and powerboats as if there is no tomorrow. Where the hell do they think the fuel is coming from—the tooth fairy? Without nukes and hydro we need that fuel to generate electricity, but they have bumper stickers like 'No More Nukes' and 'Block Auburn Dam' and then they break out the aluminum tent poles and dig caviar sandwiches out of aluminum foil. Don't they realize that aluminum is like solid electricity? Ladies and gentlemen of the press, what the fuck are the schools teaching?"

He stopped before an array of dials, positioned the flashlight so the beam helped light them up, and began jotting numbers into a notebook. Water was falling from the crown of the tunnel almost like rain, and he had to give some attention to where he held the notebook to keep it from getting drenched. He noticed a piece of plywood that Duncan must have jammed behind several pipes to shelter some of the meters and provide a dry place to stand. There was a hell of a lot of water coming in, Jeffers had to admit, and several of the readings were higher than he ever remembered seeing them. Some new cracks must have opened up—another grouting operation might be needed to seal them.

Fully a third of the meters were out of order, most of them victims of the earthquake five years earlier. The plastic tubes that led to sensors in the embankment had been pinched off or split by settlement, or the meters themselves had corroded, been mucked up by mineral deposits, or just plain worn out. Some of them never worked in the first place, or gave readings that couldn't be trusted. What a waste of the fucking taxpayers' money! He smiled at the thought of the kid who called from Los Angeles and how excited he got when he found out that the monitoring system wasn't as neat and clean as it was when the dam was built. As if a few meters on the fritz meant something. He acted as if he had stumbled onto some big deal! In the old days, Jeffers thought, we didn't need piezometers and strain gauges and stress cells and all the rest of that shit, and the dams we built then are still standing all over the country like so many Rocks of Gibraltar. Sorry, sonny, but Sierra Canyon Dam ain't going nowhere.

Sure was wet, though. Duncan should have said something. The trouble with Duncan is that he went too much by the book. Fill in the numbers, that's all he cared about, and never mind what they meant. If a boat full of fishermen somehow got sucked into one of these tunnels Duncan probably would ignore it if there wasn't a blank for it on his form. Awful wet. It was going to be interesting to see what the situation was at the end of Gallery D. If it was as bad in there as it was here, he would have to tell Bolen that corrective measures should be taken.

He tried to open the Gallery D door. The knob wouldn't turn.

"Ralph Nader," he announced to the gloom. "Oh, God, don't get me started on him. That sanctimonious pisspot really drives me wild." He dried his hands with his handkerchief. "Saint Ralph. Always looking out for the other guy, never for himself. It doesn't make sense. It isn't human. He must have an angle."

He grabbed the knob with both hands and applied his full strength to it. By hunching his shoulders and squeezing with all his might, he managed to turn the knob slowly all the way to the right.

"You . . . can . . . be . . . sure," he said, straining, "that good old Mr. Nader . . . is looking out . . . for . . . number . . . one—"

The steel door exploded open with the force of a cannon, sending Jeffers sprawling backward to the floor. Instantly tons of water landed on him, rolling him over and sweeping him down the tunnel in a flood of wild brown water. Over and over he tumbled, groping desperately for something to grab on to, his knees and elbows and head knocking against the walkway and walls as the boiling torrent rushed over him. With growing speed the water leaped two hundred feet down the bore until it struck the concrete stairs. A wave surged fifty feet up the slope before washing back down. Jeffers, unconscious and three feet below the surface, opened his mouth spasmodically and inhaled. . . .

On a rocky slope twenty miles away, far above the timberline on a ridge of the Sierra Nevadas and under a blinding sun, a drop of water had formed from melting snow. Down the slope it ran, joining with a million others to form a shimmering sheet on an immense tilted slab of granite, then into a freshet coursing between two shoulders of the mountain; gathering strength, fed by a hundred tiny tributaries, the freshet became a brook, entering the upper forests over rapids and waterfalls lined by wild flowers and green meadows. A growing stream, swollen with spring rains and a melting snowpack, rushing down the mountain, surging over boulders and around enormous logs, carrying a certain drop of water, adding its energy to Middle Reno Creek, from whose rippling surface were reflected the clouds of the sky and the pines. Down, a powerful river, crashing over granite ledges and through a dozen secret canyons, until, in one of the arms of Earl Warren Lake, in deep green water, its fury disappeared.

A single drop of water, now an infinitesimal part of a lake with a shoreline two hundred miles long, a surface area of twenty thousand acres, and a volume of more than a cubic mile, was almost imperceptibly drawn toward the intake gates of the Sierra Canyon powerhouse ten miles away—a drop of water sometimes so deep it touched the rocky bottom, sometimes so close to the surface it was caught by the propellers of powerboats and tossed into the sunlight. At the dam it was swung in an eddy away from the intake gates to the right, where six hundred feet below the surface it entered the graded rock and gravel of the upstream embankment zones. Forced by the pressure of the lake it found its way to the impervious face of the clay core, then down to the foundation rock, into a sliver-like fissure, through a twisting passageway, along the lower edge of the concrete core block, and into a hairline crack. A single drop of water entered drainage Gallery D, hung for a moment from the crown before dropping to the surface of the accumulated seepage that nearly filled the tunnel, then shot forward when the door burst open.

A minute later a particular drop of water, after three weeks of constant motion, came to rest at last . . . in the lungs of Lawrence Jeffers.

7

THEODORE ROSHEK REMOVED TWO FOLDED newspaper clippings from his breast pockets and flicked on the overhead light of the White House limousine that was returning him to his hotel. The public-relations man at the convention had handed them to him earlier, and this was his first chance to take a look at them.

ENGINEER CALLS FOR
MORE SCIENCE EDUCATION
IN CONVENTION ADDRESS

(Special to the *New York Times*)

Washington D.C.—Delegates to the national convention of the American Society of Civil Engineers heard the nation's colleges called upon to add more science courses to their liberal arts curricula.

Theodore Roshek of Los Angeles, president of an international engineering firm and incoming president of the 77,000-member, 129-year-old technical society, made the plea at the convention's opening session on Tuesday.

"Engineers and scientists," Roshek said, "are commonly supposed to be too narrowly educated. In fact, it is the liberal arts graduates who suffer that handicap. Many universities permit arts students to escape all science courses after the freshman year. Men and women are getting diplomas and thinking of themselves as educated with only the dimmest understanding of the technological society in which they will spend their lives. They don't even know how their kitchen appliances work, much less the electrical, water supply, sewerage and fuel delivery systems upon which their lives depend.

"Ask the average liberal arts graduate how his car works and you will get an explanation suitable only for use by comedians.

"Students who are never exposed effectively to the drama of science, to the challenge of scientific work, to the power and pleasure of mathematics are being tragically shortchanged by this nation's educational system. The nation is being shortchanged as well."

Roshek, 62, also urged his listeners to take a more active role in local, state, and national politics, pointing out that the great majority of political decisions involve technical matters.

"Engineers," Roshek said, "can no longer afford to be only servants of the public. We must strive to play leadership roles as well. If we don't step forward to help make the decisions that affect the future of the greatest technological power the world has ever seen, then people less qualified will do it for us, as they have been.

"This nation is too important to freedom, democ-

> racy and peace to be left entirely in the hands of lawyers."
>
> Following the keynote address, delegates attended a wide variety of technical sessions. . . .

The second clipping was an editorial from that morning's edition of the Washington *Star:*

> AN OLD-FASHIONED KIND OF MAN
>
> Theodore Roshek uses crutches to cross a room and for longer trips a wheelchair. But save your sympathy. He regards his polio-damaged legs as merely "a damned nuisance" rather than as an excuse to "slow down or sit on the porch swing." He has ignored the damned nuisance in the course of building one of the world's great engineering firms. The bridges, dams and buildings that bear his imprint are known for their strength as well as their beauty—it's as if he were striving for structures that lack the mortality he must be reminded of every time he moves.
>
> He has a direct manner that is refreshing in these days of federalese, gobbledegook and psychobabble. He'll tell you what's right and wrong and how people should act for the good of all.
>
> An old-fashioned kind of man.
>
> Rumor has it that he's in line for a government appointment. Last week Jack Anderson guessed that Theodore Roshek would be the next Secretary of the Interior.
>
> We hope the Administration has the wisdom to ask him.
>
> If asked, we hope he serves.

The limousine driver refused Roshek's offer of a five-dollar bill, but the hotel doorman accepted it with a grin. Inside the lobby an alert bell captain was at his service with a wheelchair. Good old Jack Anderson, Roshek thought as he was trundled into an elevator, wrong again.

Not Secretary of the tired old Interior, but of a brand new department, one Anderson apparently hadn't yet got wind of. Roshek had to smile at the pop psychology in the *Star* editorial. That business about his trying to compensate in his designs for his own physical deficiencies—he'd heard that before. People who believed it had simply never looked at the record. If they did, they'd find out that he had *never* compromised on safety for the sake of economy, not even when he was young and his legs were as strong as anyone's. The new attempts to save a few yards of concrete and a few tons of steel by endlessly "refining" the design with the aid of computers, the pressure to lower long-established safety factors, were not for him. Maybe his structures did cost more. Maybe they were, strictly speaking, overdesigned in the sense that they were built to standards higher than those in accepted industry practice. Fine. If you wanted a cheap dam, a cheap tunnel, a cheap airport, get somebody else. That's why he enjoyed doing business with the Arabs—they had the money to do things right.

"Here we are, sir."

Roshek struggled to his feet and arranged himself solidly on his crutches. The bell captain opened the door and handed him his key.

"Thank you," Roshek said, fishing a ten-dollar bill out of his pocket. "Here. Go buy yourself a new taxi whistle."

Roshek crossed to the far side of the room and sat down on the bed facing the windows. If he had glanced into the adjoining room of his suite, he would have seen a line of light under the bathroom door. He had accompanied his wife to the airport earlier in the evening, and assumed she was well on her way to Los Angeles. She had planned to stay with him in Washington until the end of the week, but that morning, with uncharacteristic suddenness, decided to return to California on the next available plane. She didn't explain why. Roshek noticed that she was unusually restless and withdrawn, and suggested that she should consider doing what she had often talked about, have a complete checkup at the Mayo Clinic. For some reason the remark had greatly irritated her, and had made her behave as if she could hardly wait to be out of his sight.

Roshek put the newspaper clippings on the bedside table and picked up the phone, shaking his head at the impossibility of understanding his wife. There were advantages in having her gone. One was the absence of tension in the air. Another was that he could call Eleanor from the comfort of his room instead of from a booth in the lobby. There were things he could discuss with his wife, however, that Eleanor seemed totally uninterested in. His work, for example. Were his structures more pleasing to the eye than those of his contemporaries? He hoped so, for graceful lines had been a goal all his working life. He was one of the first to take an architectural approach to bridge towers and overpass columns. He helped pioneer cable-supported roof design for large arenas, which brought elegance to what previously had been considered a problem in function and economics alone. He had striven many times in laying out such prosaic structures as chemical and manufacturing plants to lessen their effect on their surroundings, to keep them from assaulting the sensibilities of those who had to live with them. He had worried about visual pollution and environmental impact before the terms were coined. And he did these things before the scourge, the plague, the curse, had struck his legs, providing editorial writers with idiotic metaphors.

He placed the telephone beside him on the bed and dialed California. How happy she would be when she heard the news! He would try to tell her in a matter-of-fact way—too much excitement in his voice would be out of character. The initial euphoria, in fact, had passed, and he was beginning to consider it as a natural progression, as justice, that he should be chosen for a Cabinet post. He heard the phone ring at the other end, and he tried to imagine Eleanor walking across the room, tried to imagine the silken movements of her long legs, the carriage, the poise, the exquisite balance she brought to every gesture. He tried to summon up the image of her oval face, the black hair drawn tightly back, the alabaster skin, the subtle gray-green of her eyes, the smell of her, the *ambiance* of her. . . .

"Hello? Eleanor. It's Ted. How are you, my darling? Yes, I'm fine, and missing you terribly. I have some quite incredible news. To make sure you will be as happy as I am about it, I bought you something very nice I'll give you when I see you, which I hope will be next weekend. I want you to be in a proper mood for celebrating. . . ."

When she heard her husband's voice, Stella Roshek leaned toward the bathroom mirror and finished the job of redoing her makeup. Satisfied that no signs remained of the tears that had earlier reddened her eyes and streaked her cheeks, she took a deep breath and opened the door. She was going to have to confront him and she might as well do it now.

8

PHIL LIGHTLY TRACED THE OUTLINE OF Janet's body, drawing his hands across her skin from head to toe and back again. He kissed her feet, knees, furry triangle, nipples, ears, eyes, and mouth. He pressed his face into the softness of her stomach and breasts and felt her body arch with pleasure.

"Well," she said, "you seem to have lost your reticence with me anyway. With more work you may become a tolerable lover." She smiled up at him, then laughed. "Even in the candlelight I can tell you're blushing."

"The girls back at St. Jude's High School didn't talk like you."

"How did they talk?"

"They said things like 'I can't let you put your hand there because it's too much of a commitment.' "

"Really? God! I can't imagine Kansas. Nothing happens when I try to think of it."

"It's a place with lawns to be mowed and garbage to be taken out. With mothers waiting for twenty-five-year-old sons to come home from movies. Where a woman as beautiful as you would set off riots in the streets."

He kissed her.

"I'm not beautiful," she whispered. "I'm cute. I'm a cute person who likes you very much."

Phil rolled onto his back and put his hand over his eyes. "Why can't I make love to you day and night? Why does life have to include lectures from Bolen and appointments to get my ass chewed out by Roshek?"

"How did Roshek get involved? You said Bolen wasn't going to tell him. When you barged in here tonight, you were so maddened by lust—saliva running down the front of your clothes and everything—you didn't give me the details."

"Was I an animal? Sorry."

"I loved it. Before, it was like deflowering a priest."

"I called a guy named Jeffers at the dam. He called Roshek and asked who the hell I was. Roshek was damned if he knew."

Janet was moving the tip of her tongue back and forth across her lips. Phil lowered his head to touch the tip of his tongue to hers. "Roshek called Bolen?" she said.

"And told him to have me in his office the minute he gets in from the airport. From your arms to his . . . what a shock to the system that's going to be."

"It was nice, though," she said, "seducing a priest. It made me feel deliciously evil."

"I'm far from a virgin, you know. I've screwed every Miss Kansas since 1948 and most of the runners-up, along with their sisters and mothers. You are in bed with a master. Bolen called me at home after work today and lectured me on how to act with the old man. I really would like to stay in bed with you for about two weeks straight. Let's plan to do it. We could use bedpans so we wouldn't even have to go to the bathroom."

"And blindfolded eunuchs to bring food. I'll see what I can find in the yellow pages." She thought for a moment, then said: "Roshek might want to compliment you for your concern about public safety."

"What he wants to do is jump up and down on my face. Apparently he's mad as hell. Even Bolen sounded scared. He told me not to defend myself if I valued my job. I guess I'll just have to let my natural cowardice shine through."

Janet moved her hand down Phil's chest and stomach and let it rest between his legs. "I think I know why I like you so much. Because you treat me like an intellectual equal, which I am. Because you are considerate and gentle and sensuous. Because you are hung like a stud horse." She broke into peals of laughter. "You always look so shocked when I say something raunchy. You must think I'm terrible! Just because I like to talk dirty doesn't mean I *am* dirty."

"Sorry to hear that."

"Because I love sex doesn't mean my life is filled with men. I'm very particular about who I let into my laundry. *Very* particular. You have no idea how many toads I've gone out with. Until you came along, I was beginning to worry that my playpen might atrophy. Don't laugh! In the last year or so you could count the lovers I've had on the finger of one hand. As a matter of fact, the finger of one hand was about all they—"

"I don't want to hear about it! I've got enough on my mind without your other lovers."

"That's just it. There aren't any."

"Good. Okay, now I want you to do something really perverted. Let's find out how liberated you really are. I want you to hug me and pat me on the head and tell me everything is going to be all right." He nestled his head on her shoulder and closed his eyes.

"Poor *baby,*" she said, hugging him and patting his head. "Everything is going to be all *right.* That nasty old Mr. Roshek won't hurt you. If he says something that makes you cry, tell him to fuck off. You can always move in here and go on welfare."

"You are wonderful, Janet."

They made love again, then fell asleep in each other's arms.

Languorously, Eleanor James extended her arm to the bedside table and lowered the telephone receiver into its cradle. She laced her fingers across her stomach and raised her left leg in the air, foot extended, toes together, until it pointed straight at the ceiling. The skin was white and smooth. The leg was long and straight, thin but steely strong.

"It feels good to get out of my clothes and stretch after being cooped up in the car." Her voice was small, like a child's.

"I gather that was old hatchet face?"

"Yes. He thinks he's going to get some sort of government job. I wasn't really listening."

"Does he call every day?" The young man lying beside her raised his leg until it matched hers. By flexing his foot at the ankle he made the muscles ripple in his calf and thigh.

"Yes. He loves me. That's what you do when you love somebody."

Slowly she bent her left leg until the knee touched her chin while she lifted her right leg to full vertical extension. Her partner matched her movements. Their bodies were lithe and lean.

"How long are you going to string him along?"

"Until I get the money."

"Then what? Cut him off just like that?"

She watched her legs with satisfaction. "Oh, I don't know. There are advantages to being adored by a rich old man. He buys me jewelry. Did you know that he sits for hours and watches me move my legs like this? There should be more audiences like him. Change the record, would you, sweetheart? I get awfully tired of Ravel."

He strode evenly to the record player in the corner. She watched his young dancer's body through the V formed by her upraised legs. The shoulders tapered to a small waist and the buttocks were small and tight. When he returned to the bed, she noticed that he had a half erection. He lay on his side, supporting himself on one elbow. He touched her small, firm breasts. She gently closed her legs around his head.

"Why, Russell Stone," she said with a coy smile, "I do believe you want to make love again, and we've only been here an hour."

"You find that amusing?"

"Yes. Half of California thinks you're gay."

"Let them. It means that a lot of husbands trust me with their wives."

She lowered her legs and pushed herself into a sitting position. "Are you jealous of an old man?"

He shook his head. "I just don't see how you can do it. Go to bed with him, I mean. A cripple . . ."

"I want a studio of my own and he can give it to me. That's how I can do it. Besides, it's not so bad. I close my eyes and think of you. Or Baryshnikov."

"The whole thing is sick."

"I don't see him often. He can be very sweet. He's not as fierce as people think." She looked past him to the windows, to the trees, to the canyon walls on the other side of the river. "Often it's not intercourse he wants. He just wants to touch me. He treats me as if I were a fantastic work of art. He said that next to me the greatest structure he ever designed was like a mudpie."

"I give him credit for finding the key to your body: flattery."

She looked at him with round eyes. "Oh, Russell, I wouldn't talk about flattery if I were you. I've seen you burst into tears over a bad review in the *Examiner*. You shouldn't make fun of a man whose hospitality you are enjoying."

"Without his knowledge." He looked around. Through an open door he could see the enormous fireplace and the parquet floor of the living room. "It's weird, you've got to admit, making love in a room with a picture of a dam on one wall and Franklin Delano Roosevelt on the other. It's weird not hearing any traffic noises. I get the creeps when I'm not in the city."

"We're hardly roughing it. This is probably the most elaborate home in the whole valley. It even has a name, Creekwood, that's listed on county maps."

"Fancy place, all right. Still, I don't see how I'm going to stand it up here for two whole days."

Eleanor got up and slipped into a pair of jeans. "Let's take a walk by the river and fill our lungs with mountain air. You might like it."

She caught his hand and pulled him to his feet.

The river was well worth seeing. At the Sierra Canyon powerhouse ten miles upstream, the maximum amount of water was being released to generate electricity during the evening hours of peak demand. The tailrace water added to the flow pouring down the spillway sent the river close to overflowing its banks as it surged down the canyon.

It was an invigorating spectacle.

9

"WHAT HAPPENED, STELLA? DID YOU MISS the plane?"

Roshek put the phone aside and watched his wife take a chair facing the bed. Her movements were controlled, as if rehearsed, and her eyes were full of quiet strength he had never seen before. Had she overheard the whole conversation with Eleanor? He tried to suppress signs of alarm as he recalled the terms of endearment he had used and the references to a meeting and a gift.

"I let the plane take off without me," she said evenly. "I've been waiting for you in the sitting room, watching it get dark."

Roshek made an effort to smile. "You scared the daylights out of me! I didn't see you when I came in." Then with concern: "Are you all right?"

"I'm fine. Wonderful, in fact, because I have finally made a decision about something that has made me miserable for years. I came back to tell you. Suddenly I couldn't stand the thought of putting it off a minute longer. Tomorrow I am going to file for divorce."

"Oh, now, Stella, for heaven's sakes! What brought this on? You're upset about something. I'm sure if we talk about it . . ."

She shook her head with quiet conviction. "You ask what brought it on. That you should have to ask . . . I suppose that's what brought it on. You've become so self-centered, Theodore, so sunk in yourself and your work that you are completely unaware of how profoundly you've insulted me."

"Eavesdropping on my phone calls, that's what brought it on. In your mind you've twisted something innocent into—"

"Nothing about Eleanor James is innocent," she cut in sharply. "Oh, yes, I've known about her from the beginning. I was at those cast parties in San Francisco, remember, when we first met her. I saw how she played up to you, how you fawned on her. For months you talked about her and found excuses to make trips to San Francisco. Then suddenly you stopped the talking, but not the trips. I can pinpoint almost to the day when your interest in her became more than . . . paternal. More than artistic." She turned away and fought to retain control.

Roshek tightened his lips, then said, "It's on an assumption like that that you want to end a marriage that has lasted—"

"You've been seen together!" she said, facing him and speaking with a harshness in her voice. "Friends have told me how a gray-haired old man is making a fool of himself over a gold digger half his age! No, no, don't tell me she's not a gold digger. You'd have to be blind not to see it. Don't tell me how innocent you are. I heard you on the phone. I'm not deaf. I'm not stupid."

It would be worse than futile, Roshek realized, to try to defend Eleanor or himself—the effort might send Stella into the lobby in hysterics. But he would have to do something to change her mind about a divorce, at least delay the filing until after the appointment and the Senate confirmation hearings. A divorce action would hardly make his candidacy more attractive. Clampett had specifically asked if his marriage was solid. Then there were the financial consequences should Stella claim as her share of community property half of his interest in the corporation.

"Maybe I have been making a fool of myself," he forced himself to say. "I suppose it is ridiculous of me to think that a young woman like Eleanor James could find anything attractive about . . . well, about a cripple. But even if she did, Stella, it wouldn't pose any threat to *us*. My feelings for her don't match my feeling for *you*."

She waved her hand and made a sound of contempt. "You have no feelings for me. Not as a person. Not as a wife. I'm somebody you practice speeches on at breakfast. I'm your social secretary. I cater your business dinners. You think of me as another one of your employees, that's all. Well, Theodore, employees can quit. They can quit and take their severance pay and try to build a life with less misery in it. That's exactly what I'm going to do."

"You are getting all worked up over nothing. . . ."

She laughed bitterly. "You know one of the things I'm looking forward to? Not having to listen to you say things like 'You are getting all worked up over nothing.' "

"But it's true in this case! Eleanor James means nothing to me compared to you! Absolutely nothing! I'm sorry I let myself slip into a childish infatuation. I'm sorry I've been so insensitive and thoughtless. I'll change. I'll never see her again if that's what you want. A divorce? Surely we haven't come to that. Not after all we've been through together."

Clampett had warned him that he was being indiscreet in his meetings with Eleanor, and he was obviously right. For the next few months he was going to have to be very careful. Restaurants and theaters in San Francisco were out. There were remote resorts where they could meet. There was Europe and South America. He looked at his wife, who sat facing him with unwavering composure. The possibility that she would yield to tears was plainly remote.

"Even if I believed you could change, it would make no difference. Eleanor James is only part of the problem. I want a divorce mainly because you . . . because you no longer want me as a woman."

"That's not true!"

"It is true. Look at me. Am I unattractive? I'm fifty-four years old. Everyone tells me, you have told me yourself, that I look ten years younger. I still get admiring glances from men."

"You are a very handsome woman, Stella." A very handsome woman who could get a court order freezing community property, thus destroying the corporation's financial flexibility. It could take years to assess the worth of a firm involved in dozens of joint ventures around the world. A team of lawyers could make a career of the case. "I haven't been paying as much attention to you as you deserve. I've been working too hard, trying to lift the firm into the greatness we seem close to achieving. The success we've been having, Stella, the fast growth, it's a kind of vindication of everything I believe in. Eleanor has distracted me, too, made me behave, I can see it now, like a fool. Have I made you feel as though I don't want you as a woman? Please, *please* forgive me. Come, sit beside me on the bed. . . ."

"No, Theodore, you can't manipulate me anymore. It's

over. Nothing you say can make me forget the pain you've given me for four long years. Not once in four years have you touched me or shown me the slightest sign of tenderness. I can't forgive you. I can't forget it."

Roshek sighed. "A man can't be expected to sustain the same level of interest over three decades that he had during the honeymoon. Love might still be there, but it changes."

"Yes, it changes. It goes from something to nothing. Do you know why you lost interest in me? Don't deny that you did."

"I don't know," Roshek said, shaking his head and making a helpless gesture with his hands. "I'll make it up to you. I—"

"I know why. Because I had a hysterectomy. Yes, that is the reason."

"That's ridiculous!"

"From that moment I was incomplete in your eyes. Flawed. I have a scar . . . unobtrusive, but there it is, and when you saw it you turned away and never really looked at me again. You rejected me the way you would a structure that had been improperly designed."

"God, spare me the amateur psychology. I've had a dose of that already today."

"You began looking at other women differently—not as objects to impress and dominate and amuse, but as if you were appraising them. Like expensive cars. Oh, how your eyes lit up when Eleanor James smiled at you! No scars there, I could see you thinking. No missing parts—except perhaps for a brain and a conscience. You probably think of her the way you think of engineering designs you admire. I've heard you use the phrase a hundred times: a beautiful combination of form and function. You said that about Sacramento's new sewage treatment plant. Graceful lines, you said. Economical design. A beautiful combination of form and function. Do you tell Eleanor James she is more beautiful than any sewage plant? Is that what you whisper to her when she is caressing your wallet?" She rose and put her hand on the doorknob.

"Goddammit, Stella, sit down! We've got to talk this out."

"Don't raise your voice. It's a waste of energy. You don't frighten me anymore. You did once, did you know that? You are so decisive, so sure of yourself, so used to giving orders and holding hoops for people to jump through. I never knew quite where I was going or who I was, so I followed you and helped you pursue your goal, which, as I understand it, is to become the richest engineer who ever walked the earth. Well, I know who I am now. I am a piece of used, patched-up merchandise who feels that life isn't over yet. I know where I'm going, too: to the airport to catch a night flight. My luggage is waiting for me in Los Angeles. Goodbye."

"Close that door! A divorce is the last thing either one of us needs. Please, Stella . . ."

Roshek got to his feet and took several awkward steps toward her before his legs buckled. He went down on one knee and hung on to a chair to keep from falling to the floor. He grimaced. "I can't get up . . . help me. . . ."

She stood in the doorway looking at him sadly. "I never thought I'd see you resort to that," she said. "If you need help, I suggest you call the front desk."

When she was gone, Roshek cursed and pulled himself into the chair. He threw his head back and covered his face with his hands. She was going to ruin everything if she wasn't stopped. He needed a few months, then he didn't give a damn what she did. In his mind he ran through the names of attorneys she might turn to. In the morning he would call them and promise to make it worth their while if they stalled her. He would suggest going with her to a marriage counselor. He would offer to see a psychiatrist. He would send her flowers. She took a dozen pills a day . . . maybe she could be drugged in some way to keep her out of action long enough for him to . . .

He crawled onto the bed, his mind sifting through the alternatives. He needed time, and he vowed to get it one way or another. He pictured his wife, suddenly grown so hard and cold, totally unlike the woman he thought he knew. She had looked at him on the floor without a trace of sympathy. He rolled back and forth on the bed like a man in agony, eventually drifting into a sleep filled with terrible dreams.

10

A BATTERED GREEN VOLKSWAGEN BUG with a plastic daisy atop its aerial pulled into a parking space behind the Center for Holistic Fitness in Berkeley, California. A slightly built man with a thin beard got out and waved his arms several times in wide circles. His blue jeans were faded and tattered, and his T-shirt carried the message "DISTANCE RUNNERS DO IT LONGER." With a light step he walked around the one-story, cement-block building to the front door. He hesitated several times before going inside, once turning his back and taking several steps in the opposite direction.

The receptionist was impressed when he gave her his name.

"Dr. Dulotte is expecting you," she said with a smile. "I'll let him know you're here."

Scattered on a low table were sports, running, and health magazines. The man noticed that the cover of *Western Strider* was filled with a photograph of his face so twisted with pain that torturers might have been applying cattle prods to his genitals. "KENT SPAIN WINS AGAIN," the banner caption read. "See page 32 for his quick energy tips."

"Won't you have a seat?" the receptionist asked. "The doctor might be a few minutes."

"No, thanks. Sitting is bad for your lumbar."

He walked around the waiting room, studying framed testimonials from satisfied patients and photographs of smiling staff members. The Center for Holistic Fitness was a medical-mystical smorgasbord catering to a broad range of physical achievers and those wishing to be. Most of the customers were joggers and weekend tennis players, but there was a sprinkling of malfunctioning college and professional athletes as well. The building directory showed how far the services available spilled over the borders of the orthodox. Appointments could be made with a general practitioner, a podiatrist, an orthopedist, a nutritionist, a physical therapist, a behavioral psychologist, a life-style analyzer, a hypnotist, a naturopath, an acupuncturist, a foot reflexologist, a Buddhist priest (Mondays only), and a psychic schooled in astrology, meditation, and the reading of auras. The brainchild of David Dulotte, a doctor-businessman who was more businessman than doctor, the Center was under constant scrutiny by the appropriate divisions of the state government and the American Medical Association. Those on the staff with M.D. degrees didn't care what the A.M.A. thought, because they weren't members. They criticized it almost daily, in fact, for its lack of enthusiasm for wheat germ, biofeedback, and the vitamin B_{12} complex. B_{12} was one of the staples sold at the Center's adjoining store, which carried a bewildering array of health foods, sporting goods, and pharmaceuticals.

Dr. Dulotte was an enthusiastic, dapper, portly man with steel-rimmed glasses. He pumped Kent Spain's hand vigorously as he guided him into his office.

"Good to see you again, Kent, by golly! Have a chair!" He sat behind his cluttered desk and spread his arms. "What do you think of our little establishment?"

"It's not so little. You sure cover all the bases."

Dulotte chuckled appreciatively. "A guy walks in here with a complaint, or just some slob who wants to lose a belly, and he gets hit with everything under the sun. Something is bound to work, right? We give a patient a more complete workup than any hospital in the state, I shit you not. We do thermography, plethysmography, Doppler ultrasound, glucose tolerance, mineral analysis, every damned thing. We stare into their eyeballs—that's iridology—we slap 'em on a stress treadmill to see if they die of heart failure, and we make 'em swallow a Heidelberg capsule."

"Swallow a what?"

"A little gizmo that sends out radio signals as it travels through the gut. Don't look so amazed! Standard stuff you can get at a regular clinic if they have any imagination. But look how much farther we can go. We can calculate your biorhythms, ponder your alpha waves, teach you the lotus position, and flex your spine. We are the only place in the western states that does moxabustion. Sit down, will you? You make me nervous."

"I was sitting down in the car. Sitting down is terrible for you. Just what the hell is moxabustion?"

Dulotte clapped his hands with glee. "I love it! It's the very latest thing from ancient China. A jogger comes in with, say, a pain in the hip. Where it hurts, we put a little pile of wormwood leaves along with some secret herbs and spices—I don't know what exactly—and set it on fire! Honest to God! People say it helps! I think what happens is they get so distracted by the pain of the blister they forget about the original complaint. The research I've read on it suggests that it works best on old Chinese women who have never been exposed to anything but folk medicine. Unfortunately for us here at the Center, very few old Chinese women are into jogging."

"You're a quack, Doc. A regular Donald Duck."

"There are gray areas," Dulotte said with a shrug. "We use placebos just like establishment doctors, except ours aren't shaped like sugar pills. There was an article a while back in the *New England Journal of Medicine* that showed that the placebo is one of the most effective drugs on the market, with no side effects. Our policy here is to give the customer what he wants provided it can't be proven harmful in a court of law. What customers want these days is hooey from the Orient, so I'm importing everything I can lay my hands on. We're making so much money we are the envy of every clinic and medical corporation in the Bay Area. I'm thinking of selling franchises. I'll be the Colonel Sanders of holism."

From a cooler beside his desk Dulotte took a tall green bottle and poured two glasses of murky liquid. "Try this," he said. "Our newest item. Natural mineral water from Szechwan Province. Sold a ton of it already at ten bucks a quart. Can you imagine? Here's to your decision to turn pro! We'll make piles of money together. Bottoms up!"

Spain took a sip and made a face. "Tastes like dragon piss," he said, putting his glass down. "My decision to turn pro. That's a laugh, isn't it? A marathon runner turning pro? I'll be lucky if I make bus fare."

"You'll be surprised at how much you can make. Endorsements are getting to be big business. Of course, it depends on what you are willing to endorse."

"On the phone you said if I gave your shoes credit for winning a race you'd give me twenty-five hundred bucks, is that right? I'll do it. I'm thirty-three years old and I'm not getting any faster. I'm not good enough to make the

Olympics, so what the hell, I might as well make a few bucks while I can. God, when I think of the years I've spent trying to become a world-class runner! A lifetime. What have I got to show for it? Not a fucking thing. I can't even coach, because the colleges all want a high-school diploma at least. With twenty-five hundred I can get a better car and start looking for a job."

Dulotte smiled benignly. "Your problems are over if you do what I tell you. You are the biggest name I ever had a chance to work with. I made six grand for Frank Robutz last year and you've got twice the name he has."

"Six grand? Frank Robutz? Christ Almighty, he can't beat Orphan Annie."

"You are right. What kind of shape are you in?"

"Not the shape I was in a year ago. I'm only doing sixty miles a week. I used to do a minimum of a hundred. But I've been doing a lot of hill work. Every other day I do a double Dipsea. That's twelve miles, most of it either straight up or straight down."

"Can you win tomorrow."

"I should be able to beat a bunch of housewives and businessmen. Hobbyists."

"Tommy Ryan is in the field."

"Yeah? He can be tough. My money is on him."

"And my money is on you. Tell me, what's your best time?"

"In the marathon, two twenty-one, but I haven't come within twelve minutes of that for almost two years. I tell you, Doc, I'm going down the tubes."

"You will still be the class of the field tomorrow. Fifteen hundred fanatics sweating and panting in their cute little outfits and you are the favorite."

"Big deal."

Dulotte glanced at his watch. "It's a little after nine. At about this time tomorrow morning, you'll be crossing the finish line in front of the Sutterton City Hall. The banks are closed on Saturday, but on Monday, if you will sign a personal services contract I have ready for you, you can be in the bank of your choice with a check for ten thousand dollars. What do you say? Eh?"

"Come on, cut it out. You can't make that kind of money off me, not even if I ran naked with Bobby Riggs tied to one leg."

"Oh, yes, I can. Look, your best days are behind you. Everybody knows that. Your times are getting steadily worse. What if you were to turn in your lifetime best mark tomorrow? On a course that is a lot harder than Boston? While wearing and eating and drinking and using products made by Jog-Tech, which happens to be my Hong Kong manufacturing subsidiary? I could run a series of ads in the running journals that would bring the Ponce de Leóns swarming out of the woodwork by the thousands."

"Ponce de who?"

"León. The first guy to spend a fortune and bust his ass trying to stay young."

Kent Spain began pacing back and forth in front of Dulotte's desk. "How the hell am I going to run my best time? By prayer? By magic?"

"No. By cheating." He let the words sink in. "A little cheating never hurt anybody. I dare say it got you through two years of high school."

Spain put his hands on the desk and stared at Dulotte. "What do you mean, *cheating*?"

"I mean cheating. Nobody will get hurt. You get ten thousand bucks for starters."

Spain collapsed in a chair and blew a stream of air through pursed lips.

"If you can learn to talk," the doctor added, "you can make twice that on the lecture circuit even after I take fifteen percent."

Spain suddenly straightened up and struck the desk top with his fist. "I'll *do* it! Ten thousand! For starters! Holy shit! What's the plan?"

Dulotte unfolded a map and traced a line. "The race starts here, follows a highway, then a fire road, then a trail through a national forest. What you have to do is run five-minute miles for the first fifteen miles. Ryan and a few others will be trying for five seven or five eight."

Spain looked worried. "I'll burn myself out. I'll have to crawl the last eleven miles."

"No, you won't. Look at the map." He tapped a spot with his forefinger. "The trail comes out of the woods right here, goes across the top of Sierra Canyon Dam, and back into the woods on the other side. After that is a long stretch through heavy timber, downhill all the way. You'll be taking that on a bicycle, old buddy, catching your breath and whistling a merry tune, the breeze flowing through your kinky hair."

"A *bicycle!*"

"A bicycle. It's in the bushes waiting for you. Watch for a T-shirt tied to a limb. Make sure you are the first one to get there. There isn't another aid station until mile nineteen."

Spain was out of his chair again, pacing back and forth with lunging steps, wringing his hands as if he were trying to cleanse them of stubborn grease. "It won't work," he said. "It can't work. It'll never work. There's no *way* it can work."

"It'll work."

"If somebody clocks me at the dam, the monitor at mile nineteen will figure out later that something is haywire." You're nuts, Doc, totally out of your gourd."

"Which brings us to the real beauty of the concept. I am the monitor at mile nineteen."

Spain stopped and stared. "You?"

"Me." Dulotte resumed the tracing of a line on the map. "You'll be ten or fifteen minutes ahead of the field, and after dumping the bike you can sit down for five minutes and catch your breath."

"I hate sitting down."

"Walk, then. The course comes out of the woods here at the county fairgrounds. Trot the rest of the way as fast as you can. You'll be on a highway with people cheering you on. You will break the tape right here"—he tapped the map with triumphant finality—"in downtown Sutterton, the new champion of the Mother Lode Marathon, with a time just minutes off the world record. An amazing new lifetime best, achieved while festooned with Jog-Tech gimmicks."

Spain sank into a chair and watched the doctor empty the contents of a drawer onto the desk. There was a pair of ribbed rubber heel cups to guard against bruising and to provide "greater lift," a digital pedometer-watch, a Jog-Tech Living Jock Strap, a Michoelectronic Pulsometer that recorded pulse rate, blood pressure, temperature, and electrolytic balance. "This is the latest hardware," Dulotte said of the Pulsometer, "a hot item that goes for four hundred bucks."

Spain protested, "I can't wear all that crap! Must weigh ten pounds!"

"A little over a pound. You can manage. After the race you will say that your record-breaking performance was the result of being able to keep track of your body functions, scientifically adjusting your pace to your maximum feasible exertion rate. Of course, you will also say that you trained on our home treadmill—another four-hundred-dollar item—while drinking our vegetable-vitamin-almond consommé."

The runner lifted his upper lip in revulsion and turned away. "I feel sick," he said.

"We will make a killing. Sign here."

Thirty minutes later, the contract gone over and signed and the details of the race rehearsed, the two men shook hands, one beaming, one desolate. Dulotte raised a glass of Chinese mineral water to the marathoner, drained it, and smacked his lips. "You really ought to give this another taste, Kent," he said. "It's the best dragon piss in the world."

Just before lunch, Herman Bolen phoned Sierra Canyon and was told by an engineer in the powerhouse control room that Lawrence Jeffers had not yet made an appearance that day. He was expected at any time.

"He might have gone to Sacramento and forgot to tell us," the engineer said, trying to be helpful.

"You're probably right. Have him call me when he comes in."

"Sure will, Mr. Bolen. I'll put a note on his desk right now."

Odd, Bolen thought, walking slowly to the windows. Not like Jeffers to leave his whereabouts unknown. If he had found anything worth mentioning in the drainage galleries, surely he would have phoned late last night or early this morning before leaving for wherever he was. A trip to Sacramento—yes, that was probably it. Or a dental appointment. Still . . .

He returned to his desk and sat down, wondering if he should call the powerhouse again and order someone into the dam to look for Jeffers. He might have fallen down that accursedly long flight of concrete stairs and broken a leg or a hip so badly that he couldn't drag himself to one of the emergency phones. Or he might have had a heart attack despite his apparently robust health. In either case, Bolen would not appear in a very favorable light for having sent Jeffers into that dark hole at night.

Come, come, Bolen chided himself, you are overdramatizing the situation. If Jeffers was still inside the dam, someone at the site would have noticed his car. You would look pretty foolish if you launched a manhunt for a man who might come strolling into his office unconcernedly at any moment. Roshek would accuse you of overreacting to the fears of a young nincompoop by sending Jeffers on a wild-goose chase, then of overreacting again in mounting a search for him. "Jesus Christ, Herman," he could imagine Roshek saying, looking at him as if he were crazy, "haven't you got any sense at all?"

Best he wait a while longer and try to keep his imagination from soaring into fantasy. At the end of the afternoon, if Jeffers still hadn't reported in, he would make a few discreet inquiries.

He looked at his calendar. There was a meeting that afternoon at Southern California Edison's downtown headquarters about the plan to enlarge Sequoia Dam. If it dragged on, he would excuse himself at some point and make a phone call.

11

ALONE IN HIS OFFICE, THEODORE ROshek closed his eyes and touched his temples. For the first time in years he had a headache, a relentless headache that spread in waves from the center of his forehead. He hadn't slept well the night before in his Washington hotel room. The flight to Los Angeles had hit a stretch of rough air that made it impossible for nearly an hour to think about anything except the plane shaking itself apart. Even the limousine ride to the office was nerve-wracking, partly because of the congestion on the Harbor Freeway, partly because the driver seemed half drunk and nearly got them both killed with nonchalant lane changes.

At least he had had a small success with Stella. He phoned her from the airport and got her to agree not to see an attorney until they could discuss their problems further that night. The hardness in her voice, though, was unsettling. Further discussion was useless, she said, and he should make arrangements at once for moving out of the house. Surely he would have better luck with her face to face. He would play on her sympathies, and if that didn't work he would raise his voice, remind her of her own shortcomings, and exploit the guilt she must be feeling for walking out on a man who had given her a life of luxury. With luck he would break her down, make her fold up and cry the way he had on several previous occasions when they had argued. *He must not lose his temper.* If he shouted at her or threatened her, in view of the mood she was in now, he would lose all chance of keeping the marriage patched together.

He thought of the small gun he carried for protection in his attaché case. She knew it was there—it was at her insistence that he had started carrying it—and if their emotions boiled over one of them might make a grab for it. Unlikely, but nevertheless . . . He snapped the case open and removed the weapon from its velvet pocket, turning the cold steel over in his hand. The safety was on and it hadn't been fired since the day he bought it fifteen years earlier, but it still felt ominous and deadly. There might have been a reason for him to have such a thing at the beginning, before the days of airport security checks, when he was traveling alone to some of the most remote areas in the world, but hardly anymore. He hadn't even thought about the gun in a long time, and he half wondered if it still worked.

A red light flashed on his intercom. He depressed a small lever and heard his secretary's voice: "Mr. Bolen wants to know if you'll be going to the Southern Cal Edison conference. He's ready to leave."

Roshek put the gun in a drawer and felt glad to be rid of it. "Tell him I'll try to get there in an hour or so. After

I talk to young Kramer, I want Jules Wertheimer on the phone. Set that up, please."

He broke the connection and jotted down a list of questions he wanted to ask Wertheimer, the only lawyer he knew that he trusted completely. He was a corporate rather than a divorce lawyer, but he would be able to provide some preliminary guidance. Could Stella freeze the community property, thus depriving the company of its freedom of action? Were there enough assets in the estate to satisfy her rights without giving her any part of the company? Could assets be concealed, perhaps by preparing a second set of books or by making transfers to overseas subsidiaries? Wertheimer would have some ideas.

Thinking about his wife claiming half his share of the corporation he had spent his life creating angered him, and the more he thought about it the angrier he got. He would hang on to full control no matter what California's ridiculous divorce laws said. She could have the Beverly Hills house, the Sierra Canyon house, the cars, the furniture, the art, the stocks, the insurance, everything, but not the business. If her attorneys didn't think that was a fair division, they could go *fuck* themselves. He tightened his hands into fists. He would try his best to keep the marriage intact long enough to secure the government appointment, but once he had that nailed down Stella could do whatever she wanted, except stick her fingers into the company. That he would never allow. Never!

His secretary came on the intercom again. "Mr. Kramer is here to see you."

Phil crossed the carpeting and sat down tentatively on a leather chair in front of Roshek's massive mahogany desk. Good God, Phil thought when he saw the expression on the old man's face, he looks as if he's going to spring at my throat! What's he so mad about—that I didn't bring a cap I could twist in my hands while he bawls me out? If he tries to slap me the way Sister Mary Carmelita did in grade school for shooting spitballs, he's going to have a fight on his hands.

"You're Kramer? You look intelligent. Why don't you act it?"

"I beg your pardon?"

"Tell me if I've got this straight. You have no practical experience except for a few summers' work with the highway department in Kansas or some goddam place. You've never been involved in the design or construction of a dam. You know nothing about the subject except what you've read in books, which is worse than nothing. You've come up with a cockamamie computer model that makes you think you can sit in an office five hundred miles from a dam you've never seen and understand it better than men with lifetimes of experience who are sitting right on top of it. Is that right?"

Phil stared, speechless. Was Roshek kidding? Was he trying to be funny? "No," he managed to say, "that's not right at all."

"It isn't? What's not right about it?"

Phil crossed and uncrossed his legs. "I don't know where to begin. You've put the worst possible interpretation—"

"Furthermore, you had the audacity to call the chief maintenance engineer on the site and lead him to believe that his headquarters people think something is wrong with his dam."

"I did not! I called him only to get some current meter readings. He may have thought I sounded excited on the phone, but he wasn't looking at what my computer program was telling me."

"He doesn't *need* to look at what your computer program is telling you, and neither do the managers of ten thousand other dams. He doesn't *need* intimations from a greenhorn that he isn't doing his job properly. This company doesn't need and *I* don't need an employee casting doubts about one of our structures. We depend on two things for success: the ability to provide technical services of the highest professional quality, and the *reputation* for being able to provide them. Ruin our reputation and we are out of business, it's as simple as that. What you have been doing amounts to a whispering campaign against your own employer."

Phil waited until he was sure it was his turn to speak. Keeping his voice calm, he tried to make his point. "Mr. Roshek, I no doubt deserve some criticism for taking too much initiative. But the data clearly indicate, to me anyway, that some sort of investigation is called for."

"You're not an engineer. I hope you realize that. Not yet. Not by a long shot."

"I'm not a licensed engineer, that's true. In California you need five years' professional experience after graduation before you can apply. I have a doctorate in—"

"An engineer is more than a man with a diploma and five years' experience. True engineering can't even be taught in school, because it involves a man's personality, his willingness to consider every last detail, the way he respects the materials he works with, his sense of history and the future, and his integrity."

For Christ's sake, Phil thought, he's not listening to a word I say! He's using me to practice some sort of goddamned commencement address.

"Most important," Roshek went on, "is maturity. A sense of proportion. Judgment. A doctor wouldn't say to a patient, 'You probably don't have cancer. Then again, you might have. We'll know when we get the lab results. In the meantime, don't worry about it.' See how stupid that sounds? What you've been doing is along that line. Jeffers called me in Washington to find out what was going on."

"He did? I didn't mean to get everybody so upset. I didn't realize that a phone call would—"

"You didn't realize that you could have caused a panic?

What if word leaked out that we were worried about the safety of the nation's highest dam? A secretary overhears part of your conversation, a switchboard operator listens in, rumors start flying, newspapers pick it up, politicians demand an investigation, environmentalists charge a cover-up . . . I've seen it happen. Over nothing. Because a prematurely smart college student gets excited over drivel in a computer."

Phil felt his cheeks turning red. He knew he should simply let Roshek's tirade run its course without risking disaster by fighting back, but he felt he should put up some sort of defense. Silence would imply that he agreed with Roshek's distortions. Besides, he was getting mad. There was nothing in life he hated more than to be accused of something he didn't do.

"Sir, I didn't say to Mr. Jeffers that I thought the dam was failing. I showed my surprise that so many of the meters were out of order and that the seepage was so high. I did tell Mr. Bolen, in private, that my program indicated something was wrong. Maybe I should have discussed it with him first before calling the dam, but I wanted to make sure I had the latest figures." Phil let his voice trail off because his words were being ignored. Roshek's eyes were wandering around the room resting on the photographs of his projects, and he was reciting their names like a litany.

"Sinai, Maracaibo, San Luis, Alyeska. These tremendous developments are as sound as the day they were built." He gestured toward a glass display case in which was a realistic scale model of an earth and rock dam complete with tiny trees on the abutment slopes and a center stripe on the road across its crest. "Sierra Canyon Dam. Recognize it? Probably not, since your knowledge is confined to textbook abstractions. Not one of the structures this company has had a hand in designing has ever had the slightest question raised about its safety. Not one has suffered a failure of any kind. Engineered structures fail, yes, usually because foundation conditions aren't properly assessed. It was Karl Terzaghi, the father of modern soil mechanics, who said that when Mother Nature designed the crust of the earth, she didn't follow the specifications of the American Society of Testing and Materials."

I'm a dummy audience, that's all I am, Phil said to himself, wondering how much more he could take before boiling over.

"The structures I've designed will be in use two hundred years from now, if the civilizations of the future want them. Durability like that is a result of skill, hard work, intuition, and uncompromising insistence on top-quality work every step of the way. When a design philosophy like that is brought to bear, structures don't fail."

Did Roshek really believe that? Phil wondered. That if a skilled engineer did his best nothing could go wrong? The proposition was absurd on its face.

Roshek gazed with a kind of rapture at the display case. "Sierra Canyon Dam, about the supposed inadequacies of which you have developed such a lunatic obsession, has a design life of three hundred years. It is an engineering landmark, and not because of its height or its cost-benefit ratio."

"I don't have an obsession," Phil said quietly, "except possibly for a computer programmer I met recently."

"It represents an unprecedented effort to insure safety, from the thoroughness of the geophysical investigations right through to the ongoing system of inspection and maintenance. I insisted on the most extensive network of sensors ever implanted in a dam."

"Half of those sensors don't work anymore."

"There is a matter of justice involved, too. Of percentages. Of fairness." Roshek pushed his swivel chair away from his desk and looked at his legs. "I was struck by polio two years before the vaccine was developed that would have saved me. That's enough bad luck and injustice for one life." He looked up and seemed momentarily flustered by having become more personal than he had intended. Recovering, he glowered at Phil as if he were to blame for the indiscretion. "I've spent too much time on this already. I need to tell you just one thing. Stop concerning yourself with the dam. Is that clear? If you want to fool around with schoolboy computer models, use your own computers and your own time. That's all. You can go." He began assembling papers from his desk and placing them in his attaché case.

Phil had gradually slumped down in his chair while watching the older man's bizarre performance. If he understood the last remarks correctly, Roshek was saying that his structures could not fail because his legs already had, that there was a limit to the bad luck that could happen to any one man. This was the world-famous engineer, the paragon of logic and objectivity?

"Well?" Roshek said, eying him. "I said you can go."

Phil straightened up but did not rise. "Mr. Roshek," he said, "you've been very unfair. I thought you'd give me a minute at least to explain my actions. In my defense I could point out that—"

Roshek cut him off. "What do you mean, 'in your defense'? This is not a trial. I pay your salary and so I can tell you to do whatever I want you to do. I'm telling you to drop Sierra Canyon Dam. Your ignorance of it would fill Chavez Ravine. You've caused enough trouble and I want an end to it. Yesterday, as you may or may not know, I was sworn in as president of the American Society of Civil Engineers. You should read the Code of Ethics. Point number two is that engineers should perform services only in their areas of competence."

"I was president of the student chapter in college," Phil said half to himself, "and I know the Code of Ethics, too. Point number one is that engineers should put the safety, health, and welfare of the public above everything else."

"What? What did you say?"

Phil stood up, his cheeks hot and his heart pumping. In a louder voice he said, "I don't deserve to be shouted at and treated like a child," amazed that he was saying anything at all. "In the past few weeks I've been closer to that dam than you. It's true that extensive foundation borings were made before construction, but the earthquake five years ago might have changed everything. It's not true that none of your structures has ever been questioned—the dam leaked so badly after the quake two million dollars had to be spent to plug up the cracks. The reservoir was filled this spring fifty percent faster than you yourself recommended five years ago that it should be."

Roshek was so astounded by the outburst that he couldn't find his voice. His mouth opened and closed and his eyebrows rose high on his forehead.

Phil tore a sheet of paper from a notebook and dropped it on the desk. "Here are the latest seepage figures from Gallery D. In every case they are higher than Theodore Roshek said they should be when he wrote the original specifications. Somebody should go down there right now and take a look, because next week may be too late."

Roshek crumpled the sheet into a ball and hurled it against the wall. He found his voice, and it was loud. "I don't need you to tell me how to look after a dam. I didn't order you in here to listen to your sophomoric opinions! Your opinions are more irrelevant now than they were before, because you are fired! Get out! If you are at your desk in the morning, I'll have you arrested for trespassing!"

Phil tried to slam the door on the way out but hydraulic hinges made it impossible.

12

JANET SANDIFER COULD HARDLY RECognize the voice on the telephone. "Is that you, Phil?" she asked, smiling and frowning at the same time. "You sound funny. Is that a jukebox I hear?"

"I've been waiting for you to get back from lunch. That's a jukebox, all right. I'm at a bar on Figueroa Street doing some research. I'm trying to find out if it is possible to drink fifty bottles of beer and still hold a pool cue. Fifty bottles of *cerveza,* I guess I should say, this being a Mexican joint. Then I'm going roller skating on the freeway."

"What are you talking about?"

"They got one of those little coin-operated pool tables here, know what I mean? I'm locked into a big eight-ball shoot-out with the meanest-looking illegal alien I ever saw in my life. I'm two dollars ahead. I haven't played a game of pool in years! I must be naturally gifted."

"What about Roshek? Did you talk to him?"

"If you were here, you could hold the stakes. Roshek? You mean the distinguished engineer who has won any number of prestigious awards? Yes, I talked to him. Did I *talk* to him! I practically told him to go take a flying fuck for himself. I talked to him all right. The man is a mental case, Janet. It was the weirdest thing I've ever been through. I'm not kidding, somebody should rush him to a psychiatrist's emergency entrance. Christ, I knew he was ill-tempered, but I didn't know he was a madman. He talked about my cockamamie computer program and called me a sophomoric greenhorn who was trying to wreck his company. He said if he saw me around there again he'd arrest me for trespassing. It was unbelievable! I'll do an impression of him when I see you and you'll think I'm exaggerating. That old fart needs help! I had the seepage figures neatly printed on a sheet of paper so he could understand the situation at a glance, and you know what he did? Threw it against the wall!"

"Phil, wait a minute. Are you trying to tell me that you got yourself fired?"

"What I'm trying to tell you is that I got myself fired. I went in there expecting a mild raking over the coals. I thought I'd leave thinking Roshek was a nice guy after all. Instead, my God, he went after me as if I were some kind of ax murderer. The most unbelievable part of all was that I talked back to him and tried to defend myself. That was stupid. I mean, that was stupid. I was dealing with a crazy person and I should have kept my big mouth shut. But there I was, good old painfully shy Phil Kramer, arguing with him like the sophomore he said I was. It really got vicious at the end—that's when we started throwing quotes at each other from the ASCE Code of Ethics."

"Oh, Phil, I'm so sorry. I know how much you liked your job."

"I'll find another. Now I can say I have three weeks' experience."

"If Roshek fired you in anger, maybe he'll take you back when he cools off."

"I'll refuse! I liked the job, sure, before I met him. You should have seen him hollering at me, running sores all over his face, giant warts on his nose and hands, broken yellow teeth, steam and stench rising around him, green wax leaking out of his ears. Work for him again? Not a chance. Not even if he gave me a cost-of-living increase."

"So you're going to get drunk, is that it?"

"I'm going to become a professional pool player. A hustler going from town to town. You can be my sidekick. You set the suckers up, I'll fleece 'em. It'll be a wonderful knockabout life, Janet! Just the two of us, alone together on the open road!"

"I have a better idea. Come over tonight with some grass. I'll thaw something for dinner and later I'll pat your head."

"It's a deal."

In the middle of the afternoon, Herman Bolen excused himself from the conference room and made a phone call. Again he was told that Jeffers had not been heard from.

"Is Chuck Duncan around, by any chance?" The young inspector could be sent into the lower gallery to see if anything was amiss.

"Chuck is gone for the day," the powerhouse engineer said. "I think he's going fishing on the lake for the weekend. Should I try to track him down?"

"No, that won't be necessary. Just make sure Mr. Jeffers gives me a jingle when he gets in."

Bolen returned to the conference room and resumed his seat between Roshek and Filippi. The table was covered with drawings, maps, and economic reports, but

Bolen had a hard time keeping his mind on the subject under discussion: the cheapest way to raise Sequoia Dam. It was only three o'clock—if Larry had gone to Sacramento, forgetting his promise to call, he would hardly be back yet. In the meantime, there were more immediate problems to contend with, one of which was the lack of participation of Roshek, who after arriving an hour late had sat oddly subdued. At the moment, his eyes were closed and he was rubbing his forehead. Bolen himself had contributed little to the discussion beyond a few wise looks and noncommittal shrugs. Thank God Filippi had done his homework and was presenting alternatives well supported by facts. The complexity of his analysis had so far kept the Edison engineers from noticing that his two superiors at R. B. & B. were doing little more than filling two chairs. Roshek came to life long enough to point out that if the efficiency claims being made by Mitsubishi for its new turbine generators turned out to be realistic, it would be more than practical to add pumped-storage power generation at Sequoia, a good point that had, unfortunately, been gone over thoroughly before Roshek arrived. The Edison engineers heard him out respectfully, then went back to the problem of minimizing environmental impact during construction. There was no clay at the site, and unless a source could be found nearby, a long haul road would be necessary. In an effort to justify his hundred-dollar-an-hour consulting fee, Bolen suggested that it would be worth investigating a conveyor belt for the clay haul, especially if the borrow pit was at a higher elevation than the discharge point. He reminded the group that during the construction of the railroad fill across the Great Salt Lake a downhill conveyor equipped with generators had produced enough power to run the electric shovels doing the excavation.

At 2:00 P.M. Phil called Janet again.

"I've changed my mind," he said. "I'm not going to become a pool hustler. I'm three dollars behind and I think the dude I've been playing is a shark from Xochimilco. I'd break his thumbs if he weren't such a big bastard. Janet, I want a rain check on tonight. I'm going to drive to northern California. To the dam. On Interstate 5, I can make it in seven or eight hours. Don't try to talk me out of it. All I've got in life besides my health and your phone number is a computer program that the world's greatest engineers agree is a piece of shit. I want to see Sierra Canyon for myself. I'm going to try to get into the drainage galleries. If nothing is wrong, okay, a thousand pardons. What can they do to me for making one last effort to prove something is wrong? I'm already fired. If too much water is coming in, what will be the piece of shit then, the dam or the program? Me or Roshek?"

"I liked your first idea better."

By the time the meeting at Southern California Edison was over, traffic on the Hollywood Freeway had eased considerably. Herman Bolen had no trouble maneuvering his Mercedes 300SD into the fast lane. He would drop Roshek off at his home in Beverly Hills, then return to the office to clean up some paperwork before the weekend. One thing he would do was solve the Jeffers problem, even if it meant calling hospitals. Strapped securely into the seat beside him was Theodore Roshek. Roshek used the seat belt only when riding with Bolen, as a way of showing his disapproval of his partner's driving habits, which he thought were inappropriately flashy. "Your image usually suggests prudence and propriety," he had told Bolen on one occasion, "as it should, but when you are behind the wheel of a car you become as idiotic as the average teenager. I think you'd be happier as a test pilot than an engineer."

Bolen could have retaliated by pointing out that Roshek's image could stand a bit of improving as well. The gray felt hat he always wore made him look like something out of an old Humphrey Bogart movie. Without criticizing the hat directly, Bolen had once offered to buy him a new one. Roshek declined by saying that the hat he already had was fine. "It's an old friend as well as my good luck charm." "Don't mention good luck charms to our clients," Bolen had replied, and quite humorously, too, he thought, "because they might wish us to use devices and methods of a more rational nature."

"How did your chat with Kramer go?" Bolen asked by way of making conversation and to satisfy his curiosity. "Impressive young man, don't you think? Still a little wet behind the ears."

Roshek, preoccupied, turned his gaze back to Bolen. "The chat with Kramer? That went very well. I fired him." Noticing the dismay that came over Bolen's face, he added: "I know he was a favorite of yours, but he gave me no choice. He had the nerve to come into my office, look me straight in the eye, and tell me how to run my business. Never saw such impertinence in my life. He must have missed a spanking somewhere along the line."

Bolen looked straight ahead for a full minute before speaking. "He wasn't a favorite of mine, particularly," he said, using a casual tone. "It's just that I felt he was intelligent and serious-minded. I thought he might develop into a valuable employee. It surprises me that he said anything to anger you." He wondered if he should try to get Roshek to rescind his action, at least until the situation at the dam could be evaluated. It wasn't likely that emergency measures would have to be taken, but if they were it would be disastrous if the press learned that the one man who tried to sound an alarm was fired for his trouble. "Was it really necessary to let him go?" he ventured. "Seems a bit extreme." Bolen tensed himself for a possible outburst. In the last few years, the merest hint that he felt one of Roshek's decisions was less than perfect sometimes provoked a volcanic reaction.

"It was either that," Roshek replied calmly, "or turning

the company over to him to run his way while I went back to a drafting board. Maybe I was a little hard on him. He started in on his ridiculous computer model and it was more than I could stomach. I told him to keep his nose out of what he didn't understand and what didn't concern him, and before I knew it he was raising his voice to me, which wasn't too smart in his position. He should have known I wouldn't tolerate that. I had to shout at him to make myself heard. I haven't shouted at anybody in years —I mean really shouted. I almost enjoyed it."

Roshek squirmed in discomfort as Bolen, with a burst of acceleration, knifed into a gap that had formed in an adjacent lane. "Herman, would you mind cutting our speed forty or fifty percent? You aren't Paul Newman. A glance in the mirror will convince you of that."

Bolen lifted his foot from the accelerator, worked his way over to the right lane, and took the Santa Monica Boulevard exit westbound. Both men lowered visors to block the rays of a setting sun.

"I rather liked Kramer's enthusiasm," Bolen said. "Dismissing him could backfire. What I'm thinking of is—"

"We have more important matters to discuss. You and Calvin might have to run the business for the next few years."

With that abrupt announcement, Roshek began a summary of his meeting with the President's aide. He brushed aside Bolen's attempts at congratulations by pointing out that the appointment was yet to be made. "Other people are being considered. I do believe I have the inside track. There must not be any negative publicity about the firm. There must not be a juicy divorce between Stella and me, which is my main problem at the moment."

"Good heavens, Theodore! Stella wants a divorce?"

"Keep your eyes on the road. Yes, she dumped that on me last night in Washington. Her mind seems made up. I won't bore you with the reasons except to say that she has some. Tonight I get one last chance to talk her out of it."

"No wonder you were so quiet this afternoon! I thought you weren't feeling well."

"I'm not. I'm sick at the prospect of that ungrateful bitch—I'm sorry, but that's how I now think of her—pulling this on me. If she makes allegations and demands that I have to answer in court, then I think my chances of getting the appointment will be zero. I got the clear impression that what Washington wants is a wife who is a party-giver, not a mudslinger. I can't let her ruin me and the company. I *won't* let her."

The Mercedes made several turns along streets lined with forty-foot-high palm trees. Roshek's home was in the Spanish style, with thick walls, a red tile roof, and a broad lawn outlined with succulents and cactus. The car glided up the curved driveway and stopped at the front entryway. Behind a double wrought-iron gate was a carved wooden door.

"Wait until you see I'm inside," Roshek said, trying to figure out how to unbuckle his seat belt. "She might have changed the locks."

"Do you want me to push your chair?"

"No, let me struggle with it myself. If she's watching from a window, she might feel a twinge of pity. Just get the chair out of the car and hand me my crutches. How the Sam Hill do you unhook these belts?"

Bolen reached over and depressed the release catch. Silently the lap and shoulder straps were drawn into their receptacles. "You never were very good with small mechanical devices, were you, Theodore? Unless a thing has at least five hundred moving parts or is worth ten million dollars, it doesn't engage your attention."

"Then why haven't I paid more attention to my wife? She might cost me ten million dollars. Of course, she has only one moving part. Her mouth."

Bolen walked to the passenger side, removed the collapsible wheelchair from the back seat, and expanded it into position. Roshek managed to get out of the car and into the chair without assistance. As Bolen handed him his crutches, he decided to risk bringing up the subject of Kramer and the dam one last time.

"Did you by any chance take a look at the seepage figures Kramer compiled? He told me he was going to ask your opinion of them."

"He handed me a sheet of paper," Roshek said, turning his chair away from the car. "I crumpled it up."

Bolen shook his head gravely. "Seepage is high. More grouting may have to be done. I called Jeffers last night and asked him to take a look around in the lower galleries."

Roshek looked up at Bolen with mild exasperation. "What did he find?"

"I expect him to call in a report any minute."

"Let me know what he says. Now, if you'll excuse me, I have an appointment with my loving wife."

Bolen touched Roshek's arm to detain him. "We should face the possibility that Kramer has blundered onto something serious."

"Goddammit, Herman, whose side are you on, mine or that fucking kid's?"

"I'm on your side and the firm's side," Bolen said, keeping his voice low. "But it may be that new leaks have sprung up that call for grouting, overhauling the drainage system, lowering the reservoir, or whatever. We can take such corrective action quietly, without the public hearing about it, provided we don't have a disgruntled ex-employee running around shooting his mouth off. Kramer could go to a newspaper and make himself look like a hero at our expense. As you said, we don't need any bad publicity."

Roshek sagged. "Christ," he said through clenched teeth, "as if I didn't have enough on my mind."

"Suppose I tell him you are willing to give him another chance."

"You mean hire him back? Apologize to him? I'm not that desperate."

"You don't have to even see him. I'll tell him that I have your okay to assign him to the London office. I haven't met a man yet who hasn't jumped at London. That will get his mind off Sierra Canyon. Six months or a year from now we'll terminate him when it won't seem connected with trouble at the dam . . . if there is any trouble."

"Good. I like it. Just don't mention his name around me again."

Bolen returned to the driver's seat. He watched Roshek push the gates open, wheel himself to the door, and try his key. When the door swung open, he turned and mouthed the words: "Wish me luck." Bolen waved reassuringly, then released the brake and coasted down the driveway to the street.

Driving east on Santa Monica toward the freeway, he planned the actions he would take when he reached the office. Time, he learned long ago, could be spent most efficiently when priorities were set in advance. Identify the tasks that had to be done at once, those that wouldn't suffer too much from delays, and those with "float time," to use the technical scheduling term, and attack them in that order. In the present case he would phone Kramer and tell him "the good news"; he would track down Jeffers wherever he might be; and, finally, he would permit himself thirty minutes—not a minute more!—to daydreaming about what it would be like to control the company in Roshek's absence.

II

The Race

13

SEVENTY MILES AN HOUR WAS THE MOST Phil's aging Mustang would do without shuddering uncontrollably, so he held it at that speed while keeping one eye on the rearview mirror for signs of the Highway Patrol. In a racing car he could have gone twice as fast in perfect safety, for Interstate 5 through California's Central Valley was broader, straighter, and smoother than any speedway. Too broad and straight, in fact. Drivers tended to fall into a kind of follow-the-leader trance brought on by the monotony. Cars innocently parked on the shoulder were sometimes the cause of multiple rear-end collisions.

There was little chance that Phil would doze off and try to drive over the top of a parked car. He was too keyed up by what he perceived as the urgency of his mission and too aware of the significance of the region he was passing through, which he had heard his father talk about so often. He drove with both hands clamped on the wheel, leaning forward in an unconscious effort to urge the car beyond its natural limits. He read every road sign and studied every feature of the landscape, surprised at how much seemed vaguely familiar. According to his father, the Central Valley was a cradle of technological innovation and one of the world's greatest displays of engineering achievement.

Phil's father, Carl Kramer, had been Road Superintendent of Sedgwick County, a job that carried considerable prestige around Wichita, but that, Phil had discovered upon joining R. B. & B., sounded comically provincial to California ears. Phil had both loved and admired his father, and missed him now just as much as he ever had. He was a thoughtful, studious man whose honesty and warmth and intelligence had seemed as innate as the quality of his voice and the color of his eyes. His interests ranged far beyond the duties of a husband, father, and county engineer. He was a serious student of the history of engineering. If, as he had maintained, a man cannot consider himself educated unless he knows the history of his own profession, then he must have been one of the most educated men in the world. Hardly a year had gone by that both Kansas and Kansas State did not ask him to join their engineering faculties and develop a history course. Always he turned them down, although he did give several lectures a year on both campuses. He liked his low-pressure county job. He liked driving over the network of farm-to-market roads that was largely his creation and stopping to talk to farmers, ranchers, policemen, and merchants. His professional ambitions had been confined to his son. When he died, Phil was in his first year of graduate school. "Keep up the good work," he had written in his last letter. "You've got something extra and there's no telling how far you can go." He said things like that so often and with such conviction that Phil sometimes almost believed him.

Phil looked toward the east, where a thin haze obscured the horizon. Behind that haze were the Sierra Nevadas, where, his father had told him, more major dams had been built than anywhere else on earth. A dozen powerful rivers surged out of the high country and through the foothills to join the north-flowing San Joaquin, rivers like the Kings, the Merced, the Tuolumne, the Stanislaus, and the American, some of which contained so many dams that the water was almost "staircased" from one end to the other, the water behind one dam lapping at the toe of the dam upstream. Mammoth Pool Dam, Pine Flat Dam, Wishon, Courtright, Don Pedro, Pardee, and Camanche—Carl Kramer could have named them all—dams that in exchange for wild rivers generated power, controlled floods, created recreational lakes, slaked the thirst of San Francisco and Los Angeles, and supplied the irrigation water that had transformed a desert into a fantastic engine of agricultural production. Ten percent of everything grown in the United States came from the four-hundred-mile-long Central Valley, thanks to water from the mountain reservoirs, distributed by means of a vast network of canals and pipelines.

East of San Francisco, I-5 passed Stockton, an apparently unexceptional city of 115,000 that most non-Californians had never heard of. In the early decades of the twentieth century, a series of earthmoving machines were developed in Stockton that revolutionized the way land was leveled for irrigation, the way dams and roads were built, the way canals were dug, even the way wars were fought. A small Stockton manufacturing firm named Holt & Best, which later moved to Peoria, Illinois, as the Caterpillar Tractor Company, came up with the continuous steel tread that enabled farm and construction machines to work on soft and marshy ground and that led to the ubiquitous crawler tractor as well as the military tank. Several Stockton mechanics experimented with mounting steel blades on tractors so that dirt could be carved out of the ground and pushed from place to place without the need for loading it into trucks—and both the bulldozer and the motor grader were born. In the 1930s, an affable welder named Bob LeTourneau, a giant of a man, God-fearing and Bible-quoting, combined the bulldozer, tractor, loader, and truck into one machine that could dig, carry, and spread dirt without assistance from other machines. The scraper, as the hybrid was called, characterized by huge tires and an engine that overhangs the front axle, is now common everywhere in the world that earth is moved. LeTourneau later moved his Stockton fabricating shop to Longview, Texas, where in his spare time he founded a college that combined technical courses with Holy Scripture.

Phil noticed that several times in the two-hundred-mile stretch between Bakersfield and Stockton the freeway crossed or paralleled the California Aqueduct, which he had learned from his father was part of the most ambitious water redistribution system ever built. After World War II, to get water from the northern part of the state, where it wasted to the sea, to the Central Valley and the Los Angeles Basin, where it was needed, California spent two billion dollars on eighteen dams, five power plants, fifteen pumping stations, and five hundred and eighty miles of canals. The hundred-yard-wide California Aqueduct, the north-south backbone of the system, rivaled the world's greatest rivers in its capacity to carry water.

Even the freeway Phil was on belonged on a list of outstanding civil engineering achievements. Interstate 5 between Bakersfield and Modesto was the longest major highway ever built on new right-of-way—twin ribbons of concrete two hundred miles long stretched across the empty lower slopes of the Coast Range, bypassing every town and village. When it first opened, it lacked even a single rest room or gas station.

Surrounded by so many superlatives and so much engineering history, Phil wondered if maybe he qualified for some sort of list or record book himself. He was possibly the most presumptuous, reckless, megalomaniacal, and plainly ridiculous young engineer in the world. Here he was driving through a wonderland with famous projects right, left, and underfoot, headed for one of the most famous of all, to prove if he could that it was a grave threat to public safety. Phil Kramer, a sophomoric greenhorn from Wichita, Kansas. What a joke! He should have stayed home where he knew how people thought and where the things that people had built were still on a scale that could be grasped. Maybe designing curbs and gutters and living with Mom was the best kind of life for him, despite his father's dreams. A man could make mistakes in Kansas, and make a fool of himself, too, but not on the fantastic scale that was possible in California.

Once he got to the dam, what then? He still hadn't made up his mind what he would do if the people in charge laughed at him and slammed doors in his face. Maybe the whole trip was a mistake he would regret forever. He was acting emotionally, out of anger at getting fired unfairly, in the hope of finding something that would embarrass Theodore Roshek, the only person in the world he had ever hated. Hardly healthy motives for embarking on an engineering investigation. He should have stayed calm and thought things over.

How are you going to explain this to your mother, he asked himself, easing up on the accelerator, especially if you wind up in jail? How are you going to tell her that her pride and joy blew a perfectly good job by mouthing off to the company president? She's going to want you to fly home so she can press cold towels to your forehead. You must be crazy as well as stupid. And what about Janet?

She should have seen you were goofy from too much Mexican beer and talked you out of leaving town. Your father would have if he were still alive. Or would he? He believed in digging for facts, and he believed in acting on them once they were in hand.

He was passing Sacramento. Through the right-hand window of the car he could see rays of a setting sun glinting off the dome of the Capitol Building. If he was going to turn back or spend a night in a motel, this would be a good place to stop. There was an off-ramp coming up on the right. He let it go by, stepping on the gas and swinging over to the fast lane. "I *am* calm," he said aloud. "I *have* thought things over." Turning back now after coming so far would prove he was crazy. By pushing on to Sutterton, now only an hour and a half away, the worst that could happen was that he would be proved wrong. Better to be proved wrong than crazy. "When you feel you are right about something," his father had told him more than once, "stick to your guns come hell or high water."

Hell and high water. If his theory was right and he had acted too late, there was liable to be plenty of both.

The air conditioner in the window above the sink hummed valiantly, but the late afternoon heat in Stockton was too much for it. Emil Hasset sat across the kitchen table from his son, sweat rolling from his face into the creases of his neck. He had removed his holster and the jacket of his guard's uniform and rolled his sleeves above his elbows. When he lifted his forearms off the oilcloth, there was a sound like paper tearing. By leaning back in his chair he could reach into the refrigerator for two more cans of Coors. He slid one across the table.

"You're not gonna chicken out on me, are you, Freddy?"

"If you get caught, the cops will come straight to me. I'm still on probation."

"What can they prove? If you don't see the armored truck coming down the road, take the plane back to the airport and you're in the clear. Christ, look at it from my point of view. I've never bailed out of a plane before and you do it every weekend."

Freddy Hasset, a small man with thin brown hair, looked uncomfortable. He hadn't looked fully at ease since returning from San Quentin, where he had spent three traumatic years for knifing a man in a barroom brawl. "You could join the club and take a few practice jumps. If you don't, you're a cinch to break your neck."

"Not a chance. I'm going to jump out of a plane just once in my life, and that's tomorrow. With you right behind me. With two hundred thousand bucks at least."

"And with Lloyd shooting at us all the way down."

"Goddammit, let me worry about Lloyd. He'll be back at the supermarket trying to figure out how to dial the cops. He's used his gun once in fifteen years and that was to crack some walnuts with the handle. When I drive off and leave him at the dock, he'll be so surprised it'll take him an hour to find his holster. Do you want to spend the rest of your life in Stockton tapping the till at the pool hall and chasing cheap pussy and getting in knife fights? Living in this dump with your old man, who ain't going nowhere either? Mary Lou was right what she said the other night. We're losers. Now we've come up with a way to be winners . . . big winners."

"You got a steady job, at least."

"Sure I do. Twelve years, never missed a day, and they still pay me four-fifty an hour. No raises, they said. Valley Financial Transfer is a little on the shorts at the moment, they said. They'll be on the shorts at the moment, all right, when I get through with them. Oh, how they've been screwing me! Now I need you, Freddy. You're the only one I can trust. You got to do your part. If you don't land on the road to pick me up, I've had it. I've *had* it."

"I don't know, there's something funny about the deal."

"What's funny about it? When we took the other car up to the canyon, you thought it was great. Now you think it's funny? You liked the little cabin I rented and you said the clearing was perfect. A couple of months up there while things cool off and we're home free. All you gotta do is get the plane."

"I got a Cessna reserved. A two-seater."

"Is it easy to jump out of?"

"A snap. Only problem is it's a little tough to open the door against a hundred-mile-an-hour wind. So I'm going to take the door off at the airport. It's a ten-minute job with a Phillips screwdriver. You won't mind a little breeze in the cockpit, will you? You'll be strapped in with a seat belt."

Emil Hasset beamed paternally at his son, then laughed. "Oh, you gotta admit this is sweet, Freddy. The plane will crash *way* the fuck and gone and nobody will know *where* the fuck we are."

"You're sure we can find the cabin from the air?"

"Easy. Look at the maps. It's four miles downstream from a dam. Promise me you'll pick me up after I hijack the truck. Look me in the eye and promise."

"I promise. I'll be there. We got to be due for some good luck."

Freddy Hasset seldom smiled because his teeth were bad, but he smiled now. "You know what, Pop? You're gonna look awful funny floating out of the sky in your guard's uniform."

"I sure as hell will, and I'll be laughing the hardest."

14

WILSON HARTLEY, SUTTERTON CHIEF OF Police, wiped the melted butter from his chin and took the phone from his wife. Corn on the cob was impossible to eat neatly, and the same could be said for many of his favorite foods: spaghetti, artichokes, spare ribs, cracked crab, roast turkey. Whenever his wife served any of those, the dining-room table quickly took on the look of a municipal dump.

It was Karsh, the night sergeant. "Sorry to bother you at home, Chief, but I got a guy on hold who alleges that he wants to talk to you personally if at all possible. He further alleges that his name is Herman Bolen and that he is calling from Roshek, Bolen & Benedetz in Los Angeles."

"For Christ sakes, Karsh, put him through." Hartley recognized the name of the engineering firm that was in charge of the dam and assumed that some sort of security problem had arisen. He left the table and carried the phone to his desk in the next room, wire trailing behind him and a napkin dangling from his belt.

"I don't know if you remember me," Bolen said when he was on the line. "We met during the dedication ceremony ten years ago or so."

Hartley didn't remember. "Yes, of course I remember. How are you, Herman?" People tended to become tense when talking to the Chief of Police, so Hartley had gotten into the habit of using first names and a friendly manner in an effort to relax them.

"I'm fine, thank you. Mr. Hartley, a matter has come up that has to be handled with some discretion. I'm sure you know Lawrence Jeffers, our maintenance chief at the dam."

"Larry? Sure I know him. Go deer hunting with him every year. We've never come close to shooting anything, because when he starts whistling and singing all the animals run for their lives. Are you going to tell me Larry is in some kind of trouble? That would be hard to believe."

"I'll come right to the point. He's been missing all day. To put it as precisely as possible, I talked to him twenty-four hours ago and haven't been able to locate him since. He didn't show up for work and he doesn't answer his home phone. What worries me is that he promised to call me first thing this morning. Now, it may be that I'm worried over nothing. He may be missing only as far as *I* am concerned. For all I know, he's having dinner with you right now or visiting a sick friend and simply forgot to call me or tell his co-workers where he would be."

The Chief assured Bolen that Jeffers was not immediately at hand, and agreed that it was odd for a man so trustworthy to drop out of sight. "You want me to take a look around, is that it? Make a few inquiries?"

"Exactly. But I don't want to get anybody alarmed unnecessarily. I was about to start calling hospitals in the area, then I realized that you probably have a system for doing that. What I am really trying to find out is if there is any *reason* for me to be worried. I don't know his personal habits, whether he has a woman, where he goes after work. To be quite frank, I don't want to embarrass myself or him by starting a search for a man who may not be lost."

"I get the picture. Tell you what. I'll swing by his house and see if his car is in the garage and I'll call on a few of his friends around town. If I don't find him, I'll call the Highway Patrol and the hospitals to see if he's been in an accident. Any idea at all where he might have gone?"

"Maybe to Sacramento. You might also check for his car at the powerhouse parking lot."

"Right. Give me a phone number and I'll call you back in a couple of hours."

"Thanks very much, Mr. Hartley. I had a hunch you would know how to handle this."

Next, Bolen tried to reach Phil Kramer by phone. Failing, he stared absently at a pile of papers on his desk, wondering what he would do if Hartley failed to find a trace of Jeffers. If that happened, he would simply have to send somebody into the drainage gallery to look for him, even if it meant admitting that he had ordered Jeffers to make a night inspection. Would he have to admit that? He could say that he had been talking to Jeffers on another matter and heard him say he was going into the dam. . . .

Bolen frowned and picked up a sheet of paper. It was a note from his secretary:

> After you left for SoCalEd a call came in from a a Mr. Terry of the California Division of Dam Safety. He said he's seen the latest figures from Sierra Canyon and feels that a field investigation is called for, which he is going to conduct

himself tomorrow (Saturday). He was unable to reach Mr. Jeffers at the dam and wonders if you would like to accompany him. He will arrive there about noon.

Charlene

"God*dammit!*" Bolen said. Why does the *state* have to get involved? It wasn't more than a month ago that Dam Safety had made one of its regular inspections, and the new seepage figures weren't *that* bad. Now he might have to get up at dawn in order to get to Sutterton by noon, unless he wanted to fly his own plane, which gave him a backache on long flights. *Damn* that Jeffers! He picked a hell of a time to go fishing or get drunk or whatever it was he was doing. He deserved a chewing out and would get it, make no mistake about that. Jeffers was a nice man, yes, but sometimes he carried that everything-is-wonderful, whistle-while-you-work act a little too far. There's a two-hundred-million-dollar dam to be looked after, Larry, let's not forget that. Oh, I hope Hartley finds you. What an earful you're going to get! I'll show you a side of Herman Bolen you never dreamed existed.

When Phil saw the dam, he felt his sense of purpose weaken again. He drove slowly, part of the Friday-night stop-and-go traffic on Sutterton's Main Street, unable to take his eyes off the dark, looming wall that filled half the night sky. He hardly noticed the floodlit City Hall, the bandstand in the square, the Wagon Wheel Saloon, the banner stretched across the street announcing the Third Annual Mother Lode Marathon. The road across the dam's crest was marked by lights, and to take in the entire glowing line Phil had to put his face close to the windshield. The dam was so overpoweringly high and huge it was hard to accept it as man made, and it was hard to imagine the lake behind it. "Jesus," he said softly. The dam was a mountain. It would stand as long as there were mountains anywhere.

And yet, towering over a town it miniaturized, it was obviously not a mountain. The great hills and cliffs on either side were higher and more massive, but it was to the dam the eyes were drawn. It was a *presence,* intense and sullen, that was threatening in a way the mountains were not. It was alien and the mountains were not.

A few blocks from the downtown district, Main Street reverted to a country road, passed through a grove of tall pines, and climbed to the top of the canyon along a shelf cut in a rocky slope. Phil drove carefully past a line of parked construction machines and warning flares. On a promontory above the dam was an overlook where the teenage occupants of a half-dozen cars were listening to music, drinking beer, and ignoring the view. Phil parked and walked to the railing, stretching his arms and legs. It was 10:30—he had made it from Los Angeles in just over eight hours, with only a single brief break in Marysville. The cool breeze off the lake carried the scent of evergreens and fresh water and was sweet relief after the heat of the Central Valley. The only sounds were the strains of rock music from the cars parked nearby and the distant roar of the spillway water plunging into the river a thousand feet below. To Phil's right was the shining black expanse of the lake, its surface divided by a yellow trail of reflected light from a three-quarter moon, its shoreline defined by low, furrowed hills with higher hills behind them. The snowy ridges and peaks of the High Sierras were outlined against an enormous bank of dark clouds in the far distance. Breaking through the surface of the lake directly below the overlook was a doughnut-like circle of concrete that Phil knew was the top of the intake tower. Slightly to the left and only barely higher than the water was the crest of the dam and the two rows of highway lights that merged at a point on the other side of the canyon. On the valley floor below the dam was a brightly lit rectangle that was the electrical switchyard. Between that and the downstream toe of the dam, out of sight beneath a shoulder of the hillside, was the entrance to the underground powerhouse. Farther to the left, in the distance, Sutterton was a sprinkle of pinpoint lights.

Gazing at the dam, Phil began to appreciate how foolish he must have looked to Roshek and Bolen. Studying a mathematical model and drawings of a dam was one thing, confronting the reality of it was another. It was so enormous and so magnificent, so *permanent.* It spanned the canyon gracefully and seemed to resist the weight of the lake with ease, anchored so solidly in the abutments and the foundation bedrock that no force on earth could dislodge it. The computer images and columns of figures that had struck Phil as so significant suddenly seemed irrelevant, random patterns of light without substance, meaningless marks on paper. Roshek was right, it was ridiculous to think that he could gain any real understanding of a structure from a distance of five hundred miles with nothing but abstract symbols to go on. Once again he had half a notion to drive back to Los Angeles before making a bigger fool of himself than he already had. Maybe he owed an apology to Roshek.

On the other hand . . . there was always that other hand. If he had learned anything in engineering school, it was always to give proper consideration to the goddam other hand. The seepage figures were not irrelevant and abstract. The dam looked sleek and powerful and permanent on the outside, but what about on the inside? Deep within its bowels, if the meter readings were correct, were possibly fatal flaws. The dam was colossal and enormously strong, but so was the lake.

He climbed into his car and headed down the hill. He reminded himself that in recent years he had overcome most of his childhood shyness. He had found the nerve to make himself heard in groups, to introduce himself to a beautiful woman, and to talk back to his elders. He would not allow himself now to be driven back into his shell by a mere *dam*.

Herman Bolen was in the study of his home in Westwood, a phone pressed to his ear. "Yes, Mr. Hartley. I appreciate very much the trouble you've taken. Please call me at this number at any time of night should something turn up later."

He replaced the receiver on its hook. So, Jeffers's car was nowhere to be found and neither was Jeffers. He was not with friends, his ex-wife, his daughter, or his neighbors. He was not in a Sutterton bar. His car had not been in an accident of which the police or the Highway Patrol were aware. He was not in a hospital or a jail. Where was he, then? Bolen didn't like the most likely answers to that question. Either he had driven off any one of a hundred precipices that lined the mountain roads around Sutterton or he was still inside the dam. Maybe on his way from the Administration Building to the powerhouse a wasp had flown through a window, causing him to lose control and go off the road above the portal of the tailrace tunnel. He was not dead inside the dam at all, but rather dead inside his car at the bottom of the discharge channel. Dead, unfortunately, in both cases.

Before he could decide on the next step, the phone rang again. It was another policeman, this one identifying himself as Officer Baker of the Beverly Hills police.

"I'm calling from the home of Mr. and Mrs. Theodore Roshek," the voice said. "The Rosheks have been involved in a family dispute. A fight, I guess you could say. Could we put Mr. Roshek in your custody for the night? Tomorrow we will know how serious the injury to Mrs. Roshek is and whether she wants to press charges."

"Jesus, Mary, and Joseph . . . I'll be there in fifteen minutes."

15

PHIL DECIDED TO PRESENT HIS CASE TO Lawrence Jeffers. Lay out all the evidence and let the veteran maintenance engineer decide whether or not there was anything to get excited about. But Jeffers wasn't answering his phone. He wasn't answering his doorbell, either. The house, which Phil found without much trouble, was dark and apparently occupied only by a continuously barking dog. The garage was empty, and on the path from the porch to the street was the morning paper.

Plan B was set in motion from a phone booth next to a gas station. With a stack of dimes and the county phone book, Phil started in on the eleven listed Duncans.

"I'm trying to reach Chuck Duncan," he explained to the woman who answered his fifth call, "the inspector who works at the dam. Have I reached the right place?"

"Sure have. I'm his mother. Chuck went to the drive-in movie with Burt and Carla and the Peterson girl. This wouldn't be Mr. Richardson, would it?"

"Sorry. Do you expect him home soon?"

"Not hardly on Friday night. He might not come home at all, which is another story." She laughed with a twang in her voice that reminded Phil of his Aunt Lorene in Topeka. "The movie's probably out by now, seeing as how it's after ten. You could try the Wagon Wheel. They oftentimes go down there and stay till all hours."

"The Wagon Wheel?"

"On Main Street. I knew you were from out of town, which is why I thought you might be Mr. Richardson."

"Main Street. Thank you, Mrs. Duncan."

The Wagon Wheel was a kind of museum of the Old West, or at least of old Western movies. In front was a hitching post and a plank walkway covered by a low roof. Along one side was a fence made of overlapping wagon wheels. In back was a rusted tramcar, part of a display of early mining methods that had sunk into disrepair. The nature of the clientele was suggested by the vehicles that were nosed into the walkway like horses at a trough. One of the vehicles was, in fact, a horse, a handsome, well-curried beast that, judging from its twitching ears, didn't care for the music drifting through the swinging doors. Not a bad form of transportation, Phil thought as he parked and locked his car, for a person who planned on getting drunk. A horse could take you home even if you were unconscious. Most of the customers had arrived in pickup trucks with snow tires, roof racks for skis and rifles, bobbing heads in the rear windows, and plastic statuettes on the dashboards. For the first time since leaving Kansas, Phil saw a pair of fuzzy dice. He memorized a bumper sticker for use in the travelogue he would sooner or later present to Janet:

GOD, GUNS, AND GUTS
That's what made America great

It was country-Western disco night and the Wagon Wheel was packed. Phil stood inside the doors accustoming his eyes to the dim light and his ears to a noise level that was close to the limits of the endurable. Music for the evening was being provided and electrically amplified by a shaggy octet called Coley Hollenback and His Shi—— Kickers. There were plaid shirts, jeans, cowboy hats, tooled leather boots, and beards. The women as well as the men were dressed as if they were on their way to a rodeo, and not as spectators. There was singing, dancing, and shouting. Nobody fell silent and stared at the newcomer the way they did in television commercials; Phil could have secretly emptied a six-gun into the ceiling. Hanging resignedly on the walls were the stuffed and moth-eaten heads of a moose, an elk, and a buffalo.

Phil wedged his way to the bar and managed to attract the attention of the bartender, a large, unpleasant-looking man with a sunburned nose and forehead.

"Do you know Chuck Duncan?" Phil shouted over the din.

"Old Chuck or young Chuck?"

"Young, I guess. The inspector at the dam."

"Yeah. It's the old man I never met."

"Is he here?"

"Who wants to know?"

"We work for the same company. His mother sent me."

The bartender shrugged, stepped onto a case of beer, and peered through the haze over the heads of the dancers. "He's in the corner booth. The blond kid with the stupid expression. Tell him I said that."

Phil skirted the dance floor to avoid getting injured and picked his way between crowded tables to the booths that lined the wall. In the corner was a passive party of four, Duncan and, if Phil remembered correctly the words of

Mrs. Duncan, Burt, Carla, and the Peterson girl.

"Are you Chuck Duncan?"

The young man Phil addressed turned and tried to focus his eyes. His expression wasn't stupid, exactly, but was an argument against combining alcohol and marijuana. "What?" he said.

Phil repeated the question in a louder voice.

The man smiled. "Speaking," he said.

Aside from the effect chemicals were having on his mind, Duncan appeared to be no more than nineteen years old. Hardly a person you would entrust with your fears about the structural integrity of the world's highest embankment. "My name is Kramer. I'm with Roshek, Bolen & Benedetz in the Los Angeles office."

"Yeah? Well, I'll be fucked."

"Could I talk to you for a minute?"

"What?"

"I said could I talk to you for a minute? The music is so loud I can't hear myself think."

"Great, isn't it?"

"Let's go outside."

"I've been outside."

"Come on. Your friends don't want to listen to us talk about piezometers and pore pressures. It'll just take a minute." The girl next to Duncan was only partly contained by her red flannel shirt, which was unbuttoned to her waist. Phil nodded and smiled at her on general principles and to apologize for the interruption. He took Duncan by the arm and gently urged him to his feet. The young inspector yielded, mumbling, and let himself be guided through a side door.

"Let's make this fast," Duncan said when they were outside. "That goddam Burt is going to move in on Carla, I know he will." The cool night air, the streetlights, and the effort of walking had seemed to bring him out of his trance.

"Don't worry," Phil said reassuringly. "He's on the

wrong side of the table. She can't hear a word he says, anyway."

"The son of a bitch will find a way. He's done it to me before."

"Look, I don't want to take up any more of your time than I have to. Where can I find Lawrence Jeffers?"

Duncan sat on the fender of a car and crossed his arms. "Beats the shit out of me," he said. "He didn't show up for work today. Nobody knows where he is. The big bosses in L.A. are looking for him, too, I hear. His ass is going to be in a sling. Did they send you up here looking for him? God, this air feels good. It's too hot in that fucking place."

"Nobody sent me here. I . . . I'm on vacation. I'm one of the guys that looks over those sheets of readings you compile every month. I'm on my way to Reno and thought I'd stop here and see if I could get a look at the drainage galleries."

Duncan grimaced and shook his head. "You don't want to see the drainage galleries."

"I don't?"

"No."

"Why not? It would give me a feel for what those numbers mean."

"You don't want to see the drainage galleries because it is a pain in the ass. An extreme pain in the ass. You climb down two hundred steps. Then you climb back up two hundred steps. It's dark. It's wet. It's the total shits. You want to get a feel for it? Stand under a cold shower in the dark with your clothes on. Then climb up and down the stairs of a fifteen-story building with a Water Pik stuck up your rear end. That'll give you a feel for it." Duncan chuckled, pleased with the image.

"It's that bad, is it?"

"I deserve a raise for taking readings down there. Go back to Los Angeles and tell the big bosses Charles O. Duncan deserves a raise for risking his life every month. And for being a beautiful human being. Last time I went down there, I thought I was going to drown. Do I complain? Noooo . . ."

"A lot of water comes in?"

"A lot of water. You know what I call this dam? Leaking Lena. This year is the worst. I bet we pump more water out of Gallery D alone than goes through the turbines."

Phil took a notebook from his shirt pocket, flipped it open, and scribbled a few words. "I had no idea it was so bad. I definitely will recommend you for a raise. On your last monthly report there was a whole bank of meters you didn't include. Why was that?"

"I took the readings, but Jeffers told me to leave them out. They were too goofy, he said. Some were zero, some were off the high end. Every year more and more of those meters go out of whack and we quit reading them. I'm hoping they'll all conk out so I can quit going down there. Those meters are all a bunch of bullshit, anyway. Ask Jeffers, he'll tell you. I know guys who work on other dams around here and they don't have to climb down holes and read meters. Listen, I better get back inside. Burt's probably got both arms inside Carla's shirt by now."

"Wait a minute," Phil said, putting a hand on Duncan's shoulder. "Those readings from the broken meters, have you still got them?"

"Sure I got them."

"Can I see them?"

"Why not?"

"Where are they?"

"In the trunk of my car."

"Where's your car?"

"I'm sitting on it. You think I'd sit on a car that wasn't mine? Some of those guys in the saloon are *mean* bastards."

Phil followed Duncan to the back of the car, and noticed for the first time the R. B. & B. logo on the door. While Phil looked on, Duncan opened the trunk and sorted through a box full of manila envelopes, occasionally holding one up to the light and squinting at it.

"I still want to go into the dam and see the meters for myself," Phil said. "If Jeffers isn't back tomorrow, will you take me? First thing in the morning?"

"No way. Saturday's my day off. First thing in the morning I'm going to the middle of the lake with my fishing gear. Maybe on Monday."

"Monday's too late. How about right now?"

Duncan straightened up and looked at Phil in amazement. "Man, you got to be crazy," he said, slamming the trunk and handing over an envelope. "I wouldn't go into that hole in the middle of the night for a million bucks. Well, maybe for a million. You say you're on vacation? How come you look sober and talk drunk?"

"Is there anybody else who would take me in?"

"Not at eleven-thirty at night. People around here got more sense than that. I'm going back into the bar and peel Burt's hands off Carla. Nice to meet you."

Phil followed him along the wooden walkway trying to squeeze out a few more scraps of information.

"Could I go into the galleries alone?"

"Sure, if you could get past Withers."

"Who's Withers?"

"Newt Withers, the night engineer at the powerhouse. He'll look you over on closed-circuit TV, and if he doesn't like what he sees he won't raise the door. You're with the company, so he might let you in. What's the big hurry, anyway? Do the big bosses think something's wrong?"

"No, the big bosses think everything is fine. I'm just curious, that's all. I guess you're right—it's crazy to think of taking a tour tonight. If Jeffers isn't around in the morning, I'll just forget the whole idea."

"That's what I'd do. Mail the envelope to me when you're through with it, okay? And say hello to old man Roshek when you get back to L.A. I've never met him, but I hear he's a real sweetheart."

"Sure will, Chuck, and thanks for the information. Good luck with Carla."

The long-distance operator's voice was reedy: "I have a collect call for Janet Sandifer from Philip Kramer. Will you accept the charges?"

"Yes, Operator, but he's got a lot of guts."

"Janet! It's Phil! I'm calling from my phone-booth command post in the heart of downtown Sutterton. Am I interrupting anything?"

"Only a shower. I'm dripping wet."

"Don't say things like that. I'll drool into the mouthpiece and electrocute myself."

"How are things going? Found out anything?"

"I struck pay dirt, as they used to say around here in 1849, in the form of the meter-reader whose figures we've been using. From what he told me, I'm surer than ever that all hell's about to break loose. The trouble is, he was both stoned and crocked and may have been exaggerating. You should have heard him spill his guts when I told him I would recommend him for a raise."

Janet laughed. "You told him that? I'm sure your recommendation will carry a lot of weight."

"He gave me a list of readings that weren't in the last report. I know you have a terminal in your office with dial-up ports. Have you got keys to get in? . . . Okay, here's what I want you to do—feed the new figures into the program. I'll give you the phone number of the R. B. & B. computer and the password that will give you access. I doubt if they changed it just because I got fired."

"For God sakes, Phil, it's after midnight! I'm stark naked and ready for bed."

"No time for sex now. Put on one of your no-nonsense business suits and get your ass down to the office. I'll call you when you get back to find out what the new readings mean."

"I could get arrested."

"So could I. If the computer shows what I think it will, I'm going to try to break into the dam. There must be some way to break the security system and get past the control-room operator. I'm going to get a motel room now and study the plans while you do your job."

"Are you all right? You sound as if you're hyperventilating. Are you stoned and crocked?"

"I see everything with an almost mystical clarity."

"Don't give me that bullshit."

"Right. I'll give you the figures. Got a pencil ready?"

Janet sighed. "Okay," she said, "fire away."

16

THEY DROVE FOR SEVERAL MINUTES without speaking. Roshek was in the passenger's seat staring straight ahead, his eyebrows drawn together and his deep-set eyes narrow. Twice he lifted his hands as if about to make an explanation, then let them drop. Both men were uncomfortable, and neither seemed to know how to begin a conversation. Bolen glanced at his partner and was struck by the uncharacteristic aura of confusion and defeat that surrounded him.

"Do you want to tell me what happened?" Bolen asked gently. "The police were rather vague."

Roshek wet his lips and swallowed before replying. "I can't recall everything," he said in a distant voice. "That is very . . . unsettling. I've been drunk a time or two in my life with hangovers that lasted for days, but always I could remember what I did or said down to the smallest details. Not now. There are several minutes missing." He raised a hand to his forehead. "My God, maybe I should see a doctor."

After a pause, Bolen ventured to ask another question. "The police implied that you struck her and that she ran from the house. Is that true, Theodore? There was physical violence?"

Roshek took a deep, ragged breath. "We were sitting in the living room. We talked about our life together. The pros and the cons. It was like compiling a feasibility study. We both tried to be calm and not to say anything that would irritate the other. It was a terrible strain. After an hour or two of pressure we both more or less cracked at once."

Bolen turned into his driveway. The garage door opened automatically and closed when the car was inside. He turned off the engine and looked at Roshek, who was still staring straight ahead.

"I didn't know either of us was capable of such hostility," Roshek said, speaking in a monotone, "such hatred." He bent his head forward and rubbed his temples. "I don't know what made it surface. I remember feeling outraged at the way she rejected my offer to meet her more than halfway. I took the blame for her unhappiness. I offered to spend more time with her, not as a tactic but because I genuinely felt sympathy. When I saw that she was not going to yield on the divorce, I made a generous settlement offer if she would delay filing. Nothing got through to her. I suppose she thought I was trying to manipulate her, buy her off with money. I don't know. I could feel anger rising inside of me like hot water in a boiler. We raised our voices. Insults came, and curses. In a matter of seconds we were screaming at each other. At one point she said, 'Don't threaten me,' but I don't remember threatening her. I do remember calling her an ungrateful bitch and throwing a wineglass against the wall. I didn't throw it at her. I definitely did not throw it at her." He lifted his head and looked at Bolen, astonished at his own words, apparently finding it hard to believe that the story he was telling involved himself. "She ordered me out of the house, Herman. I refused to go. I told her I would not be forced out of a house I bought and paid for myself. I told her the only way I would leave was feet first in a pine box or at the point of a gun. She ran to a phone and asked the operator for the police. I lost control of myself when I heard that. I lunged across the room, leaning on furniture to keep my balance, shouting at her to hang up. A lamp got knocked over." He turned away and sighed again, deeply. "I lifted a crutch and brought it down, trying to knock the receiver from her hand. I believe I hit her wrist. Yes, that must be it. She screamed. The sound will stick in my mind forever."

Bolen studied him. Roshek's face was twisted as if he were in pain. His hands, pale and thin with prominent veins, were clamped on his knees like the talons of a bird.

"Let's go inside," Bolen said. "We'll have a brandy and talk some more if you want to."

"It's at that point," Roshek went on, "that my memory lets me down. I can see Stella on her knees clutching her arm like a wounded animal. She was looking up at me with terror in her face as if she were afraid I was going to kill her. I don't remember her running out of the house, but I see the French doors to the patio standing open. I hear her wailing in the distance and pounding on the neighbor's door. I fell into a chair and sat there like a zombie. An hour must have gone by before the police came. I agreed with them that Stella and I couldn't stay in the same house. I gave them your name." He opened the car door and swung his feet to the floor. "I can't believe any of it happened. We were both like crazy people."

Bolen got the wheelchair out of the back seat and helped Roshek into it. "The police were very understanding, I'll say that," Bolen said, pushing Roshek along an enclosed walkway to the house. "They saw the importance of trying to keep the matter private. I'll talk to Stella myself in the morning. There's to be a hearing of some kind. If she doesn't press charges, the whole thing will be quietly dropped. Naturally you can stay with me and my wife as long as necessary."

"Forgive me for causing you so much trouble. I'll be forever in your debt."

"Nonsense. It's I who am indebted to you."

In the foyer, Bolen's wife told him that two phone calls had come in for him while he was gone. One gentleman didn't leave his name; the other, a Mr. Withers at the Sierra Canyon powerhouse, wanted a return call.

Janet Sandifer, alone in a shadowy sea of deserted desks, chairs, and typewriters, opened her notebook and dialed the number Phil had given her. There was a ringing signal followed by two sharp clicks. A steady tone indicated that she had reached the Roshek computer and that it was "up." She pressed the telephone into a recessed cradle on top of a terminal housing. A row of letters and numbers silently appeared in green on the cathode ray tube, followed by

Roshek, Bolen & Benedetz
HQ   Technical bank
Los Angeles
Please identify

"At this point," Janet said to herself, "I cross the line into lawbreaking. Amazing what a basically decent woman will do for a good lay."

Her fingers moved deftly over the keyboard. One by one, letters appeared on the screen:

Philip Kramer   RB&B
Hydro Design Section
HQ   Los Angeles

When she pressed the Enter Key, the words vanished and were replaced with:

PASSWORD

Carefully, Janet typed

Grand Coulee

INCORRECT
Try again

"Whoops," Janet said after looking more closely at her notes. She had capitalized the wrong letters.

gRand cOulee

The machine responded immediately with the words

ACCEPTED
On line
Line clear
Instruct

List Column 7
Enter

Within three seconds the screen was filled with program titles. She moved the Cursor line to the seventh item on the list, the Kramer Dam Failure Model. At the touch of the Enter key the screen went blank, then displayed a message at the top:

CONGRATULATIONS!
You have reached the amazing
Kramer Dam Model
Use it in good health
Authorized personnel only
Violators will be towed away

Janet worked as fast as she could. She was breaking the law, and she didn't want to spend all night doing it.

Which laws applied to what she was doing she wasn't sure. Grand theft, probably. Or, if Phil's program turned out to be worthless after all, petty theft. Unlawful entry, maybe. If impersonating an engineer was a crime, then she was probably guilty of that. Since she was female and the engineer she was impersonating was male, there was an element of transvestism involved as well. Fortunately, she thought, trying to comfort herself, that wasn't illegal in California.

Recall values of
5-22-81

5-22-81
Values recalled

Add new values
Meter bank 9
Gallery D
Sierra Canyon Dam

Ready

Piezometers
A 17
B 35
C 0
D 0
E 35
F 29
H 21
I 35

Strain gauges

Ready

A 0.2
B 0.2
C 0.5
D 0.7

E 2.5
F 4.1
H 9.1
I 0.0
J 0.0

Observation wells

Ready

A Overflow
B Overflow
C Overflow

Mode Four
Best Case
Evaluate
Instruct

One moment, please
I'm thinking

Janet leaned back and waited. It took the computer three minutes to evaluate the condition of the dam under the most optimistic assumptions.

BEST CASE
Begin lowering reservoir
Make visual inspection
Galleries C & D

She jotted down the response, then bent over the keyboard and made another request:

Mode Five
Worst Case
Evaluate
Instruct

When the response came on the screen five minutes later, she couldn't help smiling. Phil had told her what he had put in the program to indicate a failing dam that was beyond salvation:

RUN FOR YOUR LIVES!

When she got back to her apartment, it was after 1:00 A.M. and her phone was ringing. It was Phil.

"I'm calling from the beautiful Damview Motel in Sutterton, California, Gateway to a Mountain Wonderland," he said cheerfully. "If you project the plane of the surface of Earl Warren Lake in a southwesterly direction, I am under seven hundred feet of water."

"Sounds like a good spot to be. If your theory is right, you are doomed."

"Janet, remember when I told you not to remind me of your body because I might drool into the telephone and electrocute myself? I want to take that back. I've been thinking it over. The wattage used in telephones is so small you wouldn't even get a shock, much less a fatal incident."

"I wasn't worried. From what I've noticed, you don't drool with enough accuracy to hit something as small as a telephone mouthpiece. Is that why you called?"

"You know why I called, sweetheart. I've been calling every ten minutes. Were you able to rape the Roshek computer?"

"Sure was."

"And?"

"And I got a hell of a scare. It was creepy being in an empty office building. That is, I *thought* it was empty. I was glued to the terminal when I heard a noise. I looked up and here were these three black dudes advancing on me with clubs and rocks! Actually, they were janitors and they were carrying mops and buckets. They apologized for scaring me. They turned out to be really nice. When I left, the oldest one, a dignified man with white hair, walked me to my car to make sure I'd be safe."

"That was nice of him."

"I thought so, too. So I invited him home. He's here with me now. One thing is leading to another, and in a few more minutes I'll be pregnant."

"I hope he won't mind if we talk business for a second. What did the computer say?"

"What I'm sure you knew it would. It suggests that you run for your life."

"Did you ask it for the most likely points of failure?"

"Yes. It said there weren't enough data to be precise, but that it would courageously make a guess. Got a pencil? Upstream, between stations fifty plus seventy-five and fifty plus ninety-five, elevation five six five. Downstream, between stations fifty plus forty-three and fifty plus nineteen, elevation three seven five."

Phil read the numbers back to make sure he had them right. "Sounds like the contact between the fill and bedrock. Water must have found a way through the grout curtain under the core block at Gallery D. I've been studying the plans, and if I can get into the dam I'm sure I can find the place."

"What's next?"

"I'm going to call Bolen at home. He's a reasonable man and he thinks I'm only half crazy. He should be interested in finding out that nobody knows where his chief maintenance engineer is, that three observation wells are overflowing, and that the inspector who reads the meters says it's so wet in the lower galleries he needs scuba gear. Maybe Bolen will authorize me to make an inspection. He knows I know more about the dam now than anybody other than Roshek. I'm not going to call Roshek because he is a paranoid schizophrenic as well as a turd."

"What if Bolen tells you to mind your own business?"

"I'll make an inspection anyway. If I can't bluff my way in, I might go down the intake tower. There's a little elevator, a man-cage, inside. The problem would be getting to the top—it sticks up twenty feet above the water. I was thinking of stealing a yacht and climbing the mast."

Janet groaned. "This is sounding worse and worse. You'll get caught and thrown in jail if you don't kill yourself first. Either way there is nobody to take me out to dinner."

"Why not look on the bright side? You are a very attractive woman and you will have no trouble finding yourself another engineer."

"Don't make me laugh. I learn from my mistakes."

17

PHIL TURNED ONTO THE POWERHOUSE access road and immediately had to hit the brakes: both lanes were blocked by a double chain-link gate. "Shit," he muttered. "Duncan didn't mention this."

He left the car with the headlights on and the engine running to examine the obstacle. The hinge posts were four-inch steel pipes set in concrete. The padlock in the middle weighed at least three pounds and looked smugly impregnable, and the length of chain it joined in a loop would withstand a week of hacksawing. The good news was that there were no electrical connections anywhere on the gate or adjoining fence, which meant that if he could somehow force it open, alarms wouldn't go off up and down the Pacific Coast.

He returned to the car and sat behind the wheel pondering the alternatives. Climbing over the fence and walking the half mile to the tunnel portal would be no problem, but that is hardly the way an inspector from the Occupational Safety and Health Administration would arrive, and it was a federal OSHA representative he had decided to impersonate. The United States government didn't send its agents slinking along lonely roads in the middle of the night like escaped felons. He could try picking the lock with a piece of wire. No, that would take all night. If the local police had a key to the gate, maybe he could bluff them into opening it. No, too risky. He had to act fast if he was going to exploit Bolen's absence—his wife had told him on the phone that he would return home within the hour.

With his arms folded on the wheel, Phil lifted his eyes from the gate to the massive bulk of the dam looming in the background. The great structure seemed to be asleep, bathed in faint light from a moon that now was high in the sky. Dams for Phil had always been the most inspiring and admirable symbols of the engineer's art—stunning, audacious, thrilling. Sierra Canyon was different. There was something sinister about it and dangerous. The longer he gazed at it, the more uncomfortable he felt. Calm down, he cautioned himself, there is no immediate threat. The uneasiness you feel is an emotional response to the knowledge you have of the dam's inner workings. The dam was so goddam big! An enormous jungle cat, sleek and muscular, crouched in the canyon, its back arched against the force of the lake. Phil felt like a gnat in comparison. If he advanced any closer, that big cat might choose to obliterate him with a flick of a paw.

But dams and jungle cats, Phil told himself in an effort to keep his determination from eroding, can have physical problems that don't show on the surface. The most powerful and ferocious beast can be hobbled by a thorn and killed by a ruptured artery. He put the car in reverse and slowly backed away from the gate. "What I need," he said aloud, "is a way to get this car past that gate. Something simple and elegant that would honor the holder of a doctorate from one of the Midwest's finest institutions of learning."

When the car was a hundred and fifty feet from the gate, Phil stopped, checked his seat belt, shifted into low, and raced the engine. Grabbing the wheel tightly and bracing himself, he let out the clutch. Tires squealed. "Something subtle and sophisticated," he said as the car shot forward.

A speed of forty miles an hour proved sufficient to break the gate apart, cave in the grill, flatten the front tires, rip off the front bumper, and smash one headlight. The nice thing about driving an old car, Phil thought, shaking off the effects of the impact, is that a few more scratches don't make any difference.

Set into the base of a vertical wall of rock was a steel hangar door that marked the mouth of the powerhouse access tunnel. Next to it was a concrete panel into which were countersunk a microphone and a loudspeaker. Phil, a roll of plans under his arm and a clipboard in his hand, pushed a large black button. A red light went on and a hiss came over the loudspeaker followed by a voice.

"Control room."

"Is this Mr. Newt Withers?" Phil asked crisply.

"This is Withers."

"I'm Charles Robinson of the Occupational Safety and Health Administration." It was the biggest lie Phil Kramer had told in his entire life. When the state of Kansas was admitted to the union in 1861, Charles Robinson was elected Governor.

"Come again?" Withers asked.

Phil repeated his *ad hoc* name and affiliation. "I trust

you've been expecting me," he added.

There was a pause. "What did you say your name was? Robinson?"

"Mr. Withers," Phil said with mock impatience, "didn't Mr. Jeffers or Mr. Bolen tell you that there might be an OSHA night inspection this weekend?"

"I'm sorry, nobody said anything to me. I'm not supposed to raise the door without authorization."

"What time did you go on duty?"

"Ten o'clock, sir."

"Nobody left a message for you?"

"Not that I noticed. May I ask how you got through the upper gate?"

Phil raised his voice slightly. "With a key that Herman Bolen gave me earlier today in Los Angeles. Your communications seem to be less than adequate. It makes me wonder what else might be. I told Larry Jeffers yesterday and Herman Bolen this morning to be sure that all powerhouse personnel were notified of the new OSHA program. They assured me there would be no problem and that I would be admitted at any time of the day or night."

"I don't know what to say," Withers said defensively. "My standing orders are—"

"If I'm not let in after clearing the visit with the officers who are in charge of the structure, I'll have to assume there's something you're trying to hide."

"It's not that. We had an OSHA inspection a few months ago. We got high marks."

"The marks were not as high as you apparently think. There were questions raised about air quality—the air you have to breathe, Mr. Withers. There were lights burnt out in the inspection galleries. The subcontractor replacing the rotor of the Unit Three generator was not conforming to standard safety procedures. Excuse me, I don't mean to blame you for the failure of others to keep you informed. Here's what I want you to do—call Lawrence Jeffers and Herman Bolen at their homes right now. I'll wait here. Don't worry about waking them up; tell them I ordered you to call. They will confirm our recent discussions and give you the okay to let me in. If they don't, I'll have to file a report with my superiors in Washington as well as with the State Division of Dam Safety."

"Yes, sir. I'll do that right away."

The red light went out and the loudspeaker fell silent. With luck, Phil thought, Bolen won't be home yet and nobody will answer Jeffers's phone. Withers will be on the spot then and will probably yield. Phil turned away and looked up at the dam. "No need to look so surly," he said, addressing it as if it were alive. "I'm only trying to help. If you have a thorn in your paw, it should be taken out—don't you agree? Then we can be pals."

After several minutes two floodlights went on above the panel, illuminating Phil like a singer on a stage. He turned and squinted.

"Would you stand on the center of the platform, please," Withers asked over the loudspeaker, "and look at the camera?"

For the first time, Phil noticed a camera housing on the rock wall five feet above his head. He saw the lens retract to put him in focus.

"May I ask what the cylinder is you are carrying?"

"This? A set of plans of the dam's instrumentation and inspection tunnels."

"Would you unroll them, please?"

Phil did so, realizing that Withers wanted to make sure he wasn't concealing a rifle or a bomb. He held the sheets toward the camera. "You can see the Roshek company seal in the lower corner," he said.

"Yes, I see it. Are you carrying any metal?"

"Just a belt buckle."

"What about the clipboard?"

"Plastic." It was in fact a children's item Phil had bought in the School Daze section of an all-night grocery store.

"If you are carrying any other metal, an alarm will sound in the Sutterton police station when you go through the detector. I'm going to raise the door high enough for you, Mr. Robinson, but not for your car. You'll have to walk down the tunnel. If you have instruments that are too heavy to carry, you'll have to come back in the morning when my boss is on duty."

"Fair enough."

There was a rumble as the ponderous door rolled upward. It stopped with the lower edge five feet above the pavement. Phil ducked inside and heard it thunder shut behind him with reverberating finality.

"This is Herman Bolen speaking."

"Oh, yes, Mr. Bolen. Newt Withers here. Thanks for returning my call. Excuse me for calling so late, but I had a question to ask and I couldn't locate Mr. Jeffers."

"Is everything all right up there? No sudden leaks or anything, I hope." Bolen laughed briefly.

"Everything is fine, as far as I know. Nothing shows on the board."

"Good. I must say I was surprised to get the message that you called, because I was about to phone the powerhouse myself. Something came up and I had to leave the house for a time. I'm trying to find out what happened to our Mr. Jeffers. He's been missing for over twenty-four hours."

"I know he didn't come in today. The local Chief of Police called earlier to ask if I knew where he was."

"Withers, I have to tell you that I'm a little worried about what might have happened to him. It may be that his car has gone off the road somewhere . . . that's what I'm most afraid of. Another possibility is that he's had some sort of accident in the lower drainage tunnels. When

I talked to him on Thursday night, he said he was thinking of checking a few meters before going to bed. No reason to get excited," Bolen added quickly when he heard Withers's low whistle. "All of this is just supposition on my part."

"If he was in the dam, wouldn't his car still be here? I didn't see it in the lot when I came in."

"Good point. Still, I'd like to have somebody take a look around down below. What I want to avoid is a general alarm, missing-person bulletins on television, and that sort of thing. That would be embarrassing to the firm and to Larry, too, if it turns out that he has simply wandered off somewhere without telling anybody. Can you take a break and go down to the lower galleries?"

"Well, I'm not supposed to leave the control room for longer than ten minutes. Going down to the bottom and back would take a half hour. The OSHA inspector said he was going to check Gallery D. That was twenty minutes ago. . . . When he gets back, I'll ask if he—"

"What OSHA inspector?"

"The one you talked to this morning. The one you gave the key to the upper gate to. The reason I called you a few minutes ago was to make sure he had proper authorization. You and Jeffers were out, and he seemed to be getting hot, so I decided to let him in."

"I don't know any OSHA inspector. My key to the upper gate is locked in my desk."

Withers moaned. "Oh, God, no. He said his name was Charles Robinson. He said he was here to make a night inspection and that you knew all about it."

"I don't know anybody by that name. He must be the fellow who tried to reach me when I was out. He knew I was gone, that's why he told you to call me. The man is a phony."

"If he's a phony, he sure knows his business. He knows this dam inside and out. He even had a set of R. B. & B. plans of the tunnels. Should I call the cops?"

"He had a set of plans? What did he look like?"

"Tall guy, maybe six foot two. About twenty-five years old. Reddish hair."

"Does he take big steps when he walks, like a farmer stepping over two furrows at once?"

"Yeah, I guess you could say that."

Bolen cursed quietly. "It sounds like Kramer. Can you turn on the parking-lot lights from where you are? See if you can find his car with your camera."

"Just a second. Let's see . . . yep, that must be his car, right next to mine. Wait till I focus. Got it. Looks like a Mustang, six or seven years old, pretty banged up."

"Call the police. Your OSHA inspector is Phil Kramer, an engineer Roshek fired about twelve hours ago. He is convinced that the dam is going to fail any second. He's absolutely possessed by the idea, which is why we had to let him go."

"Is he violent? Jesus, I'm in here alone."

"I don't think there is any chance of violence. As far as I know, he is perfectly rational except when it comes to the dam. Unless I miss my guess, when he comes up from below he's going to want you to declare an emergency. He's never been inside a dam and has no idea of how much leakage there is. When he sees the way water comes in, he'll think it's about to bust."

"I hope the cops can get here before he gets back."

"Withers, if it can be arranged, I don't want him charged with anything. Best for us is if the police restrain him and keep him from going to the newspapers until I get there. I'm coming up to meet a Dam Safety inspector from Sacramento at noon. We don't want rumors getting started about the dam. See the point? I'll take charge of Kramer when I get there. I'm sure I can talk some sense into his head. Let's keep this quiet if we can."

Bolen had been talking on the wall phone in the kitchen of his home. When he hung up, he turned to his wife and Roshek, who were having coffee at the kitchen table.

Roshek had obviously grasped the entire picture from hearing only one side of the conversation. There was color in his cheeks and the fire had returned to his eyes. He looked almost normal.

"We should throw the book at that kid and try to keep him behind bars for life. He's a menace to the company."

Bolen nodded tiredly. "We'll talk about it in the morning. Let's all try to get some sleep. I'll wake you, Theodore, if Withers calls with any unusual news."

18

PHIL SQUEEZED PAST THE CAR THAT was parked behind the sixth turbine. Was there a workman of some kind in the tunnels, he wondered, despite the hour? If there was, he would bluff him the same way he bluffed Withers. He sprinted up the flight of steel stairs and pulled open the door marked "DANGER, NO ADMITTANCE." He grabbed a flashlight from the rack and headed down the tunnel at a half trot. He couldn't help smiling at the success of his acting début. His officious and faintly irritated manner had completely fooled Withers. The poor guy was kept on the defensive by a barrage of questions about working conditions, handrails, fire extinguishers, first-aid kits, and anything else that had popped into Phil's mind. Withers never had a chance to demand identification or to ask questions of his own.

The tunnel was better suited to screams of fear than to smiles of satisfaction. It was no bigger than the culverts under his father's county roads, so poorly lit by the widely spaced overhead bulbs that he had to turn his flashlight on, and so wet he had already ruined his shoes. God, he wondered, casting his light onto the mineral-stained walls and the swiftly flowing rivulet in the gutter along the walkway, if there is this much water coming in at the elevation of the river what's it going to be like a hundred and fifty feet lower?

The air was stale, and the tunnel seemed to get smaller the deeper into it he advanced, although he knew that was just his imagination. For the first time since childhood, he felt a touch of claustrophobia, not enough to make him turn back, but enough to make him remember with unsettling clarity being held in a closet at the age of five or six. His tormentors were a group of laughing playmates who were unmoved by his terror—they were moved, finally, by his mother, who heard his muffled screams from the backyard. Now Phil had the feeling that the fear that overcame him then was lurking deep within him still, and would surface again if he let it. He pushed on, each footstep making a splashing sound that reminded him of the way he used to stomp around in the puddles that formed after summer rains in Wichita. He wished he could be transported suddenly to Kansas and out of the dreary tunnel whose walls seemed to be pressing in upon him—Kansas, where the horizons were always miles away.

At an intersection with a cross tunnel, Phil unrolled the plans and rested them on his upraised knee. He hardly needed to refer to them again, but the sight of the detailed technical drawings, complete with dimensions, cross-sections, and explanatory notes, helped him keep his intellect in control rather than his emotions. There was no mystery about the tunnels, the drawings seemed to say, and nothing to be afraid of. You aren't lost in Hell or the sewers of Paris.

To the right was the inspection tunnel that penetrated the rock of the north abutment. Straight ahead was the way to the base of the intake shaft. To the left, that's where he wanted to go.

The side tunnel was definitely smaller, Phil thought, proceeding with more caution—no more than seven feet in diameter. Jesus, I can see why Duncan hates to come in here. A man could shout his lungs out and shoot off a cannon and not a living thing would hear him. At least in the sewers of Paris there would be rats to take notice, or maybe gendarmes. If I really was an OSHA inspector, I'd raise hell about these tunnels—not enough light, terrible air, treacherous footing—and maybe I will anyway. Something should be done to make seepage water come in through the underdrains and the radial collector pipes, where it's supposed to, instead of through cracks and joints in the tunnel walls. This is a hell of a mess. . . .

Phil stopped at the top of the main stairwell, which descended at a steep angle. The beam of his flashlight had little effect on the gloom below him. There was a faint sound of rushing water that he felt sure could not be normal. He stood very still and listened. Water was dripping and trickling around him and flowing in the gutter alongside the walkway, but the sound that held his attention was deeper and stronger, like that of a waterfall plunging into a pool.

He started down, taking the steps as quickly as he could. According to Duncan, there were two hundred of them. If he tripped, he would never stop rolling.

Two hours after midnight on Saturday morning, the bars of Sutterton were closing. Two police patrol cars were on duty, one stationed across from Randy's Roadhouse south of town, the other across from the Wagon

Wheel Saloon. Experience had shown that as the patrons of the town's two largest establishments debouched onto the streets, the sight of police cars hastened the onset of sobriety.

Car Two was at the Wagon Wheel. Officers John Colla and Lee Simon were relieved at the display of temperance and good behavior. Nobody seemed interested in disturbing the peace or anyone else. Nobody needed police assistance to stand or walk.

There was a rush of static on the two-way radio as the dispatcher asked for their location. Colla, behind the wheel, picked up the microphone. "Car Two at the Wagon Wheel. Quiet as a church picnic."

"We've got a two two three at the powerhouse. Engineer on duty is Withers. Proceed NFS."

The policemen glanced at each other. Two two three was the code for a trespass under way. NFS meant no flashing lights or siren.

"Which Withers is that, Chet?" Colla asked. "Newt?"

"Yes. The intruder is thought to be one Phil Kramer, who used a false name and story to get in. Purpose unknown. Suspect is somewhere inside the dam and doesn't know we've been called. Newt has locked himself in the control room and will raise the door when you ring the buzzer."

Colla started the engine and pulled away from the curb. A U-turn put him on the way to the dam. "Weapons?"

"Nothing showed on the metal detector. Suspect has no known record. May be unstable. Known to be a fanatic about the dam and thinks it's going to fail."

"What about the upper gate?"

"Your key number fifteen should open it. If not, Newt has some of his people on the way who can let you in."

"Sounds tricky. Are we getting any other help?"

"Highway Patrol is sending a car."

"Roger. Out."

Officer Simon unlocked the glove compartment and

removed a ring of keys. "We might have a psycho on our hands," he said.

"Sounds like it. I hope he's one we can sweet-talk."

His hope for using psychology rather than force was undermined by the sight of the demolished upper gate.

After saying good night to Roshek, Herman Bolen waited in the hallway outside the guest bedroom to see if he would go to sleep or sit up working himself into a temper. When the slit of light under the door turned black, Bolen sighed in relief. "At least I've got *him* out of my hair for a while," he breathed, going down the stairs to his den. He sat at his desk and dialed the powerhouse.

It was amazing how complicated life had suddenly become. Questions about the safety of Sierra Canyon Dam were raised by the latest inspection reports; one of the company's most reliable employees was inexplicably missing and guilty at the very least of gross thoughtlessness; Roshek announced that he might abdicate his throne for a few years, then proceeded to terrorize his wife and get evicted from his own house by the police. Now this thing with Kramer. It was surprising enough that Kramer had talked back to Roshek and gotten himself fired, but going to Sutterton and lying his way into the dam was almost unbelievable. That kid will wind up in jail if Roshek has his way. Bolen was disgusted with himself for making such a terrible character judgment, and wondered if there was mental illness in the young engineer's background. A call to the boy's family or the Menninger Clinic might turn up something.

"This is Herman again," he said when Withers answered. "Any developments?"

"The cops are on their way but not here yet."

"Good. Kramer hasn't showed up again?"

"Still down in the hole, I guess."

"Don't let him in the control room. If he throws a fit in there, he could really do a lot of damage."

"You think he'll throw a fit? Christ, I'm glad these big windows are bulletproof."

"I don't know what he might do. I completely misjudged the man. I don't think we have to worry about bullets, though . . . unless the police get excited and start shooting. I hope they'll use minimum force. I've been thinking about my last conversation with Kramer. He was particularly upset about what he regarded as excessively high seepage in Gallery D. Can you tell me anything about conditions there from where you sit?"

"Gallery D? There are a few remote-reading pore-pressure sensors, I think. I'm strictly electrical, you know, not trained in hydraulics. Hang on while I take this on another phone—the lower gallery panels are on the other side of the room. . . . Mr. Bolen? There are three dials here for Gallery D. Two show zero, and the third is stuck on the high end. I think they're out of order. I've worked here six months and the readings never change. I can check the current drain for that reach of the electrical network . . . one second. Let's see, looks like about a third of normal. I would guess two of the three pumps aren't working."

"Two pumps out? That means there might be a few inches of water standing on the tunnel floor. If there is a break in the high-pressure line from the third pump, Kramer will think the lake is coming in. Don't let him scare you."

"I understand."

"One more thing. If those pumps are out, get somebody to put them back on line immediately. We don't want the inspector from the state to find a pile of broken-down machinery."

At the bottom of the steps, Phil found himself in darkness standing in water that came to his thighs. Don't get excited, he told himself, just because the overhead lights are out and the pumps aren't working. The situation was hardly normal, but there was no proof that a catastrophe was pending. What he wanted was proof. Leaving the roll of plans on a dry step, he waded forward toward the sound of surging water, the beam of the flashlight penetrating only as far as the next veil of water dripping from the tunnel crown. Fifty feet from the foot of the steps, he found what he assumed was the main source of the flood —a vigorous upwelling of water from beneath the surface. He groped with one foot to try to determine if it was erupting from a boil-out on the floor or from a broken pressure pipe, but the force of the jet was too great. His foot was knocked aside and into a submerged object that seemed roughly cylindrical and covered with canvas or cloth that was snagged on the tunnel wall. It yielded and rolled away as he pushed past it.

Deeper in the tunnel, Phil's flashlight illuminated a rectangular chamber. On the left wall was a half-open steel door marked Gallery D. There, he knew, he would find the proof he needed.

He kept fear in check by concentrating on the technicalities of the job to be done. He already felt vindicated for breaking in. The fantastic amount of water demonstrated beyond argument that the drainage, pumping, inspection, and monitoring procedures that Roshek was so proud of were inadequate. Further, his computer program, while perhaps far from foolproof, had at least revealed that *something* was haywire. Even if the submerged jet was the result of a ruptured discharge pipe, he was justified in sounding some sort of alarm. For one thing, if emergency pumping was not begun at once, the water level would rise so high that all the pumps and monitoring devices in this section of the structure would be put out of action. He had evidence enough now to wipe the look of contempt off Roshek's face and to dissolve Bolen's attitude of condescension. But Phil wanted to check his larger theory as well, that the dam as a whole contained fundamental weaknesses. For proof of that, he wanted a look at the meters in Gallery D that were still above water and functioning.

The passageway behind the door descended gradually and after only eighty feet Phil was in water up to his chest. He stopped and shined his light ahead, wondering how much farther he had to go to reach the meter bank. Twenty feet away he saw a shimmering horizontal band that made his mouth open and his flesh crawl: a sheet of water under extreme pressure was jetting from one wall of the tunnel to the other from a jagged crack. The volume of water grew as he watched it, and he saw several small pieces of concrete at the base of the stream scoured loose and shot across the tunnel with the force of rifle bullets.

"That's not seepage," he said, taking several backward steps and trying to swallow, "and that's not a broken pipe. That's a fucking *breach*. . . ."

He turned and waded toward the main tunnel as fast as he could, wondering if he could make faster progress by swimming, aware for the first time how slippery the footing was. Slippery? Holding the flashlight aloft in one hand, he lowered the other to the walkway, having to submerge his head and shoulders to do it. He scraped the side of his palm along the concrete and brought it to the surface. The flashlight confirmed his suspicion: his cupped hand was filled with clay. The incoming water was carrying with it part of the embankment. He poured the clay into the pocket of his shirt and fastened the button. Ten feet away, sudden waves of water in the main tunnel began closing the door to Gallery D. With a desperate lunge he was able to jam his arms through the narrowing gap and force the door back far enough to pull himself through. He no longer was worried about verifying a theory, or saving his career, or getting the last word with Bolen and Roshek. All that mattered now was escaping with his life. Gasping, he pushed his way toward the steps. Blocking his way was the submerged fountain, which was gushing upward now with ten times its earlier force and sending a boiling mass of water against the tunnel crown. Phil plunged wildly forward and into the cold, stiffened arms of Lawrence Jeffers.

In the powerhouse, needles on two dials assumed to be inoperative rose from zero to the high ends of the scales.

Theodore Roshek couldn't sleep. He fumbled in the darkness for the lamp on the bedside table. When the light was on, he lowered his feet to the floor and put the telephone in his lap. He would call Eleanor. She had never been particularly sympathetic when he wanted to discuss matters she considered "heavy," but maybe when she heard what he had gone through she would forgive him for waking her and say something to cheer him up. Just hearing her voice would make him feel better. Unfortunately, there was a busy signal when he dialed Creekwood, the house on the Sierra Canyon River. She had probably turned in for the night and, as usual, had taken the phone off the hook.

He put his head on the pillow and lay staring at the ceiling.

In the kitchen downstairs, Herman Bolen was at the stove making another pot of coffee and waiting for the phone to ring.

19

WHEN THE SMALL JET OF WATER IN the tunnel floor erupted into a full-fledged geyser, the increased force dislodged the snagged body of Jeffers and rotated it upward in a sudden cartwheel, the arms projecting grotesquely. Before the body landed on him, Phil caught a flash of glassy eyes protruding from a death mask that was frozen in an expression of terror even greater than his own. Phil hurled himself backward in fright, dropping the flashlight and losing his balance. His hoarse shout was stopped by the water that closed over his head as he fell. When he regained his footing, he was in total darkness. He waded toward the sound of the upsurging water, again encountering the body, which was floating face up and blocking his way. Phil filled his fists with the cloth of the dead man's shirt and pushed the body ahead of him. Taking a deep breath and ducking his head beneath the surface, he drove forward using the body as a shield and as a way of keeping his balance. Once past the jet, which was shooting upward like the stream from a broken hydrant, the water level came to his waist—a foot higher than it was on his way in ten minutes before. Phil struggled forward, pushing the body, orienting himself by keeping one foot on the edge of the walkway. At the base of the steps he looked up and saw faint lights far above him. Thank God, he thought, the lights are out only at the bottom. He began the upward climb one step at a time, pulling the ungainly body behind him. After advancing twenty feet he released his grip and sat down gasping for breath. The body slipped down several steps and became wedged in the gutter between the walkway and the curving wall of the tunnel. Phil tried to clear his thoughts. Was there time to drag the body out and save himself as well? What was the point of risking his life to retrieve a corpse? He felt a coldness growing on his legs and wondered if it was a sign that he was going into shock. Peering down through the semi-darkness, he saw that the stairwell below him was completely flooded. Silently rising water was creeping over his feet, calves, and knees. He rolled away from it and clambered up the steps on all fours toward the distant lights.

Withers cursed his own stupidity. Why did I let that guy in? Raise the door only for people you know or who have authorization arranged in advance—that's what the orders are. Oh, Jesus, it's going to be my ass when Jeffers gets here, or Bolen, or any of a half a dozen other people. But I thought it would be my ass if I *didn't* let him in! How was I supposed to know he was a phony? He knew all the right things to say. Anybody would have done what I did.

There were four closed-circuit television screens

mounted on the wall. One displayed the access tunnel entrance and parking area, one the electrical switchyard, one the generator deck, and one the turbine deck. The last two were usually focused on dials, but they could be panned remotely to take in any part of the chambers. By manipulating two small levers, Withers trained Camera 4 on the door leading to the inspection galleries. He moved his eyes back and forth from 1 to 4, hoping that the police would appear before the intruder.

A buzzer sounded and a light flashed on the hot-line phone to Pacific Gas & Electric's Power Control Center in Oakland, from which the power grid in northern California was monitored.

"Sierra Canyon."

"Power Central. Rancho Seco may have to cut back in a few hours. We'll need an extra twenty megawatts from you during the morning peak. I guess you can handle that? We show you at eighty-six percent of capacity, not counting Unit Three. Are you spilling? What's your afterbay elevation?"

"We're spilling two feet, but the afterbay is drawn down. An extra twenty will be no problem."

On the fourth television screen, Withers saw Kramer burst through the door at the end of the turbine and drape himself over a steel railing, apparently trying to catch his breath. He was gulping air, his shoulders and chest heaving. Or was he vomiting? Squinting, Withers couldn't tell. Where were the goddam cops? "Can I get back to you?" he asked the dispatcher.

The voice from Power Control Central went on in a monotone: "Checking our printouts on Sierra Canyon, there seems to be a frequency fluctuation during the last thirty minutes or so. Nothing serious, just a hair. What do you indicate at your end?"

"Look, I'm awful busy right now. I'll call you back in about thirty minutes. . . ."

"At three in the morning you're busy?"

"I got a slight problem here. I'll explain later."

Withers hung up and rose out of his chair staring at the monitor. Kramer's clothing and hair looked wet. His eyes were wide and his mouth was hanging open. "Holy Christ," Withers whispered, "a pipe must have burst and hit him with spray. He looks like he's flipped his lid completely." As he watched, Kramer closed his mouth and swallowed with difficulty, glancing behind him as if he were being pursued. He lunged down the short flight of steps to the floor of the turbine deck, out of the camera's view.

Withers lowered himself into his chair and swiveled toward the windows that lined one wall of the control room. He would have to stall Kramer until the cops arrived. Remain calm and reason with him. Hope that he wouldn't go beserk. Withers ground his teeth at the thought of how much damage a madman could do. Unit 3 was off line and the generator deck was strewn with tools and equipment that could as easily be used to destroy as repair. A sledgehammer or a bucket of bolts thrown into one of the spinning rotors would cause a terrible amount of damage. If something like that happened, Withers realized, because he had admitted a man without clearance, he would be out of a job and could forget about ever getting hired again as a powerhouse operator.

The apparition that appeared on the other side of the windows was like something out of a bad dream. Kramer's clothes were soaked and torn and his face was streaked with blood from a cut on his scalp. The expression on his face was that of a man who was in a desperate battle with private demons, a man who had only a tenuous connection with reality. He ran drunkenly across the tile floor, skidded to a stop, and pressed his hands against the glass. The voice Withers heard over the intercom was high-pitched and breathless.

"The dam is failing! We've got to sound the alarm! The dam is failing!"

Withers nodded sympathetically but did not move.

"Can you hear me? The dam is failing!"

Withers leaned forward to bring his lips close to a microphone on the counter top. "Yes, I can hear you."

"The lake is breaking into the tunnels. . . . One man is dead already. . . . We've got to warn the town. . . ." Kramer looked wildly around, then hurled himself to the end of the windows and tried to open the control-room door. "Unlock the door! What's the matter with you? The dam is failing!"

Withers concentrated on presenting an unruffled appearance even though his pulse was racing and beads of sweat were forming on his forehead. He was gripping the edge of the counter so tightly the tips of his fingers were white. Did Kramer say a man was dead? "I can't open the door," he said. "It's against regulations. Clearance would have to be obtained from—"

"Fuck regulations!" Kramer shouted. "This is an emergency! We've got to do something right away, warn people, get our asses out of here. . . . Are you crazy? Isn't one corpse enough? Maybe the dam can be saved . . . we've got to get on the phone. . . ."

"Calm down, Mr. Kramer. You are all excited."

"Sure I'm excited! Jesus Christ!" He frowned. "You called me Kramer. How did you know my name was Kramer?"

Withers hesitated, hoping he hadn't made another terrible error. "I talked with Herman Bolen a few minutes ago. He was able to identify you. When you say 'corpse,' do you mean—"

"Get him on the phone! Let me talk to him. When I tell him what I've seen . . . Call him! Call anybody! You goddam dummy! Do something!"

"Mr. Bolen will be here at noon. You can talk to him then."

Kramer shook his fists. "By noon the dam may not be here! Sutterton may not be here! Unless you get in gear, you'll be floating around in that chair in the middle of

San Francisco Bay. *The . . . dam . . . is . . . failing.*" He rolled his eyes in disbelief at the lack of effect the words had on Withers. "The dam is failing and I have to deal with a robot." He whirled around and saw the row of offices that lined the opposite wall of the lobby. He ran from one to another trying the telephones, throwing them aside when he couldn't get a dial tone.

"The phones are dead," Withers said. "The switchboard is turned off when the staff leaves at five. Mr. Kramer, you've got to get hold of yourself. Why don't you sit down at one of those desks and take a nap? We'll talk things over later." Where the hell were the cops?

Kramer tightened his fists and walked back to the control-room windows. "You think I'm a raving fucking lunatic, don't you?" he said. "Bolen told you I had a fixation about the dam failing and that I wasn't to be taken seriously, is that it? Protect the company's reputation."

"You *think* the dam is failing. You don't *know* the dam is failing. If the dam was failing, the instruments would—"

"The instruments are out of order! Ask Duncan, he'll tell you. This whole joint is out of order. I *know* the dam is failing. With my own eyes I have . . ."

Kramer slapped both hands over his face, digging his fingernails into his forehead in frustration and apparently not feeling the blood on his cheek. His shoulders were trembling. Withers stood up, studying him, hoping he was about to succumb to some sort of seizure.

Kramer lowered his hands. He had managed to erase the tension from his face. The men stared at each other through double panes of bulletproof glass. When Kramer spoke again, it seemed to Withers that he was making a great effort to keep his voice from cracking and to keep from talking too fast.

"I am not a crackpot," Kramer said, making precise gestures. "Until yesterday I worked in the hydro design section of Roshek, Bolen & Benedetz in the Los Angeles office. I have been worried about the structural integrity of this dam for three weeks. I got fired because I explained my suspicions to Roshek and lost my temper when he wouldn't take them seriously." He stopped for a deep breath. "I came here to see if I was right or wrong. I lied to you to get in because it seemed like the only way. A thousand pardons, Mr. Withers, for the trick I played on you." His voice and face had become calm. As he continued, he gave a convincing impression of being utterly relaxed. "I was just down in the lower drainage galleries and I found that my worst fears were true. The lake is breaking in under pressure even as we stand here having this friendly discussion. I saw two breaches. Each one is bringing water in at about five or ten thousand gallons a minute, I would guess."

Withers gradually realized that Kramer's voice and expression had taken on a patronizing quality, as if it were he, Withers, who had to be humored.

"I'm sure you realize, Mr. Withers, as an engineer, that water coming in under pressure is— how shall I put it?— bad news."

"I . . . I'm not an engineer."

"I am. I have a Ph.D in civil engineering. My area of special interest, as luck would have it, is the prediction of dam failures. Some people immerse themselves in hydrangeas or collect miniature whiskey bottles. I study dam failures. One thing you learn when you pursue such an interest is that it is a poor sign when leakage is under pressure. Another poor sign is the presence of clay, which shows that the impervious core is not as impervious as might be wished, and is being scoured away by the water under pressure, to which I have just alluded." He dipped a finger into his shirt pocket and extended it toward Withers. "See? I scooped this up from the invert in the lower gallery. From under four feet of water." He drew a gray line on the glass between them. "That's clay from the core." He laced his fingers together. "What this all means

—the pressure, the clay, the rapid increase in flow—is that the dam is failing. That's it in a nutshell!" He smiled as if pleased at himself for finding words that even the dumbest child in kindergarten could comprehend. "As simple as that. The dam is failing! Now, Mr. Withers, what should two intelligent adults do when confronted with a failing dam?" His face clouded over and his voice began to rise. "Should they alert the authorities or should they converse like two fucking idiots? *Get on the phone!*"

"I'm not an expert or a specialist on hydraulics . . ."

"*I* am an expert and specialist on hydraulics!" Phil shouted. "I am a foremost goddam authority!"

". . . and I'm not going to cause a furor just because you are telling me things you may be making up or imagining, or that are based on misinterpreted data. In the morning the appropriate people can check out what you say."

"Fuck the appropriate people! There may not be any morning! We don't have time to go through channels, you dumb son of a bitch! You know how much time was lost at Baldwin Hills because the first people on the scene went through channels? We may have hours and we may have minutes. This dam may be ready to split open like a watermelon dropped from a truck." Phil pounded his fists against the windows. "One man is dead already and we may be next! You want to stay here? Fine. Then open the outside door so I can get the hell out. Otherwise I'm going to grab a crowbar from downstairs and tear this place apart. I'll smash these windows and knock your teeth out!"

Withers was sweating profusely. "What man is dead? Who is dead?" Could it be that Jeffers had had an accident in the inspection gallery? Kramer might have blundered into a broken pressure main and found Jeffers unconscious while snooping around in Gallery D. That would scare anybody half to death; no wonder he was so agitated.

"How should I know? The guy whose car is parked behind the turbines, I guess."

"Did you see him?"

"He landed right on my head! Did I see him? My God, I *danced* with him."

"What did he look like? A high forehead?"

"He looked terrible! He looked dead!" Phil lifted his eyes to the television screens behind Withers. His eyebrows rose. "Hey, did you call the cops?"

Withers turned to the monitors and saw a police car in the parking lot. A touch of a button switched the camera to close focus. The face of a policeman appeared on the screen. "Newt? This is Lee Simon. You okay? What's going on?"

Withers picked up a second microphone. "I'm okay, Lee. I'll raise the door. Drive to the end of the tunnel and come up the steps to the control room."

"You got a trespasser?"

Phil pounded on the glass again. "Don't let them in! Tell them to wake up the town!"

"Yes, but no trouble so far. He's on the control-room deck."

"Is he armed?"

Withers looked at Kramer, who was holding the sides of his head as if to contain an explosion. "I don't think so." He pushed the button that raised the roller door at the mouth of the access tunnel.

"You've got to be out of your mind," Phil said, edging away. "We'll all drown. . . ."

"Look, Kramer, the police aren't going to charge you with anything. Bolen just wants you held until he gets here. Stay cool and everything will be fine, okay? Do us both a favor. . . . Where do you think you're going?" He cursed when he saw Kramer run for the stairs to the lower decks. He picked up a microphone and shouted into it: "Touch those generators and you'll spend the rest of your life in jail! That's a promise!"

20

A CAR FROM THE COUNTY SHERIFF'S Department arrived within minutes of the police. Withers told the deputies to post themselves at the portal of the access tunnel in case Kramer tried to escape in that direction, then turned his attention to officers Colla and Simon, who were standing in the control-room lobby awaiting further instructions.

"He's back in the inspection galleries," Withers said. "See those stairs? Two flights down is the turbine deck. Go to the far end of the chamber and you'll see a steel door. I saw him go through there on the monitor."

"You're sure he's not armed?"

"Almost positive."

"Can he cause any damage?"

"Not if you keep him away from the generators. He could break some instruments and pull out some wiring, but nothing too bad."

"We'll stand guard downstairs until some of your people get here who know the tunnels."

"Right." Withers's attention was caught by a red light flashing on an instrument panel to his left. "Wait a minute. . . . Christ, he's in the elevator."

Although Withers had never been in it, he knew there was a man-cage inside the walls of the intake tower. He should have realized that Kramer would be aware of it. The red light showed that it was in use, and a dial showed that the cage was at the seven-hundred-foot level and was rising steadily toward the top landing at eight hundred and thirty feet. With a slight smile, Withers reversed the position of a toggle switch labeled "Override." The arrow stopped and began to swing slowly to the left. It would take the cage about five minutes to return to the bottom of the shaft, and when it got there the intruder would be met by Withers and the two policemen. He unlocked the control-room door and ran toward the stairs. "Come on!" he shouted, waving for the policemen to follow him. "He's trapped in an elevator. We've got him now!"

The footsteps of the three men as they ran down the steps masked a faint, throbbing vibration in the hum made by the generators. In the control room, a series of lights went on indicating a drop in frequency, then went out as circuits were shorted out by water. Two phones began to ring.

The elevator was little more than an open framework built over a three-foot-square platform. A waist-high grillwork fence shielded the passenger from the concrete walls of the shaft. One wall of the shaft was covered with water pipes, ventilation ducts, and bundled electrical conduits;

another, in a two-foot-wide, two-foot-deep vertical inset, carried the steel rungs of a ladder that ran the full height of the tower.

Phil reviewed in his mind the drawings of the tower he had studied at the motel. At the highest landing was a flight of stairs leading to a hatch cover. Once he got past that, he would be outside, twenty feet above the surface of the lake and about two hundred feet from shore.

As the cage rose, it rattled disconcertingly against its steel guide channels. Phil steadied himself against the railing and looked upward. The steel doors through which the reservoir intake gates could be reached were eighty feet apart, each one marked by a light. He kept one hand on the control handle, pressing it hard against its upper stop in an effort to force the cage beyond its fixed and agonizingly slow speed. With enough of a head start, he felt sure, he could swim to shore, find a phone, and sound an alarm before Withers and the police figured out where he had gone.

He kept his eyes on the last light, now about a hundred and fifty feet above him, and watched it slowly approach. With a lurch, the cage stopped moving. "Now what?" he said aloud, rattling the control handle. His first thought was that water had risen high enough to short out the generators . . . but no, the lights in the shaft were still on. Maybe power was only temporarily interrupted. "Come on, you bastard!" he shouted, kicking the grillwork fence and slamming the handle back and forth.

When the cage began to descend, Phil guessed that Withers had discovered where he was, and was using some sort of emergency hookup to bring the elevator to the bottom. He climbed to the top of the railing, caught hold of one of the ladder rungs as it went by, and stepped out of the cage. He flattened his body against the ladder until the upper framework had passed on its way down, then began climbing. The rungs were so wet from water trickling down the wall that he had trouble keeping his footing, and the steel was so cold he was afraid his hands would stick to it if he stopped moving. He kept his eyes fixed on the light above him and tried not to think about what would happen if he lost his grip.

After several minutes of steady hand-over-hand progress he reached the top landing. He stepped off the ladder and through a rectangular opening in the concrete wall. The clanking and creaking pulleys and cables stopped—the cage had reached the bottom. The faint sound of excited voices, confined in the narrow shaft, drifted up to him. The committee that had been waiting to welcome him was disappointed.

Phil ran up the stairs, pushed open the hatch cover, and climbed outside. With a profound feeling of relief in escaping from what could have been a death trap, he sank to his knees to catch his breath and look around. He was on the outer rim of the tower, the structure that had looked like a concrete doughnut floating on the lake when he first saw it from the overlook. The moon was in the western sky and would soon be out of sight, but it was still bathing the valley in light and casting a trail across the water. The sky was full of stars and there wasn't a trace of movement or sound in the air. The dam, visible as a low wall that stretched away as far as the eye could follow, seemed to be a natural part of the landscape.

It was a scene of such tranquility that Phil began to wonder if his brain was playing tricks on him. Had he simply imagined what he had just been through? For more than an hour, he had been trying to escape from a surrealistic nightmare, his bloodstream laced with adrenalin and screams never far from his lips. But under the starred canopy of the night sky and in the silence of the surrounding forests there was nothing but perfect peace. His feelings of terror, panic, and impending disaster seemed almost absurd. Perhaps a flawed and failing dam existed only in his mind. Perhaps Withers, the bloodless robot-clone, was right to ignore the ravings of a hysteric.

If I'm nuts, he thought, getting to his feet, they can lock me up. If I'm not, I'd better get a move on. The water I saw jetting into the lower galleries was no illusion. I didn't imagine that dead body—I can still feel the clammy arms around my neck. I've got to get to a phone. . . . The cops are probably already on their way to head me off.

Phil placed his car ignition key in the right side of his mouth between his cheek and his gum. In the left side he put two dimes he had in his pocket—they would be handy if the only phone he could find was in a public booth. He removed his shoes, socks, shirt, and slacks, and folded them in a neat pile. "If things work out right," he said to his clothes, "I'll come back for you."

He turned and leaped off the edge of the concrete, cupping his testicles in one hand and pinching his nose shut with the other. The shock of the cold water gave him new energy, and he pulled for shore with clean, strong strokes.

21

HERMAN BOLEN LAY ON HIS SIDE IN bed scowling into the telephone. The connection was poor and he had to strain to hear the words. "He said he saw a dead body?"

"Yes, sir," he heard Withers say. "It must be Jeffers. When I went with the police to the elevator, I saw his car behind the last turbine."

Bolen collapsed onto his back and stared at the ceiling. Jeffers! Dead! Dead because I sent him into the hole in the middle of the night . . . or was he? "Is it Jeffers or not?" he said in sudden exasperation, throwing the covers aside and sitting on the edge of the bed. "Is there a body or isn't there? Didn't you go down to make sure?"

"Things have been so hectic around here I haven't had a chance."

"Send somebody else, then! Have you called Cooper and Riggs?"

"They got here a little while ago. They're outside helping the police—"

"Goddammit, Withers! I want somebody to go down below *right now!*" Bolen covered the mouthpiece with his hand and turned to his wife, who was standing on the other side of the bed pulling on a robe. "The *stupidity* of this guy," he said in a strained whisper, shaking his head in amazement, "is absolutely incredible." He turned back to the phone and asked Withers what else Kramer had said.

"He said water was jetting in all over the place and bringing the dam in with it. He dug some dirt out of his shirt pocket with his finger and streaked it across the glass, as if that was supposed to prove something."

"Good Lord!"

"I didn't let that bother me because you already told me he was going to say the dam was failing. My dials showed two pumps were out, so I knew water was accumulating. When he saw a dead body, or thought he saw one, I figure he got hysterical. You should have seen him screaming and waving his arms. He's definitely psycho. I don't think his version is going to have much relation to the way things really are,"

"For everybody's sake, Withers, I hope he was hallucinating. What's your version of the way things really are?"

"Looks like all three pumps are out in the lower gallery. I'm getting no current drop on the sump circuit. The remote sensors in Gallery D have shorted out, too. My guess is that Gallery D is flooded."

"Wonderful," Bolen said with heavy sarcasm. "Just wonderful. And Kramer? You say the police have him cornered?"

"They saw him run across the road by the left overlook wearing nothing but his shorts. He's hiding in one of the buildings in the construction yard. They think they'll have him in a few minutes."

"What construction yard?"

"Mitchell Brothers has a contract with the county to widen the road."

"Get hold of Leonard Mitchell and give him the job of pumping out the lower tunnels. We've got to get those three sump pumps back in action, and I mean immediately. My God, we've got a guy from Dam Safety coming in at noon! Tell Cooper and Riggs to leave Kramer to the cops. I want a report from them on what's going on down below. I'm going to leave Beverly Hills right now." He looked at his bedside clock—it was 5:30 A.M. "I think I can be there in three hours. There's no commercial flight until eight o'clock and there's no airport at Sutterton for the company Lear, so I'll take my own plane. I'll land on top of the dam."

Bolen hung up and began dressing hurriedly. "I'll try to be back by late this afternoon," he said to his wife. "When Theodore wakes up, tell him I had to go to Sierra Canyon because of the Kramer situation and that I'll call him as soon as I can. Would you mind calling Stella? See if you can get her not to press charges."

In the guest bedroom downstairs, Roshek carefully replaced the receiver of the extension phone. He pulled himself out of bed into a chair and stared into the darkness, his jaw muscles tense and his lips pressed into a thin line.

After scaling the rocky slope from the lake to the road, Phil stood shivering, wondering which way to turn. Sutterton was at least a mile downhill to the right. The overlook was closer, up the road to the left, but he didn't recall seeing a pay phone there. Across the road were fuel and water tanks, what appeared to be an asphalt plant, and several corrugated-metal buildings. Against the sky he could see wires fanning out to the buildings from a nearby pole. One could be a telephone line. He trotted across the road, cursing under his breath whenever his bare feet landed on a pebble.

Just before he reached the shadows on the other side of the road, a car rounded a curve. For an instant, Phil was caught in the beam of the headlights. He sprinted between two parked crawler tractors, hoping he hadn't been spotted, and tried the door of the largest building. It was solidly locked. He ran to the rear of the building, which was set close to the steeply rising mountainside, and saw a row of horizontal windows hinged at the top. He broke one out with a rock and climbed carefully inside, and as he did so he heard the car slide to a stop in the gravel. The crackle of a two-way radio and fragments of a conversation confirmed his fears—it was the police.

"Suspect in construction yard on Sterling Road. Negative, cliff is too steep to climb. Maybe inside one of the buildings. Look, just send everybody up here, all right? We'll keep him from getting out."

Phil hugged himself in the cold, his eyes gradually becoming accustomed to the darkness. Looming over him were the shapes of two off-highway earthmoving trucks with tires eight feet high and cabs that could only be reached by ladders. One was on blocks with its rear wheels removed. On a workbench beneath the windows was a pile of oily rags. He grabbed a handful and dried himself, smoothing down the goose bumps on his forearms. What appeared at first glance to be a man standing against the wall staring at him turned out to be a pair of white coveralls on a hanger. He put them on, knocking over a rack of tools in the process. Outside, a second car arrived, and a third. In a momentary flash of headlights, Phil got a look at his surroundings—in the far corner was an office partitioned from the main area by walls of glass and plywood. He picked his way toward it, feeling the floor with a toe before each step.

"No shooting," he heard an authoritative voice say. "There's fuel tanks all over the place and maybe dynamite, too."

"Yes," Phil whispered, groping forward, "let's have no shooting. The suspect hates shooting."

In the office was a desk and on the desk was a phone. He raised the receiver to his ear and closed his eyes in relief when he heard a dial tone. Sixty seconds later Janet Sandifer was on the line.

"Phil, my God it's five in the morning! Where are you? Did you get in the dam?"

"Getting in was easy, getting out was the bitch. The cops are after me and they've got me cornered in a garage. The dam is failing, I'm sure of that now. Water is pouring into the tunnels under pressure. You've got to sound the alarm. . . ."

"What?"

". . . and raise all the hell you can. The dam is failing and I can't get anybody to believe it. I'm about to be arrested for trespassing or some goddam thing. Tell everybody the dam is failing. Call the towns downstream, call the Sheriff, call your mother. The state has some sort of disaster office . . . call that."

"The dam is failing? You mean right now?"

"Right now. What I am faced with here is a dam in the failure mode."

"You're putting me on. You sound funny. Your voice—"

"I'm not putting you on! If my voice sounds funny, it might be because I'm scared shitless! I'm surrounded by cops with guns! There are thousands of people asleep below the dam and I'm the only one who knows its failing. . . ."

"Can't the cops see it failing?"

"There's nothing to see unless you know exactly where

to look. Water is probably oozing out of the downstream face right where the computer said it would, but it's still dark and I can't get anybody to listen to me. You're my only hope. . . . This is the only phone call I'm going to be able to make. I may sound funny but I sure as hell don't feel funny. I feel like crying, if you want to know the truth. Janet, there's still time to evacuate the town. You've got to believe me! I know I'm right! I'm not joking! You've got to do what you can . . . please, please, please!"

"I believe you. I'll do what I can. How much I can accomplish from Santa Monica I don't know, but I'll do my best. Phil? I'm worried. About you. Don't take any more chances. You've done enough. Okay?"

Phil closed his eyes in relief. "Whew! I knew I could count on you. I've got to hang up. Good luck!"

"Don't take any more chances! Promise?"

"Just one more. Then I'm through. Then it's up to you. There's one more stunt I can try. . . . Read about it in the papers tomorrow."

When Chief Hartley arrived at the construction yard, a patrolman apprised him of the situation. Prints of bare feet had been found leading to the rear of the main building, where a pane of glass had been broken. A sheriff's deputy trying to look inside with a flashlight had nearly been hit by a wrench thrown by the suspect.

"Give me the bullhorn," Hartley said, "and I'll see if I can talk him out." He crouched behind his car with several aides and raised the bullhorn to his mouth. "This is Wilson Hartley," he said, his voice booming through the still night air and echoing off the cliff behind the building. "Sutterton Chief of Police. You might as well give yourself up, Mr. Kramer. Just stroll through the door with your hands up and you won't be hurt. Don't make us throw in a cannister of tear gas. You won't like it at all."

He lowered the horn and listened for a response. Surprisingly, he got one. Six times in his thirty-year career as a peace officer he had been involved in capturing runaway teenagers, escapees, and burglars who had hidden themselves in buildings of one kind or another. Never had one replied to his initial appeal for surrender.

"Do you promise not to shoot?" came a call from within the building.

Hartley widened his eyes at the deputy next to him. "We don't shoot trespassers in Caspar County," he said into the bullhorn. "My men won't shoot unless I give them a direct order."

"Good," was the muffled reply, "because I don't have a gun. You have a big edge on me there. I hate guns and shooting. Guns and shooting are inimical to life."

"What did he say?" Hartley whispered to the deputy.

"I didn't catch it. Something about life."

"If you can get them talking," the Chief went on in a whisper, "they usually won't do anything crazy. Setting up lines of communication is the key."

"I heard that," said the voice from inside the building. "Communication works both ways. Get a policeman talking and he usually won't do anything crazy, either. How do you like police work? Does your wife worry?"

Hartley frowned at the bullhorn and flicked the switch on the handle back and forth several times. "We can talk about that later," he said, once he was satisfied that he understood the mechanism. "Right now we want you to come out before somebody gets hurt. There are a lot of men out here who would like to go back to their regular duties."

"So would I," said the voice. "I know we can talk later, but we should talk now. The dam is failing, did anybody tell you? I know because I am a civil engineer. Kansas State. You and your men should be waking up the town instead of terrorizing a civil engineer who is trying to do everybody a favor and who is sure he is right and whom you can't help liking once you get past his shyness that is a carryover from God knows what in his childhood."

"Jesus," Hartley whispered, "this guy is a real fruitcake."

"I heard that," said the voice. "I am not a fruitcake. I resent that."

Hartley shook the bullhorn angrily. "How the fuck does this thing work, anyway? How do you turn the goddam thing off?"

"Must be stuck," said the deputy.

"The reason I am talking so much," said the voice, "is that I'm stalling for time. I'm checking a few things out in here. I'm not quite ready to come out, but almost. There, I think I'm ready. Are you ready, Sheriff?"

"I'm not the Sheriff, I'm the Chief of Police. We're ready. Take it nice and slow. Keep your hands over your head."

"I will not keep my hands over my head. That is a self-incriminating posture that would prejudice my chances for a fair trial. I intend to appeal this case all the way up to the Board of Direction of the American Society of Civil Engineers. See the garage door, Sheriff? I'm going to push a button that opens it. Then I'm coming out. I mean, I'm coming *out*."

Before Hartley could respond to what he sensed was in some way a rejection of his ultimatum, the door, suspended from a track at the roofline, rolled to one side with a rumble, revealing an opening large enough to pass the largest construction machines. Hartley peered into the shadows inside the building and was startled by the sight of two headlights winking on. There was the roar of a diesel engine and a fifteen-ton dump truck leaped into view. One of the huge tires caressed the Chief's car and knocked it aside as if it were made mostly of fiberglass rather than steel, which was in fact the case. Before anyone could react, the truck was out of the yard and turning left on the highway.

A deputy raised a rifle. "Say the word," he murmured, aiming.

"No shooting," Hartley commanded, jumping into his car. "He might lose control and crash into a house. Try to pass him and stop your car across the lanes. I'll radio ahead for a roadblock. He won't get far in that thing."

Hartley stepped hard on the gas and took off in a cloud of flying gravel. He turned on his roof lights and his electronic siren and overtook the truck in less than a minute. As he tried to pass on the left, the truck swerved right onto the narrow road that crossed the dam. "Where the hell does he think he's going?" Hartley said, braking and cramping the wheel hard right into the turn. "He'll never make the hairpin curves on the other side."

The deputy beside him had rolled down his window and was aiming his rifle again. "Let me take his tires out, boss."

Hartley pursed his lips in indecision. "Jesus, I'll bet those big fuckers cost five thousand bucks apiece. Well, okay, go ahead. . . . Wait, he's stopping! He's raising the dump. . . ."

He slammed on the brakes and hung tight to the wheel as the car skidded to a stop with its nose under the tail of the truck.

"Come on," Hartley said, "let's get him."

But before they could open their doors the car was jolted violently as ten tons of crushed rock slid out of the upraised dump and landed on the hood and engulfed the sides. By the time the two men had crawled out of the rear windows, a line of seven police and sheriff's cars had formed behind them and the truck was lumbering away, its upraised dump outlined against a graying sky.

22

PHIL STOPPED THE TRUCK WHEN HE saw the numbers 50+00 stenciled on the concrete shoulder of the crest road. According to the figures Janet had relayed to him when he called her from the motel, the most likely point of failure on the downstream face was between nineteen and forty-three feet past this point. He climbed down the ladder from the cab to the ground. He was dressed in the white coveralls he had found in the garage and a pair of ill-fitting rubber knee boots. A quarter of a mile away approaching headlights and a siren told him that one of the police cars had gotten around the pile of rock.

He climbed over the guardrail and looked down at the face of the dam, which angled downward at a two-to-one slope into the shadows and mists far below. The only sound was the thunder from the bottom of the spillway. In the left distance at the base of the dam on the other side of the river was the parking lot for the switchyard and the powerhouse. There were half a dozen cars there now, including his own. Despite its two flat front tires and its crumpled front end, the sight of his beloved jalopy was comforting, a link with his carefree past. His tongue touched the ignition key—still wedged between his cheek and gum.

The crest of the dam was a thousand and fifty feet above sea level, the predicted failure point at three seventy-five. He had a long climb ahead of him. From a distance the face of the dam looked as smooth as a tabletop—in fact it was composed of rough chunks of quarried rock measuring several feet on a side that protected the underlying layer of compacted earth from erosion. Phil swung himself over the guardrail, hung for a moment from the edge of the concrete road platform, and dropped five feet to the top of the slope. Above him he heard a car stop and doors open. He clambered downward as quickly as he could without losing his balance.

"Get back up here," a voice shouted, "or you're going to be in a whole shitpot full of trouble!"

"I'm already in a whole shitpot full of trouble," Phil replied, scampering downward across the rocks.

"Stop or I'll shoot!"

Phil stopped. Two policemen were looking down at him from twenty feet above. "You wouldn't shoot a harmless, unarmed engineer. The Chief told you not to shoot without a specific order from him. Aren't you going to follow me? I want you to. I want to show you where the dam is leaking. Then you'll know I'm not the nut you imagine. Well?"

"Son of a bitch. John, radio that he's going down the dam about two hundred yards from the spillway. Send some men to the bottom. I'll chase him down. You stay here in case he doubles back."

The policeman vaulted the rail and dropped to the top of the slope. He cupped his hands to his mouth and shouted at the figure scuttling down the rocks below him. "I'll give you one last chance to stop. If you make me climb all the way down this fucking dam, I'll wring your neck when I catch you."

There was no answer.

Power Control Central was on the line again. "Rancho Seco has to cut back more than we thought," the dispatcher said. "We need forty extra megawatts from Sierra Canyon, not the twenty we asked for earlier."

"No problem," Withers said, filling his voice with confidence, "We got plenty of water here."

Riggs and Cooper had arrived and let themselves into the control room. "Hang on a second," Withers said to the dispatcher. He covered the mouthpiece with his hand and told Riggs and Cooper that Bolen was on his way. "He's really pissed. He wants you to make a visual inspection of the galleries and have a report ready when he gets here."

Riggs, the older and heavier of the two, groaned. "The *lower* galleries?"

Withers nodded. "Gallery D. Look for a dead body. The kid said he saw one. Could be Jeffers. Get going, I've got Power Central on the line."

The mention of Jeffers galvanized Riggs and Cooper. They looked at each other and left for the tunnels on the run.

"Okay," Withers said into the phone, "so you need some extra juice. Forty megawatts? No sweat. Want it in a lump?"

"Feed half onto the line in thirty minutes and the rest thirty minutes later."

"Right. Gotcha."

"Are you having some kind of trouble up there? You said you were going to call me back and you never did."

"Trouble? No trouble. Well, we had a little trouble with one of our employees. Ex-employee, actually. He was sick and I told him to go home but he wouldn't go and started throwing up all over the place and it was a mess around here, I want to tell you! He's gone now and everything is quiet." Withers looked at one of the television screens and narrowed his eyes. A thin line was coming from the half-open door at the end of the turbine deck, a sparkling line like a piece of tinsel. Was that water?

"Good," said the dispatcher. "Glad to hear it. One other thing. We definitely have a frequency problem in the foothills sector of the grid. Could be Sierra Canyon, could be one of the automatic plants downstream. What do you show? Give me the readings for each of your units."

Withers swiveled his chair to the right and glanced at the bank of frequency meters. All arrows were on zero.

"What the goddam hell—?"

"Beg pardon?"

Withers was half out of his chair, leaning toward the dials. "I can't quite see them from here. I'll call you back in a minute. I'll check the graph traces, too, for the last couple of hours."

"Do that."

He hung up and ran to the generator meter bank. He tapped his finger on the glass dial coverings and gave the panel housing a rap with the heel of his hand. Nothing flickered. Every dial within his field of vision indicated zero. "That goddam son of a bitch," he said, running back to his chair. "He must have tripped all the circuit breakers or some damned thing." Cursing, he made a series of connections to try to find out how much of the system was affected. The overhead lights dimmed, then came on more brightly than before as a backup diesel-electric generator in the next room coughed into life. On the television monitor behind him, the silver strand he had seen emerging from the turbine deck doorway grew into a small waterfall that bubbled down the short flight of concrete steps. Through the windows he saw Riggs running toward him shouting and waving his arms.

Phil stood on a flat rock and slowly turned in a small circle. As closely as he could estimate, he was standing on the coordinates that the computer program indicated was the likeliest point of failure. But there was no failure. There was no leak. The sky was light enough now to enable him to examine the face of the dam for a hundred feet in every direction. There wasn't the slightest trace of moisture anywhere. It was as dry as Death Valley.

"Well, shit," Phil said, glancing at the policemen who were working their way toward him from both above and below. "So much for mathematical models." He sank to a sitting position, put his arms wearily on his knees, and hung his head. He noticed soreness in his legs. Two hours of climbing up and down stairs and ladders, running through tunnels, swimming across lakes, and climbing down dams was having its inevitable effect. He should never have given up jogging.

The policeman who had been chasing him from above arrived first. He stood beside him for a moment catching his breath and looking at him with an expression of revulsion that turned down the corners of his mouth. He said: "I'm Officer Lee Simon, badge one four six three, and I place you under arrest in the name of the Sutterton Police Department. I'm forced by law to caution you that any statement you make can be used against you, and sure as hell will if I have anything to say about it. Couldn't you give yourself up at the top instead of making me climb all the way down here and rip my pants, you goddam cocksucker?"

Phil sighed profoundly. He looked up with misery on his face. "I made you climb down here to show you the leak in the dam. As you can see, there is no leak, which puts me in . . . an unfortunate light. There is an old proverb in the computer industry: 'Garbage in, garbage out.' What that means is—"

Hands landed on each of his shoulders. There were three policemen around him now, the two new arrivals breathing hard and not looking friendly.

"See these?" the first policeman said. "Handcuffs. See this? A nightstick. Put out your hands so I can snap on the cuffs or I will introduce the stick to your head."

"Well put," Phil said, "but handcuffs won't be needed. I give up. I'm sorry I put you to so much trouble."

"I'll bet you are," the policeman said, locking Phil's wrists together. "I'm going to be so sore I won't be able to walk for a week. Let's go."

Phil was pulled to his feet. He winced at the pain he felt in his calves and thighs. "Suppose I go limp," he said. "Would you carry me to the car?"

"Go limp and we'll kick you along the ground like a soccer ball."

At the bottom of the dam they walked in single file along a path formed by the juncture between the embankment and the natural hillside.

"Looking at the dam bathed in the dawn light," Phil said, "you'd never guess it was about to burst apart, would you? It looks impregnable."

"Jesus, what a job," one policeman said, ignoring Phil's remarks. "I was going fishing today. Now I'll have to spend hours writing a report on our apprehension of this fucking asshole."

"Appearances can be deceiving," Phil went on. "Fact is, the dam is hemorrhaging. Whether it can be saved by fast action, I don't know, but if the success I'm having in warning people is any indication, I'll lay you eight to five it won't even be here at noon."

"Would you knock it off, kid? Explain yourself in court on Monday. We're going to put you in a nice jail. The nicest jail we've got. You can talk about the dam to all the new friends you'll meet there."

"You don't have to put me in jail. It would be a waste of the taxpayers' money. Just drop me off at the bus depot."

"The jail's already there, so we might as well use it."

"You look like intelligent men. All hell is breaking loose inside the dam. The lake is pouring into the inspection galleries right now. Sooner or later it's going to find its way to the downstream face. Start counting minutes then. Instead of hauling me to jail we should all be sounding an alarm."

"Tell it to the judge."

The policeman leading the way warned the others of a muddy patch ahead.

"You can't put me in jail," Phil said in a voice edged with alarm. "I'll be drowned. I haven't done anything. I'm a first offender. I'll never break into a dam again, I promise. I didn't steal anything or cause any damage."

"No damage, eh?" said the policeman behind him, poking him in the shoulder. "You totaled the Chief's cruiser by burying it in rocks, that's all."

"I did? It was an accident. I pushed the wrong button. I was trying to turn on the radio. My God, don't put me in jail now!"

"There's more than when we came up," said the policeman in the lead, jumping over a rivulet. "Shit, my shoes are soaked."

Phil stopped walking. "What's the elevation of the jail? Is it below the inundation line for a catastrophic failure of the dam?" He looked down at the feet of his rubber boots, which had sunk partly out of sight in mud. Crossing the path ahead of him was a stream of brown water several feet wide and an inch or two deep. He traced its course with his eyes to the point where it emerged from the lower edge of the rock blanket on the dam's face. He was poked on the shoulder again by the policeman behind him, who told him to keep moving. Phil stood rooted, looking back and forth from his boots to the dam. His expression changed from desolation to triumph. "Wait a minute! This is it! This is the leak! The dam is failing!" He jumped in the air. "Hallelujah, the dam is failing! I *told* you I wasn't nuts, but you wouldn't listen!" The smile left his face and he slowly covered his mouth with his manacled hands. "Holy God," he said in an awed whisper, "the dam *is* failing!"

He was grabbed by both arms and pushed roughly forward. "Spring water," one of the policemen said. "Lots of springs in the hills this time of year."

"This is no hill, this is a dam," Phil said, trying to twist free. "Spring water is clear, this is muddy." He was being hustled along the path so quickly his feet were barely touching the ground. "You know what's going to happen? The leak is going to get bigger and bigger until there'll be no stopping it. . . . We've got to tell the authorities. . . . Let me go—"

"We are the authorities."

They had arrived at a group of waiting police cars. Phil was thrown into a back seat. He lunged to the far door and tried to open it, but there was no handle. He rolled onto his back and saw Officer Simon pointing his nightstick at him.

"You are going someplace where you can calm down," the policeman said. "If we run into an engineer, we'll tell him we saw a trickle."

"I am an engineer," Phil yelled, "and I'm telling you that that trickle won't be a trickle for long! The town has got to be evacuated! Can't you see that? Are you completely stupid?" He instantly regretted using the word "stupid."

Simon shouldered his way into the car and pushed the end of his nightstick against Phil's upper lip until his head was bent back against the seat. "You run your business and we'll run ours, okay? Yours is trespassing and destroying city property. You're not an engineer as far as I'm concerned. To me you're just one more piece of shit." He twisted the end of the stick slightly and Phil's lip along with it. "Now, either you apologize for what you just said or I'll give you some purple knobs."

"I am sincerely sorry for what I just said."

Simon glowered, then backed out of the car and slammed the door. Phil rolled his face into the upholstery and made no sound during the ten-minute drive to the Sutterton city jail. His feeling of misery derived not only from his failure to convince anyone that a disaster was impending and from his aching legs and smarting lip. When Officer Simon's nightstick was telescoping his nose, he had swallowed his car key and twenty cents.

Janet Sandifer poured herself a glass of orange juice and carried it along with her phone to the dining-room table. She sat down and positioned two sharpened pencils alongside a sheet of paper on which she had made a list of the agencies she would call. First was the State of California. If the highest dam in the country was folding up, the state would surely want to be among the first to know.

Dialing 411 brought the patronizing recorded voice that always infuriated her: "You really can help reduce phone costs by using your directory. If the number you need is not listed, an operator will give it to you. Please make a note of it."

"Why should I make a note of it, you jerk," Janet said, "so I can report dam disasters every day?"

A female voice came on the line. "Directory assistance for what city?"

"Probably Sacramento, but maybe Los Angeles."

"For Sacramento Directory Assistance, dial 916-555-1212."

"I know that. Maybe the state department I want has a branch down here."

"What department is it?"

"I'm not exactly sure. I want to report an imminent dam disaster. An impending dam disaster."

"How do you spell that?"

"Either way it starts with 'I.' Who should get such a report?"

"For state offices beginning with 'I,' I have Immunization and Inheritance Tax."

"How about 'D' for disaster? Doesn't the state have something called a disaster office?"

" 'D' as in Donald? I have the Diagnostic School for Neurologically Handicapped Children and the State Board of Dental Examiners."

"I guess I better try Sacramento."

"Is the dam in Sacramento?"

"No. Sacramento is flat. Thanks for your help. I don't know how the phone company gets such good people to work so early in the morning."

"If you are unable to find the state office that you need, dial 916-322-9900."

"That's the state's information number?"

"It's just listed as 'If you are unable to find the state office that you need.' "

"Thanks very much. Jesus Christ."

An operator in Sacramento reminded Janet that most state offices were closed weekends and would not even be open weekdays at five-thirty in the morning.

"There must be somebody open in state government besides yourself."

"A very few."

"Name one."

"Janitorial."

"No good. What else?"

"Emergency."

"That's it! That's it exactly. I've got an emergency to report. A big dam is failing and I thought somebody around there might want to do something about it. Like get out of the way."

"You don't sound serious."

"I'm deadly serious! I'm also exasperated. I've been on the phone for five minutes and still haven't been able to get through to anybody. The biggest dam in the country is in terrible trouble and I can't find out who should be told."

"Well, all right, I'll put you through to the Office of Emergency Services."

"Marvelous."

"There are numbers for radiation hazards, earthquakes, war, and so on."

"Anything! Hurry!"

There was a buzz followed by a deep voice that was clipped and all business. "Emergency Services. Hawkins."

"I'm calling to report a failing dam. Have I reached the right office?"

"Sure have. You're on the oil-spill hotline."

"I can't help that. Sierra Canyon Dam has been breached. Sutterton should be evacuated at once."

"Are you calling from the dam?"

"No, Santa Monica."

"Is this the Southern California Disaster Center?"

"Oh, God. I sometimes think of myself in those terms, yes, but at the moment I'm a private citizen trying to warn you about a leaking dam."

"All dams leak, lady. How did you get on the oil-spill hot line?"

"Would you forget that, for Christ sakes?"

"You're a long way from Sierra Canyon. You had a vivid dream, is that it?"

Janet inhaled and exhaled between clenched teeth before replying. "An engineer at the dam called me and asked me to alert the state. He told me water was breaking into the drainage galleries and that it was only a matter of time before it found its way through the whole embankment."

"It was nice of him to call you. Funny he didn't call us. Or the police."

"He didn't call the police because . . . because the police were calling *him*. Everybody up there has his hands full, don't you see? The engineer had only time for one call, so he asked me to sound the alarm."

"Sorry, that's not how it's done. I'm not going to order an evacuation and mobilize disaster relief at the suggestion of a housewife in Santa Monica who didn't sleep well. I think you're a practical joker and I ask you nicely to get off the oil-spill hot line."

"I'm not a housewife and I don't give a shit about the oil-spill hot line! You mean you're not going to do anything? What the hell is the Office of Emergency Services for? Wait till the newspapers hear about this!"

"Tell your engineer to notify the local jurisdiction, which in this case would be the Sutterton Police Department or the Caspar County Sheriff's Department. The local jurisdiction will appraise the problem and take the necessary steps, which might include contacting this office to activate the state's warning and coordination functions."

"My engineer didn't notify the local jurisdiction," Janet shouted angrily, "because the local jurisdiction has its head up its ass! As far as *your* ass is concerned, it will be in a sling if you don't do something!"

"I don't appreciate that kind of language from a lady."

"Then you are a sexist pig as well as a schmuck klutz and you can fuck off!"

Janet slammed the receiver down and stormed around her apartment cursing the State of California, the Office of Emergency Services, and the cruel gods that brought Phil Kramer into her life. After several minutes of raging she sat down and dialed the next number on the list, vowing never again to get involved with a man who felt strongly about anything. While listening to the ringing signal, she decided to try a slightly different tack; the plain truth was apparently not persuasive enough.

23

WITHERS WATCHED RIGGS RUN PAST the control-room windows and stop at the door, fumbling with his keys. The phone rang and he answered it automatically. It was Leonard Mitchell, the contractor.

"Yes, Mr. Mitchell, thanks for returning my call. Would you hang on a second?"

Riggs burst into the room, gasping. "Water . . . water is pouring from the gallery entrance . . . got to shut down. . . . Water is running into the turbine wells. Shut everything down. . . ." He ran to the master panel and started throwing switches. Withers leaped after him and grabbed his arm.

"What are you doing? We can't shut down. . . . I've got to start feeding in an extra forty megawatts—"

"Water . . ."

"What water? What water are you talking about?"

Riggs pointed at the television monitors. "That water. I hope we can save the generators. . . ."

When Withers looked at the screens, it was his turn to gasp. Water a foot deep was surging through the doorway and splashing on the floor of the turbine deck. As he watched, stunned, a horn began to sound rhythmically.

"There goes the warning horn," Riggs said, manipulating the controls that would bring the massive generator rotors to a halt. "Give me a hand, will you?"

"Where's Cooper?"

"In the tunnels to see if he can find where the water's coming from."

Withers swallowed hard. "The dam is failing. That's what Kramer said."

"Look," Riggs said sharply. "Water is coming into the turbine deck, that's all we know. Could be a ruptured discharge line. Could be a crack on the upstream side of the core block, like the one we had five years ago, or in the abutment granite. Could be a dozen things that don't mean the dam is failing. We've got to shut the place down and find out what the problem is. Come on, we've got work to do."

Withers nodded and picked up the phone. "Mr. Mitchell? We need a dozen of your men and some pumps. Got any pumps at your yard across from the south side overlook?"

"A few small ones. How much water have you got? Did I hear something about the dam failing?"

"No, no, nothing is wrong with the dam. Water is coming into the powerhouse, and we've got to get it under control before it damages any equipment. We think what happened is three of our own pumps stopped at the same time. The horn? A warning that something is wrong in the drainage system. We've got water at the rate of—oh, ten cubic feet a second. Can you handle that?"

"I'll round up some men and equipment and be right over. How are you going to pay for this—cost plus fifteen percent, or what? I'll have to bill this out at weekend labor rates, you know."

"Just keep records on everything. Mr. Mitchell, keep this under your hat till we know what we're up against. We don't want a panic."

"I understand. I'm on my way."

Withers showed Riggs the banks of inoperative gauges. Everything relating to sections of the embankment lower in elevation than the generator deck was dead.

"Christ," Riggs said, grimacing, "that really puts us in the dark. No way of telling what's going on. Water must have gotten into the utility conduits and shorted everything out."

They were interrupted by Cooper, who was red-faced and puffing and whose clothes were drenched. "I got as far as the centerline intersection," he said, collapsing into a chair. "Lights went out, so I came back. Couldn't tell if the water was coming from the intake tower or the lower gallery stairwell. Could the lower tunnels be flooded and the stairwell, too? Doesn't seem possible."

Riggs pulled a set of engineering drawings from a rack and spread them on a table. He turned the sheets until he came to a cross-section of the embankment that included the intake tower. "I'll bet the kid did something when he was running around loose. Maybe when he was in the tower he managed to open one of the bulkhead doors and let the lake in."

"That might be it," Cooper said, nodding, then shaking his head in dismay. "If it is, we'll have to lower the reservoir to the level of the bulkhead to get it closed. That'll take a week. The water districts and the P. G. & E. will love it."

"We'll look like a bunch of fucking clowns." Withers groaned. "Especially me."

"Can you stop the goddam horn?" Cooper asked. "It's driving me nuts."

Withers cut the horn circuit. A heavy silence settled over the control room. With power production stopped and the generators stilled, there was not even the customary electrical hum. "Well," he said, looking at the other two men, "do you think we should tell the Sheriff and the Chief of Police we've got a crisis on our hands?"

"Not yet," Riggs said. "Maybe with Mitchell's pumps we can dry everything up and keep the whole thing quiet."

"How are we going to keep it quiet," Cooper said, "when we've shut the plant down? I think we should assume the worst."

"Call Roshek," Riggs suggested, "and ask him what he wants us to do."

"Not me," Withers said. "I'm not going to let him chew my ass out."

"Call Bolen, then."

"He's in his plane on his way here to take charge of Kramer."

Riggs walked to the door. "Turn on the phones in the offices. I'll call the air communications center in Oakland and see if they can reach Bolen by radio."

"Let's call the police, too, just in case," Cooper said.

Riggs disagreed, insisting that it should be Bolen's decision.

When Riggs was out of the room, Cooper again urged Withers to alert the police. "We should start lowering the reservoir, too," he said.

"You want me to drop the spillway gates? Not unless somebody tells me to with more authority than you. There's two feet of water going over the top now. If I drop the gates, there will be twenty-two feet. That would cause a good-sized flood all by itself. It would take out Sutterton's Main Street Bridge, for starters. Let's see what Bolen says. If we can't get through to him, then we'll decide."

Cooper jumped to his feet and strode to the door. "I'm not going to sit here twiddling my thumbs. I'm going to drive around outside and look things over. If I see anything that isn't a hundred percent normal, Newt, I'm sounding an alarm whether you guys want me to or not. Piss on the company's reputation."

The phone rang. Withers answered it while waving goodbye to Cooper. On the line was Bill Hawkins of the Office of Emergency Services in Sacramento.

Hawkins said with a trace of amusement in his voice, "We just had a call from a woman in Santa Monica who said that the dam you have there is busting up. Now where do you suppose she got an idea like that? Hello? Are you there?"

"A woman from where said what?"

"A woman from Santa Monica said poor old Sierra Canyon Dam is on its last legs. A friend of hers, she said, called her from there and told her that water was coming in on all sides. Just a crackpot, eh? Thought I'd give you a jingle anyway. Amazing, the rumors that get started."

Withers whistled. "Kramer must have gotten to a phone. . . ."

"Come again?"

"We had a nut up here a while ago and we had to call the cops on him. He must have a girl friend who's trying to make us look bad."

"So everything's okay? Water is not coming in on all sides?"

"No, just into the powerhouse."

"Just into the powerhouse. Water is coming into the powerhouse." Hawkins repeated the words slowly, as if he were laying them on a table for examination.

"We've got a flow that may not be normal. A crew is on its way to check it out. We've shut the plant down."

"If enough water is coming in so that you've had to shut the plant down, it sure as hell is not normal. Say, I'm glad I called! This is only the Office of Emergency Services. I suppose if your dam is dissolving we'll hear about it on the eleven o'clock news."

"We are having a problem, that I grant you, but we don't think it is serious. We'll know in a few minutes. I'll call you. I know the emergency procedures. Your number is on a list we have posted on the wall, just after the local jurisdictions."

"Yes, leave us not forget the local jurisdictions."

"Excuse me, I've got a call on the other line. Be talking to you."

On the other line was an irate dispatcher from Power Control Central.

"What's wrong up there? We just got a big drop in frequency. Are you ready to start feeding in the extra power? Why didn't you call back with those readings?"

"I was just going to. Say, about that extra power. We've got some percolation—well, it's more than percolation; it's an actual flow—coming into the turbine bays and we've had to shut down the plant. That explains the drop in frequency."

"You've *what*? My God, for how long?"

"Don't know. We've got to pump out the drainage galleries before we can find out what the problem is."

"Is the dam in danger?"

"Oh, hell, no. Oh, shit, no. Listen, soon as I get a report I'll get right back to you."

"If you aren't back on stream in thirty minutes, we're going to have one hell of a brownout."

"Thirty days is more like it."

"You're kidding! Tell me you're kidding!"

Withers hung up and took the next call. The monitor showed that the flow into the turbine deck had slacked off. Maybe the leak or rupture was self-clogging.

"Newt? This is Luby Pelletier over at the Butte County Disaster Office in Oroville. Remember me? We met last year at the Public Safety Conference."

"Yes, Luby, I remember."

"How is everything up your way this fine day?"

"Wonderful, terrific. Say, would you mind—"

"The dam isn't falling apart or anything, is it?"

"Well . . ."

"We just got a weird call from a woman in Santa Monica—"

"Jesus! She must be calling everybody in the whole goddam state!"

"You know her? She said she was a psychic who just had a vision of Sierra Canyon disappearing and swarms of people running naked into the woods. Who is she?"

"We don't know, exactly. A friend of hers used to work here."

"I guess that's how she knew so much about the dam. She mentioned the intake shaft, the drainage tunnels, stuff like that. Came to her in a flash of light, she said. I could hardly keep from laughing."

"Look, Luby . . ."

"She said predicting the future was her main gift and that she had a special fondness for disasters. The big stuff. I told her I didn't put much stock in that bullshit, but that I'd check out what she said."

"As it turns out, we do have a small problem. At least, we hope it's small." Withers kept his eyes on the television screen. The flow seemed to be increasing again.

"Of course, I didn't actually say 'bullshit.' People who claim they can see the future have terrible batting averages. One lucky guess for every five hundred misses. Nobody remembers the misses."

"Luby, I'm awful busy and I'm going to hang up. We may have to evacuate the town." From the other side of the lobby, Riggs was nodding to him and holding up a phone. Apparently he was getting through to Bolen.

"Look at the philosophical pickle it puts you in," Luby Pelletier rattled on, chuckling. "If you foresee something, you can make sure it doesn't happen. So what was it you foresaw? See what I mean?" He paused, then added,

"What did you say about evacuating the town?"

"I'll call you later. Don't make any plans for today."

As Withers took the next call—the phone rang the instant he hung up—Riggs shouted to him over the intercom that air traffic controllers had located Bolen in his plane over Fresno. Withers acknowledged the news with a wave. Lee Simon was on the phone.

"Your friend Kramer led us on a merry chase," the policeman said, "but we've got him under lock and key now."

"Great. Keep him out of everybody's hair till my boss gets here."

"Did he wreck anything inside the dam?"

"We don't know yet. He may have opened some valves. We've had to shut the plant down while we check things out."

"Yeah? That skinny son of a bitch is a good argument for police brutality. Say, Newt, we saw a wet spot at the bottom of the dam a while ago. Thought I better mention it to you. A spring, probably. Been raining a lot lately."

"A wet spot? Where?" Like the caress of a feather, goose bumps advanced across Withers's shoulders.

"About a hundred yards from the riverbank on the north side. Your friend Kramer got all excited when he saw it, but he gets excited about everything."

"Is it just a wet spot or is there a flow of water?"

"Sort of a trickle. About as much as you see in the gutter when somebody up the block is washing a car. Think it means anything?"

"Cooper is in his car right now. I'll call him on the radio and have him take a look. Lee, are you at home? I know you worked all night, but don't go to bed yet. I got a horrible feeling we've got big trouble. Stay by the phone and I'll call you back."

Withers got on the radio, reached Cooper, who was on his way to check the gauges in the tailrace valve house, and directed him to a vantage point next to the switchyard parking lot. Withers's phone was ringing again, but before answering it he jotted down the names of people he had promised to call back.

"Powerhouse, Withers speaking."

"This is the news desk of the Sacramento *Bee*. We're tracking down a rumor that Sierra Canyon Dam has been mined by former members of the Iranian Secret Police. According to our source, the blasts are set to go off in thirty minutes and Sutterton should be evacuated."

"Is your source a woman in Santa Monica?"

"You know her? Anything to what she says?"

"I'll call you back."

Cooper's voice came over the radio loudspeaker announcing that he had arrived at the overlook.

Withers leaned into his microphone. "Can you see the toe of the slope from where you are? On the north side? See anything odd?"

"What am I looking for?"

"A wet spot. A trickle of water about a hundred yards up from the riverbank. Look along the seam between the natural ground and the toe of the riprap."

"I've got a clear view, but that's a quarter of a mile away. Let me put the glasses on it."

In the silence that followed, Withers drummed the side of his fist lightly against the counter top at a rate that matched his heartbeat. He glanced at the wall clock and saw that it was ten minutes after seven. Riggs came through the control-room door and began to report on the conversation he had had with Bolen, then froze at the sound of Cooper's voice on the radio:

"A boil-out, Newt . . . Jesus God, must be five hundred or a thousand cubic feet a second. . . . We've lost her, we've lost the whole goddam thing. . . . Christ God Almighty, the dam is a goner. . . ."

III

The Failure

24

HERMAN BOLEN HAD A PAIN IN THE ass. He shifted around in the contoured seat of his handmade airplane to center the bulk of his weight on his left buttock. That helped the pain in his ass but intensified the pain in his neck. The heat in the cockpit remained constant. He peeled off his Eddie Rickenbacker goggles and scarf and used them to fan his perspiring face. Through the side window he gazed dully at the blanket of fog that filled the Central Valley. The sun was above the Sierra Nevadas now and the reflected light was blinding.

To take his mind off his discomfort, he tried to calculate his precise position. His ground speed was approximately two hundred and fifty miles per hour. . . . The last checkpoint was . . . The wind speed and bearing was . . . In thirty seconds he realized that his mind had dropped the numbers and equations and once again had settled on the pain in his ass. He was somewhere around Fresno, that was close enough. At least he was five thousand feet *above* Fresno and not actually down *in* Fresno, which was something to be thankful for. He was seized with the wish to be elsewhere, anywhere but in his sickeningly expensive toy five thousand feet above Fresno. Immersed in a hot tub, perhaps, while his ample belly was kneaded by the jets of a Jacuzzi, or spread-eagled on a nude beach in Brazil.

Five years—five years!—he had spent designing and building a personal airplane with the help of friends who were engineers, mechanics, orthopedists, and pilots, and still it wasn't right. It was, in fact, a torture chamber. The chair, the cockpit, the whole plane had been designed around the size, shape, and weight of his body—that's where the dream broke down. The plane was perfect, but his body had failed to adhere to its original specifications. You can let the seams out of a suit, but not a plane. The plane was tailor-made for a Herman Bolen who no longer existed. The seat was a precision fit for a memory.

"Aircraft N nine seven three zero seven, this is Oakland Center. Can you read me?"

Bolen was so lost in thought that the voice on the radio didn't register. His mind wandered over the thousands of hours he had spent in his home workshop fussing with Posa injectors, chrome-moly tubing, cadmium-plated tie rods, and the custom-built power plant that could hurl the plane through the sky at two hundred and ninety miles an hour. Never mind maneuverability, he wanted *speed.* Of course it couldn't reach two hundred and ninety now because the weight of his own body had drifted so far beyond the design assumptions.

"N nine seven three zero seven, Oakland Center. Can you read? Over."

Maybe he should start over. Use an Emeraude fuselage

with slotted Frise ailerons and Fowler flaps. That would catch the eyes of the ladies at the meets and rallies. If only his *own* fuselage looked a little racier and had a lower fat content. Any flashing female eyes his plane attracted tended to be turned away by the pear-shaped blob that struggled out of the cockpit. Cosmetic surgery was a possibility. He would look into it. Maybe he could find a quack who did tummy tucks on a truly gigantic scale.

Something in the back of Bolen's mind nagged him. He picked up his microphone. "Excuse me, Oakland Center. Did you say N nine seven three zero seven? I read you."

"We have a call from Sierra Canyon Dam."

"Can you patch through a direct line?"

"No, but I can relay both sides of a conversation."

Bolen hesitated. If there was an emergency, did he want everyone at Oakland Center to know about it as well as all the ham operators who happened to be tuned in? Withers was such an idiot he probably wouldn't have the sense to speak indirectly. "Tell him to call me on the telephone through the mobile operator."

"Do they have your number?"

"I don't want to give it out on the air. Tell him it's listed in the company directory under my name."

Bolen looked at his watch, wondering if the message had to do with Jeffers, Kramer, or the dam itself. It had to be something serious if they couldn't wait another forty-five minutes for him to get there. His sweep second hand made four revolutions. At exactly five minutes before seven a buzzer sounded on his instrument panel.

"Herman Bolen here."

"This is Burt Riggs, Mr. Bolen, one of the maintenance engineers at Sierra Canyon. We seem to—"

"Did you find Jeffers? Did you check Gallery D?"

"We couldn't reach Gallery D. Water is flowing out of the access tunnel into the turbine wells. It may be that the lower galleries are flooded. Jeffers might have got caught down there."

As he listened to the description of the incoming water, the inoperative meters, and the plant shutdown, the goggles and scarf slipped from his hand to the floor. Before Riggs finished, Bolen cut him off.

"Have you told the police Sutterton has to be evacuated?"

"No, we thought we'd better let you decide that."

"Jesus Christ, man, how much evidence do you need? Can't you see how everything ties together? I think the core block has been breached. Listen to me. What you do in the next few minutes could save a thousand lives. Call the police, the Sheriff, the county disaster headquarters, and the State Office of Emergency Services—the numbers are on the wall—and tell them there's a possibility we could lose the dam. Bypass as much water as you can around the turbines from the penstocks directly into the outlet works. Drop the spillway gates."

"Withers says that will cause pretty heavy flooding—"

"I don't care what Withers says! Do what I tell you!"

"Yes, sir. Mr. Bolen, I can see the television monitors from where I'm sitting and it looks like a crew from Mitchell Brothers has arrived in the parking lot with pumps."

"If you can get rid of the water faster than it's coming in, fine—that will let you into the tunnels to find the source. Maybe we'll get some good luck and find a leak that can be plugged. A quick-setting chemical grout might work. . . . Get Mitchell's opinion. But if the embankment is breached it's probably all over. Are you listening? Put at least six men on the downstream face to look for signs of water. If a boil-out occurs, I want everybody out of the tunnels. If you have to abandon the powerhouse, take every monitoring record with you that you can find, because when this is over we're going to have to figure out what went wrong."

Bolen made Riggs repeat the instructions, then broke the connection. He gazed once more through the side window. The fog below him looked soft and firm enough to lie down on and go to sleep. In the far distance to the northwest he could make out the rounded tops of Mount Hamilton and Mount Diablo; to the right was the snow-covered backbone of the Sierra Nevadas. The vault of blue sky that arched from horizon to horizon was cloudless and clear. It was a magnificent spectacle, but cold and remote, like the view of a planet from an orbiting spacecraft. The steady roar of the engine was comforting; it was an engine so finely tuned it brought a glow of appreciation to the face of every mechanic who heard it. At the controls of his handcrafted machine Bolen felt isolated from the concerns of the human race, which at this altitude seemed not to exist, and he wished he could stay there forever.

Dapper Dr. Dulotte eased his station wagon around the huge truck that was inexplicably parked on top of the dam. Before reaching the far side he had to slow down again, this time to follow the hand signals of a policeman. A wrecker was extracting a police car from a pile of gravel.

"What happened, Officer?" he said, rolling down a window.

"No stopping," the policeman replied curtly, waving him on.

The road left the dam and gained several hundred feet in elevation before joining the county road at a T intersection. Dulotte nodded in satisfaction when he saw the arrows and signs marking the entrance of the trail into the woods. The Route Committee had done its jobs well. Only the most thickheaded and delirious runners would lose their way. He parked. It was 7:20. The race would start at 8:00, and about an hour or so after that, if everything went according to plan, his boy, Kent Spain, would be the first to cross the dam and disappear into the woods. He'd be reeling and ready to quit, Dulotte imagined, but the scent of money would drive him on.

From the back of the station wagon he dragged a three-wheeled pushcart called the Dulotte Trail-Barrow, the rights to which he was close to selling to the State Department of Parks and Recreation, not to mention the Forest Service and the Bureau of Mines. Into it he loaded a collapsible table, a director's chair, four five-gallon bottles of water, a clipboard, a pad of record-keeping forms, a stopwatch, a first aid kit, a crate of oranges, and a lunch bucket. Ten minutes later he was striding briskly through the woods on the wide, well-defined trail, the cart rolling along ahead of him. He smiled appreciatively at the pines, the moss on the rocks, and the wild flowers on the open slopes. Drifting to his ears from the distance were the meaningless sounds of sirens and church bells.

The T-shirt was still on the branch. Behind it the bicycle was ready to go. Dulotte strode on, humming "The Impossible Dream." Even though the trail was level and the cart offered little resistance, he was soon panting. He pinched the flab around his middle and shook his head. He really should start working out.

In Stockton, a hundred miles south of the dam, Emil Hasset admired himself in the mirror before leaving for work. He tugged at the visor of his cap until it was square on his head, straightened the tie around his short thick neck, and patted his holstered gun. Behind him in one of the twin beds, his son Freddy watched sullenly. Emil turned around and spread his arms. "How do I look?"

"Same as ever," said his son. "Stupid."

Emil laughed. "Is that any way to talk to your father?"

Freddy Hasset rolled and faced the wall, the gray sheets falling away from his mottled back. "Valley Transfer uniforms make everybody look stupid. That's what you always say. Loomis guards look snappy, which is something else you always say. I think they look just as stupid. Why anybody would work as a cop or a guard is beyond me."

"The need to eat drives people to do crazy things. You'll find out when you stop sponging off me." He put his hand on the doorknob, looking at the bed. "Shouldn't you be getting ready to go to the airport? To warm up the plane and so on?"

"Plenty of time."

"Don't talk with a blanket in your mouth. How many times have I told you that? I'd feel better if you were up and showing a little pep. This is a big day for us."

"Lay off, Pop. I said I'd go through with it and I will. My word is good."

"That's a change for the better. Okay, see you later. In the wild blue yonder."

Phil Kramer clamped his hands around the bars of his cell door. A short distance away, Night Sergeant Jim Martinez sat at his desk doing paperwork, a task which, judging from his expression, left him less than thrilled.

"Let me out of here," Phil shouted, rattling the door. "This is an emergency! Let us all out! Every minute counts!"

"Shut up," somebody said behind him.

Phil looked over his shoulder. There were four cots in the cell, three of them filled with blanket-covered lumps. From one extended a bare leg so scrawny and wizened it looked like a stick of beef jerky. "I will not shut up," he said, addressing the cots. "I am trying to save your necks as well as mine." He turned to Martinez. "Maybe you weren't paying attention to what I was saying when I was dragged in here, so I will run through it again. I am a world-renowned authority on dam failures. Ask anybody. I have just finished inspecting Sierra Canyon Dam. That's the one you can see out the window, Sergeant, if you'd care to look."

"Shut up," the voice behind him said again. Similar sentiments could be heard from other cells.

"Listen to what I'm saying, everybody," Phil said, rattling the door again. "The dam is failing. Tunnels inside of it are filling with water. . . . I saw it happening with my own eyes. A leak has started on the downstream face. You know what that means? It means that a great big lake is going to come crashing down on our heads, because once water finds its way through an embankment you can kiss it goodbye."

"Hey, we're trying to get some sleep," a gravelly voice said.

From an adjoining cell: "Pipe down, would you please?"

A third voice: "But what if the dam did break? We'd be trapped in here like rats." To which somebody replied, "Don't call me a rat, you motherfucker."

"Exactly," Phil said. "We'd be trapped in here like rats. The water is going to keep boring a bigger and bigger hole until it cuts a slot all the way to the top. Then *splooey!* That's what happened to Baldwin Hills in 1963 and Teton in 1976."

At the door of the cell opposite Phil's, a prisoner appeared dressed in a business suit decorated with dried vomit. "Hey, Martinez," he said with an air of exasperation, "can't you do something about this guy? There are people here with some very serious hangovers."

Sergeant Martinez sighed, put down his pencil, and got to his feet. He walked down the corridor and studied Phil, standing just beyond arm's reach. "This is an emergency," Phil said to him. "You've got to get us out of here and yourself as well. Turn us loose on the street if you have to—otherwise we're dead ducks."

There was a crash that made Phil turn around. A giant of a man with a protruding belly and a tangle of long blond hair had gotten out of one of the cots, knocking it over along with a cardboard box that served as a bedside table. He took two strides and dropped a huge hand on Phil's chest, gathered the front of his coveralls into a fist, and lifted him off the floor. His breath smelled of garlic, tobacco, chocolate, marijuana, whiskey, beer, stale air, and feedlots. "I thought I told you to shut up," he said.

"Put him down, Haystack," Martinez said. "I'll handle this."

The man called Haystack glared at Phil from a distance of two inches, then released him. He righted his cot and fell on it, almost instantly snoring.

"Kramer, you got to knock off this crap about the dam," Martinez said. "Everybody is getting all excited. We could have a riot."

"Good! That might help. I'm trying to save our skins."

"There are several things I could do," Martinez said thoughtfully. "I could transfer you over to the county jail where they got isolation cells. I could knock you out with a club. I could have Haystack force-feed you some little pills we keep on hand for troublemakers."

The phone on Martinez's desk rang.

"The dam is failing," Phil said.

"The dam is not failing. If the dam was failing, I would hear about it."

"The dam is failing," Phil said.

"I'm going to answer the phone," Martinez said. "When I get back, unless you have stopped talking and let these good people go back to sleep, I'm going to say a certain code word that makes Haystack go wild. Think about it."

Haystack stopped snoring and sat up on the edge of his cot. He needed a shave and his eyes weren't in focus. "If I strangled the turd," he said, "it would be justifiable homicide. The Governor would invite me to brunch."

Martinez walked back to his desk and picked up the phone. Phil watched the expression on his face change as he said, "Yeah? It is? Now? We are? No bull? You mean everybody? Are you sure? Right. Okay. Christ." He hung up slowly.

"What is it?" Phil shouted. "What's happening?"

Martinez ran his fingers through his hair and shook his head. "They think the dam might go out," he said. "A school bus is on its way to pick us all up." He pushed a button that set off an ear-shattering alarm bell.

Phil grinned at his cellmate. "Pack your bags, Haystack, we're getting out of this joint."

25

THE BEGINNING OF THE MOTHER LODE Marathon was an elbow-to-elbow melee. At the crack of the starter's pistol, nearly fifteen hundred people surged forward, a fantastic, colorful swarm of arms, legs, and bobbing heads. Kent Spain was in the group of fifty top seeds who were given priority positions at the front, but once the race was under way he felt just as engulfed by humanity as he would have in the rear with the week-enders, school kids, geriatrics, and maniacs in wheel-chairs. He hated the dilettantes, even though he knew they were the reason Dr. Dulotte could pay so handsomely for corruption. The sheer weight of their numbers, added to their clumsiness, ignorance, and enthusiasm, was a threat to the serious runner's life and limb. You never knew when one of the goddam fools was going to collapse under your feet or run up the back of your legs. Once early in his career, Kent Spain lost three minutes by absent-mindedly following some creep off the marked course into a weed patch where the guy stopped, squatted, and took a shit.

The first couple of miles was more like a steeplechase than a cross-country run, a process of jumping over barking dogs, dodging dropouts who were walking back to their cars with ashen faces, and watching for chances to pass the scores of puffing laggards. For several hundred yards he matched strides with a long-legged, black-haired young woman who had the number 38 pinned to her bulging shirt. He reluctantly gave up the view by passing her. "Is the thirty-eight a measurement of anything?" he asked as he went by.

"Yeah," she answered without looking at him, "it's the caliber of the gun I carry."

At the two-mile mark, where the course left the highway and entered an expanse of grazing land below towering outcroppings of rock, the runners were strung out in single file about fifteen feet apart. Kent was never able to catch sight of all those ahead of him, but he guessed there were at least a dozen. In the next thirteen miles he would have to pass every one of them, for if Dulotte's plan was to work he would have to be first across the dam. Most of the competition would probably fold on Cardiac Hill at the ten-mile mark, if not before. Only two runners figured to be trouble—Tom Ryan, immediately ahead of him, and Nabih Yousri of Ethiopia, a world-class marathoner who had entered at the last minute. If Yousri was following his usual strategy, Kent thought, he was probably already in the lead, his bald black head glistening in the sun like a polished eight ball and his sinewy legs flicking back and forth like licorice whips. His policy was to start fast and hang on at the end to win. Passing him would take a maximum effort.

Ryan was a different kind of runner, a crafty calculator with a great finishing kick. Trailing Ryan and letting him set the pace was a sure way of getting a good time, but it was no way to win, because in the last thousand yards nobody in the world could keep up with him, much less pass him.

With steady effort, Kent pulled to within five feet of Ryan. After half a mile of lockstep, he pulled up on his heels and said, "Honk, honk."

Ryan, unworried, moved to the left edge of the trail and glanced at Spain as he went by. "What's the hurry? Still early in the day."

"Gotta catch a plane."

"Crazy. You know better. You'll burn out."

"Maybe."

In the next seven miles Kent passed ten runners, none of whom he knew, who were showing the effects of the blistering early pace. It was a pace far faster than he had ever taken himself, and he felt twinges in his calves and an ominous tightness in his midsection. He should have trained harder, especially at the fifteen-mile distance. What he had to do in this race was expend ninety-five percent of his strength over a course eleven miles shorter than he was accustomed to. Only if he succeeded would he reach the bicycle first.

Cardiac Hill was a mile-long grade that led to a ridge overlooking Warren Lake. It was the best place to catch Yousri, for at the top, where the trail curved right, there was a two-mile level stretch that was ideal for the Ethiopian. Yousri wouldn't expect to be challenged on the most punishing section of the course.

Kent spent a few seconds at the ten-mile checkpoint and aid station at the bottom of the grade. As he sponged off his face and neck with cold water, he asked the man behind the table how many were ahead of him.

"Four," the man answered, handing him a paper cup. "Yousri's in the lead, about a minute and a half ahead of you."

"I'm going to catch him." He drained the paper cup, then spat out a mouthful of green liquid. "God, Gatorade! Don't dish out that sweet shit this early . . . gimme some water." He drank the water while picking up speed and entering the shade of the woods. The trail rose cruelly through tall evergreens. He felt a definite soreness in his calves. The tightness he had noticed earlier in his stomach was becoming a palpable knot. He drove his legs hard, setting his internal metronome to a tempo better suited to a sprint than to a marathon.

"You can do it, old buddy," he said, addressing his body in a strained whisper. "Come through for me one more time, just one more time. I know it's tough, oh, it's tough, then we'll take a long rest, just the two of us. No, don't tell me to stop, no, no, no. Think of the money. Money, money, money. Push, push, push, push . . ." He timed the words to the impact of his shoes on the ground.

Five hundred yards from the top of the slope he had passed everybody but Yousri, who was still not in sight. The first runner he went by was sitting on a rock gasping; the second fought him briefly, stride for stride, before yielding and falling back; the third was almost standing still, taking tiny, shuffling steps. Kent put Yousri out of his mind temporarily while he concentrated on breaking through "the wall," that half-physical, half-psychological barrier that stood in the way of a peak performance. Never before had he encountered the wall so early in a race. His calves were red-hot pokers and his stomach a mass of cables stretched to the breaking point. It was the worst he had ever experienced, and the thought came to him that if he didn't pull up and walk for a while, he might hurt himself seriously, possibly even die of a heart attack. He kept on going, refusing to listen to his body.

The secret was to ignore the pain and keep on ignoring it until the body gave up sending pain signals and unlocked its secret stores of energy.

"Push, push, push," he muttered, his teeth and fists clenched, "money, money, money, money."

Behind him he heard footsteps getting closer and closer. He turned for a quick backward glance and saw a blond teenager approaching at what seemed to be fifty miles an hour, with legs working effortlessly and only a faint trace of sweat on his arms and face. On his chest was the number 1027, which meant that he was unrated. Kent lowered his head and drove himself forward, trying to find something extra to beat off the threat of a goddam kid who looked like he was running after somebody who stole his surfboard. The kid sailed past him, then eased up and let Kent draw even.

"Excuse me, sir," 1027 said, scarcely breathing hard, "where's Cardiac Hill?"

Kent Spain's face was a mixture of agony and loathing. "At the top . . . of this slope . . . the trail swings left," he said in a desperate effort to rid himself of a new menace, "through a field of ferns. Half a mile more . . . you'll see an International House of Pancakes. That's the start of Cardiac Hill." It was hard to talk. He couldn't seem to get enough air in his lungs.

"Thanks a lot," the teenager said, pulling away. He looked back with sympathy and added, "Hang in there, old-timer, you'll make it."

Two minutes later Kent labored to the narrow, tree-studded grassland on the top of the ridge and followed the trail to the right. The area called Fern Gardens was on his left, and on a hillside beyond it he could see number 1027 striding powerfully along a path that Kent knew led only to an abandoned ranger station.

Feeling pleasure for the first time since the race began, Kent let out his own stride. Through the trees and below he caught glimpses of the lake. Rounding a curve, he almost stumbled over Nabih Yousri, who was down on one knee tying his shoe. The African jumped up and bounded away like a frightened jackrabbit, his legs showing the springiness for which they were famous. Kent smiled grimly and shifted into his highest gear. He didn't have a devastating kick, but he could sustain a fast pace for a short distance, especially at twelve miles out rather than twenty-six. Lashing himself with the fury of a madman, he gradually closed the gap.

Yousri wouldn't yield the right-of-way. When Kent tried to pass on the right, Yousri moved to the right. When Kent moved left, Yousri moved left.

"Let me pass, goddammit. . . ."

"No pass," Yousri said. "Not right for you. You poop out."

"Let me by!"

"No. Stay back. You thank me later."

"Move over, you goddam freak foreigner fag!"

The black man's reply was to quicken his pace and try to draw away. Kent Spain, teeth clenched and a maniacal look on his face, matched him step for step. For two hundred yards they ran in synchrony within three feet of each other. It was a draining duel witnessed only by the passing trees and shrubs, and both men knew that if they kept it up for very long they would collapse and be passed by the trailing herd. Kent fastened his eyes on the shoes ahead of him that were snapping back and forth like the pendulum of a high-speed clock. Timing his move nicely, he leaned forward and slapped one sideways so that it caught on the back of the opposite ankle. The great Nabih Yousri, a well-oiled running machine feared throughout the world, crashed to the ground in an explosion of twigs, pebbles, and incomprehensible curses.

At last, at mile thirteen, Kent Spain was in the lead. He was running downhill now through a hillside of scrub oak and manzanita toward the crest of the dam. In a few minutes he would emerge from the woods at the right overlook . . . provided he hadn't overexerted himself. He felt dizzy. The ground was undulating like the floor of a fun house. A roaring filled his ears. His mouth was hanging open and he was sucking and blowing air like a steam locomotive.

A persistent knocking woke Theodore Roshek, who had fallen asleep in the chair beside his bed. The door opened and Mrs. Bolen put her head into the room. "Theodore? There's a call for you from Sierra Canyon. A Mr. Withers. You can take it on the bedside phone."

Roshek listened to Withers with disbelief and rising alarm, and he pressed him for details. "How much water is coming through? Have you seen it yourself?"

"No, but I just got a radio report from one of our maintenance engineers who estimates it at five hundred or a thousand second-feet." Withers hesitated, then added. "He thinks the dam is lost. I thought I better call you. Your wife told me where you were."

Roshek exploded. "Are you bulldozing rock into the breach upstream and down? Have you dropped the spillway gates? Have you told the police?"

"We've dropped the gates and the police are evacuating the town, but as for bulldozers—well, there just isn't anybody here yet who knows exactly what to do. Mr. Bolen is on his way, but Mr. Jeffers is, we think—well, dead."

"Where's Kramer?"

"Who?"

"Kramer! The engineer who's been trying to tell us something was wrong. . . ."

"In jail. Locked up."

"Unlock him."

"Unlock him?"

"Who else around there knows more about what's going on than he does? Maybe he has some more smart ideas."

Roshek hung up and dialed Creekwood. Eleanor was in danger. If the unthinkable happened and the dam . . .

was it possible? Images of well-engineered dams that had failed crowded into his mind—St. Francis and Baldwin Hills in California alone, Malpassant in France, Vega de Tera in Spain, Teton in Idaho. In 1963 a landslide into the reservoir formed by Vaiont Dam in Italy sent a wave of such size down the valley that the town of Longarone was destroyed with a loss of twenty-five hundred lives. The catastrophes were as vivid to him as the anguish suffered by the responsible engineers, many of whom were his friends. "Acts of God," "standard industry practice," "inescapable unknowns"—phrases like these came up over and over in the inquiries that followed every disaster. Certainly it was impossible to eliminate every unknown and pin down every variable; certainly nature was capable of dreadful surprises, and yet . . . Roshek couldn't help feeling that if a man paid enough attention to detail, if he had enough strength of character to resist compromise, then— A busy signal told him that the phone was still off the hook. Eleanor was either asleep or had forgotten to hang up the phone when she arose.

Could Sierra Canyon Dam fail? Was the secret contempt he held for designers of inadequate structures to be turned around and applied to himself? Perhaps the extent of the downstream leak was exaggerated. It was hard to estimate turbulent flow. Maybe it was in the order of a hundred second-feet instead of a thousand, in which case it might be possible to stop the unraveling of the embankment. If it wasn't, then no force on earth could stop the inevitable, and the name of Theodore Roshek would be attached forever not to dreams but to nightmares.

With the dam destroyed, Eleanor would be even more important to him than she was now. Her beauty, her ability to create beauty, and the sweetness of her affection for him, these things and these alone would make life worth living. He would go to her and warn her of the danger. When she saw that he went to her before the dam, that he put her above the technical achievement that in many ways defined his life, her affection would surely turn to love.

He dialed the number of Carlos Hallon, the corporation's pilot. There was enough time to reach Creekwood even in the worst possible case. Most of the ten miles of canyon between the dam and the house was rough and twisting. The water would be carrying a heavy load of silt and debris and would advance at no more than ten to fifteen miles an hour. If the dam held out for at least an hour and a half—a conservative estimate in view of the density of the embankment and the presence of the massive concrete core block—then he could reach Eleanor well before—

"Carlos? Theodore. We've got an emergency in northern California and you've got to get me there as fast as possible. Is the Lear ready to go? I'm leaving for the airport immediately. It'll take me longer than you, so I want you to arrange for a helicopter to meet us at the Yuba City airport. . . ."

Roshek slipped from the chair to the floor and, by using his hands, scuttled across the room to the closet. He pulled on his trousers while lying on his back.

"Marilyn," he called to Bolen's wife, "get dressed. You've got to take me to the airport. . . ."

26

PLUMP, GRAY-HAIRED, AND SWEET-faced, given to granny glasses and sensible shoes, Elizabeth Lehmann looked more like a spokesperson for a line of frozen pies than Caspar County Disaster Control Officer, but such she was and proud of it. She threw off the robe she was wearing when the call came from the Sheriff, and hurriedly put on the black slacks, the blue blouse with the bow, and the black jacket with the wide lapels. All dark colors that never looked soiled, all half polyester to hold a crease. If the dam did fail, she might not get back home for days and she didn't want to look like a frump. Getting men to accept orders from a woman was as much a matter of *looking* as it was *acting* businesslike and professional.

In the bathroom she attacked her hair and face with a deft efficiency born to forty years' experience, then swept everything on the counter into an overnight bag. Her mind raced as she ran to the kitchen for last-second fortifications from the refrigerator. Now she would find out if all those practice sessions paid off. Once a month she forced grumbling local officials to spend an afternoon in the Operations Room of the Disaster Office reacting to hypothetical atomic explosions, chemical spills, earthquakes, hurricanes, prison breakouts, train wrecks, riots, and terrorist attacks. Every unpleasantness she could think of was proposed to make sure everybody knew what kinds of things had to be done and who had to do them. Of course it was impossible to have a detailed plan for every conceivable calamity, but at least general procedures could be established, resources identified, and priorities agreed upon.

While finishing a cup of coffee, she tried to anticipate the problems that would arise if the entire valley below the dam had to be evacuated, problems of communication and transportation that she had never found the time to work out fully. Time was short because Elizabeth Lehmann was Caspar County Disaster Control Officer only in the mornings. Afternoons she was Chief Stenographer in Purchasing. Some California counties had as many as half a dozen people working full time on it; others, like Caspar, complacent and penny-pinching, relied on a part-timer from the steno pool. Planning for disasters was a waste of county money, in the opinion of the Board, because God in his wisdom doesn't announce which disaster among the hundreds at his disposal he is going to unleash or which parcel or parcels of land he is going to unleash it against. Or when. Not to mention plague and pestilence.

A failure of Sierra Canyon Dam was certainly something God might be considering, in Elizabeth Lehmann's opinion, and she had spent a lot of time preparing for it.

One serious inconvenience would crop up right off the bat. The County Disaster Control Office was located in the basement of the building housing the Sheriff's Department where it had always been, six blocks from the center of Sutterton. When the Board of Supervisors was reminded of this fact, a ruling was made that since it would cost X amount of dollars to move it to higher ground, let's not do it now. Thus the disaster most likely to befall the town would give the people trying to cope with it the handicap of being under five hundred feet of water.

While relocating her office was voted down monthly, Elizabeth, through two years of raising hell, had managed to get enough money to put the county's radio equipment into a van. Now the nerve center could be moved quickly to wherever it could function most efficiently. She was proud of her command car, which was equipped with a powerful two-way radio, medical supplies, road flares, and, most important, a "resource file" that listed the location of everything from doctors to sandbags and included checklists for setting up field kitchens, medical centers, and refugee camps. It was a rolling Pentagon from which she could supervise the county's response to almost any upheaval.

"Thank God this is happening on a weekend," she said to herself as she ran down the porch steps, pushing a piece of toast into her mouth. "No school kids to contend with, at least."

In the darkness of the garage she reached for the door of her command car. It wasn't there. The garage was empty and so was the driveway. Nothing was parked at the curb. She clutched her head when she remembered that the car was at the office. The previous week, the Board of Supervisors, faced with declining income year by year since the passage of Proposition 13, decided that employees could no longer take county vehicles home with them, a prohibition that included the Disaster Control Officer. In other words, from now on disasters would have to occur during regular office hours.

Cursing Howard Jarvis, Elizabeth ran into the street and looked both ways for help. Next to an abandoned kitchen stove in a weedy yard two doors away knelt Norman Kingwell polishing his motorcycle. Kingwell was a teenage good-for-nothing whose main function in life seemed to be revving his engine. She had not spoken to him or his rotten parents for two years, not since the day he turned fifteen and removed his muffler. She ran toward him, waving. "Crank that beauty up, Norm baby," she called, "you are taking me for a ride."

South of Monterey in the depths of Los Padres National Forest, a man looking absurdly out of place in a business suit hurried along a leafy pathway in the Zen Center at Tassajara Hot Springs. Across a lovely Japanese bridge he went, startling a black-robed acolyte, and down a series of stone steps to the open-air enclosures of the mineral baths. He dropped to one knee and peered into the steam rising from the surface of the murky water.

He found what he was looking for—a thin, naked man, submerged except for his eyes, nose, and mouth. The wan face was reminiscent of the image of Christ on the Shroud of Turin.

"You're going to have to leave," the kneeling man said in an urgent whisper. "There's an emergency in Caspar County."

The Governor of California lifted his head, blinking and blowing water from his lips. "*Caspar* County?"

"Sierra Canyon Dam has sprung a leak. It looks bad."

"Can't they plug it?"

"Apparently not. Sutterton is being evacuated."

"Hard to believe a state as big as this that spends so much money on the university system doesn't have people who know how to plug a leak."

The Executive Assistant to the Governor shrugged. "I'm just relaying the news. If you leave right now, you can get there for at least the tail end of what promises to be a first-rate catastrophe."

"Okay," the Governor said with a sigh of resignation, pulling himself out of the water. "I'll get dressed, and you see if you can get the Plymouth started."

"A helicopter is coming to take you. You'll do a flyover, declare a couple of counties disaster areas, and talk to the press. You can bet the press will be there in battalion strength."

The Governor put on a terry-cloth robe and stepped into a pair of sandals, dabbing at his face with a towel. "What tack should I take with the press—corporate greed, ecological insult, the Big Energy boys, spaceship earth, or what? Can we blame it on the Republicans?"

"The dam was built during your father's administration."

The Governor smiled slightly, which was the most he ever smiled. "He'll kill me if I mention that. God, do you suppose all our dams are going to start falling apart on us right and left? We've got a big enough P.R. problem as it is."

"Hardly. With the press, stick to concern for people who are dead and homeless. Show that you care about them and that the state government cares."

"And that the state government will do all it can to help, within fiscal and statutory limits. Yes, that's good. How about an attack on dams? Might be a good chance to work in a plug for solar and wind, how smaller is better, breaking the grip of foreign oil, and all that."

The two men climbed the steps, walking quickly.

"Simple concern for suffering is the ticket for the first day or two," the Executive Assistant insisted. "You are deeply moved as a person, see what I mean? You are a feeling, caring human being. Don't get technical. Display some basic, heartfelt emotion."

"You're right," the Governor said after some thought. "I'll go with that. In fact, I like it."

* * *

Two yanks of the cord and the outboard came to life. With one hand on the tiller, Chuck Duncan guided his small, flat-bottomed boat out of the secluded inlet where he kept it tied. There was little wind so early in the morning and the surface of the water was smooth. Duncan set a course for the widest part of the lake, five miles above the dam. When he got there, he would cut the motor and begin a lazy day of drinking beer, listening to soft rock, salivating over the photographs in *Oui,* fishing, and working on his suntan. Next to his teeth, in his opinion, his worst feature was his complexion. A suntan helped a lot, and this summer he intended to invest whatever time it took to get a good one.

He leaned back, turned his face to the sky, and closed his eyes. The sun wasn't warm enough yet to do much good, but he was tired and wanted to relax. He had a hangover. His muscles ached. He had spent most of the night wrestling with Carla—God, she was strong—trying and failing to get her clothes off. She giggled through the whole session as if it was some sort of goddam game. Maybe next time she would tire out. Now he looked forward to getting smashed on beer and catching up on his sleep, drifting wherever the current took him.

27

THE FOUR STEEL TRUSSES CROSSED THE river on piers of quarried granite. At the approach closest to the town was a concrete monument on which was inscribed:

Main Street Bridge
Sutterton
Erected A.D. 1933

Never had the structure been put under such stress, not even in the Great Flood of 1956, when the water crept to within three feet of the roadway. It was within two feet now and rising, a broad, swift tide.

A yellow school bus filled with prisoners from the city

jail groaned to a stop beside the monument. "Holy Toledo," said the driver, "look at the river! Think it's safe to cross?"

Beside him was a guard carrying a shotgun, who stooped to see through the windshield. "I don't think so, but I'm not a goddam engineer."

"I'm a goddam engineer," said Phil Kramer, coming down the aisle in his white coveralls and rubber boots, "and I don't think so, either. Look how fast the water's coming up. Soon as it hits those horizontal stringers, the bridge has had it."

"Siddown," said the guard.

The other prisoners, squeezed into the undersized seats, craned their necks and looked around worriedly. Haystack was stretched out at the back of the bus snoring like a foghorn.

"Fuck," said the driver, striking the steering wheel with the heels of his hands.

Two police cars arrived. One knifed in front of the bus to block its access to the bridge, the other stopped alongside. Suddenly policemen were everywhere, setting up barricades across the approach and redirecting the cars that were lining up behind. The air was filled with flashing lights and radio static. Wilson Hartley emerged from one car and waited for the bus driver to open his window.

"Where to now, Chief?"

"The high-school gym in Sterling City. Take 191. Don't go back up Main—too much traffic and people running around. You got Phil Kramer in there?"

The driver twisted in his seat. "Is one of you guys—"

"I'm Kramer," Phil said, pushing his way to the front.

The door folded open and the guard stepped aside to let Phil pass, then pointed the shotgun menacingly at the other passengers, some of whom were half out of their seats with notions of following.

Phil was uneasy when he saw Officer Lee Simon waiting

for him. He extended his hand. "I want to apologize again for—"

Simon grabbed him by the wrist and armpit and walked him on his tiptoes around the front of the bus. "Hey, what is this?" Phil protested. Before he could say anything further, he found himself shaking hands with a silver-haired policeman with a powerful grip and a familiar voice.

"Wilson Hartley, Chief of Police. We should have listened to you last night."

"Well, I—"

"All charges against you are dropped. We need your help."

"You do?"

"They tell me that until the bigwigs get here you know more about what's going on than anybody."

"Well, I—"

"For starters we need an estimate on how long the dam is going to hold."

Phil shook his head in amazement, then tried to adopt a professional manner. "I'll have to see how much worse the leak has gotten. Can you take me somewhere where I can see it? How about the powerhouse parking lot?"

He was interrupted by a loud popping and grinding noise from the river. All eyes turned. The water had reached the underside of the bridge roadway, and the force had broken the connection between the two center spans and the pier on which they rested. The roadway bowed left and the entire bridge began shuddering. At that moment a motorcycle hurtled onto the far end.

"Look at that crazy bastard!" someone shouted. "He'll never make it!"

Several inches of water were flowing across the pavement of the second span. The motorcycle crossed it like a speedboat, sending waves to each side. The bridge lurched downstream a foot when the bike reached the fourth span, almost upending it, but with a sudden thrust of his leg the driver managed to keep his balance. When he reached solid ground, he swerved to a stop, knocking over a barricade.

"You goddam fool!" Hartley shouted. "Didn't you see the roadblock on the other side? Are you out of your fucking mind?"

Norman Kingwell looked at the Chief with a half smile. "The devil made me do it," he said, jabbing a thumb over his shoulder.

Behind Kingwell, the Caspar County Disaster Control Officer climbed off the seat. "Whew!" she said. "That was invigorating!"

"Mrs. Lehmann!"

"It's okay, Wilson. I ordered him to take me across. Everything I need is in my car and I've got to get to it. There goes the bridge. . . ."

Water was piling up against the roadway from one abutment to the other, boiling over the railing and sidewalk. With a deep wrenching sound, the two center spans began to slip off their supports. The venerable old bridge seemed to make a final effort to hang on, but yielded when struck by a mass of floating trees and debris. The center spans folded together in slow motion, pulling the side spans after them and rolling under the water. Within one minute everything was out of sight, and the only indications that a bridge had once been there were the three equally spaced rapids formed by the tops of the piers.

Elizabeth Lehmann got back on the motorcycle behind her teenage chauffeur. "I've got to move the radio van to high ground," she said to Hartley. "Would the right overlook be safe?"

Hartley looked at Phil, who assured them both that the right overlook, being on solid rock, was perfect.

Mrs. Lehmann turned her attention to Phil for the first time, eying his coveralls and boots. "And you are?"

"For the time being," Hartley said, answering the question for her, "he's the technical expert in charge of this event. Anything he says goes."

"The right overlook it is, then. Let's go, Norman, we've got work to do."

Kingwell kicked his motorcycle to life and revved the engine noisily as the woman behind him threw her arms around his waist. He took off with a roar, smiling and giving the finger to one and all. It was the first time in his life he had had any function or status.

The Cessna rose quickly from the highway, banking right. "I'll go west out of town," Freddy Hasset said, "to throw off anybody who might be watching, then swing around the foothills."

On the low side of the plane, his father pointed through the open doorway at the armored truck he had abandoned on the shoulder of the highway. "The truck sure looks little," he said. "Like a bug that's been blasted with Raid." He smiled, unveiling a row of square, cigar-stained teeth. "Lookit, not a car anywhere! Nobody chased me. Got away as clean as a whistle!" He chuckled. "You shoulda seen Lloyd when I drove away and left him on the dock! I told him I had to run an errand and would be back in a minute. Oh, God! I watched him in the rearview mirror running a few steps this way and a few steps that way, wondering whether to shit or go blind! Then he just stood there with his feet apart and his arms spread as if he was getting ready to catch a sack of potatoes. Jesus, it was funny! I was laughing so hard people on the sidewalk were staring at me. I betcha that dumb bastard is still waiting for me to get back from the Laundromat or wherever the hell he thinks I went with a truck full of money." He turned in his seat and patted the two gray canvas sacks he had brought aboard with him. "Must be a hundred thousand in there, Freddy, my boy, maybe more, most of it in twenties and smaller." He broke into song, never coming close to a right note:

> *"I'm in the money! I'm in the money!*

"Excuse me, Freddy, that should be

> *"We're in the money! We're in the money!*

"How does the rest of it go? And what's that other one?

> *"It's a great day for chasing the blues,*
> *It's a great day for drinking the booze."*

He slapped his son on the knee. Freddy wasn't sharing his father's joy. He kept his hands on the controls and his eyes straight ahead.

"What's the matter? You should be as happy as I am. We're rich! We made it! We're in the clear!"

"We're not in the clear, not by a long shot," Freddy said grimly. "We still gotta find the goddam cabin from the air, we gotta get you to the ground in one piece, we gotta hope the plane flies by itself for a hundred miles at least, we gotta hope nobody sees the parachutes and comes around asking questions, then we gotta live together for months without killing each other. You think we're in the clear? Shit."

"Aw, cheer up. Everything is going to be terrific. Don't worry about me being hard to live with, because I'm a new man. Money does that to people. Now that I'm rich I love everybody, even you, my own son, who never gave me anything but trouble. Ha, ha! *Sure* I slapped you around a little in the old days, but you deserved it! Let's see a smile! Okay, then, don't smile. You're not gonna spoil my day. You know what, Freddy? I've never been so happy in my whole goddam life. That's the truth! It's not the money so much as it is the fucking I'm giving the company. Oh, that feels good!"

Emil Hasset tore open his collar and broke out again in an approximation of song:

"Happy days are here again,
The sky is full of beer again,
Let us eat a box of Cheer again,
Happy days are here again.

"God, I wish I knew the words to those great old songs, 'cause I sure feel like singing."

The plane completed a long turn to the east and leveled off toward the morning sun. The pilot's eyes were narrow and his hands were tight on the wheel.

Phil Kramer stood with a group of men at the corner of the powerhouse parking lot scanning the lower reaches of the dam with binoculars. The boil-out was easier to find than when Mort Cooper had stood on the same spot an hour earlier. It was a torrent now, flowing from a hole thirty feet in diameter and scouring a ditch down the hillside to the river. Phil adjusted the focusing knob. "A couple of hours ago it was hardly more than a mud puddle, now look at it. Must be thousands of cubic feet a second coming out of there."

"How long have we got till the whole thing blows?" Lee Simon wanted to know.

Phil handed the glasses to the man next to him, contractor Leonard Mitchell. "No way to tell for sure. Dams are as different as people, as Roshek put it in his textbook."

"I talked to Roshek a little while ago," Newt Withers offered. "He said maybe the flow could be pinched off by dumping rock on it."

Phil dismissed the suggestion with a shake of his head. "Too late for that. Maybe three or four hours ago, before piping started. Dumping stuff on the upstream side might slow it down a little, but the dam is going to fail no matter what we do."

"There must be something—"

"There's nothing."

"How long have we got?" Simon asked again. "That's all I want to know. We've got a town to evacuate."

"If the water is going *under* the core block," Phil said, thinking out loud, "through the foundation rock and grout curtain, that's one thing. If it's coming *over* the core block—"

"How long in minutes?" Simon insisted.

"The embankment is three-quarters of a mile thick at the base, so it's going to take a while. The hole is going to keep caving in until a notch is cut all the way to the crest. That's when the lake will come shouldering through in a big wave."

"How long have we got, goddammit!" Simon was losing his temper and turning red.

"I'd just be guessing. I've seen films of dams failing, but—"

"Take a guess, then!"

Withers put an arm across the policeman's chest. "Cool it, Lee," he said. "He's not God."

"He can take a guess, can't he? His guess would be better than mine, wouldn't it? Or yours? He's written a fucking *book* on the subject, hasn't he?"

Phil raised a hand. "A doctoral thesis. I'll take a guess. Where we're standing now could be under hundreds of feet of water in as little as forty-five minutes."

Simon threw Withers's arm aside. *"Forty-five minutes!"*

"Might take two or three times longer than that. Forty-five is minimum. At Baldwin Hills, for instance—"

"Shit, with forty-five minutes we'll never be able to knock on every door in town, which is what we're trying to do now. We'll be lucky to cover the side streets with a sound truck. . . ." He reached through the window of his car for the radio microphone.

"Suppose I keep an eye on the breach and keep giving you updated estimates?"

"Good idea. We'll put you on the right overlook where the radio van will be."

"I'll take you in my pickup," Mitchell said to Phil.

Riggs, Cooper, Withers, and a group of men from the Combined Water Districts ran for the powerhouse to complete the job of removing files and records that might later reveal the cause of the failure.

Minutes later, Mitchell swung off the county road onto the top of the dam. Ahead, the crest road stretched across the valley like a taut white ribbon. "Jesus," Mitchell said, pointing through the windshield, "look at that! Some fool is trying to land a plane on the dam."

Phil followed the contractor's gaze and saw a small plane approaching in the distance pursued by a police car. Several other cars had pulled over to the curbings and stopped to give the plane as much room as possible. The plane lost altitude rapidly, rose to clear the truck Phil had abandoned in the middle of the night, then touched down smoothly.

"I hope he sees the gravel," Phil said.

"What gravel?"

"I stole one of your trucks last night, and to slow down the pursuit I dumped a load of gravel on the road."

Mitchell squinted at his passenger. "You stole one of my trucks?"

"Well, I borrowed it."

The plane, a small sport model painted a bright red and decorated with racing stripes and painted flames, was taxiing rapidly toward them when the landing gear hit the gravel. The tail flipped upward, the fuselage balanced on its nose for a second, then toppled over on its back.

By the time Phil and Mitchell got there, two highway patrolmen were cutting the pilot out of his seat belt, from which he was suspended upside down. "I'm all right," said the pilot, a heavy, balding man, but clearly he wasn't. A contusion the size of a fist showed where his forehead had hit the windshield. "I'm all right," the pilot said again as he was revolved into a sitting position. His lips were drawn away from his teeth in pain and his eyes were tightly shut.

"Can't take him to the hospital downtown," one patrolman said. "That's being evacuated."

"How about the right overlook?" the other patrolman suggested. "Old lady Lehmann's setting up a medical tent there."

When the pilot was right side up, Phil recognized him. "Mr. Bolen! My God, it's Mr. Bolen!" He clambered out of the truck.

"Who?"

"Herman Bolen of Roshek, Bolen & Benedetz, one of the people who designed the dam. Oh, man, Mr. Bolen, am I glad to see you!"

Bolen forced an eye open and looked at Phil's boots, coveralls, and face. "Do I know you from somewhere?"

"I'm Phil Kramer. Roshek fired me yesterday, remember?"

Bolen closed his eye. "That was a mistake," he said, wincing. "We need you in London." He tried to get up, then sat down quickly. "Maybe I'm not all right."

"We'll see that you get first aid," a patrolman said. "If you're still not all right in thirty minutes, we'll run you over to the hospital in Chico for X-rays. You could have a skull fracture."

More cars had arrived and a circle of onlookers had formed. The patrolman asked if anyone was willing to take Bolen to the right overlook.

A man behind the wheel of a van volunteered. Phil and Mitchell helped Bolen to his feet and walked him slowly across the highway. He was handed a gauze pad to hold against the wound on his forehead.

"Kramer," Bolen said, "I'll apologize later for yesterday. Right now you've got to listen. Block this road except for emergency vehicles. When the breach reaches elevation seven five five, get everybody off the dam because it will go fast from there."

The rear doors of the van were opened and the two men helped Bolen inside. He sat against the wall with his legs extended in front of him, pressing the gauze against his head.

"Get everybody out of the powerhouse," Bolen went on in a strained voice. "Close the access tunnel door and brace it with trucks on both sides. It might hold."

Mitchell's eyes went back and forth between Bolen and Phil. "Then you think the dam is definitely going to let go?"

Bolen rolled his head toward the front of the van to hide the tears that were leaking from his eyes. "The dam is lost."

"There must be some way to save it," Mitchell insisted. "Suppose we dump rock in the lake over the point the water's getting in? I've got a loaded barge tied up at the quarry dock that I could have towed into position in half an hour. . . ."

"Useless," Bolen said, "even with a bull's-eye. In about half an hour a whirlpool will be forming. You'll lose the barge and everybody on it, all for nothing. Too late now. Too late, too late."

A patrolman closed one of the doors.

"We'll drag your plane off the dam," Phil said. "We'll save that at least."

Bolen lifted his hand weakly. "Forget the plane. I'm too old to fly. Dump it over the side to clear the road." He motioned for Phil to lean close. "If Roshek shows up, keep an eye on him. This may be more than he can take."

Phil nodded. "I'll do that."

"You still work for us," Bolen said. "You'll get a raise. Enough to buy some decent clothes. Did he say a fractured skull? I may pass out."

The second door was closed and Phil watched the van depart. He climbed into the pickup. Now there were tears in *his* eyes.

28

THE HELICOPTER SKIMMED THE TREE-tops at the bottom of the valley ten miles below the dam. Roshek spotted the green lawn surrounding Creekwood and pointed. With a nod the pilot made a slight course correction.

The river didn't look good . . . already out of its banks and dotted with driftwood. Roshek hoped Eleanor had heard the news and was already gone. If not, he was prepared to sacrifice himself for her. He would tell the pilot to lift her to safety, then come back. If the wave arrived in the meantime, too bad. Better she survive than him, if it came down to a choice. He was an old man physically, and fast falling apart. His career, which just days before was on the verge of reaching unprecedented heights, was falling apart as well. Not that there was much chance that he would have to sacrifice himself. He could see several miles up the canyon and there was no sign of a wave. The helicopter could easily make two trips to high ground.

The house came into view. There was a car in the driveway and it wasn't Eleanor's. If he was not mistaken, it belonged to Russell Stone, the dancer she was living with when Roshek came into her life.

Good Lord, Roshek thought, surely they aren't in the house together, not after she had sworn she was through with him. Stone had come alone—yes, that was it—and she had loaned him the key.

"Set her down?" the pilot shouted as he approached the lawn below the house.

"Hover," Roshek shouted in return.

The front door opened. A slim, well-muscled young man wearing shorts stepped onto the porch and shielded his eyes. It was Stone, all right, Roshek was sure, and he felt a rush of anger. He didn't like the idea of a rival spending the night at Creekwood even with Eleanor's permission . . . especially with Eleanor's permission.

A woman appeared in the shadowed doorway. "Don't let it be Eleanor," Roshek whispered, "please, please . . ."

But it was Eleanor, dressed in the silk pajamas he had given her for Christmas. She glided into the sunlight and slipped an arm around Stone's waist. He put an arm around her shoulder and pulled her close as they stared at the helicopter together. Roshek saw her hand move to shield her eyes like a bird rising to a limb. Even her simplest gestures were so graceful and elegant that he—

"Up," he said to the pilot abruptly, pointing upward, "take her up."

As the helicopter soared up, Roshek was seized by convulsive sobs. He buried his face in a handkerchief and struggled to regain his composure.

"Hey," the pilot said, "you all right?"

Roshek nodded, blew his nose noisily, and took several deep breaths.

When the helicopter reached an elevation of fifteen hundred feet, it tilted slightly and swooped forward on a level course toward the northeast. In the distance was the shining surface of Warren Lake. The lake tapered to a narrow finger above Sutterton, where a tiny brown patch that was the dam held it back like a cork in a bottle.

The right overlook was a two-acre flat area paved with asphalt and lined on the canyon side with coin-operated telescopes. It was a hundred feet above the crest of the dam, and on summer weekends was filled with the cars of as many as two hundred sightseers. Phil, equipped with a two-way radio and a pair of binoculars, established himself at the outermost point where two reaches of guardrail met atop a rock outcropping that was shaped like a ship's prow. It was a spectacular vantage point. To his left the deep green water swept smoothly over the lowered gates into the spillway, which angled downward directly below. At the bottom, far to his right, the torrent dissolved into a continuous explosion of spray as it struck a field of massive concrete blocks—energy dissipaters designed to pass the discharge into the river shorn of its capacity to gouge and tear.

At the far side of the river was the electrical switchyard and the powerhouse parking lot, empty now except for Phil's battered and nearly inoperable Mustang, which he had decided to abandon. As Bolen had suggested, the powerhouse had been evacuated and a protective wall of trucks set up in front of the access tunnel door in an effort to spare the generators from the costly indignity of total immersion.

Near the bottom of the dam embankment just beyond the spillway was a circular area a hundred yards in diameter that was glistening with moisture and looked soft and spongy. The lower edge was a ragged gash thirty yards long from which a powerful flow of brown water was pouring steadily and cascading down the hill.

Holding his radio close to his mouth so his words would be heard over the roar of the water, Phil reported on the progress of the failure: "Upper edge of breach now at elevation five hundred. Volume of flow has doubled in the last five minutes. Saturated area is growing and may erupt at any time. Now estimate main collapse in thirty-five minutes."

In the right distance was Sutterton, the lower sections of which were being nibbled away by the rising river. Three brick warehouses dating from the gold rush that had withstood countless floods had been pushed over and submerged. Through binoculars Phil watched a dozen wood-frame houses twisted off their foundations, up-ended, and smashed to pieces. A large white building with a cupola on top was magically lifted off its moorings and carried downstream without a sign of listing or turning, a grand Victorian excursion boat embarking on a leisurely tour of the Thames. At the turn the river made south of town, the cupola dropped straight down as the building collapsed in on itself and quickly sank.

Phil felt like a spotter in a war relaying battle information to generals at a field headquarters behind the lines. Field headquarters in this case was just a few feet away, for the overlook had been transformed into a kind of alternate seat of government. One of the first to arrive was Mrs. Lehmann, driving a car so loaded with equipment that it almost dragged on the ground, followed by a van that bristled with radio antennas. Next came cars carrying the Sheriff, the Chief of Police, the Fire Chief, and the head of the local Red Cross. Highway patrolmen kept one area clear for helicopters bringing in officials from Sacramento, though the first helicopter to arrive carried a television news crew.

Mrs. Lehmann set up shop on a card table behind the radio van, with maps and lists spread out before her. She kept a steady stream of information flowing to communities downstream, relaying reports on traffic conditions as soon as she received them from the Highway Patrol. She made sure city and county officers knew where the refugee centers were being set up and that they were being staffed with appropriate personnel. Her voice had a hard edge to it, and Phil could hear almost every word she said over the cacophony of roaring water, vehicle engines, shouts, and loudspeaker static. She was obviously well prepared and was attacking her job with tremendous energy and effectiveness. To a remark from Wilson Hartley that she seemed almost to be enjoying what she was doing, Phil heard her reply: "I'll cry if it will help any."

The idea spread that Phil not only had predicted the catastrophe but that he was the greatest authority on dam failures in the world. He was deferred to and treated as the ultimate authority. It was to him, for example, that the television reporter and his cameraman were drawn.

Hearing a well-modulated baritone voice behind him, Phil turned and found himself looking into the lens of a television minicamera. Next to the cameraman was a man in a butterscotch sport jacket speaking earnestly into a microphone: "On your screen is Bill or Phil Kramer, the heroic young engineer who spent the night sounding the alarm and who is now providing on police wavelengths a minute-by-minute account of the dissolution of the mighty Goliath that for ten years has tamed the once-rampaging Sierra Canyon River, and which, or so it seems, will rampage again, this time with a vengeance and worse, and who is credited with giving officials enough warning time so that the cost of the disaster, if and when it comes, will be greatly minimized, at least in terms of wasted lives." He thrust the microphone in Phil's face and asked him to give the viewers "an up-to-the-minute update."

Phil waved him away in irritation. "Jesus, mister, would you mind? I'm awful busy. We've got a dam failing here."

"Gradually, as I understand it," the reporter said.

"Water will come out faster and faster until the valley is flooded, is that it?"

"No. In about half an hour the dam is going to get washed out and a wall of water will go down the valley like a bulldozer."

"A bulldozer how high?"

"Depends on the width of the valley. Five hundred feet high in narrow spots, a hundred in wide spots."

"Traveling fifty or a hundred miles an hour? What a spectacle that will be for our strategically placed cameras."

"It might go a hundred down a straight concrete canal, but this is a valley with twists and turns. Turbulence and the load the water will pick up will cut the speed down to ten or fifteen miles an hour. Now if you'll excuse me . . ."

"I'm told you spent some time in jail last night. How did you feel about that?"

Phil was rescued by Mrs. Lehmann, who shouted shrilly at two policemen: "Get those clowns away from Kramer!"

He turned and scanned the lake through binoculars. "Looks like all boats have made it to shore," he said into his radio. "Wait, I think I see one about a quarter mile from the spillway. He must have missed the warnings. Is there a helicopter or powerboat that can get out there? No sign of a whirlpool forming yet."

He swung the glasses down the valley. "On the rim of the canyon, below town, where the river bends, I see half a dozen people. They should be removed from that area. When the wave hits the hillside, it might surge all the way to the top."

Wilson Hartley put his hand on Phil's shoulder. "Did I hear you say the flood would only move at ten or fifteen miles an hour?"

"Just a guess, but I can't imagine it going much faster. There's a couple of narrow spots and some sharp turns."

"Shit, a man could drive down the canyon a lot faster

than that. Make sure everybody has been moved out."

"Yes, I suppose—"

"Not the kind of risk I'd want to order a man to take, though. I'll do it myself. I'll take our best car, the one we use to track down speeders."

Phil stared at the policeman in disbelief. "Are you serious? I don't know for *sure* how fast the water will go. It might—"

Hartley turned away. "You just keep talking into that microphone so I know how much time I've got left. . . ."

A clap of thunder pulled Phil's attention to the dam. A tremendous upwelling had blown out the circular saturated area. A geyser exploded upward and fell back, and viscous brown water gushed out like blood from a wound.

"A major blowout," Phil reported excitedly. "Flow coming through for the first time at what looks like full pressure. Spurting out like a fountain. Cave-ins on upper side of breach to about six seventy-five. The breach is now about fifty yards wide and a hundred long. Won't be long now, maybe twenty minutes. If anybody's still in town, they should get out now and fast."

On the surface of the lake three hundred yards from the spillway, a column of bubbles broke the surface and a circle of water began to revolve slowly around it.

From Roshek's helicopter, the town, the lake, and the dam presented a scene of picture-postcard splendor. Sutterton looked as sleepy and peaceful as any New England village, and only by close observation was it possible to see the lines of cars fleeing it on every available road. The lake sparkled in the sun, and the foothills rolled away from it toward the snowy high country like a rumpled green blanket. Looming ever larger as the helicopter approached was the dam, a colossal wall that swept from one side of the valley to the other. On the left side, like a silver bracelet on a suntanned arm, was the spillway, and beside it, half as high and twice as wide, was an ugly, seething mass of brown water. Roshek stared at the rupture as he might at a beautiful woman whose face was scarred, or at a painting ripped by a madman's knife. Minutes before, he had felt overwhelmed by sorrow and pain at the discovery of Eleanor's treachery and his eyes were still stinging from the tears. The tears came again at the sight of Sierra Canyon Dam in its death throes. The great structure that was as much a part of him as his heart or his brain was sprawled beneath him, broken and bleeding.

Roshek lifted his eyes and stared unseeingly at the horizon. He wanted to return to the Lear waiting for him at the Yuba City airport—what was the point of watching something you loved die at close range?—but he found himself unable to give the command. He couldn't speak or make a sound or lift a hand.

He was aware by the forces on his body that the helicopter was landing, but when it came to rest and the rotor stopped he did not move. Words spoken by the pilot came to him as from a great distance and he couldn't focus his mind on their meaning.

The door opened and he felt himself being lifted to the ground. Men surrounded him whose faces were familiar but whose names and functions he could not place. He put his arms automatically into his crutches and walked at the center of a small group. He felt a wind, and he paused to pull his hat down close to his ears.

Men were standing shoulder to shoulder at a guardrail. They parted to make room for him and said things to him he didn't hear. He looked over the edge. A powerful tide of water, green and glassy, was surging in from the lake across the lowered spillway gates and hurtling down the smooth concrete channel in perfect laminar flow, gradually changing to white turbulence exactly as the hydraulic formulas and scale model tests predicted it would. It was beautiful and hypnotic the way the power of the water was guided and controlled by the precisely calculated angles and curves of the spillway walls. It was a photograph in an engineering textbook.

Beyond the spillway, where there should have been nothing but the smooth, tawny flank of the embankment being warmed by the sun, was a raging brown beast from a nightmare, savage and roaring and gnawing a fatal cavity in one of the man-made wonders of the world. The gusher heaved and spouted, lashing like the tail of a crazed animal that was trying to back out of a hole. When it did succeed in wrenching itself free, it would be submerged immediately in a flood of unimaginable proportions.

It was all wrong, Roshek thought, shaking his head while tears streamed down his cheeks. Sierra Canyon Dam was designed in part to lift the spirit and nourish the soul. To superimpose a hideous eruption on it was insane, it was a crime, it was a grotesque contradiction. He remembered with sudden clarity the rage and frustration he had felt as a young engineer when a paper he had written was botched by a technical journal. An intricate analysis had ended with a single equation, the result of thousands of observations made in the field, and somehow it had been hopelessly mangled. Because of the stupidity of people he had never even met, an insight of great value had been transformed into something ridiculous. He had wanted to go to New York and strangle the editors with his bare hands. He felt the same urge now.

Through no fault of his, Sierra Canyon Dam was unraveling before his eyes. The smooth skin was being ripped apart. Forces of nature were at work. Since there was nothing he could do to stop them, there was nothing to be gained by becoming emotionally involved. He withdrew to an infinite remoteness and watched as he would a film from a soundproof booth. The hands of an insolent young ballet dancer with a nearly perfect body were caressing Eleanor James and she was smiling in response, but what was that to him? Eleanor was out of his life now and soon the dam would be as well. He had done his work as best he could and others had wrecked it. She was not the Eleanor he had loved and this was not his dam. He had worshipped perfection. The Sierra Canyon Dam he designed and built would not cave in like a sand castle to provide entertainment for a gathering of ghouls.

Wind tugged at his clothes. His hat was snatched from his head and catapulted into the air like a clay pigeon. Roshek watched it soar high in the sky, then fall in a long arc, spinning, shrinking in size until it became a hard-to-follow dot. After what seemed like minutes it disappeared against the background of the river that was cascading down the face of the dam.

He relaxed his hands and let his crutches clatter to the ground. To keep from falling, he closed his fingers around the cold steel pipe that formed the top railing of the fence. If it weren't for his withered legs, he could have hurdled it in an instant. He became aware then of a voice that sounded somehow familiar, and he turned slowly to his right. Ten feet away a man in white coveralls peered through binoculars and held a radio to his lips. Roshek had seen that face before. "I can see a whirlpool forming in the lake," the man was saying. "A definite depression in the water and a clockwise turning about three hundred yards northeast of the spillway. That's a hundred yards closer than the mathematical model predicted. Top of breach now at seven hundred feet."

The voice was too dispassionate. Sierra Canyon Dam was failing—weeping was called for and screams of pain. Roshek stared, trying to place the man. What was it about the sight of him and the sound of his voice that stirred such feelings of hatred in his heart? He worked his way along the guardrail to get closer, sliding his hands along the railing and ignoring the men who had to step back to make way.

"Main break only ten minutes or so away," the man said into his radio. "I still see people standing on the ridge below town. They may be goners if they stay there."

The man turned, lowering the radio and binoculars. "Mr. Roshek!" he said in astonishment. "Oh, Jesus! God, I'm so *sorry*. . . ." He gestured toward the dam. "It's . . . it's a great structure, a magnificent structure. There was nothing wrong with the design. . . . The studies will prove that, I'm sure. . . ."

"It's Kramer, isn't it," Roshek said, pulling himself close. "Yes . . ."

The younger man drew back slightly, as if afraid he was about to be spat upon or struck.

"You were lucky," Roshek said in a quavering voice, "incredibly lucky. It was a chance in a billion that the dam would fail and you would blunder in when you did." The roar of the water was so loud he had to raise his voice to be heard. "Your idiotic computer program had nothing to do with it. . . . Sheer stupid luck." He let go of the railing and took hold of Kramer's shoulder. "Before you came, there was no problem. You made this happen, yes, somehow you let the water through—don't deny it! Sabotage . . . to prove your crazy theory, to attract attention to yourself, to tear me down . . ." Roshek was shouting to make himself heard over the surrounding din, but his voice was thin and cracking. He had a powerful urge to try to wrestle Kramer over the edge and fall with him into the flood below, but he forced himself not to yield to it, knowing that the effort would fail. The boy was strong and young and would fight him off and would be helped by the men who were crowding close. An assault would do nothing but provide still another spectacle for the jackals who were watching.

Roshek felt a strong hand on his arm. He turned and saw a man with his head wrapped in bandages who was shouting his name. "Can't you hear me?" he was saying. "Don't you recognize me?"

It was Herman Bolen. Roshek evaluated the situation coldly. If I don't answer him, he reasoned, he will think

I've lost my mind. I must put him at his ease. . . .

"Of course I can hear you, Herman. What happened to your head?"

"I tried to break the windshield of my plane with it. I just got out of the medical tent. Took six stitches. For a while there I was bleeding like a stuck pig."

"Like the dam," Roshek said. "You'll kill yourself eventually with your driving and flying."

There was a deep, rolling thunder from the dam. A great triangular block of the embankment near the top gave way and sank into the river of water surging beneath it. The lake seemed to leap forward into the slot that now reached from the bottom of the slope to within a few yards of the crest, fighting its way through with an awesome frenzy. Directly above the breach, the crest roadway began to show a noticeable sag.

Roshek turned away. He leaned his back against the guardrail and held out his hands. "Where are my crutches?" When they were handed to him, he swung himself between the cars and trucks toward his helicopter. "I don't want to watch," he said to Bolen, who had to hurry to keep pace. "I'm not a masochist. I'm going back to Los Angeles. Carlos is waiting for me in Yuba City with the Lear."

Bolen helped him climb into the passenger's seat. "Wouldn't it be better, Theodore, if you stayed till this was over? The press is here and they want to talk to you. We should agree on some sort of statement."

"A crippled old man crying," Roshek said, buckling his seat belt. "That would make a nice thirty-second spot on the noon news, wouldn't it? No, thanks. You talk to them. Say whatever you want."

Bolen wouldn't let him close the door. "Are you sure you are . . . will you be . . ."

"I'm perfectly all right, Herman. Stop worrying. I got a little . . . well, unhinged when I first saw the dam and Kramer, but I'm okay now. Everything is under control, believe me. We'll have a talk when you get back to Los Angeles. Especially about Kramer. The press is going to make a hero out of him, I'm sure you realize. We have to think of a way to turn that into a gain for the company."

Roshek concentrated on speaking rationally and on presenting himself as a man who had been subjected to crushing pressure but who had enough strength of character to recover from it. He smiled and nodded reassuringly as he lifted Bolen's hand off the door.

Bolen hesitated, then backed away.

The helicopter lifted off vertically. When it was above the tops of the surrounding trees, it tilted and veered away toward the southwest. Roshek watched Bolen looking up at him and saw him almost bumped into by a jogger, who appeared from the woods with no apparent idea of where he was going. He twisted in his seat for a last glimpse of the ravaged dam. The breach now dwarfed the spillway and the final breakup was obviously near. Tens of thousands of tons of water per second were pouring through in a flood that was like a slice of Niagara Falls and three times higher. He watched in spite of himself, and he watched until a mountainside mercifully obstructed his view.

29

THREE TIMES DUNCAN PULLED THE cord and three times the motor failed to start. "Shit," he said. The boat had drifted much more quickly than usual toward the dam, which was now only a quarter of a mile away. He decided that the spillway gates must have been lowered during the night . . . the pull wouldn't be so strong with only two feet going over the top. Not that he was in any danger. There were trash racks on the lake side of the gates—large steel grilles—designed to retain debris so that it wouldn't damage the spillway, and a hundred feet from the dam was a long string of logs chained together that prevented private boats from running aground on the upstream slope of the embankment. But Duncan didn't like being so close to the dam. He saw enough of it during the week, and fishing was better farther upstream.

He tried again to start the motor—this time it caught. He swung the boat around and set a course for the center of the lake. Tilting his head back, he drained the last drops from a can of beer, then held it over the side until it filled with water. He dropped it and leaned over the edge to watch it sink. Usually he could follow a can fifteen or twenty feet down, sometimes farther. The water in the lake was mostly melted snow and extremely clear, but this time the can faded from view after a few feet. Weird. He had never seen the water so murky in this part of the lake, where it was eight hundred feet deep. Something must be stirring up the sediment.

He sat up and looked around. There was a man standing on the crest of the dam waving his arms. Was he waving at *him*? Duncan waved back. The right overlook was full of cars and trucks. What was that all about? Maybe something to do with the marathon. He noticed that he was even closer to the right side of the dam than he had been before. "Well, for Christ sakes," he said aloud, moving the throttle to full open and redirecting the propeller thrust. He kept his eyes on a fixed onshore point to check his progress—he was *still* losing ground.

He shifted in his seat and looked toward the spillway. If the current was so strong, maybe the best way to escape was to run with it, angling slightly to the side so that he would reach the shore at the right abutment. From there he could surely make his way back upstream by sticking close to the canyon wall. He pointed the boat toward the spillway, and for the first time became aware of a muffled roar. Usually on the lake it wasn't possible to hear the sound of the water at the bottom of the spillway, because the dam acted as a sound barrier. They must be spilling the whole twenty-two feet, he thought, otherwise I'd never be able to hear that noise. He had visions of his boat being drawn against the trash racks and held there like a stick of wood on a sewer grating. If that happened, he and the boat would have to be lifted out with a crane.

He saw a helicopter leave the overlook and disappear to the southwest. A minute later another helicopter rose from the same point and headed directly toward him. His boat was picking up speed and the tiller angle had no effect on his direction. First he was drawn toward the dam, then parallel to it, and now he was being swung in a broad arc *away* from it. He noticed then a depression in the surface of the water about a hundred yards away, a depression around which a large section of the lake was revolving. "Jesus," Duncan said, "I'm caught in some kind of goddam eddy. . . ." He managed to turn the boat so that it was facing away from the depression, and watched with rising fear as he was swung in a wide circle, returning to the same point a minute later but ten yards closer to the center. His outboard motor was useless against the speed and power of the quickening spiral current. After two more revolutions, he was within fifty feet of the center and his boat was angled steeply downward. It was as if the surface of the water were a rubber membrane that was being pinched and pulled downward from below.

Whirlpool! The word dropped into his mind like a snake. In a panic he saw that he had been drawn so far beneath the surrounding surface of the lake that he could no longer see the dam or the shore. The boat spun in ever-tightening circles until it was so close to the deepening spout of the funnel that Duncan could have pitched an oar into it. The helicopter appeared above him, descending, the pilot half out of the door gesturing for him to try to grab one of the landing runners. The helicopter hovered in a fixed position as the boat made two twisting passes beneath it. Both times Duncan, kneeling on the seat, reached as high as he could but missed making the connection. As the boat careened around the banked curve for a third approach, Duncan rose unsteadily to a crouching position, trying not to lose his balance and capsize the boat. This time, he vowed, he would catch hold even if he had to leap upward to do it.

He never got the chance. Striking a half-submerged log, the boat was upended and Duncan was pitched into the center of the vortex, where he was instantly sucked out of sight.

The helicopter lingered, turning slowly, before lifting away.

Kent Spain wondered how much longer he could last. Staggering out of the woods onto the right overlook, he ran into the side of a parked police car. Rebounding, he nearly knocked over a fat man with a bandaged head. As he threaded his way through sawhorse barricades that were so ineptly placed they hindered his progress rather than guided it, he felt both nauseous and dizzy. There were a lot of spectators, but for some reason they didn't greet him with the spontaneous cheer usually given to the runner in the lead. Several people shouted congratulations of some sort when they saw him, others were looking in the wrong direction.

Reaching the pavement of the road across the dam and ducking under a chain that somebody had stupidly stretched across it, he saw a cop waiting for him with a hand extended. Spain had no intention of stopping for a handshake. The cop, apparently not wanting to be denied, lunged at him as he passed. The runner sidestepped and slipped out of his grasp with a shrugging motion of his shoulder. Now the cop was chasing him and shouting words he couldn't hear because of the head-splitting roar that filled his ears. The dumb bastard probably wants me to stop and give him an autograph, Kent thought, marveling at the general thickheadedness of the human race. Legs churning, he increased his speed as much as his remaining strength would allow, which was enough to leave the cop behind.

A few minutes earlier, as he had come down the hillside to the dam, the trees shimmered and the ground undulated like a flag in the wind. He had heard roaring then, too, but it was nothing like the thunder that filled his skull now. The road here was not so much undulating as it was quivering and at one point seemed to sink beneath his feet so that he had to run downhill into a trough and up the other side. Stop for a minute, an inner voice told him; sit on the curbing and wait for the roaring and quivering to go away. No! He would keep going if it killed him. Perseverance was the mark of a champion. He would not allow his body or his brain to talk him into taking a rest. The only thing that would bring him to a halt was if his body came unhinged at the joints and fell into a pile of separate parts.

There were people at the other end of the dam, too, clutching at him as he ran by and shouting things at him he couldn't decipher. The sign marking the point where the trail left the road and entered the woods had been knocked down. Good. That might delay runners who didn't know the route.

Soon Kent was alone again among the trees, jogging determinedly along a trail that followed the contours of a side canyon. At the end of a long switchback Dulotte would be waiting. He was beginning to feel a little better and he kept his eyes open for the white cloth that marked the hidden bicycle. His breathing was not as ragged as it had been coming across the dam. The roar had diminished and the ground had almost come to rest. Then his legs failed. They simply turned to rubber. In the space of five strides he was transformed from a man running to a man face down in the dirt. He clutched the ground as he would a life raft and gasped like a beached fish.

It's all over now, he thought; I've blown it. Yousri will come flying by first, maybe stopping to kick dirt in my eyes, then Ryan, then the panting, sweating, salivating herd. If I don't roll over into the weeds, I'll be trampled to death.

After several minutes of lying still, strength seeped back into his limbs. He sat up. It was eerily silent. Nobody was coming down the trail. He must have had a bigger lead than he realized. With some effort he got to his feet and brushed himself off. A few cuts and bruises. His left kneecap was bleeding slightly. He walked for a while. A cool breeze felt good and he began to jog, tentatively at first, then with a trace of vigor.

He stopped when he saw a Center for Holistic Fitness T-shirt dangling from a limb. Still there was nobody on the trail. "Christ," he said as he parted the bushes, "I must have left those assholes miles behind." The bike was there, gleaming and beautiful. He dragged it into the open and bounced it several times before climbing aboard.

When Dulotte saw the bike coming, he stepped from behind his table and held out his hands. Kent skidded to a stop.

"Not so fast," Dulotte said with a smile. "At this rate you'll break the world record by ten minutes. How are you holding up?"

"A few minutes ago I thought I was dead, now I feel terrific. How far ahead of the field am I?"

"I don't know. Back in this canyon there's nothing but static on the radio. Did you make use of the pedometer-watch, the Pulsometer, the—"

"No. All that shit broke down a couple of miles out. And the way my crotch feels, I think the Jog-Tech Living Jock died, too."

"Well, nobody will ever know. Leave the bike here and jog the rest of the way. Your time has to be in the realm of reason."

Kent got off the bike and gave it a push into the weeds. "Anything you say, Doc." He drained a cup of water and helped himself to a peeled orange. As he trotted away, he looked over his shoulder and waved. "So long," he said, "see you Monday at the Bank of America."

* * *

Officer John Colla sped through the side streets of Sutterton with his siren wailing, stopping at every third house to tell anybody he could find to head for high ground after first warning the neighbors. When he heard Kramer's radio report that the major break would come in as little as twenty minutes, he realized that at his present rate he was never going to be able to cover the section assigned to him. He switched to stopping at every fifth house. Most of the houses were already empty, thanks in part to a plane equipped with a public-address system that had spent forty-five minutes flying a low crisscrossing pattern over the town broadcasting the evacuation order. The plane was from Sutter County. Mrs. Lehmann, bless her heart, had obviously talked somebody into releasing it.

Colla found one man who didn't want to leave because the baseball game he was watching on television looked headed for extra innings. Colla argued with him only briefly before running back to his patrol car. As he made a U-turn in the street, he saw the man come out his front door and head for his garage. "I'm leaving," he shouted to the policeman. "Power failure. Lost the picture."

When the break was estimated at five minutes away, Colla abandoned his efforts and took one of the roads leading to the tablelands above the town. On the way he stopped to tell Mr. and Mrs. Orvis, who were trying to tie an upholstered chair to the roof of their car, to give up and clear out. Colla was satisfied, based on what he had seen himself and reports he heard on the radio, that Sutterton was almost entirely empty. He would be surprised if more than a dozen people out of the population of 6,500 were unaccounted for when the flood was over.

At the edge of town, where the road turned sharply uphill, he stepped on his brakes. Two kids not more than ten years old were sitting quietly in a tree.

"What the hell are you kids doing?" he shouted out of his window.

"The dam is breaking," one of them called down. "We can watch the water come out from here."

Colla got out of his car and ordered them down, telling them they'd drown if they stayed where they were. "Where are your mom and dad? In the house?"

"Dad's divorced," the older of the two boys said, working his way to the ground. "Mom's upstairs fixing her nails."

"Hasn't she heard the sirens and the bells and people shouting and the airplanes?"

"She said it was awful noisy today."

"Get in the car."

"Really?"

Colla fired two shots in the air. A woman's face appeared in an upstairs window. When she saw what looked like an arrest of her babies, she started screaming.

"The dam is failing!" Colla shouted. "I'll wait thirty seconds for you, then I'm getting the boys out of here."

The woman raised her eyes and looked across the rooftops toward the dam. What she saw made her mouth fall open. She was running down the front walk twenty seconds later, a cat under each arm, a fur coat over one shoulder, and purses swinging from both elbows. She was a good-looking woman, Colla noticed as he helped her into the car, even without makeup and wearing a housecoat. He filed away a mental note to look her up when it was all over.

"Look out," an excited voice on the radio was saying, "here it comes. . . ."

From Phil's vantage point it looked like the end of the world. With deep-throated booms and crashes, great chunks of the dam fell into the breach until a ragged V-shaped notch had been opened all the way to the top. A section of the crest roadway hung like a suspension bridge over the torrent before dropping, seemingly in slow motion, as a single piece. The lake, sensing that it had an unobstructed path to a level a thousand feet lower, pushed forward like a suddenly energized green glacier. The lower sections of the breach, where brown water was still erupting like lava from a volcano, was obliterated by hundreds of thousands of tons of white water landing on it from above. The massive tide quickly blasted a wider and wider path for itself as the once stubborn dam seemed to lose its will to resist. The concrete spillway was undermined, sagged sideways, and was torn apart from the top down, one ponderous block after another. Phil took several steps backward instinctively, fearing that the solid rock abutment on which he was standing might be the next to go. He had intended to continue describing the scene before him, but his radio was no longer working—it was soaked with water, as were his clothes. He had lost the power to speak anyway, so stunned was he by the way the unleashed reservoir smashed through the dam. He had seen films of other dams failing, smaller dams impounding smaller reservoirs, but there was nothing in his experience or his imagination to prepare him for a display of destruction like this. It was like watching a mountain range breaking up or California sinking into the sea.

The ground beneath his feet shuddered as it would in an earthquake when a section of the dam a thousand feet wide and four thousand feet thick at the base detached itself from the rest of the embankment. A crack appeared halfway between the breach and the far end of the dam, revealing itself by a new eruption of water. Fully a third of the dam, a mass containing at least thirty million cubic yards of material, began to edge downstream as a unit, unable any longer to hold back the weight of the water pushing against it. As it moved, it slumped until water was sweeping over the crest and down the face as well as boiling around the sides, and when that happened it slowly lost its shape, sinking and spreading like a pile of mud.

A river wider than the Columbia pushed through the

opening, sloping downward as it streamed to a new, lower level a quarter mile downstream. The widening flood fan from the first break was overtaken and overwhelmed by an avalanche of new water hundreds of feet deeper. In minutes Sutterton was crushed and obliterated by a fury that would scour the valley down to bedrock from one end to the other.

The main wall of water, unobstructed, rolled over the town at fifty miles an hour. When it struck the hillside below the town where the river and the canyon turned right, a mighty sheet of water surged up the slope like the crash of surf against a seawall. It was a splash of death. When the wave fell back into the main flood, the slope had been swept clean of trees, topsoil, houses . . . and sightseers.

30

KENT SPAIN WAS FEELING FINE, STRIDING long, and breathing free. And smiling. Only a mile more to the steps of the Sutterton City Hall, where he would break the tape for a stunning new Mother Lode Marathon record. After coming so close to dropping out, the big bucks, the fame, the cars, the clothes, the women, and the food would be his after all. Downhill the rest of the way, along a lane on a hill above the town, to the fairgrounds, down a steep gravel road to the city limits, then up the length of Main Street waving to the cheering throngs.

A helicopter clattered overhead, the fourth he had seen since crossing the dam. Sure a lot of hoopla for a relatively obscure cross-country run. The sport was getting too big for its own good. Rounding a corner, he saw people standing with their backs toward him. They were in the pathway, on the grassy slope above the pathway, and on the ridge in the distance, people with suitcases and laundry bags and boxes, people in clusters with their arms around each other. Children were crying.

"Keep this lane clear!" he shouted, sidestepping his way through the strangely silent crowd. "There's a race going on! Let me through. . . ."

"Stupid goddam fool," he heard a man say.

Responding with curses of his own, Kent left the path and picked his way along the hillside to get around the congestion. When he saw what they were looking at, he stopped in confusion. He was on the edge of an inland sea. Where he expected to find the gravel road that descended into town, there was only water, water that stretched to the hills on the opposite side of the valley a mile and a half away.

"Where am I?" he shouted, bouncing up and down on the balls of his feet to keep his circulation going. "I must have made a wrong turn. Where's Sutterton? Which way do I go? What the hell is wrong with you people? What's going on? Are you deaf? Which way to City Hall?"

A woman raised her arm and pointed toward the center of the lake, where floating debris revealed a swift current. "There is Sutterton," she said in a small voice, "under the water. The dam broke. Everything is gone."

Kent stopped bouncing. He turned in a slow circle as the truth of the woman's words sank into his brain like a deadening gas. The desolation on the faces of the people around him made it clear that the loss he had suffered was trivial compared to theirs.

Sitting on the grass next to him were a man and a woman and three children, all sobbing quietly. Beginning to sob himself, he sat down beside them and lowered his face into his hands. Sitting was bad for the lumbar, but Kent Spain didn't care anymore.

* * *

Freddy banked the plane to give his father a view of the clearing. "There it is," he said. "You jump first. When you're on the ground and out of your chute, I'll drop the moneybags to you, point the plane toward Mexico, and jump myself."

"You gotta be kidding," Emil Hasset said with a smile that was threatening to become permanent. "Me jump before the money? No way."

"You think I'll head for Vegas or someplace without you, is that it? What'd I tell you? We ain't even out of the plane yet and already we're at each other's fucking throats."

"Who's at anybody's fucking throat? Not me. I'm happy. I feel like a million bucks. But when I go out that door, the million bucks is going with me, one sack under each arm. Leaving you up here with all the loot is just not good business, with all due respect."

"Pop, you can't jump with the money. When your chute opens, you'll get a jolt and you'll drop the bags in the trees or the river and we might never find them. If you did manage to hang on, you'd be so heavy your legs would break like pretzels when you hit."

"I'm not leaving you with the loot, period. It's a temptation even the Virgin Mary would snap at. I know you, Freddy! You once tried to split my forehead with a pool cue." He took off his cap. "Lookit, I still have the scar."

Freddy sighed. "That was ten years ago. Okay, here's another idea. I circle low and we drop the sacks close to the cottage. Then I go up to about fifteen hundred feet and you bail out. I'll jump from two thousand because I got to make sure the plane clears the ridge."

"Ain't fifteen hundred a little low for me? I'm just a beginner."

"Plenty high. Can't take you higher because you don't know how to steer. If a wind comes up, you might land in Minnesota or some fucking place."

Emil fingered the harness on his chest. "How does this work, anyway?"

"Simple. That thing there's the ripcord. Soon as you're outta the plane, pull it. When you hit the ground, don't try to keep your feet. Go limp. Crumple up and roll with the punch."

"Sounds easy enough. Let's get it over with." Emil put a hand on his son's shoulder. "Look, kid, I'm sorry if it sounded like I don't trust you. It's just that I—"

"You don't trust me," Freddy snapped, pushing his father's hand away. "So what? That's nothing new. Always you think I'm going to fuck you over in some fucking way."

"Maybe because you *have* so many times. I know I haven't been the greatest dad a kid ever had, but in the next couple of months you're going to see a new man. You'll see I'm not such a bad guy. Maybe when the heat is off, you and I can—"

"Oh, bullshit. You're in this for yourself and for the money, and the same goes for me. When the heat's off, I'm splitting. Forget the family stuff. I don't want to hear that shit."

"Okay, okay," Emil said, raising his hands. "Calm down. Sure, I'm in this mainly for myself. That doesn't mean we can't forget the old days and all that ancient history. Why can't we start over?"

Freddy refused to continue the conversation. Instead he pointed at the moneybags and told his father to move them into position in the open doorway. Freddy's aim with the bags was excellent. When he said "Now," his father pushed them out of the plane and they landed within twenty feet of the cottage. His aim with his father was just as good. Emil Hasset, struggling to open a parachute pack that had been sealed shut with a few twists of a pliers, dropped like a rock into a clump of small trees at the edge of the clearing where his body would be out of sight and yet easy to find.

Freddy banked in a wide circle, then straightened out for another jump run. Adjusting the controls carefully, he trimmed the plane for straight, level flight. Floating under his canopy thirty seconds later, Freddy watched the Cessna, climbing gently in response to its reduced weight, disappear over the ridge. It would go two hundred miles south at least, maybe twice that far, with any luck at all. It looked as though luck was finally running with Frederick N. Hasset.

He guided himself to a patch of ground free of rocks, tumbling expertly on impact. Regaining his feet, he unbuckled and slipped out of the parachute harness, gathered the billowing folds into a ball, and carried it to the cottage. The keys were where they had left them—under a coffee can on the porch. After throwing the chute inside he paused, looking and listening. There was nobody around. No nosy fishermen, hunters, hikers, wardens, or neighbors. A clockwork heist. The newspapers would be talking about criminal masterminds.

He retrieved the canvas sacks, dragging them into the small front room and leaning them against the sofa. They were heavier than he thought they would be and he was anxious to count the contents. No time for that now, though. He had to conduct a simple, non-religious burial service.

The garden tools were in a storage crib outside. He selected a spade and carried it to the clump of trees at the low side of the clearing. The ground was wet and soft, and his father's body was pressed into it face down like some kind of broken swastika, the arms and legs protruding awkwardly. There was blood oozing from the collar and cuffs of the guard's uniform.

Freddy worked quickly, digging a shallow grave. When it was long and deep enough, he used the point of the spade to turn the body into it. In returning dirt to the hole, he started at the head end in order to cover the grin that was frozen on his father's face.

As he worked, he became aware of a distant rumble, like that of a train crossing a bridge. There was no railroad in the valley. The sound grew steadily louder. Freddy straightened and rested his hands and chin on the top of the shovel handle. He had heard a sound like that once before at an air show at Travis Air Force Base near Sacramento when a squadron of World War II bombers was approaching from behind a hill.

An odd wind sprang up in the trees, odd because it was without gusts . . . just a steady stream of air from the northeast moving at about fifteen miles an hour and carrying with it a suggestion of moisture, like a breeze off the sea. It didn't smell like the sea, though. The smell was more like the San Joaquin River at flood stage, a combination of fish, sewers, and fresh-cut grass.

The wind grew stronger. A hundred birds rose from the trees and headed down the valley.

Leaving his father half uncovered, Freddy dropped the spade and walked uphill to the side of the cottage. From there he could see a mile upstream. More birds took to the air. A rabbit dashed crazily across the clearing.

The horizon was formed by the tops of the hills where the valley narrowed to nearly vertical cliffs that followed the river around a sharp bend. The sky was clear and blue, but rising from somewhere beyond the bend was an enormous black cloud of dust. An avalanche was the only explanation Freddy could think of. A mountain had caved in and frightened the animals. But that growing roar . . .

The wall of water flashed into view, coming around the turn in the canyon like the head of a snake with scales that reflected blacks and browns and silvers. It collided against the outside of the turn, rising high on the cliffs before folding back on itself. The roar increased a thousandfold and Freddy was hit by a blast of wind so strong that he was almost knocked backward off his feet. He dropped to all fours and stared at the apparition the way a dog that was frozen with fear might stare at an approaching locomotive. He was in the grip of a terror so great he was unable to move or breathe. A seething mass of water hundreds of feet high was hurtling toward him like a fantastic wall of surf, boiling with debris, a great, rolling wall of water that nearly filled the canyon to overflowing, ponderous, thundering, impossibly huge, a monster from a psychotic nightmare, leaping, writhing, roaring, crashing, every part in motion, always falling forward.

Freddy managed to get to his feet in the face of a gale-force wind that filled the air with dust, pine needles, and the branches of trees. He staggered up the slope, unable to tear his eyes from the mountain of moving water that now filled half the sky and resembled a constantly collapsing building that was being pushed forward from behind. He ran into a tree and threw his arms around it, embracing it with all his strength, knowing he would be engulfed so quickly that trying to reach high ground was utterly useless.

The flood was so close now he could pick out details —a billboard, the side of a house, entire trees, a truck trailer—all of it boiling with a million other pieces of debris, sliding down the face of a towering waterfall only to be revolved back to the top and thrown down again. Freddy could see the trees on the floor of the valley being knocked over toward him in great rows like weeds before a scythe, partly by the down-crashing water and partly by a great mass of debris that was being pushed ahead like a rolling windrow of trash in a bulldozer blade. He tightened his grip on the tree and closed his eyes. His heart stopped beating. Just before he was hit, he did the only thing he could think of, and that was to hope that the roughness of the bark against his hands and cheek was the real world while the world that was exploding around him was madness.

Forty-five minutes after the destruction of Sutterton, Police Chief Wilson Hartley was ten miles below the dam, careening down the county road in his police cruiser, stopping at every campgrounds and dwelling that didn't require a side trip. He had managed to pound on the doors of at least thirty cottages, house trailers, and camper trucks, almost half of which were occupied by people who hadn't heard a thing about the approaching flood. He had sent three fishermen and a dozen members of a Sierra Club hiking party scampering up hillsides to safety. No telling how many unseen campers and hikers had heeded the warning he broadcast over and over on the car's public-address loudspeaker. To make sure one house was empty, he had to shoot an attacking German shepherd that had been abandoned by its owners in their haste to flee.

The advance of the water was being monitored from planes and relayed to the communications van. Hartley heard Mrs. Lehmann's voice, cut by static, report that the wave had just hit the fish hatchery at Castle Rock. The hatchery was a mile and a half upstream.

He braked to a stop at the driveway leading to Creekwood, Roshek's imposing summer home. He debated with himself whether he had enough time to check it out . . . he was between five and eight minutes ahead of the wave. He had seen Roshek arrive and leave the overlook in a helicopter, so chances were the old man himself had made sure there was nobody at the house, but still . . . Hartley had been at Creekwood only once, when Roshek had hosted a stiff and proper lawn party on the day of the dam dedication. The driveway was about a quarter of a mile long, he remembered, and fairly straight. It would only take twenty seconds each way, and when he got back to the main road he would still have at least four minutes to spare. From there to the mouth of the canyon it was a straight shot he could take at top speed, putting some breathing room between himself and disaster. Two miles downstream, just across the bridge, were three different roads he could take to high ground. With his siren turned to high, he turned in to the Creekwood driveway.

From the top of the massive stone chimney curled a peaceful column of smoke. A man and a woman who obviously had heard him coming were watching him from the porch. Hartley was relieved to see that they were young and healthy; otherwise he would have had to take them with him. He wanted as much room in his car as possible to pick up stragglers he might meet in his final sprint to safety.

"The dam has broken!" Hartley shouted, stopping at the bottom of the porch steps and waving his arm. "A flood hundreds of feet deep will be here in minutes. . . . Go up the hill all the way to the top . . . right now, get going. . . ."

The couple looked at each other in amazement, then back at Hartley.

"The dam has broken!" Hartley shouted again, cutting the siren to make sure his words were understood. "You've got to climb the hill as fast as you can." With the siren off it was possible to hear a distant rumble, so faint it was hardly more than a whisper. Hartley pointed upstream. "Hear that noise? That's the flood coming down the canyon. . . . Look, you can see the dust it's raising. Run up the hill, run as hard as you can and keep running. . . . It's your best chance . . . good luck!"

Hartley made a hard U-turn on the lawn, the tires cutting black gashes. He paused for a few seconds to watch the frightened pair running up the grassy slope behind the house. They bounded forward like gazelles and were plainly in remarkable physical condition. Probably athletes of some kind. There was no question that they would make it to the top. He floored the accelerator and shot down the driveway, confident that he had saved two more lives; now he would concentrate on saving his own.

The two miles between Creekwood and the mouth of the canyon he took at seventy miles an hour. Just before the road crossed the river and intersected with a state highway he had to slam on the brakes. Four cars were stopped ahead of him. The Sierra Canyon River, out of its banks and carrying a heavy load of flotsam, had taken out the bridge. Hartley got slowly out of his car and collapsed against it with his arms on the roof, staring at the gap in the road where the bridge had been. There was no way he could climb to safety on foot, for this part of the valley was lined with nearly vertical cliffs. The drivers and passengers from the other cars ran to him and surrounded him. A screaming woman clutched at his uniform and pointed at the river. Her husband restrained her, explaining in a voice broken by sobs that the bridge had collapsed just minutes earlier and that in a car that had been swept away with it were their daughter, their son-in-law, and two grandchildren. Any notions Hartley might have had about bursting into tears himself or falling to his knees in prayer had to be set aside. Ten people close to hysteria were crowding around him, shouting questions and expecting him to give them answers. They wanted to be told what to do. More than once in his career he had managed to calm people down simply by adopting an authoritative pose. Doctors did the same thing when they pretended to know more than they possibly could. He raised his hand and asked for silence. "There's a Forest Service fire road a half mile upstream!" he shouted. "Get in your cars and follow me."

Driving back up the canyon in the face of a steady head wind, Hartley saw in his rear view mirror the caravan of cars following him. What he saw through the windshield made it plain that they were all on a journey of futility. Above the trees was a cloud of boiling dust that turned the morning brightness into a deepening and ominous gloom.

The fire road was little more than a wide dirt path, rutted from spring runoff and blocked to bikers and hot-rodders by a horizontal steel beam that was hinged to a post at one end and padlocked at the other. Hartley ran to the barricade and shattered the lock with two shots from his service revolver. As he climbed back into the car, wind whipped his clothes and hurled dirt and pine needles at him with such force that he had to close his eyes to keep from being blinded. A continuous and growing roar told him that the wave was no more than half a mile away.

The car lurched forward, weaving from side to side as the wheels spun in the dirt, bouncing over the ruts and scattered rocks. He eased up on the accelerator until the tires achieved traction, then gradually pressed it to the floor. The high-powered V-8 engine, capable of sending the car down a freeway at a hundred miles an hour, enabled Hartley to leave the other vehicles far behind, but he wasn't thinking about them. He didn't risk taking his eyes off the treacherous roadway to glance in the mirror. He didn't look over his shoulder, either, afraid that he might see the source of the thunder that had grown so loud it blotted out every other sound. He jerked the wheel right and left to avoid the worst gullies and boulders, smashing through fallen limbs and hoping that he wouldn't find the way blocked by a ditch or an upended tree. A light splash of water struck the windshield, instinctively he flicked on the wipers.

The fire road followed a sidehill course, rising at a constant grade of twelve percent. For a full minute Hartley plunged recklessly ahead, gaining at least two hundred feet in elevation. Even though one tire had gone flat and the oil pan had been lost to rocks, he kept the accelerator floored. The feeling came over him that he was going to make it after all. One more minute, that's all he needed, just one more minute.

The road, always pitched steeply upward, curved to the right and entered a crease between two mountain shoulders. Hartley was traveling directly away from the river now. To his left was the steep mountainside on the other side of the draw, brown in color from a layer of humus and decayed needles and dotted with widely spaced pines and rock outcroppings. Looking left and upward, Hartley could see far above him on the opposite slope a diagonal line—that, he knew, was the fire road after it had rounded the switchback at the end of the side canyon. If he could reach that elevation, he would be safe.

With stunning speed, the brown slope turned white. A sheet of foam swept over it from left to right as if a bucket of soapy water had been dashed against a wall. At the same time, a river of water several feet deep surged uphill around and under the car, sliding it ahead and causing the rear wheels to lose their grip. The engine died. Within seconds a powerful backwash streamed over the hood and roof, turning the car until it was facing downhill and pinning it against the slope on the high side of the road. Water boiled over the windows.

Hartley set the emergency brake and waited, hanging tightly on to the wheel. The car was totally submerged and water was squirting through crevices in the floor, the dashboard, and the doors. He wondered if this was the worst of it. Maybe the flood would subside before the car filled with water, maybe . . . He felt a current dislodge the car and give it several gentle shoves along the ground, like a box being nudged by a giant paw. He realized then that he was sobbing, not from fear of pain or death but because of his utter helplessness. There was absolutely nothing he could do but grip the wheel and hope for the best. As a policeman, he had long ago come to terms with the possibility that he would die before his time, but he had always assumed that if it happened to him it would be swiftly, most likely by gunfire—not this way, not trapped in a car under water, my God, not by drowning.

A tremendous force lifted the car, revolved it slowly end over end, and dropped it on its side to the ground. Hartley was dazed when his head struck the doorpost, but he clung to consciousness. His reasoning powers continued to function with eerie coolness. Two windows were broken and water was jetting against him. He moved a hand toward the buckle of his seat belt. An air bubble will form near the rear window, he told himself. If the car stays where it is, I can last for an hour and maybe more. The water will have dropped by then. No bones broken. If I run out of air, I'll push myself through a window and swim to the surface.

The car was picked up again and pulled swiftly in a long arc out of the draw and into the main canyon. With a profound sense of hopelessness, Hartley realized that he was caught up in the flood's main current. The force of acceleration was so great it pressed him against the seat. The car was rolling over and over and was quickly filling with water. When Hartley felt the coldness on his face, he held his breath. There was no sense of panic. He was simply a boy again on a carnival ride. He was being drawn with delicious anticipation to the top of the roller coaster, ready for the big plunge that would make the girls scream and the boys hang on to their caps. Suddenly the car was hit by a counterforce that sent it straight down. He braced himself the way a man would in an elevator that was dropping in a free-fall toward the bottom of a shaft.

Along with a thousand other pieces of debris, the car was hurled against the canyon floor from a height of two hundred feet, crushed to no more than a fourth of its original size, then rolled along the ground like a wad of paper on a windswept street. Again the car was drawn upward by circular currents in the flood wave, this time almost to the surface, and propelled downstream in a broad sweep through the mouth of the canyon. The second time the car dropped, it was driven like a stake into the loam that lined the Sacramento River. In the following three hours, as the tide rolled over it with decreasing energy, it was buried under thirty feet of silt.

31

IT WAS TWELVE MILES FROM THE DAM to the mouth of the canyon, where the Sierra Canyon River emerged from the foothills and followed a meandering course through the flatlands of the upper Central Valley to a confluence with the Sacramento River at the town of Omohundro. The flood fought its way down the twisting canyon like a thing alive, a lengthening serpent, surging from one side to another and gathering into itself everything that wasn't solid rock. The sides and bottom of the flow, retarded by the rough surfaces presented by the indented hills, rock palisades, and side canyons, and the work of scouring and uprooting, advanced more slowly than the main mass of water, which was constantly flowing downward from above and pounding the valley floor with an endless series of hammer blows. In the hour it took the flood to reach the canyon mouth, it picked up so much debris that only half of it was water—the rest was dam embankment material, topsoil, river gravel, trees, logs, telephone poles, structures ranging from houses to bridges, farm animals, and at least fifty miles of wiring and fences.

Those who saw the advance of the wave from hilltops and planes were later to describe it in a variety of ways.

"The first thing I saw was the dust cloud," said Kitty Sprague, a Forest Service trail worker. "I thought it was smoke, and radioed that a huge fire had broken out. A few minutes later I saw the flood, which was like a rolling mountain of water pushing a city dump. The front of it was half hidden by mist, but I could see a fantastic squirming, with whole houses being tossed around."

An orchard handyman named Knox Burger had a narrow escape. "I was running up the hill as fast as I could. Behind me was my brother Kurt carrying his three-year-old boy. The wind was so fierce it near ripped my shirt off, and I saw a barn get flattened as if somebody stepped on it. When I looked down below, I couldn't believe my eyes—a monster as big as the valley was sliding along making a noise like World War III. We thought we were high enough to be safe, but a splash of water landed on us and tried to drag us down. I grabbed a tree and kept my feet, but the boy was torn out of Kurt's arms. He let out a bellow and jumped in the water, and that was the last I saw of either of them."

Evelyn Frances Hayes, state assemblywoman from Sausalito, was camping with a group of Girl Scouts on McFarland Peak above the mouth of the canyon. "The odd thing was that it was such a beautiful day," she told the Sacramento *Bee*. "One would expect the end of the world to come with the sky full of thunderclouds and lightning flashes. That's what I thought, that Armageddon had arrived. All of nature's destructive forces seemed turned loose. God was destroying the world without giving anybody time to pray. It never occurred to me that a dam had failed, because the devastation was taking place on such an enormous scale that it seemed beyond anything human beings could be responsible for. I gathered the girls into a group and we all put our arms around each other. We watched the flood come out the canyon and fan out across the orchards and rice fields like a stain growing on a piece of cloth. When it reached Omohundro, the houses got pushed together as if somebody was sweeping toys into a pile. Then they got folded under and we couldn't see them anymore."

Tim Hanson, an operatic tenor who lived in Omohundro, told his story several times on national television hookups from his hospital bed in Chico. What viewers saw and heard on their screens was a man whose face, hands, and arms were covered with bandages, whose gestures seemed intended for audiences in the upper balcony, and whose voice was full of dramatic tension. "I didn't hear the warnings because I was in a soundproof booth I built in my bedroom so I can rehearse without the neighbors calling the police. I was working on the role of Lindoro in Rossini's *The Italian Girl in Algiers*, which I'm doing next month in San Francisco for Pippen's Pocket Opera.

"When I felt the house shaking, I left the booth and looked out the window. Three blocks away a tumbling wall of rubbish was coming toward me knocking down trees and houses. I didn't see any water at all, just a churning mass of trash and trees and pieces of buildings. A couple of miles away, though, I could see water—it was pouring from Sierra Canyon like syrup from a pitcher.

"I ran up the stairs to the attic and climbed through a skylight to the top of the roof. I sat with my arms around the chimney and watched the houses down the street get crunched one after the other. When my house got hit, it stayed in one piece and started rolling over. It must have rolled over three or four times before it broke up, with me climbing to stay on the high side like lumberjacks do on logs in a river. The noise was terrific, the roll of a thousand drums with the sound of trees and boards splitting. I ended up getting swirled downstream hanging on to a piece of an outside wall. A woman I know who works at the bank came floating by on a barrel. I called her name and she turned and nodded as if nothing unusual was happening. She sailed by as if she knew exactly where she was going, and I never saw her again.

"Where I was going was down the Sacramento River. I didn't know where I would end up, but I had visions of eventually going right under the Golden Gate Bridge. Finally I got snagged in some bushes and people with ropes helped me get to solid ground. I was covered with cuts and bruises and was taken here to the hospital. I'm going to sing in that opera even if I have to dress like *The Return of the Mummy.*"

The San Francisco *Chronicle* in its coverage quoted a retired army colonel named Tom Stewart, who had witnessed the destruction of Sutterton. "When the water subsided, the town had disappeared without a trace. The valley was nothing but wet bedrock. Everything had been shaved off clean as a whistle, including building foundations. I got in my car and drove north along what used to be the edge of the lake. I was in a daze. I think I was *looking* for the town, expecting to see it around every turn. All I saw were mud flats and boats on their sides. In some places the lake had dropped so fast fish were trapped in puddles. Hundreds of them were flopping around. I saw two kids going after them with sacks."

Roshek was seen leaving the overlook in a helicopter and he was seen at the Yuba City airport boarding his company's private jet. When he landed in Los Angeles, the press was waiting. Jim Oliver was appalled by both the size and the bad manners of the crowd. He had thought he might have to compete with three or four people at the most, not a swarming pack of thirty. Reporters and cameramen surrounded the wheelchair like pigs at a trough, extending microphones, firing flashbulbs, and shouting questions. Oliver jotted a line in his notebook about the change in the engineer's appearance. His face was as hawklike as ever and his heavily browed eyes just as intense, but his chin was close to his chest instead of defiantly thrust forward. His body didn't seem to fill up his clothes. He looked like a man returning from a long stay in a hospital.

At curbside, when Roshek was being helped into his limousine, he showed a flash of his old personality. With a sudden thrust of a crutch he knocked a camera to the sidewalk.

"You son of a bitch," a photographer said, stooping to pick up the pieces.

"Sue me," Roshek said. "My attorney needs the money."

Before the door was closed, Oliver managed to elbow his way to the front. "I'm Jim Oliver," he said through the clamor. "I interviewed you five years ago when an earthquake hit close to the dam. Remember? The Los Angeles *Times*. Could I call you for an appointment?"

Roshek didn't look at him. "I read the Anaheim *Shopper* myself. Now there is a hell of a paper."

Oliver straightened up and stepped back. Roshek had said something similar to him five years before, and he had included it in his article. It wasn't the same this time. The line was delivered now mechanically, as if Roshek were playing a role that was expected of him. He was impersonating himself. Oliver made another entry in his notebook.

The limousine rolled ten feet down the street and stopped. The front door opened and the driver got out. "Jim Oliver of the Los Angeles *Times*?"

Oliver raised his hand. The driver motioned him inside the car and held a rear door open for him.

"Thanks very much for singling me out like that," Oliver said when the limousine was under way again. "I can certainly understand why you might not want to talk to the press right now."

Roshek waved his hand to indicate that pleasantries were unnecessary. Oliver noticed that his business suit was flecked with mud, that his collar was starched and one size too big, that his skin was as white as typing paper, and that he wasn't wearing his hat.

"I singled you out because I remember that last article you wrote about dams. It was one of the least ridiculous pieces ever to appear in a newspaper on an engineering subject. Why do papers have science editors and not engineering editors? People are touched by engineering every minute of the day. Cars, television, frozen food, plastics—these things are more the artifacts of engineering than science. Newspapers should—"

"Did you see the dam fail?" The question stopped Roshek. His mouth closed and his eyes drifted into the distance. "Could you tell me how it made you feel?"

"Imagine," Roshek said in a quiet, unemotional voice, "looking into a mirror and seeing brown water gushing from a socket where one of your eyes had been. Imagine looking at your stomach and seeing it slowly split open and your guts spill out on the floor."

Oliver swallowed. His pencil was momentarily paralyzed.

"My feelings aren't important," Roshek went on in the same voice. "If you are intending to write a so-called human interest story featuring my feelings, you can get out of the car right now."

"Your feelings *are* important. I don't intend to feature them, but I would like to ask a few questions about—"

"I don't care about your questions. I have a message to give to the American people. That's why you're here."

"I see. The American people. The American people are going to want to know why the dam failed."

Roshek was stopped again, and a shadow of pain crossed his face. He covered his eyes for a moment before answering. "The dam failed because of me. Because I thought it couldn't. I believed that nothing I designed could fail. I still believe that, but only if I stay with the structure to make sure it is properly cared for. Because I thought the dam was invulnerable, I turned it over to others who didn't recognize the dangers and who didn't keep on top of the details, as I would have. As the saying goes, if you want something done right, do it yourself. The world is in a hell of a mess today, wouldn't you say, Oliver? You know why? Because God sent his only begotten son to earth to save the human race and the job was botched. He should have gone himself. See the parallel? God's mistake was that he sent a boy to do a man's job."

Oliver eyed the man who was slumped in the corner of the seat, wondering if he was losing his grip on reality. He certainly looked broken physically. Maybe his mind was going as well.

"I don't mean to compare myself to God," Roshek said, "if that's how that sounded. I was a creator—small 'c.' I accept part of the blame for what happened. At the same time, though, God is partly to blame, if you want to use that term. In designing the dam, I applied the mathematics as perfectly as God could have done it himself. God is to blame for providing misleading geophysical data."

"I'm afraid I—"

"I didn't know the fault was there. The one that caused the earthquake five years ago. We had brown water coming into the lower drainage galleries on that occasion, too, did you know that? No, because we managed to keep it quiet. We didn't want the public to get excited over nothing. We thought the problem was minor and we corrected it. It's obvious now we were wrong. You are probably looking for a villain to make your story easier to write. An incompetent designer, a contractor using substandard materials, a corrupt politician pushing through a pork-barrel dam project that made no sense. It's not that simple. The dam made a lot of sense. If there is a villain, it is the unknown, which we can never eliminate entirely. What we knew and what we were able to find out, we took into account. What we didn't know destroyed us."

Oliver looked up from his notebook. "Let me see if I have this straight. You say an earthquake weakened the foundation. You thought you fixed it. The weakness reappeared five years later and wasn't noticed because . . . Why wasn't it noticed? Aren't there instruments in the dam that—"

"It wasn't noticed because of an incredible string of human and mechanical breakdowns," Roshek said, gesturing, his voice getting louder. "Instruments failed, instruments gave wrong readings, instruments weren't read, instruments were ignored by a chief inspector who was suffering from what can only be called terminal optimism. When we knew something was wrong, we sent him below, when the dam still could have been saved, and he died of a heart attack or some goddam thing. As if that wasn't enough, we had a nincompoop of a control-room operator who didn't grasp what was happening until it was too late." Roshek's eyes were flashing, and he was opening and closing his fists in frustration. "The timing was another thing. The state was due at the site today to take a look . . . today! Yesterday and the whole mess wouldn't have happened. Another terrible thing is that this happened in California, which has the best system of dam safety regulations in the world, regulations I fought for years to get adopted. . . ."

Roshek turned his face to the window. Oliver spent five minutes catching up on his notes, then asked the engineer if it was true that a young employee of his sensed something was wrong and spent the night fruitlessly trying to sound an alarm.

"If you can't have a villain, you want a hero—is that it?"

"I'm only trying to verify rumors I've heard."

"A young employee," Roshek said with distaste, "tried to sound an alarm that would have been sounded anyway."

"But not as soon. Because of him a couple of hours were gained, isn't that so?"

"Five minutes is more like it. No, I take that back. Just because I detest Kramer doesn't mean I should run him down. What he did was remarkable. Maybe two hours is fair. Ask somebody else. I can't be objective."

"Is it true you fired him for telling you the dam was in trouble and that you had him jailed for trying to prove he was right?"

Roshek's response was so explosive spittle flew from his lips. "It's also true I had him released from jail when I knew he was right. I ordered him put in charge. And when I saw him a few hours ago I had the urge to kill him. Why? Because the whole thing was so goddam unfair I couldn't stand it. The greatest engineering structure ever built was failing, a structure that was as much a part of me as . . . as these goddam crutches. Because it was failing, an arrogant young puppy who still doesn't realize how incredibly lucky he was and who has contributed *nothing* to the building of this nation—absolutely nothing!—is to be idolized, while I . . . My life and my career are wrecked. My . . ." He clapped a hand over his eyes and bared his teeth as if trying to withstand a terrible pain without crying out. He fell back into the corner of the seat. The driver of the limousine turned around with an expression of concern, lifting his foot from the accelerator, but Roshek with irritation told him to keep going, that he was all right.

The limousine swung off the Harbor Freeway at the

Wilshire exit. When Roshek spoke again, he was calm. "Just because a man is a hero doesn't necessarily mean he is likable. Kramer is still with our firm and we have big plans for him. He puts the lie to the impression the public has of engineers as mechanical men without hearts."

"I don't imagine you want me to write that you had an urge to kill him."

"Write what you want about me. If you want to trivialize your story by dealing with personalities, go ahead. Gossip may be what the American people want, but it's not what they need."

"What is it that they need? What is it you want me to tell them? Assuming I can get their attention."

Roshek leaned toward Oliver and spoke with great earnestness. "The American people need safe dams. There are nine thousand dams in this country that would cause extensive damage if they failed, and a third of them don't meet modern safety standards. It's like having three thousand bombs waiting to go off. One survey concluded that it was between a hundred and a thousand times more likely that a dam would fail and kill a thousand people than that a nuclear accident would do it. Unbelievable as it seems, there are states where a real-estate developer or a farmer can build a dam without even applying for a permit! Without hiring an engineer to design it! When it's built and forgotten about, there is no requirement for periodic safety inspections. Not more than thirty states have even a half-assed set of rules and regulations on the books backed up by an adequate enforcement. How many people are going to have to be killed?"

The limousine pulled up in front of Roshek's office building.

"I care about dams, you see," Roshek said. "When one fails, it is a reflection on engineering, on engineers, and on the whole idea of dams. That this country tolerates unsafe dams is because of politics, not engineering. Engineers know what has to be done, but politicians won't give us the green light or the money to do it. That's where you come in, Oliver. There will be a big clamor now about dam safety, but it will die down the way it did after the failure of Teton and Taccoa. Don't let it fade! Keep beating the drums! Make the states face up to their responsibilities before there's an even worse disaster than the one we just suffered through. If the states won't act, make the federal government step in."

"That's a big order. I'm just a reporter and feature writer."

"Promise me you'll do what you can."

"I'll do what I can. It sounds like a worthy campaign. I can't imagine that things are quite as bad as you say."

"They are far worse, as you'll find out."

On the sidewalk, Roshek made a show of being his old self, sitting erectly in his wheelchair and shaking the reporter's hand with vigor and decisiveness. Oliver watched through the building's glass doors as Roshek wheeled himself across the lobby to the elevators. He was surprised to realize that he liked the sharp-edged old man. He felt he almost understood him. He felt something else as well—that he would never see him again.

32

PHIL KRAMER TOOK A LAST LOOK. Downstream from where the dam had stood, the valley was denuded. Above the damsite were deeply fissured beds of sediment through which a placid Sierra Canyon River meandered, sparkling in the noon sunshine. On the far side of the canyon was the apparently undamaged intake tower, rising from the mud like an elevator shaft without its skyscraper. All that was left of the dam was a section of the embankment extending about a thousand feet from the opposite abutment. Phil could see Herman Bolen's airplane on the crest roadway, still lying upside down where it had been left.

He turned when he heard his name, and saw the television reporter in the butterscotch sport coat. "Mrs. Lehmann says it's okay to talk to you now," he said. "Everybody agrees you are the key to this story, so we'd like an interview. Maybe in depth."

Phil walked slowly away from the railing and sat down on the front bumper of a truck. "I don't want to be interviewed. I need a couple of days of sleep." He hung his head and closed his eyes. "My legs are killing me. My back is killing me. I feel sick. My car is gone. I'm hungry. I want to go home, but I don't have my clothes or my shoes or my billfold."

"If you could just tell me how you got arrested, and then how you got *un*arrested. . . . Hello? Are you asleep?"

Phil raised his head. "Say, are you the guys with the helicopter?"

"Yes. We call it the Telecopter."

"Tell you what. I'll give you an interview, in depth or any other way, if you'll do me a favor."

"What kind of favor?"

"See that thing sticking up out of the mud that looks like the world's tallest silo? That's the intake tower. It's eight hundred and forty-five feet high. My shoes and watch and clothes and billfold are up there in a neat little pile."

The reporter eyed him narrowly. "On top of the tower? How did they get there?"

"That will emerge during the interview. I also want you to take me to a phone so I can call Santa Monica and ask a certain special someone for a date, whose name will also emerge during the interview."

"Mr. Kramer, I don't know if you're joking or not, but I do know I can't give you a ride in the Telecopter. Crew only. No outsiders under any conditions. I could lose my job."

Phil shrugged. "Okay. I'll give the interview to someone

else. Why not channel seven? I see some guys over there with sevens on their jackets."

The reporter cursed under his breath. He pointed at the helicopter. "Get in," he said.

The phone call to Janet was made from a booth in Chico. Phil sat on the sidewalk holding the folding door open with his shoulder. A group of television and newspaper reporters waited nearby, anxious to resume questioning him.

"Phil, is that you?" Janet answered before the first ring was completed. "I'm so glad to hear your voice! I saw you on television a few minutes ago and you looked . . . well, exhausted."

"That's probably because I'm exhausted. I feel like a washrag that's been wrung out and thrown in a corner. All I want to do is collapse in a bed. Preferably yours. Jesus, Janet, what I've been through in the last twenty-four hours has been . . . I can't find words. I'll say this, though, I don't think I'll ever smile again."

"I'll make you smile . . . with my magic fingers."

"I'm smiling again."

"I'm so proud of you! What you did was absolutely fantastic!"

"You weren't so bad yourself. The guys in the control room said they got phone calls from all kinds of agencies asking about a crazy woman in Santa Monica."

"I had to act crazy to get anybody to take me seriously. When I acted serious, they thought I was crazy. The problem, I think, and I'm embarrassed to admit it now, is that I was afraid I was making a fool of myself. I was only three-fourths sure you weren't hallucinating. When you woke me up and said you were surrounded by cops, you sounded—well, overwrought."

"I was overwrought, all right. Whatever you did worked, because you sure stirred everybody up. God, I'm so tired! I'm totally knocked out. I can hardly hold the phone."

"What are you going to do now? When am I going to see you?"

"Soon as I get a few hours' sleep, I'm going to get on the first plane headed in your direction. I'm going to wrap my arms and legs around you and stay that way for about a month. After that, I don't know. According to the network nerds who have been following me around, I could spend the rest of my life appearing on talk shows. I don't want that. I can't see myself as a star of stage and screen. Give me a desk somewhere and let me sit in peace adding and subtracting numbers."

"For Roshek, Bolen & Benedetz?"

Phil laughed dryly. "No, not for Roshek, Bolen & Benedetz. Bolen says I still have my job, but I don't want it as long as Roshek is running the company. He's not only weird, he hates my guts. I can't help feeling sorry for the poor bastard, though. It must have been the shits for him to see the dam getting wiped out. I'm not thinking about a job right now. I'm thinking about sleep and I'm thinking about you. I don't ever want to be more than five minutes away from you again. Excuse me for going all mushy, but that's how I feel."

"You're a sweetheart, you know that? Do you mind if I call you sweetheart? And darling? And honey?"

"Music to my ears."

When Janet was off the line, Phil didn't bother hanging up. He let the receiver slip out of his hand. Dangling from its cord, it swung away and rattled against the sides of the booth. He waved at the newsmen and told them to get lost. Then he rolled face down and fell asleep on the sidewalk.

"I came in as soon as I heard the news."

"Thank you, Margaret," Roshek said. "I knew I could count on you." It looked to him as if his secretary had powdered her face to cover the traces of tears.

"Some of the men are here, too. Mr. Filippi is downstairs. Shall I tell him that—"

"No, I don't want to be disturbed."

"You have a ton of messages. Everybody under the sun has been trying to reach you, including your wife."

"Tell them I'm in a meeting."

Roshek locked his office door behind him, got two white towels from the bathroom, and shifted himself into the swivel chair behind his desk. He gave his wheelchair a push and watched it roll silently across the rug and bump into the wall fifteen feet away. He wouldn't be needing it again.

A touch of a button turned on the television set next to the door. The three network channels were presenting flood coverage, and he lingered for a minute or two on each one. The Sacramento River was out of its banks and the capital was bracing itself for a water level at least five feet above flood stage. No serious threat was posed to the Rancho Seco nuclear plant. Ranchers in the delta region were sandbagging levees even though state officials were assuring them that that far downstream the effects of the flood would hardly be noticeable. Suisun Bay, San Pablo Bay, and the northern half of San Francisco Bay were expected to turn brown for a day or two, but marine biologists did not foresee a major fish kill. The towns of Sutterton and Omohundro were thought to have been evacuated in time. Most homes and summer cottages in Sierra Canyon were also emptied, thanks in part to a still-unidentified and still-missing policeman who raced down the valley one step ahead of the wave. Property damage would go over a billion dollars. Fifty-six people were known dead and twice that many missing. The Governor credited the amazingly low death toll to the well-organized emergency service programs in the affected counties, which were set up with state assistance and coordinated with disaster control offices at the state level.

The Governor is right about something for a change, Roshek thought as he turned off the set. In any other state thousands of people might have been killed. Eleanor . . . had she survived? To reach her, the daredevil policeman would have had to go quite a distance off the main road. Well, it didn't make any difference.

He turned on his recorder and dictated a long memo to Herman Bolen, giving him suggestions on how to act as president of the corporation and giving him his thoughts on the firm's most important contracts. Because of insinuations that might be made by certain rival engineering firms, Roshek warned his colleague, clients should be assured that the failure of the dam had nothing to do with design deficiencies. Roshek advised that Bolen and Filippi should immediately pay a personal visit to every major client, particularly those with whom contract negotiations were under way.

"With regard to Kramer," Roshek said, speaking crisply into the microphone, "it is absolutely essential that he remain with the firm. For him to join a competitor would have a devastating effect on our image. During the next few weeks, he is going to get a great deal of media attention, and it should not be surprising to you if he is invited to appear on the popular talk shows to narrate film clips of the failure. By giving him a promotion—say, to the head of a new department of dam safety investigation—any acclaim he gets can be shared by the corporation. Keeping him is the key. Offer him fifty thousand a year if you have to.

"As you know, Herman, I regard Kramer as a presumptuous young twerp who just happened to be in the right place at the right time. Seeing him in a position of prestige and seeing him honored by the engineering societies would make me sick. Fortunately, I'm leaving.

"You're a good man, Herman, all things considered. Best wishes."

Roshek picked up his fountain pen. On a sheet of company stationery he wrote: "I, Theodore Roshek, president of Roshek, Bolen & Benedetz, Inc., being of sound mind, as unlikely as that may seem to some, declare this to be my Last Will and Testament, written in my own hand, and hereby revoke all other Wills and Codicils previously made by me. I direct that my just debts be paid and all that sort of thing and that my body be cremated and disposed of without participation of the clergy. I direct that my entire estate be given to my faithful wife, Stella, who deserved better treatment from me than she got in the last few years.

"I do not wish any part of my estate to go to Eleanor James of San Francisco, who in my previous Will was provided for so generously and foolishly. Let me phrase that another way to make sure there is no misunderstanding: I want my wife to get everything and I want Miss James to get nothing. If Miss James gets so much as one dime of my money, I will come back from the grave and make those who let it happen so miserable they will wish they were dead instead of me.

"To my wife I want to say I'm sorry.

"As far as bequests to individuals and institutions are concerned, my wife, if she chooses, can follow the directions I gave in the last Will we prepared together."

Roshek signed and dated the sheet and added a line for his secretary to sign as a witness. Next he dictated a letter to his attorney.

"Dear Jules: Enclosed with this letter is a handwritten Will. I trust you will make sure the terms are carried out and that my previous Will, which was drawn up against your advice, is junked. I don't know if Eleanor survived the flood or not. If she did, she may contest my cutting her off by claiming that I am not mentally competent, as evidenced by my suicide. I assure you I know exactly what I am doing and am not off my rocker by any reasonable definition. On the contrary, taking my life now proves my sanity. It will save everybody a lot of grief and pain, including especially myself, and will, I suspect, add to the sum total of human happiness. My body is giving me more and more trouble and would not last more than four or five years in any case at the rate it is deteriorating. I am not going to spend my declining years in courtrooms testifying in the endless damage suits that even now are being concocted in offices like your own.

"Should you be called upon to *prove* my sanity on this day, you can put the Will into evidence. Note the strong, smooth handwriting. Not that of a crazy person, is it? Or play the tapes I have just recorded. Experts will find nothing in my voice that suggests tension or strain. It's my normal speaking voice. Not the voice of a man who is desperate or distraught. Far from it. Knowing the end is near, I'm almost happy.

"It's been nice knowing you, Jules. If you want to remember me, insult somebody who deserves it."

Roshek turned the television set on again and changed channels until he found a newscaster who resembled an actual human being. While listening to "updates on the disaster situation," he spread one towel on his desk and folded the other one into eighths. He removed the gun from the drawer and checked to make sure it was loaded and the safety was off. There were only five bullets. Five would be enough.

"Coming in the next hour," the newscaster said, "will be an exclusive interview with Philip Kramer, the heroic engineer who is being credited at this hour with saving the population of Sutterton, the stories of an opera singer and two ballet dancers who had close calls but lived to tell about it, and a replay of some of the most incredible film footage ever taken. Right now we take you live to the campus of Cal Tech, where our Linda Fong is in the office of engineering professor Clark Kirchner. Linda?"

Roshek arranged every article on his desk so that the edges were parallel with each other. A photo of Eleanor went into the wastebasket, a photo of Stella was turned face down.

A mustachioed man on the television screen was holding forth on the design of Sierra Canyon Dam. "I maintained then and I maintain now that it should have been able to resist a quake of six point five at four miles rather than five miles. The slope of the upstream face, considering the materials used, was at least ten percent too steep. This was the highest embankment dam in the world, remember, and should not have been used to test so-called progressive design theories that—"

The bullet entered the center of the screen, which imploded with a vacuum pop and a shower of silvery glass needles. The next bullet shattered the glass that covered a painting of the dam.

Roshek heard Margaret scream. She was a dignified woman who had been his secretary for twenty years. He had never heard her scream before. He looked with respect at the weapon in his hand. A remarkable invention, the gun. It gave a man the godlike ability to hurl lightning bolts, like Thor, and its sound was the sound of thunder.

On the right side of the office was a framed cross-sectional view of the underground powerhouse. The third bullet smashed its glass into a thousand pieces. Men were shouting and trying to force the door open. Roshek could imagine Margaret, having found her key, running to unlock it. No matter. They would never get to him in time. The glass display case that housed the scale model of the dam collapsed with a satisfying crash.

One bullet left. Roshek picked up the padded towel and held it against the left side of his head, leaning forward over the towel that was spread on his desk. He positioned the muzzle solidly against his right temple, adjusting the angle so that the bullet would strike squarely. He didn't want to graze his brain and turn himself into a vegetable. This had to be a suicide, not an attempted suicide, and it had to be neat, clean, and efficient. No more failures. Sierra Canyon Dam was enough for one life.

When he was sure the gun was close to perpendicular to the side of his head, he pulled the trigger without hesitation.

Author's Note

I am deeply grateful for the help I received from J. Barry Cooke and his miracle-working daughter and office manager, Bonnie. Cooke has served as a consulting engineer on the siting, design, construction, and operation of nearly a thousand dams worldwide. Discussions with him and access to his remarkable library are in large part responsible for whatever air of technical authenticity the text projects.

I am grateful, too, for the friendly cooperation of Dr. Bruce Tschantz, Chief of Dam Safety for the Federal Emergency Management Agency and professor of civil engineering at the University of Tennessee; James J. Watkins of the California Office of Emergency Services; Charles Von Berg of the California Department of Water Resources, Oroville Field Division; Thomas Struthers, Butte County (California) Civil Disaster Coordinator; Larry Gillick, Sheriff-Coroner of Butte County; Richard Stenberg, Undersheriff of Butte County; and Paul Girard,

Pacific Gas & Electric Co. The drawings were made by Mark Mikulich of Windsor, California.

For reading parts of the manuscript and making many valuable suggestions, I wish to thank Leonard Tong, Don McGinnis, Bob Jewett, Janice Davis, Mark Van Liere, Gooch Ryan, David Parry, Julia Reisz, Sally Culley, Kent Bolter, and Madeleine Bouchard.

None of the above-named is in any way to blame for the plot of this novel, for the characters, or for the views the characters express, which were entirely of my own devising. The characters are not patterned after anybody I ever knew or heard of.

Sierra Canyon Dam, which does not exist, shares a few design features with Oroville Dam, which does. The similarities were adopted for convenience and are not intended to imply anything about anything. Oroville Dam is as safe as it can be.

Not all of America's fifty thousand dams are as safe as they can be. In 1981 the Corps of Engineers will complete a four-year survey of the nine thousand nonfederal dams that would cause the most damage if they failed. Results so far are alarming: a third of the dams are unsafe. In West Virginia, South Carolina, Tennessee, Georgia, and Missouri, according to figures in the Corps study, more dams are unsafe than safe. Nobody wants to pay the cost of repairs.

Existing dams are one problem, future dams are another. Amazingly, in most parts of the country there is little to impede construction of still more hazardous dams. Very few states have adopted anything resembling the design, construction, and inspection regulations urged by the United States Committee on Large Dams. Readers who don't like catastrophic man-made floods should write to their legislators and demand action.

Robert Byrne
San Rafael, California

ROBERT BYRNE was born and raised in Dubuque, Iowa, and now lives in Marin County, California. He has worked as a railroad section hand, cabdriver, pool hustler, civil engineer, and trade journal editor. As a technical journalist, he covered the construction of more than two dozen large dams in the western states. His magazine pieces have appeared in *Saturday Review*, *Sports Illustrated*, and *Playboy*. *The Dam* is his sixth published book and third novel.